BROKEN DREAMS

STORMS OF NEW ENGLAND, BOOK 4

KARI LEMOR

RYCON PRESS

BROKEN DREAMS © 2020 by Kari Lemor

Cover Art by: Karasel

First Electronic Edition: August 2020

ISBN - 978-1-7348335- 2-2

First Print Edition: August 2020

ISBN - 978-1-7348335- 3-9

All rights reserved under the International and Pan-American Copyright Conventions. No part of this book may be reproduced or transmitted in any form or by any means, electronic or mechanical, including photocopying, recording, or by any information storage and retrieval system, without permission in writing from the publisher.

This is a work of fiction. Names, places, characters and incidents are either the product of the author's imagination or are used fictitiously, and any resemblance to any actual persons, living or dead, organizations, events or locales is entirely coincidental.

To my daughter, Kasey, who has so much love and patience for my beautiful but active grandchildren. God Bless You for being such a wonderful mother.

SERIES BY KARI LEMOR

Love on the Line
Wild Card Undercover
Running Target
Fatal Evidence

Storms of New England
Elusive Dreams
True Dreams
Stolen Dreams
Broken Dreams

ACKNOWLEDGMENTS

I am so appreciative of all the people who have given me support and encouragement in writing my stories.

My husband and children for always believing in me. Jeff for all the vampire and Dracula information. My sisters, Allison and Cindy for sharing with me the stories of their children and the challenging road dealing with ASD. To the Fab Four and Teri for all the weekly motivation to keep writing.

To my talented editor, Emily Harmston, for making me sound incredible. To Kris for always being there and having the right words. To Meredith, my CP who pushes me to be the best writer I can be. You three ladies are essential and I couldn't do this without you!

CHAPTER ONE

"Congratulations! It's a boy."

Nathaniel Storm closed his eyes and shook his head before he opened them again. When he did, Helene Castleton-Billingsworth, formerly Helene Castleton-Storm, still stood on his front porch.

"Helene, what are you doing here? It's Christmas Eve. I figured you'd be getting ready for one of your swanky parties with the beautiful people." Not here on the outskirts of tiny Squamscott Falls, New Hampshire.

She might already be decked out. Her fur-trimmed cashmere Burberry coat, the one he'd spent a few months' salary on, covered her outfit. Her blonde hair was swept up in a fancy do, and her feet were shod in the newest Louboutins. Jewels shimmered in her ears and on her hands.

"This is Tanner." She pushed a small boy with a mop of blond curls forward. "He's yours. I need you to take him."

Nathaniel eyed the child and scowled. "What are you trying to pull, Helene? I'm guessing this is the kid you got knocked up with when you were screwing around with Bryce."

She took in a deep breath, letting it out slowly. So she didn't lose control. Helene had been all about control. Too bad she hadn't used it to keep Bryce Billingsworth out of her pants when the man had been Nathaniel's law partner.

"We recently had some medical testing done on Tanner and discovered his blood type is O positive."

Nathaniel's blood type was O positive. Was that too common for a child of a Billingsworth? "Lots of people have type O blood, Helene."

"Yes, but I'm type A, and Bryce is AB. It's genetically impossible for Tanner to be Bryce's child."

Shit. He'd wondered about that possibility, but Helene had insisted Bryce was the father. Now what the hell did they do? Share the child?

"What do you want? Child support? Because you can kiss my ass if you think I'm paying you anything when you have millions at your disposal."

Helene's lips pinched, letting him know she disapproved of his language. Or of him. Who knew with the Ice Princess?

"I need you to take him. I can't keep him anymore."

"What do you mean, take him? He's your son." The kid stood quietly next to her, his eyes focused intently on the spinning tires of a Hot Wheels.

"Bryce…" She cleared her throat and looked over her shoulder at the limousine parked in front of his house. "Bryce doesn't want to raise another man's child."

"I always knew he was a bastard. The fact he was sleeping with my wife while we were still married kind of confirms that. But thumbing his nose at a child he's raised for what… three years? That's cold."

"Nathaniel, please. Bryce hasn't spent much time with Tanner due to his work commitments, so he's not attached. I'm giving custody over to you."

The cold-hearted weasel and Helene deserved each other.

"You're giving me custody? *Full* custody?"

Her glacial stare skimmed to the child, then returned as icy as ever. "Yes. Bryce doesn't want him living in our house."

"What kind of mother gives up her son? God, Helene, are you seriously that frozen inside?"

Another peek at the boy standing next to her, then her smile thawed slightly. "I mean, if you and I were to get—"

"Get back together," he finished for her. "Are you out of your mind? Not in a billion years. You're a lying, cheating tramp, and I'd rather be married to a flea-infested alley cat. I want nothing to do with you."

She shrugged, his words bouncing off the cashmere of her coat. "I didn't think so. Simply checking. But the fact remains that I can't have Tanner in the house with Bryce."

"You're not even going to want visitation?" He wasn't a family lawyer, but he knew she was screwing her parental rights if she gave the boy up completely. If this child was his —and with Helene's previous deceit, he had reasons to doubt —he'd make sure she never saw him again.

She shook her head, making sure not to upset the expensive coiffure.

"I guess you need to follow the money. That always was your first love." At one time, he'd thought it was him. *Fool me once...*

"Yes, well…here are his things." She stepped aside. Several large suitcases sat behind her, along with a car seat and a box of toys.

Seriously, there was enough for a dozen children. "His things."

Leaning down, she scooped a black and white stuffed dog from the top and handed it to him. "This is his favorite toy. He likes to sleep with it. It can get ugly if he doesn't have it at bedtime."

The child, Tanner, his son, never even looked up. He'd

been standing there without saying a word this whole time. Did he not understand his mother was deserting him? Essentially throwing him away and giving him to some stranger he didn't know? Was he able to hear her? She'd said something about medical tests.

"Helene, what exactly were you looking for when you had the blood tests done? I assume Bryce wasn't doubting the kid's paternity now. Is the boy sick?"

Her gaze flittered away, and she squared her shoulders, a fake smile appearing on her perfectly made up lips. She was about to lie to him. Too bad he hadn't noticed those tells earlier. Like before they'd gotten married.

"No, he's perfectly healthy. There are a few odd behaviors that the doctor wanted to check out. Nothing serious, I'm sure."

Nothing serious. The child—Tanner. *Tanner.* Tanner hadn't done anything except stare at the spinning wheels of the car. Nathaniel was no child psychologist, but he didn't think most kids did that. Tanner was about the same age as Matty, his cousin Erik's adopted son. Matty jumped and yelled and couldn't sit still all that long.

A beep from the limo had Helene pressing her lips together and glancing nervously over her shoulder. "I have to go. We've got a private jet waiting to take us to the Vineyard. Bryce will be quite dismayed if they've started it up, and it wastes too much fuel."

"Yes, let's not waste jet fuel. You're seriously going to walk away from your child? Do you know what this will do to him? Do you even care? I know nothing about him. What am I supposed to feed him? What does he like to do? When does he go to bed? What are his routines?"

"I don't know, Nathaniel. The nannies took care of all that. I really do have to go."

"Is there a nanny who'd work for me that he's familiar with?" Tanner needed someone in his corner who knew him.

"It won't matter. You'll see." She bent and stroked the boy's hair. "Be good for your daddy, Tanner." Then, she skirted the bags and stepped down the porch stairs. As she got to the bottom, she turned and said, "Oh, Dr. Malachite in Boston is his pediatrician. I'm sure he'd be happy to send his medical records to whatever doctor you choose for him. Merry Christmas, Nathaniel."

Nathaniel stood in the doorway until the limo cruised away and the bitter nip in the air woke him from his stupor.

What the hell just happened? And what in God's name was he supposed to do now? Tanner still stood there with the toy car, unfazed that his mother had left him with a stranger. Left him for good. Holy shit. He had a feeling those words would be repeating over and over for a while.

"Hey, Tanner. Let's get you inside where it's warm, okay?"

He took the boy's hand and led him into the house. Tanner looked around, like he'd only now realized he wasn't home. Would he start screaming for his mom?

Nathaniel's heart beat triple time, about to pound out of his chest in frustration, anger, and terror. He couldn't do this by himself.

Leading Tanner into his study, he placed him on the large leather chair and handed him the stuffed dog. The child tucked the animal under his arm and started rolling the car along the seat cushion.

Pulling his cell phone out of his pocket, Nathaniel pressed number one on his speed dial. When the call connected, his voice sounded weak and pathetic to his own ears.

"Mom, I need your help."

CHAPTER TWO

"You are rocking that bride look, Sara."

Darcy Marx grinned at her friend, then brushed the skirt of her fancy pastel bridesmaid dress and did a little twirl in front of the mirror. God, it was like she was in an old Doris Day movie with the soft colors and lace trim. Black and leather were more her thing.

But this was Sara's wedding. Sara was good people and made the boss happy. That made Darcy happy.

TJ Bannister had given Darcy a job over three years ago, even though her resume had been tragically thin and the references she'd listed on her application had long since moved and changed phone numbers. Oops. But he'd taken a chance on her, and she'd be ever thankful. For that and giving her more hours each week as she'd proven herself, and then a raise every six months.

"Thanks, Darcy. And thank you so much for being in my wedding and wearing the dress without any complaining."

Darcy squinted at her friend. "Oh, there's been plenty of complaining. It's just all been in here." She pointed at her black spiked hair. "But you know I'd do anything for you and the boss."

The matron of honor, Sara's sister-in-law, Tessa, pushed open the door and came back in, sighing. "Okay, let's see if we can get through this wedding without me having to pee again."

The woman was six or seven months pregnant and kind of a nervous sort. Super quiet. Of course, Darcy didn't know the woman's backstory. Everyone had a backstory. Some more dramatic than others. You never knew what baggage people were carrying, and Darcy tried not to judge anyone without knowing what that history was.

"You'll be fine, Tessa," Sara reassured her sister-in-law. Hopefully, this day would go exactly as she'd planned. So far, Sara looked the part of the beautiful blushing bride. Her blonde hair tucked in a twisting design under her long lace veil, and the wedding dress was perfect for Sara's sweet personality. It had cap sleeves and a lace bodice that hugged her figure. The skirt flared out and trailed behind her for what seemed like yards. Sara's future husband, TJ, made tons of money as the songwriter, James True, so could afford for his bride to splurge on all that fabric.

"It's time to head out and get this party started, girls," Molly Storm, Sara's adorable mother called into the church's back room. "The guys are all ready to escort you down the aisle."

"Oh, yay," Darcy mumbled under her breath. Time for the fashion show.

The cousin she'd been paired with was in the running for Cary Grant wannabe and GQ model of the year. With an attitude to match. Light brown hair, cut in a stylish conservative fashion, a face most women would drool over, and a suit that fit his tall, lean frame like a well-tailored glove. Pretentious didn't even cover it.

At the rehearsal last night, he'd almost choked when he'd seen her. Of course, the black on black ensemble might have been a little over the top, even for her. But if she was gonna be standing on her feet for a while, she needed her combat boots. They were totally broken in to her feet. The sheer black blouse was feminine, and she'd actually worn a tank top underneath. No free peeksies. Nothing to complain about. Her cutoff shorts might have been a little skimpy, but she'd worn opaque black tights. The bottom of the shorts hid her ass, and the rhinestones on the back pockets made them quite festive. Mr. Billion Dollar Suit could keep his opinions to himself.

As the wedding party exited the small room, they all gave Sara hugs. Sappy. When it was her turn, Darcy planted a kiss on her cheek, then made a face. "How come you couldn't have hooked me up with that first groomsman? With the sandy blond hair? He looks like he's a bad boy through and through."

Sara laughed, which was the result she'd been going for. "That's my brother, Luke, and I wouldn't wish him on my worst enemy. I love him, but he doesn't stick around long with any woman."

Darcy tipped her head and winked. "You only need them long enough for one thing."

Sara blushed. "Go line up with Nathaniel, so I can finally get married to the man I love."

"Only for you will I endure that stick in the mud. And only for today."

The music started to play, so Darcy sashayed toward Nathaniel and held her wrist up like she expected him to kiss her hand. His eyes narrowed, he shook his head, then held out his elbow for her to grasp.

"If that's the way you want it, fine. I'm Darcy, by the way."

He looked down his nose, his very straight and haughty

nose, and his lips tightened. "We met last night. Do you honestly not remember?"

She grinned. "I do. Wanted to make sure you did, too."

"You're pretty hard to forget."

"That I am. Now, let's do this thing." It was their turn to march down the aisle, and she made sure to step slowly and gracefully. Couldn't have the other bridesmaids outdoing her.

As Sara and TJ spoke words of love and forever, Darcy's gaze wandered around the church. It still amazed her that families like Sara's existed. Mom, Dad, brothers, aunts, uncles, and a bazillion cousins, all seeming to like each other. Then, there were TJ's rock star parents on the other side of the church trying to blend in. Celia Muñez and Abe Bannister. Yeah, that wasn't happening. Even in traditional wedding attire, they stood out like a sore thumb. And why did a sore thumb stick out? Where did that saying even come from? Unless the thumb was bleeding, it shouldn't look any different from the other fingers.

Finally, all the readings were done. The bride and groom had been joined and allowed to kiss, which meant it was time for her to join up with the old stick in the mud again. Oy. He might be fun to play with for a day, but it was a good thing she wasn't marrying into this family, or she might have to see him often.

As Sara and TJ greeted the rest of the guests, the bridal party stood to one side of the church vestibule. Darcy reached into her pocket, giving thanks that Sara had chosen dresses that had them, and pulled out one of her cigarettes.

"I got to have a smoke. I'll be right back."

GQ man stared at her, his mouth hanging open. She winked and took a few steps to stand outside the doors. As she placed the cancer stick in her mouth, Nathaniel stormed over to her and leaned down, his mouth near her ear.

"Can you seriously not wait until we get to the reception to do that? Not everyone wants to inhale your secondhand smoke."

"Like you?" She pulled the cigarette out of her mouth and blew air in his direction.

His head cocked, and he squinted at her fingers. "That's a candy cigarette. You smoke candy cigarettes?"

"Two pack a day habit. I've gotten it down from three. But I figure if I have to socialize with all these people, the least I can do is have minty fresh breath. Don't you agree?"

For the first time, the man actually smiled. Then, laughed. He turned around and headed back into the church shaking his head. That was fun. She should do it more often. Who was she kidding? She did it very often.

The ride to the reception hall was quick as it was only around the corner, but with fancy dresses and high-heeled shoes, they'd rented a few limousines. The groom had enough money to buy this town, so he could afford it. If she'd known who he was when she first got hired at Tea and Tales, his coffeeshop/bookstore down in Hyannis, she would have asked for more money. She'd never complain, since he paid her more than any of her other pitiful jobs ever had, plus benefits to boot.

The pictures took forever, or what seemed like forever, but luckily she only had to be in the wedding party ones. The family ones took even longer with Sara, her parents, grandparents, three brothers, sister-in-law, and Erik and Tessa's two kids, who didn't always stay as still as they should for the photographer.

As she stared at the bridal couple being photographed with TJ's famous parents, Nathaniel appeared at her shoulder.

"A little awestruck, are you?"

"Not in the least. They've been in the store and around

the Cape for a while. We're like this." She crossed her first and middle finger together. "Are *you* all aflutter?"

Nathaniel's lips curled up. "Not my type of music. I prefer classical."

"Of course you do, Biff. What else would you listen to?"

"Biff?"

"If the Italian leather shoe fits, wear it."

"At least it's not black combat boots."

Sticking her foot out, she showed off her boring white pumps. "No combat today. Guess we're under a cease fire."

"And here I forgot my white flag, so I guess you're the one surrendering."

"In your dreams, Biff."

"If you're in them, they'd be classified as nightmares, Goth Girl."

"For your information, my style is not Goth. It's authentic Darcy Marx."

"Your own style. Wearing all black. Original."

"I don't always wear all black. Last night was a special occasion. But today, I'm festive. See? Pink dress, pink eyeshadow, and even red lipstick." Okay, most of her eye makeup was black, and heavy, but she'd added special curlicues to the corners of her eyes, so it would stand out from her typical fare.

GQ Man squinted as he leaned to look closer. Holy Pop-Tarts, he smelled good.

"That's red?"

"Yes, dark red. It's called Blood Moon."

He chuckled. "Perfect name for a vampire."

"A vampire in pastel lace and white pumps? Seriously? Have you not seen any Dracula movies?"

"Only the classics. Most of them are in black and white, so I wouldn't be able to tell if something was pink."

"A real vampiress doesn't wear pink. At any time. And I'm out in the daylight, thus…not Dracula's bride, genius."

He looked about to respond when a high-pitched screech shot from the edge of the garden area they were standing in. Mr. GQ closed his eyes and sighed heavily.

"Who's that?"

When he opened his eyes, his jaw was so tight she wasn't sure he'd be able to speak. But he did.

"My son."

"Your son?" He had a kid. "Wait, someone actually married you. Is she as stuck up and in love with herself as you are?"

As he walked away, he looked over his shoulder at her. "Even worse. I know. Hard to believe."

At least he admitted it. Self-deprecation kind of looked good on him. He should wear it more often, but she doubted he would.

A small, toe-headed child careened across the path, away from the building. Nathaniel scooped him up before he could do any damage and carried him back. A slim, blonde woman raced after the boy and stopped short when she saw Biff with him. Was that his wife? She looked a bit too…mature, unless he was into much older women.

The child hung over his arm crying and kicking his feet. Had mom…or grandma…not let him have a piece of the wedding cake yet? Was he as spoiled as his dad?

The photographer called out, "Okay, folks, all done. Time to line up and be introduced. I'll be inside the door taking pictures from there."

The wedding planner shuffled them all inside and to a room off the main reception hall. Where was her partner in crime? Maybe if he wasn't here, she could skip this part. One could only hope.

At the last second, Nathaniel rushed over and held out his

elbow to parade into the room with her. His entire body was stiff, and he kept glancing to the side to check on something. His kid? She'd give him a hard time, but he already seemed totally wigged out about the crying episode.

"Is it nap time and someone's tired?" Her way of asking without throwing shade on anyone.

He swallowed, and his Adam's apple bobbed up and down. Why the hell was she finding that sexy? And on Mr. Biff GQ himself? *Not cool, Darcy. Get a grip. You've been wearing pink too long.*

"Something like that. My mom's got him for now. Hopefully, he'll calm down."

Okay, so the cool blonde lady was his mother. They had a good relationship, if their interaction was anything to go by. But, of course, all these Storms loved each other. They were the friggin' Brady Bunch and Happy Days all rolled together.

But if mom had the kid, where was wifey-poo? Her hair appointment was more important than a cousin's wedding? Seemed about right for this dandy.

When Sara and TJ began their first dance, Nathaniel whispered in her ear. "I'll be right back."

"Holding my breath," she mumbled as he trotted away. But he'd heard. That little side eye and smirk were all for her. Didn't she feel special?

Not as special as the little boy who was held in his grandmother's arms in the doorway behind them. That damn GQ model had to go and touch the child sweetly on the head and whisper something to him. He pulled an item from his pocket and handed it to the boy, who immediately reached for whatever it was and settled down.

She could see Nathaniel's shoulders rise and fall from here. Soon, he was back at her side and pulling her into his arms when they called for the rest of the wedding party to join in a dance.

His hand was warm against her back, and the other one tingled where it held hers.

"What did you give him? It seemed to quiet him right down."

Leaning in closer, Nathaniel said, "My key chain. It's got a flashlight on the end he loves to play with. Of course, it'll probably be dead by the end of the night. If he doesn't lose the keys first."

Minty breath floated across her cheek. Had he puffed on a candy cigarette, too? Must be the reason she was going all gooey in his arms. The addiction to her smokes was cutting in.

"You're taking the chance he'll lose your keys? Risky business, Biff."

"It'll keep him quiet, and I don't want him wrecking Sara's wedding. I've got another set at home if I can't find them."

Frack. Why'd he have to go and do something nice? Now she couldn't rag on him quite so much. And he was still checking on the child even while they danced. He kept spinning her around so he could face where his mom and kid sat at a table furthest from the dance floor.

"What's his name?"

"My son? Tanner."

She couldn't hide the snort that escaped from her mouth. "Of course, it is."

His eyes darkened, and he took a deep breath. "I didn't name him."

"You didn't even put up a fight? You just let the old lady choose something pretentious."

The music ended, and he stepped back. "She'd already divorced me and married someone else. So no, I wasn't involved in naming him. I didn't know he was mine."

With that, he turned and headed to the table his mom sat at. *Open mouth. In you go, boring white pumps.* She'd gotten fairly good at that recently. Too bad it wasn't an Olympic sport. She'd win gold.

As the rest of the guests settled into their seats for the meal, Darcy sat at the head table with an empty chair next to her. Nathaniel still crouched next to the back table talking to his son. Tanner.

This rich GQ wannabe might be pompous and snotty, but it seemed he at least attempted to be a decent father. How long had he known the child was his? She'd have to do a little snooping today.

While father and son sat together jangling the key chain in the air, Darcy thought about her own childhood. If you could call it that. Her mother's biggest worry was her next fix. She had never played with them or cared if they were entertained. She could barely remember to feed her children.

As Darcy watched the love and family all around this room, she knew even a fraction of it was more than her mother had ever done for her and Zane. And sadly, more than she'd ever done for a child. Reaching for her champagne glass, she took a big sip. Thankfully, it was running free today.

NATHANIEL CLICKED the flashlight on his key chain off again, then back on, making a shape on Tanner's leg with his fingers. The boy waved his hand over the shadow again and again. He'd seen him do this for hours, and Nathaniel wasn't sure he had it in him right now.

"Honey, why don't you go and talk to some of your cousins for a while?" his mother suggested as she settled back in her chair. What would he have done without Anna Storm? The woman had been a godsend. "I'll play with my grandson for a while. Aunt Luci can keep me company while your father and uncles discuss electricity."

Kris Storm, along with his two brothers, Nick and Pete, owned and ran Storm Electric. It was a lucrative business, and often they'd be found chatting about a project when they should have been doing family stuff. The business had put all their kids through school and kept food on the table, so Nathaniel wasn't going to complain. However, that had never stopped their wives.

"Thanks, Mom. Wave me over if you need a break, although I'm not sure what good it'll do. He seems to be calmer for you than for me." That effect his mother had was the only reason Nathaniel had gotten a few quick bites of the expensive meal Sara and TJ had paid for. For once, Darcy hadn't given him any lip about not keeping her company.

"Thirty years of working with children gives me some advantage, honey. Don't worry. He's only been with you a little over four months, and he's gone through quite an upheaval in his young life. You'll get there."

Wandering over to the bar, he wondered if he ever would. His mom had worked at a child care center right in Squamscott Falls for most of his life. Part time when he'd been little, and then full time once his younger sister, Amy, had started school. She knew how to deal with children with all kinds of needs. And he had to face facts—Tanner had special needs.

When he'd first called his mom for help, she'd spent a ton of time with Tanner. Those odd behaviors Helene had wanted checked? Yeah, turns out Tanner was on the Autism Spectrum. He'd bet big money she'd already known the child's diagnosis, and the bitch couldn't run away fast enough.

He'd run right to a lawyer friend and started the process of being named Tanner's legal guardian. The DNA test took some time, but it came back with absolute certainty the boy was his son. Once that was established, he'd wanted Helene stripped of all parental rights. She swore out an affidavit stating that she had no desire to contest his petition, but unfortunately, the judge wasn't so easily convinced. A child needed his mother. Yes, he did. But not one who wanted nothing to do with him.

Helene had appeared in court last month and announced to the judge she was expecting another baby with her husband, this one absolutely his. They'd already done genetic testing that showed this child would be born without any abnormalities. Nathaniel's lawyer took the opportunity to remind Helene and inform the judge that, because scientists had yet to discover what causes it, Autism is a disorder that cannot be predicted before birth. Helene barely batted an eyelash. Like a robot, she reiterated to the court that Nathaniel had the right to take care of and make decisions for the child.

The judge had been horrified. She hadn't completely stripped Helene of her parental rights. She allowed that, if Helene ever wanted to see Tanner, she needed to give him at least two weeks' notice, with the proviso that he could deny her access at that time if it wasn't in the best interest of the child. All legal and medical decisions would be Nathaniel's and only Nathaniel's. And he was able to legally change the birth certificate to list him as father and change his son's name from Tanner Bryce Billingsworth to Tanner Nathaniel Storm. He kept the first name for Tanner's sake, but there was no way in hell he'd allow his child to carry the name of the bastard who betrayed their partnership and slept with his wife.

The sad thing was he didn't even miss Helene. She was the perfect woman who was supposed to finish out his grand plan. Job in a great law practice, lovely wife, beautiful house, respect in the community.

He still had respect in the community, much of that coming from the Storm name. His parents and grandparents had been in Squamscott Falls their whole lives and were a vital part of the town. He'd started his own law practice and was doing exceedingly well as a corporate attorney for some of the state's biggest companies. He had sold the ostentatious monstrosity Helene had insisted they build in Rye and bought his four-bedroom house on Exeter Pond on the outskirts of town.

The only thing missing was the wife. And he wasn't ready to jump into that pile of horse manure again anytime soon.

Now, if only he could get a nanny to actually stay working for him. He'd lost the third one only two days ago. He had a lead on another, one from England, who had reportedly worked for one of the lesser royals. For what she wanted in salary, she'd better be able to take good care of his son.

Leaning against the bar, he sipped his water as his cousin, Alex, joined him and ordered a beer.

"Designated driver today?"

He frowned. "No, but I need to be ready if Tanner decides to have one of his freak-outs."

They both stared at the little boy playing with his mom. Darcy had gone over, chatted with them, then sat on the floor in front of where Tanner was rolling his toy car. She didn't seem to care about her fancy bridesmaid dress.

"How are things going there?"

His lips tightened. "I've gone through three nannies already. Thank God for my mom, but she can't keep coming to my rescue. I need to get a handle on this, but I have no idea how to do that."

"Darcy looks like she's getting some good reactions."

She did, which was surprising. He'd never have guessed

she was a kid person. Tanner actually looked up at her a few times. Eye contact was not his forte. With anyone.

"Yeah, she does. Maybe she can give me some lessons. I can't get any kind of positive reaction from him."

"Give it time." Alex patted his shoulder.

It had been four months, and Nathaniel still had no better idea how to connect with the boy. Apparently, having the same blood didn't guarantee you'd understand each other. The books he'd read on ASD hadn't been super helpful either, since every Autistic child had his or her own personality and quirks. Just when he thought he'd figured out one of Tanner's, something else would pop up that threw the kid into a tailspin.

"Sure." His gaze moved to the door where Gina, Alex's friend…girlfriend…whatever she was to him, stood. Typically, she looked like a bohemian vagabond, but today she'd fit right in with Helene at the country club. "And maybe Gina could give Darcy some lessons on metamorphosis. That's quite a change. Did she do that for you?"

Alex shrugged and walked toward Gina. The man was so whipped, but Nathaniel wondered if he actually knew it. Probably not, poor bastard. Gina was as opposite as you could get from Alex.

Kind of like him and Darcy. She was the exact opposite of anything he'd look for in a woman.

And how'd that work for you the first time?

Whatever. He and Darcy rubbed each other the wrong way, and they weren't anything more than partners in the bridal party today. But his hand rubbing along her back while they danced had been surprisingly nice.

Original Darcy Marx style. It was something. Her short black hair was spiked in every direction, with the exception of one long clump that swooped down over her right eye. Every now and then she'd tuck it behind her ear. The one that had half a dozen sparkling jewels embedded in it. The other ear was a matching set. A smaller stud glistened on the side of her nose. He wondered if she was pierced anywhere else that didn't show.

And why the hell had his mind even gone there? He wasn't into the tattoos and piercings, although the only tattoo he could see on Darcy was a small set of wings on her back. When she'd been placed in front of him during pictures, he'd managed to see what it was. The word HOPE with a heart in place of the O and the wings were on the H. Maybe someday he'd ask what it meant. Or maybe not. There was no reason for them to associate with each other after today.

The music stopped after a vigorous fast number and a laugh crossed the floor. It was Darcy, and Tanner was almost in her lap. What the heck? His son never willingly touched him or sat on his lap unless Nathaniel put him there.

Tipping her face, Darcy smiled and let Tanner touch her cheek. His fingers trailed down her diamond studded ears and then traced the fancy scroll work on the outside of her eyes. It was different from yesterday's darker makeup that had surrounded her eyes, both top and bottom. It was possible she might be of Asian descent, but with that much makeup he honestly couldn't tell. She was definitely an odd duck.

And Tanner seemed taken with her for some reason. Leaning back against the bar, he kept his eye on them. Maybe if he watched them long enough, he could learn something.

CHAPTER THREE

Nathaniel put his car in park and shut it off. Sara and TJ pulled into his driveway only moments after.

"Perfect timing," he said as he gave his cousin a kiss on the cheek and shook her husband's hand. "I appreciate your meeting me here instead of my office. I hate leaving Tanner too long. I'm not too sure about this newest nanny."

"Well, your office in Portsmouth is further away anyhow, so it's easier to come here." TJ guided his wife up the stairs to the porch.

"What's wrong with this one?" Sara asked. "I thought she had all sorts of great qualifications."

"She did. She does, but I'm not sure they're the right qualifications to take care of Tanner."

Before he even opened the front door, he heard it. The humming of Tanner's repetitive cry. God, not again. It broke his heart every time the child had a meltdown. Especially since he didn't seem to be able to stop them. He'd seen his cousin, Erik, with his kids many times, and usually scooping them into his lap and snuggling worked almost immediately to calm them down.

Tanner didn't want to be picked up or cuddled. The black hole in his chest expanded every time the boy stiffened in his arms. What good was he as a father if he couldn't help his child when he was in distress? Would it have been different if he'd raised his son from a newborn? Damn Helene and her selfish, lying ways.

"Mr. Storm, thank goodness you've arrived home." Mrs. Taverton squealed in her high-pitched voice. That alone probably sent Tanner off the deep end. "He's been this way for hours, and he won't stop. Doesn't matter what I threaten him with, he refuses to stop crying."

Heat rose to his face, and he clenched his jaw. "Why didn't you call me at work? I would have come home early."

Her shoulders pushed back on her thin frame. "It's my job to care for the child and discipline him. He needs to learn to listen when an adult speaks to him."

"Mrs. Taverton, we've had this talk before. Tanner is on the Spectrum, which means he doesn't respond the same way other children do."

Her eyes opened wide, and her mouth turned down. "Well, he needs to learn. We cannot have a child being disrespectful to his elders."

"What did he do?" Nathaniel didn't even want to know.

"He refused to eat the sandwich I gave him at lunch and threw it across the table. When he tried to get down to play with his car, I insisted he apologize first. I took his car away and told him he'd get it back when he picked up his ruined lunch. Instead, he flung it onto the carpet in the family room. When I took out the vacuum to clean it up, he began that horrible caterwauling."

Nathaniel closed his eyes and counted to ten. He might have counted even higher, except Tanner was still whimpering, and he needed to see to him first. The noise from the vacuum cleaner always sent him into hysterics.

As Nathaniel moved down the hall past the kitchen and dining room, he stopped short. His son stood by the floor-to-ceiling windows overlooking the lake, his face pressed against the glass. The sobs had diminished, but small whimpers still erupted every few seconds in rhythm.

"Where's his car?" It didn't matter. He'd stuck several of them in various locations throughout the house in case of an emergency. Tanner liked certain ones, but in a pinch the others sometimes worked, too.

Pulling one out of the kitchen drawer, he trotted down the few stairs into the family room, knelt down next to him, then scooped the child into his arms. "I've got your car, buddy. It's okay."

Tanner didn't even turn his head to look at him. He rarely did. When Nathaniel placed the car on the window near his face, the boy grabbed onto it, his gaze zeroing in on the moving wheels.

Sara and TJ had followed him in but stood back near the hallway. Once Tanner stopped sobbing, Sara eased closer. "I'll sit with him if you want to deal with this." She canted her head slightly to indicate the nanny. Guess he'd better.

TJ joined Sara and Tanner on the couch that faced the fireplace on the field stone wall. Nathaniel scrambled back up the stairs to find Mrs. Taverton getting her purse out of the closet.

"I don't think this is working."

Her head snapped around, and she focused her intense gaze on him. Had she looked at Tanner this way?

"Of course it's not, since you insist on spoiling that child and allowing him to get away with rude behavior."

He clenched his fists to keep from wrapping his hands around her scrawny throat. "You may have wonderful experience with most children, but you obviously know nothing about dealing with children with special needs, and I can't have you terrorizing my son and taking away the only thing he has to soothe himself. I'll forward your last paycheck to you tomorrow. Thank you."

Her pointy nose stuck right in the air as she slung her purse strap over her shoulder. "I can assure you, I had no plans to return here again. I will see myself out."

His fists tightened into balls, and he closed his eyes to keep himself from screaming. Good riddance. But now what the hell did he do?' It was only the first of June, and his mom was still in school for another few weeks.

Before he went back to the family room, he detoured to his office and grabbed a small globe from his desk.

"I'm sorry about that. You didn't drive all the way from the Cape to listen to my nanny bitch about my kid." As he settled into the large recliner, he held out his hands for Sara to give him Tanner.

Once the boy was in his lap, he handed the globe to him. No happiness or excitement, he simply took the small orb and began spinning it on its axis.

"It's okay, Nathaniel." Sara adjusted her skirt, then took her new husband's hand. "We were visiting Gram and Gramps this afternoon, then stopped in to see my parents and check that Alex was all right. One stop shopping, you know."

"God, Alex. How's he doing? My mom's been keeping me updated, but I haven't had a chance to stop in and see him." He gazed at Tanner, the reason he'd been stuck at home so often lately.

"He got home from the hospital a few days ago. He needs rest and a little pampering."

Nathaniel thought back to Alex, and how he'd reacted to Gina's transformation at the wedding. Right before someone tried to burn down Gina's house with the two of them in it. "I'm sure Gina will take care of him. She was in a little better shape, right?"

Sara frowned. "Yeah, she's in New York City right now. Something about work. I think Alex is afraid she might not come back. But that's something they'll have to work out. Is everything all right with the nanny?"

"I canned her. I'm sure you heard. I can't have someone here who doesn't understand Tanner's needs. Heck, I don't understand his needs, but at least I don't make him eat food he doesn't like or run the vacuum, knowing loud noises set him off."

"You seem to be doing okay right now," TJ pointed out the child with his gaze glued to the spinning sphere.

Nathaniel laughed. "I only use this as a last resort. The globe came from India and cost a small fortune. But watching it spin is mesmerizing for him. It often distracts him from what was originally bothering him." The fact Tanner sat quietly on his lap meant nothing, though. Nathaniel wasn't deluding himself. He'd put the child there so he had some feeling of being fatherly. "I never even asked. How was your honeymoon?

Sara blushed and looked down. "It was amazing. We had a great time."

"What did your parents do when you showed them the prenuptial documents?" The question was addressed to TJ, who grinned widely.

"It took them a few minutes to understand the legal mumbo jumbo, but when they realized the agreement was written so Sara got all of my money in case of divorce, and I got all hers in that event, they went a little ballistic."

"I'm still not sure why you wanted it written that way."

Sara gazed at her husband with such love, Nathaniel was

humbled. Helene had cared more for his money and what his status could do for her. It was never about him.

"We only did a pre-nup because they insisted. But I figure if Sara gets all my assets and I get all hers, then honestly, I'll get the better end of the deal. This talented lady will be worth more than me someday."

"You're such a goof." Sara rolled her eyes but leaned closer and touched her lips to TJ's arm.

TJ placed the large manila envelope onto the coffee table. "It's all signed, notarized, and legal, and yours to keep a copy of."

"Happy to help."

Sara tipped her chin, indicating Tanner. "Is there anything we can do to help you?"

"Not unless you want to move back here and babysit for me. Except I can't even do that here. This place needs major renovations. It's so old I'm worried about possible lead paint. The windows all need replacing, and I think some of the electrical and plumbing aren't up to code. Storm Electric can do the rewiring, but not the rest. Plus, I need railings along the kitchen and dining room. Those drops are too steep with a child in the house."

His family room was sunken and took up the entire east side of the house facing the lake. A small set of stairs rose up the middle to the area with his kitchen on the left and his dining area on the right. The rooms dropped off with nothing to stop anyone from falling. It was only a few feet, but for a three-year-old it was too high.

"I've hired John Michaels to do the renovations, but it's going to take at least a month or two to get it all done. My parents' place at the adult community doesn't allow children and isn't large enough for all of us. I may have to either rent an apartment or stay at a hotel."

"You can't stay here while the renovations are being

done?" Sara glanced around the room.

"A lot of the stuff that needs to be done will require cutting holes in walls and there'll be dust everywhere. I don't want to expose Tanner to that."

TJ looked down at Sara and tilted his head. She nodded and grinned. "You're welcome to come stay with us while the house is torn apart. We've got five bedrooms, and we're right on the beach. The weather will get nicer from here on out."

"But work…"

"We've got wifi, and it's only a two-hour drive, if you need to meet with a client."

He sat and thought for a few minutes. Could he possibly do it? A number of the companies he represented took the summer at a slower pace, so his presence wasn't needed as much.

"I'll be there to help keep an eye on Tanner when you have work to do." Sara stared at his son. The kid sure was adorable. Blond curls, bright blue eyes, turned up nose. Luckily, he didn't have too many of Helene's features. He had more the look of Nathaniel's brother, Kevin, when he'd been younger. His mom seemed to think so, too.

"I might be able to arrange things so my business partner can handle any of the in-person contact, and I can deal with the legal end." His new business partner was a fifty-year-old woman. Efficient in every way, and most likely not in the market for a fling. Not that Nathaniel had anyone he'd been flinging with lately.

"Then, you should come down. It'd be nice to get to know Tanner better. Maybe he could even hang out with some of the kids from Story Hour. I do that every Tuesday, Thursday, and Saturday morning. TJ's dog, Freckles, even joins us. Does Tanner like dogs?"

He looked at the boy in his lap, still focused on the spinning globe. "He has a stuffed dog that he absolutely has to sleep with. I have no idea about real dogs, but I guess we'll soon find out."

"Great. Let us know if there's anything special you need, and we'll make sure to get it before you arrive."

"Thanks, Sara, TJ. Appreciate this. It's been a little rough lately. Especially since I've had to go to work every day and leave him with someone else. I'm due some time off. Maybe I can use that time to get to know my own son."

Darcy snapped the lid on the coffee cup and handed it to the customer with a, "Have a groovy day."

If only she could have the same. A groovy day, not a cup of coffee. It was Story Hour day again. The day she looked forward to yet dreaded at the same time. Maybe she should ask TJ not to schedule her the mornings when the kids were all here. Brats, the lot of them.

"Hey, Darcy, just a heads up," TJ said, coming in from the back room where he'd probably been rearranging coffee covers and napkins. Something he did too often.

"My head's up. What's it doing there, boss?"

"Sara's cousin is going to be staying with us for a while this summer due to house renovations, so Sara might not be here as often as she usually is. Do you want the overtime, or should I see if those new hires want extra hours?"

"Don't give those yahoos more hours than they already have. They'll call in sick on the good beach days, and I'll end up covering for them anyway, except then I'll be pissed because it will be my day off, instead of scheduled overtime. Which you'll be paying me time and a half for, correct?"

"Yes, that's correct. But make sure you let me know if the hours are too much. You need to have some time for yourself, too."

Sure, time for herself to sit in her crappy little apartment worrying about how she'd pay the rent and for everything her brother needed.

"Hey, boss, which cousin is coming to visit?" Darcy had gotten along great with all of them. Well, all except GQ. Sara's cousin Sofie seemed the coolest. She could see them hitting a dance club or two together. When she wasn't working her overtime.

"Nathaniel."

What the heck?

"The guy can afford to buy a whole new house to stay in if he needs to. What's he doing coming down here and mooching off you two?"

"He did some legal work for us, and Sara wanted to pay him back. Plus, he's been having some problems with nannies for his kid, so this way Sara can help him with Tanner while he works."

Frack. She didn't need Biff and his GQ attitude hanging out anywhere near her space. Could she take the summer off? Hell, she'd just told TJ she'd do overtime. Oh, and there was rent and therapy for her brother she needed to find money for.

TJ smirked as he poured himself a cup of cinnamon tea. "I figured with you and Nathaniel being good buddies and all, you'd be thrilled."

She threw him the look. The one she'd learned from Mary, day manager and mother figure to many of the staff here. TJ included. "Don't quit the day job to go into comedy, boss. You'll starve."

"But I might need you to do Story Hour once in a while, if Sara's unable to. You'd be okay with that, right?" He peeked at her from behind his mug, his eyes sparking with mischief.

"Story Hour? With the rug rats? Are you serious? You know kids aren't my jam."

"Really? Because seeing you with Tanner Storm at the wedding was something to behold."

She let out a soft, "Pfft."

"I've also seen you watching as Sara reads to the kids. If I didn't know any better, I say that you, Darcy Marx, might even like children." He pivoted and went back to work.

And wasn't that the crux of the problem. How much she liked, even loved children. But they could only rip your heart out and leave you bleeding alone on the cold hard floor.

She thought about Nathaniel Storm and his son. She'd asked around, and Sofie had given her the dish on Nathaniel's nasty wife, who'd cheated on him with his business partner and got knocked up. Only it ended up being Biff's kid and one that had a special need. That lying sack of shit ex of his should be covered in honey and left to be fed off by the buzzards and wild animals.

When you were able to take care of your child, you did. That woman didn't have a good excuse for deserting her kid. Maybe that was why Mr. GQ seemed like he had a stick up his ass. Being denied your kid for three years, or any amount of time, was painful. No matter the reason.

At least now he was able to be with his son. Not everyone had that opportunity. Of course, some people did stupid things and lost their kids. Like her mother with her drugs and...

"Hey, Darcy." Jodie Benedict, one of the Story Hour moms, walked over to the counter. "How are you today?"

"Peachy keen. All good with you and the family?"

"Thankful every day for all we've been given." Jodie gazed back at the children starting to congregate on the rug. "You know if you ever need anything at all, we're more than happy to help. Just give us the word."

Darcy picked up a rag to wipe the counter. Why weren't there more customers right now? Didn't the other parents want coffee while they waited? TJ should insist they buy something while their kid got free entertainment. Maybe she'd suggest it.

"I'm totally good. Looks like you are, too." She glanced over at Jodie's daughter sitting quietly on the carpet, waiting for the rest of the children so they could start. "You're doing a great job raising that little girl, and that's the most important thing you can do. It's all that matters."

"You should talk to her today, Darcy. I bet she'd like that. She always comments on your hair and all those earrings."

"I'm good. I've got to get back to work. It's great that you bring her in every week." Why she did this to herself, she didn't know. Glutton for punishment? Or maybe she should call it penance. For all her sins.

"I've got some new pictures of her we took on vacation a few weeks ago. I'll send them to you."

"Sure." As Darcy turned away, her eyes started to prickle and her vision blurred. Dust from all the books must be kicking up again. She threw a "thanks" over her shoulder, but Jodie had already moved past the colorful rug to settle on one of the couches, and Sara started her first story.

The kids sat mesmerized by how she emphasized certain words and used a variety of voices for each character. Freckles, TJ's spaniel, practically sat in Sara's lap, as did Eddie. His sister Jasmine hugged Sara's other side, while the twins, Harrison and Benson, were front and center. Elliott occupied the middle of the carpet, back straight, eyes ahead, and next to the bouncy, redheaded Fiona sat Hope. The shy little thing clasped her hands together and watched, leaning forward slightly like it would get her deeper into the book. Her dark hair was pulled into two braids that framed her face with the help of the bangs that hung in her eyes. Eyes that were the same shape and almost an exact replica of the ones Darcy stared at every morning in the mirror.

CHAPTER FOUR

Nathaniel flipped his blinker on a second before he turned onto TJ and Sara's road. Man, this was a great neighborhood. It was right on the beach. Sarah had mentioned their place had five bedrooms, but he hadn't realized how big the other houses were.

"Almost there, buddy." Tanner had fallen asleep shortly after he got on the road and was just starting to stir. Hopefully, they could get to the house before he woke up completely. The stuffed dog had slipped to the seat during the drive, and Nathaniel couldn't reach it while maneuvering through the streets of Hyannis.

When he pulled into their driveway, Sara came scurrying out of the house, a massive smile on her face. She bounced over and pulled him into a hug as soon as he got out of the car.

"I'm so excited you'll be staying with us. It'll be like when we all stayed at Gram and Gramps' up in Maine over the summer, except we won't have to all bunk in the same room."

Those days had been fun. The boys' room had been a hive of activity, with six boy cousins all together, while the four girls had shared the smaller bedroom. But they'd made it work. God bless their grandparents who allowed them all to stay at the same time, while their parents had gone back to New Hampshire for a mini vacation.

"Do you want me to grab your bags, or should I see if Tanner will let me carry him? He seems like he's still drowsy."

"You can try. I'll get our things."

Sara reached in and unbuckled the straps, then pulled Tanner into her arms.

"Dog," the child yelled, his hands extended.

Nathaniel grabbed the stuffed animal and thrust it in the boy's arms as quickly as he could. Hopefully, that would hold him until they got in the house. After picking up the other bags, he followed Sara into the house.

"Let me show you your rooms first, then I'll give you the grand tour."

She kept hold of Tanner all the way up the stairs and stepped into the first room on the right.

"I gave you both of the front rooms. They have a great view of the ocean and are connected through a bathroom. I figured that way you could get to Tanner if he needed you in the middle of the night."

"That's thoughtful. He's actually a great sleeper. Once he's in bed, he won't get out of it until I get him in the morning. I usually leave a few cars within reach, so he can play if he wakes up before me." He dropped the bags on the bed. He'd sort the stuff out later.

"Hey, Tanner, this is your room." Sara crossed through the bathroom and twirled around in the second bedroom. "I hope you like it."

"Dog." Tanner yelled, swinging the black and white beast in the air. Sara snuggled him close and kissed his cheek. It went totally unnoticed.

"You look good holding a child."

"I love kids. That's why doing Story Hour at the bookstore is one of my favorite things. We'll have to bring Tanner there tomorrow. He can meet some of the other kids."

Nathaniel wasn't sure that was a great idea. He hadn't tested the boy with other children yet and wasn't sure how he'd react."

"Are you and TJ thinking of starting a family soon? You've got plenty of space."

"Oh, God, no. We've got time. I want to focus on my singing career for a bit. TJ had the entire cellar redone into a sound studio, so I can record. My manager wants me to cut an album, so TJ's been furiously writing songs for me. Then, I'll do a few shows this fall to promote it."

"I'm sure they'll all be big hits." His cousin had a gorgeous voice.

"Thanks," Sara replied, then stepped into the hallway, still carrying Tanner.

"I appreciate your letting us stay here. It could be a while until the house is ready. You're sure TJ doesn't mind?"

She stopped in the hallway and grinned. "During the summer, he's at the shop a lot so it doesn't matter. Plus, he wants me to be happy."

Wouldn't that be nice? A spouse who cared about your happiness. *Bitter much, Storm?* Even when he and Helene had first been married, he didn't think they were ever that happy. There was always something missing, something more she needed to make her life 'just right'.

"There're two more bedrooms across the hall. If your rooms don't work for some reason, you're welcome to use any of these."

"I'm sure the front ones will be fine."

Sara nodded and skipped down the stairs, showing him the rest of the house. And he'd thought his place was big. Five massive rooms downstairs. The living room in the middle, with four rooms surrounding it, one in each corner. The front right corner had floor-to-ceiling windows and a huge grand piano in the center. Nothing else.

"This is my favorite room." Sara twirled Tanner around the wide-open floor. "But I'd bet you could guess that."

"Is this where all the magic happens?"

An impish expression twinkled on her face. "All the music magic, anyway."

Wow. That wasn't at all the Sara he remembered from childhood. But then she'd traveled with a rock group and gotten married all in the last year.

Quickly, she showed him the dining room in the back-right corner, then the master bedroom on the other front corner. They finished up in the kitchen.

"Are you hungry? I've got the fixins for sandwiches."

"Dog." The word came out of Tanner's mouth louder than any he'd heard.

Sara knelt down and placed the boy on the floor as a black and white spaniel padded into the room. "Yes, sweetie. This is Freckles. She's our dog. Like you have your dog."

Tanner plunked his butt down on the floor and stared at the spaniel, his own dog clutched in his arms.

"Dog. Dog."

Freckles sat next to him, then stretched out to place her head in his lap. Nathaniel watched closely, ready to move in at the first sign of Tanner getting upset. To his knowledge, the child hadn't been in contact with any animals before. Not that he knew what the boy had experienced, since Helene refused to talk to him at any length. Was it because she missed her son? He'd like to think she wasn't so cold that she could simply forget she had a child, but then why give up all contact with him? He'd told her they could make arrangements if she wanted to see him.

More than likely, she wanted to keep Bryce happy. He was her meal ticket. Even though she came from a prominent family, her father was old fashioned and fairly misogynistic. To him, women didn't belong in the work force. They organized fundraisers and then hung around afterward as decoration. He'd expected her to marry a successful man who could provide for her, and even though Nathaniel had a great job and a generous paycheck, he didn't come from a moneyed family. Thus, her seduction of Bryce.

"Dog."

Sara patted the animal's head. "Her name is Freckles. Can you say that? Freckles?"

"Fwecko."

"Yes, Freckles. That's right. She's a nice dog. You can pat her if you like. See, like me." Sara stroked her hand over the dog's back.

"Fwecko." Tanner took his stuffed dog and plopped it on Freckles' head.

"Tanner, be careful." Just what he needed was the dog biting his son.

Looking up, Sara said, "I wouldn't worry too much. Freckles is used to all the kids at Story Hour. She's given many a stuffed animal a piggyback ride."

"Fwecko wide."

"Yes, Freckles can give your animal a ride. But be gentle. Soft, okay, Tanner?"

Sara gazed up at Nathaniel as she helped Tanner pat the dog. "We think Freckles is pregnant. The neighbor's dog got loose about a month ago and somehow managed to get under our backyard fence. TJ hadn't gotten her spayed yet, because he always keeps her in the yard or with him. She's got an appointment with the vet next week."

"What kind of dog? Will they be a strange mix?"

"It was a tan Cocker spaniel. Freckles is a Springer. The

puppies would probably be a little smaller than her and a combination of black, white, and tan. The owner felt bad and offered to get her fixed, but we'll wait and see."

At least, they knew for certain who the father was before the puppies were born. Bitterness rose again.

Sara took the stuffed dog and gently passed it over the real dog's head and back. Tanner stared, and Nathaniel almost saw a smile touch his lips. His heart picked up, and he wanted to freeze that moment.

"What's your dog's name, Tanner?" Sara asked, patting the fake one.

"Fwecko." Tanner held up his stuffed dog again, his other hand flapping in the air.

"I'm not sure his dog has a name. He hasn't called it anything other than *dog* since he's been with me. And he's not great at answering questions."

"How much does he say?"

Nathaniel shrugged. "I've heard maybe a few dozen words. Usually not more than two in a row. The pediatrician says it's behind a typically developing child, but not uncommon for a child on the Spectrum."

"Maybe at Story Hour, when he sees the other children, he'll pick up some more. Do you read to him a lot?"

Plopping into a kitchen chair, he ran his hands through his hair. "No. Helene didn't send over any books, and I haven't had time to buy any. Besides, I've been doing everything I can just to figure out how to deal with him. I know that's a lousy excuse, but I'm not too proud to admit I'm floundering in the parenting department."

"You're doing fine, Nathaniel. Give yourself a break. Most people get to ease into it with babies and learn as they go. You kind of got tossed into the deep end without a life preserver."

"You aren't kidding."

"As for not having books for Tanner…just so happens TJ owns a bookstore. We'll see what kinds of books Tanner likes tomorrow and bring back a whole stack."

"Thanks, Sara. I may need to get a few myself on parenting. Like potty training. Tanner's going to be four in September, and he still hasn't shown any interest in using the toilet."

"We'll take the next month or so to figure out the best way to interact with Tanner. Have you spoken to his pediatrician about it?"

"I've only seen her once. It took a while to get his files transferred from the doctor Helene had him with in Boston to a local one. She suggested I take him to the school district for testing. My mom said the same thing. Once a child is three, they can be put into the public school system and receive special education services. Since the school year is almost over, I figured I'd wait until fall to enroll him. I should have enrolled him before now, but my head was all over the place trying to get proof he was my child. He should have qualified for early intervention before age three, but of course, Helene didn't realize there was any problem."

"That makes sense. Well, we can ensure he has a great summer here on the Cape with the sand, sun, and sea."

"And maybe we can get him out of diapers before he starts school. I can't imagine they'll let him in, otherwise." He let out a huge sigh, and Sara reached out for him.

He sat next to his son, who simply stared at Freckles. His little hand rested on the dog's back. His fingers moved in and out, in and out.

"You're doing the best you can, Nathaniel." Sara patted his arm. "You have your dad as a great example. Uncle Kris is fabulous, and I'm sure he was a good role model."

"Yeah, but he never taught me how to potty train a kid. The hardest thing has been that I'm not home much during the day, and I've had to rely on nannies. I don't know why I thought hiring women with super strict tendencies was the right thing. I guess I assumed, wrongly, that they'd know how to handle a child like Tanner."

"Maybe you've been channeling Mr. Banks from Mary Poppins too much. You need the wind to come along and blow all those old nasty nannies away and wait for Mary Poppins to drift in on the new breeze."

"I sure could use Mary Poppins. Do you happen to know her?"

The grin on Sara's face made him nervous. "I don't, but I did notice how well Darcy interacted with Tanner at our wedding."

Yeah, he'd noticed, too. But the idea of working with Darcy and her flip lip wasn't appealing. Couldn't he find someone with her skills who wasn't her?

THE STORE BUSTLED WITH CUSTOMERS, which Darcy typically loved. When it was slow, she had too much time to think. But today was Saturday. Story Hour day. The day all those kids arrived, happy and eager to be entertained by Sara. Or sometimes Mary or TJ. Never her. As long as she called them rug rats and said they were all brats, TJ kept the job of reading to them away from her. Which suited her just fine.

Unfortunately, her job during the stories was always the coffee counter. Direct line of sight to the children's area, and all the adorable little kids and their smiling faces.

The bell above the door tinkled, and her gaze automatically flew to the entrance, looking for one particular child. Her stomach clenched but not for the reason it usually did.

Mr. GQ Storm strolled in, his hand holding that of his son, Tanner.

The little boy sure was cute with his blond curls and big, blue eyes. Eyes that right now focused on the stuffed dog tucked under his arm. It had been cool hanging with him at Sara and TJ's wedding a few weeks ago. He was an interesting kid. He had a lot of the same quirks her brother, Zane, had when he was younger.

Now, the father. He was another person of interest. Today, he was slumming it in dark jeans and a navy button down, with the sleeves rolled to his elbows. Why did her gaze automatically zoom in on those bare forearms? Because the last two times she'd seen him, he'd worn long sleeves. Because he had the perfect amount of hair on them, and she was a huge fan of arm porn.

One more thing for the *'can't hate you for this'* column. Ugh.

When he looked her way, she shot him a super goofy smile that she usually reserved for people who ticked her off.

"GQ? Of all the gin joints, you had to walk into mine."

His eyes narrowed, but his lips twisted up at the side just a touch. Yep, he was trying to hide a smile. "Sorry, Elvira, I thought this was a coffee shop. I must have stumbled into the blood bank by mistake."

"Your being in here is definitely a mistake. We don't sell Dom Perignon."

"As long as you sell coffee, I'll be good."

"You could try."

"You're back to the mourning clothes again." He tipped his chin at her black jeans and snug concert T-shirt. "Who died? No, wait, let me guess. You killed off the pink bridesmaid dress."

She pressed her lips together to keep from laughing. The guy could be humorous when he wanted. "The pink outfit had it comin'."

"So the bad attitude wasn't because of the lace? It's an everyday thing with you?"

"All part and parcel of the whole Darcy gig. And you don't even have to pay extra."

"Lucky me. You wouldn't have anything a kid could drink, do you? You know, without caffeine."

Reaching into the small fridge behind her, she pulled out a carton of milk, a little bottle of orange juice, and one of apple juice. She placed them on the counter, then smiled at Tanner.

"Hey, there. Which one would you like? Can you point? Maybe your dad can lift you up to see better."

Biff eyed her strangely, but he picked the boy up and moved closer to the drinks.

"Milk," she said pointing to the white and blue carton, then the others. "Orange juice. Apple juice."

"I think he'll have—"

"He can choose. It's his drink." Maybe this guy hadn't been a dad all that long, but he needed to let his kid do things on his own. She'd spent years trying to teach Zane how to make good decisions.

Leaning over, she rested her elbows on the counter and repeated the drink choices slowly. "Milk. Orange juice. Apple juice." Since most of the customers were here for books, and Becca, the assistant manager, was taking care of the coffee counter, she figured she could let him take his time.

After a minute, Tanner reached out and touched the golden bottle. "Ahppoo."

"Apple," she repeated. "Excellent choice, young man. Here you go. I'll even get you a straw to go with it."

As she turned around to put the other drinks away, Biff tapped her hand. "Thank you."

"Don't thank me yet, GQ, I could still spit in your coffee."

His look made her squirm. The man had an attitude, but holy hotness, was he supermodel sexy.

"Let's get you settled in a chair, buddy, while Daddy gets his coffee." He walked Tanner over to a table, set the apple juice on it, then lifted him into the chair.

Darcy picked up a cup, then realized she didn't know what kind of coffee Biff wanted. She poured him dark roast black and brought it over to their table. He'd unwrapped the straw and inserted it into the apple juice bottle.

"I got you high test. If you want any cream or sugar to soften it up, you'll have to come get it. But then your manliness goes way down in my book."

"Black is fine. What do I owe you?"

As she set the cup on the table, Sara caught her eye and mouthed, 'no charge' in between greeting the children.

"My treat."

Sara caught the lie and chuckled but didn't call her on it. One of the things she liked about the lady boss. She allowed Darcy the opportunity to be Darcy.

"Oh, we can't accept—"

"Sure, you can. Anyway, it's not for you, it's for Tanner. All I want is a high five." Perched in the chair next to the boy, she placed her hand, palm up, on the table. "Smooth. Can you give it to me smooth, Tanner?"

Without looking up from his drink, Tanner placed his hand in hers and slid it slowly across her palm, then placed his like hers. She dragged her hand across his, then tickled his palm with her fingertips.

When Tanner giggled, Biff stiffened and stared. His lips tightened, but she'd swear his eyes were a little damp.

Standing, she said, "He's got smooth moves, this one."

"How did he know to do that?"

"If you must know, GQ, I taught him at the wedding. I

think he likes the feeling of the palms sliding against each other."

"You can call me Nathaniel, you know."

She thought about it for a minute, then replied, "Sure, Nate."

His eyes narrowed. "Nathaniel. No one calls me anything else."

"Then, they all have more time to spare than me. 'Cause, seriously? It's four syllables. There's no need to be so pretentious. Nate works fine."

"Not for me, it doesn't."

"Fine, *Biff*, whatever floats your boat."

"Nathaniel."

She smirked and shuffled back to the counter to help with a few customers. More of the children showed up, and she kept herself busy behind the counter. Saturday always brought more of the kids for the stories, so she glanced to make sure they all had enough space. Poor Hope was so shy she didn't always speak up for herself and often got pushed out of her favorite place to sit.

As Story Hour began, the line at the counter disappeared, and the parents found seats in the coffee area with their cups and pastry. TJ trotted down the stairs, checked in with Sara, said a few words to GQ, then headed her way. Once she finished with her customer, he angled against the counter.

"Hey, Darcy, I hate to ask—"

"But you will anyway." She threw him a squinty-faced look.

He knew her too well to even respond to her sarcasm. "Can you possibly sit with Tanner during Story Hour? Nathaniel was hoping to find some parenting books. He'll need to go through them to see if they're what he wants, and that could take a while."

"I'm kind of busy, boss." She took a page from his book

and started fiddling with the coffee stirrers and napkins. He'd done that so much when Sara first started working here, to pretend he wasn't watching her. It was adorable. She doubted she looked that way.

"I'll take care of the counter, and Becca will do the bookstore register. You know Fiona acts up if her mom is too close, and you seem to have the magic touch with Nathaniel's son."

Darcy let out a huge sigh. TJ wouldn't take no for an answer. Of course, he had no idea why sitting with the kids was taboo.

"Fine, but you owe me."

"And I'm sure you'll make me pay."

Slipping off her apron, she hung it on the hook by the door into the back room, then moseyed her way to the colorful children's carpet.

"Guess I'm elected to be babysitter today while you go on your book journey, Nate."

His head whipped up at the name, but he didn't correct her. Score one for her.

"Appreciate it." He knelt next to the boy, who sat on the back corner of the rug. "Tanner, I'm going to be right over there. Darcy will sit with you while Auntie Sara reads the books, okay?"

"Auntie Sara?"

"I know technically they're cousins, but she's a different generation. It's a title of respect. Our whole family does that."

Darcy wouldn't know what normal families did. She didn't remember her father, and her mother had barely been conscious most days. Who knew if she had aunts and uncles out there somewhere?

Hunkering down cross legged on the floor, she placed her hand on the carpet and whispered, "Smooth."

Tanner slid his hand over hers. "Fwecko."

BROKEN DREAMS

TJ's dog had wandered into the area. Tanner started flapping his arms, repeating, "Fwecko, Fwecko."

"Freckles. Pretty dog."

"Pwetty dog." More arm flapping.

Would Nate be okay with the dog sitting with his son? They were staying at the same house, and Tanner knew the animal's name, so it must be okay.

"Freckles, here girl." She usually sat near Sara, but maybe being near Tanner would help him.

Sara looked over and scratched the dog's ears. "Go see Tanner."

When the animal wandered over slowly, Tanner lifted his stuffed animal and placed it on Freckles' head as she sat.

"Gentle," she warned quietly.

Tanner slid the stuffed dog easily over Freckles's head and said, "Gento."

"Great job, Tanner. Now, let's listen to the stories."

After the first story, Darcy felt movement behind her. Hope had scooted over until she was on the other side of Freckles. Good for her, asserting herself. But her proximity had Darcy on edge.

As Eddie picked a story for Sara to read, Hope tipped her head at Tanner and whispered, "I like him. What's his name?"

God, her voice was perfect. So sweet and angelic. Darcy had never heard it from this close before. The little girl didn't usually say much while she was here.

"His name is Tanner Storm."

"Like Sara. Her name is Storm."

"They're part of the same family, though Sara's new last name is Bannister, because she married Mr. B." The kids always abbreviated TJ's name.

"My last name is Benedict. Both my Mamas have that name Benedict. And they gave me that name, too, when they got me. But Hope is the name I got from the mama who I got borned from."

Hope scrunched forward and patted Freckles, unaware of the bomb she'd dropped.

Darcy froze, but inside she was a quivering mass of Jello. Hope knew she was adopted. Jodie had said they'd tell her when she was old enough, but she was only five. Was that mature enough to understand? Darcy still didn't.

Sara started her next book, and the kids all quieted again. Hope kept peeking at Tanner, giving him a little wave. No response. Finally, Darcy slid her hand onto the carpet and softly said, "Smooth."

Tanner pressed his hand to hers and slid it across, then laid his hand for her to reciprocate and tickle his palm. A tiny giggle erupted from his mouth. Hope watched enthralled.

"Try it." She wanted to take Hope's hand and show her, but if she touched the child, she wasn't sure what would happen.

Luckily, the girl had been taking careful note and put her hand on the carpet, then whispered, "Smooth." Tanner took a moment to assess who said it, then proceeded to give Hope a smooth high five.

"Now, he'll do it. You can tickle his hand a little at the end." The child took her advice, causing Tanner to utter a small laugh. A huge grin lit Hope's face. Darcy's heart pounded faster in her chest.

"Hope, did you want to choose a story today?" Sara called out, having finished her last book.

The little girl next to her ducked her head, shaking it.

"I think Tanner would like one about dogs," Darcy suggested. The boy shook his stuffed animal when she said this.

Nodding, Sara shuffled through a pile of books and

pulled one out. As she started to read, Darcy saw Hope place her hand on the carpet again and whisper, "Smooth."

The thought she'd actually taught the little girl to do something, and something good, twisted at her insides.

When the hour was through, Sara wrapped up the last book, typically one all the kids could say together. Hope sang with the rest of the children. She even said the words louder so Tanner would know them. Except the boy didn't pay much attention to the story, merely patted Freckles.

"Time to go, Hope," Jodie said, as the rest of the parents claimed their kids.

"Mama, this is Tanner. He's my new friend. He likes to sit with Darcy and Freckles."

"I noticed you moved over to be closer to him. Hopefully, we'll see him again at Story Hour."

Darcy rose and took Tanner's hand. "He and his dad are staying with Mr. and Mrs. B. for a month or so. I'm guessing he'll be here again."

"Yay," Hope squeaked, clapping her hands. Tanner copied her movements.

"Why don't you say thank you to Darcy, and if you want, you can give her a hug before we go?" Jodie patted the girl on the shoulder.

Darcy's whole body quivered as Hope wrapped her arms around her waist. The pleasure and pain mixed and built to an agony she didn't think she would ever experience again.

It had been more than five long years since she'd held her daughter in her arms.

CHAPTER FIVE

Nathaniel flipped through yet another book on parenting. This one had lots of suggestions on disciplining a child, but not necessarily a child like Tanner. Moving down the row, he glanced at more titles, then skimmed the back covers.

Here was one on tips and tricks for dads of kids with autism. Like it was written just for him. After peeking at the index, he thumbed through the pages. This one might help. Quick, easy stories and basic steps on what to look for in your child and how to respond to certain behaviors. Hopefully, these worked. But his mom had reiterated, if you knew *one* person with autism, you knew *one* person with autism. It was called a spectrum for a reason.

He tucked the book under his arm and continued perusing the others on special needs children. As he looked yet again to where Tanner sat with Darcy, he noticed one of the little girls had joined them. She beamed at Tanner, her eyes filled with excitement. Would he ever see his son with that kind of look in his eyes? Or gazing at him with interest?

"Are you finding anything?" TJ came up behind him and leaned against a shelf.

"Found one that looks good. It takes a while to skim through them. Thanks for asking Darcy to sit with Tanner. I'm not sure he'd stay there by himself yet. Maybe once he gets older."

"Happy to help. Darcy seems to get a good reaction from your son. Not sure why. She always complains about the kids and refuses to even consider doing Story Hour."

"That little dark-haired girl moved closer to her. She can't be all bad." Only annoying to him.

"Darcy's an enigma. One I haven't figured out yet. And the little girl is Hope. She's been coming here for about three years. Almost never misses a Story Hour. But she's pretty shy. Took a while for her to warm up to everyone. Even Sara."

Sara seemed like the Pied Piper when it came to the kids. The ones here all wanted to sit near her and get her attention. Except the one little girl who was focused intently on Tanner. Hope. Like the tattoo on Darcy's shoulder.

"Is Darcy related to Hope? An aunt or cousin or something. They have similar features."

Shrugging, TJ pushed off from the shelf. "I don't remember Darcy ever mentioning any relatives, except her brother. Actually, if Sara's not around and you need someone to keep an eye on Tanner, you might think about asking Darcy. I pay her a decent wage plus overtime, but she's always looking for more money. I think her brother has medical issues. I'm not sure. She isn't one to talk much about herself."

"I'll keep that in mind." If he wanted to drive himself crazy, that is. He and Darcy didn't mix too well. She brought the snarky side out of him, and he'd never realized he had one. Not in recent years, anyway. Maybe when he was younger. He and his brother, Kevin, would tease the crap out of each other and then team up on their little sister, Amy. She'd had to grow a tough skin to deal with them.

The kids all stood and milled around, looking for their parents. Except Tanner. He didn't seem to care if Nathaniel was there or not. God, it sucked so much. He'd always wanted a son to look up to him like he looked up to his dad. The worst part was having missed so much of his early life. It killed him to think of his child being raised by nannies and not a loving mother or father. The fact Helene could walk away from her child so easily…

She was never any kind of mother.

After grabbing a different book that looked informative, he nodded at TJ and walked back to the colorful rug.

Sara finished straightening the area and glanced up at him. "You should pick out a few books that we can read to Tanner back at the house. Any idea what he likes?"

"Cars." He retrieved one of the Hot Wheels he'd stashed in his pocket and held it out. Tanner reached for it and started rolling it back and forth along the side of a shelf.

"I'd also get him some books on dogs. He loves Freckles," Darcy said.

"Dogs and cars. Got it." Sara dug through some of the shelves that housed the children's books.

Darcy stepped closer. "I'd also make them mostly pictures, with only a word or two on each page. It'll be easier for him to understand."

"What are you implying? That Tanner can't learn beyond a few words?"

Instead of the sass he anticipated, her eyes actually softened. "I'm not saying that at all. When children are learning language, sometimes it's easier to learn new words if they're by themselves. It's harder to identify them when they're mixed in with lots of other words. Once his vocabulary grows, he can be introduced to longer sentences."

"How do you know this? And how do you know what to do to get Tanner to respond to you? I've been trying everything I can think of."

Darcy's gaze flittered around the room, then she looked down at the floor. Tanner continued to push his car around. When she glanced up, she let out a deep breath.

"My brother, Zane, has some developmental delays. Some of his tendencies aren't that different from Tanner's."

So that was the probable medical condition TJ had mentioned. "And you learned about language acquisition because of him?"

Her eyes rolled up. "The social workers were lucky if my mother was conscious when they stopped in. Same with the therapists when they showed up. So I paid attention to what they said in order to help my brother."

Man. Didn't sound like a great life. Maybe explained the dark makeup and funky clothes. He'd try to be more thankful for his own parents. There were times when he'd been embarrassed by them. His prep school friends had laughed at his blue-collar father, but at least his parents had been together and had provided for their children.

"Didn't these social workers and therapists ever let the authorities know that your mom wasn't well?"

"Wasn't well? Now, there's a charming way of saying it. Must be the lawyer in you. And yes. They'd report her, and Zane and I would be pulled out of our home and stuck in foster care. But after a few weeks, my mom would run out of drugs, get slightly cleaned up, and we'd be right back with her."

"Where is she now? Does Zane still live with her?"

Her eyes turned cold. "She died about three years ago. Drug overdose. Go figure. Zane lives with me."

"How old is he?" Was he a minor child and Darcy was his guardian? That was a lot for any one person to undertake.

"He's twenty-five."

"Does he have a job?" Would Tanner be able to handle a job once he got older? And why was he asking so many questions? He wasn't interested in Darcy, though TJ was right. She was an enigma.

"Zane's had jobs in the past." Her jaw tightened and pain resonated from her eyes. She held herself stiff as she continued. "Right now, he stays with an elderly neighbor during my work hours. It's good for both of them. Zane keeps Mr. Peabody company and does chores around the house. Mr. Peabody helps Zane with manners and common-sense stuff he doesn't always catch onto."

"Is he older or younger than you?" And at what age had she taken up the responsibility for her brother? It put a whole new spin on the Darcy Tilt-A-Whirl.

"I'm twenty-four, if you need to know."

Sara strolled over as she said this, a pile of books in her hands. "Darcy is ten days older than me. We're almost twins."

Darcy grinned, took one of the books, and bent down to show Tanner.

Twins? Sure. His cousin Sara and Darcy were about as far apart as people could get.

~

"Thanks so much for helping me with Tanner today, Darcy. I appreciate it." Sara swept her fingers over the keyboard of the honking grand piano that sat dead center in the music room of the home she and TJ lived in.

On the floor, installed in Darcy's lap, Tanner stared at the large instrument as music drifted around the room.

"You know I'd do anything for you and the boss. Is Freckles okay? You said the boss was taking her to the vet."

"We think she's pregnant. She's got all the signs, and we had a visit from the neighbor's dog recently, so there's a possibility."

"Wait, the neighbor's dog simply shows up and does it with Freckles? Did she consent? Can you press charges against that beast?" No one should have that forced on them, not even a dog.

"She was in heat. Not quite the same." Sara's laughter intermingled with the music. "Tanner seems to like classical the best. It soothes him. I'll have to make sure to mention it to Nathaniel. He's been trying to figure out what to do and what not to do with his son."

As Tanner swayed back and forth in her lap, Darcy tousled his curls. "Where did Biff go?"

"Biff?"

"Biff. GQ. Or if I must call him by his real name…where did Nate go?"

"He had a meeting with a client in Boston." A loud laugh erupted from Sara's mouth. "Did you seriously just call him Nate?"

Shrugging, she said, "That's his name."

"No one calls him anything other than Nathaniel. He'd throw a huge fit if anyone tried giving him a nickname."

Yeah, Darcy had experienced that firsthand. She rocked back and forth along with Tanner. The movement did seem to have a soothing quality to it. "Why does he have such a big stick up his as…butt?" She could hear TJ's stern, lecturing tone. *Language, Darcy. It's a family friendly store.* They weren't in the store, but there was a kid present.

Shaking her head, Sara tried to hide a grin.

"I mean, he's related to you, and you don't have one."

"Thanks, Darcy. I know Nathaniel can be a bit stuffy at times, but he's a nice guy, and he'd do anything for any of us."

"But that big stick…"

Rolling her eyes, Sara pressed her lips together, then took a deep breath. "I don't like gossiping about my cousin."

"But you will, right?"

The crinkle in Sara's nose let Darcy know she'd fold like a maid on laundry day.

"Fine. Only because you're helping with Nathaniel's son and should maybe have some background."

Yessss. Backstory. Hopefully, it was something juicy.

"I don't know everything, but my oldest brother, Erik, is the same age as Nathaniel, as well as our other cousin, Greg."

"Dang, how many cousins do you have? Never mind, I saw them all at your wedding. They're all beautiful and in love with each other and all that family crap."

"We are pretty close, but we grew up in the same town and spent lots of time in the summer up in Maine at our grandparents' place. It's the house Erik and his family live in now."

Darcy didn't need a blow by blow of the amazing times the Storm family had. They were too perfect. She'd never be able to understand people like that.

"Nate?" Could they get back to the gossip on GQ?

"He, Greg, and Erik were all in school together and hung out when they were young. He was great. But Nathaniel's super smart and got a scholarship to Brookside Academy in town. It's very exclusive, very expensive."

"So, he wasn't always rich and pretentious?"

"No. We grew up middle class. Our dads are electricians, and even though they've done well, we certainly weren't wealthy. Nathaniel changed after he went to the Academy. He hung out with rich kids whose parents could afford the tuition. He's six years older than me, so I don't remember everything, but I do know Erik hated that they grew apart."

"So, he became a douche to everyone in the family."

Sara rolled her eyes, and her lips pinched. "Not quite that bad, but he distanced himself from us. Suddenly, money and clothes and the right kind of cars were all he cared about. Appearances were everything."

"Yeah, he nearly fell over when he saw I was his partner at your wedding. I'm not exactly the country club type."

A grin took over Sara's face. "I bet you'd be lots of fun at the country club. Not that I'd know. I've never been to one."

"The boss has tons of money. You could join one, if you wanted to." Darcy didn't see Sara or TJ at a posh club. They were two of the most down to earth people she'd ever met.

Sara shook her head. "I don't think so. But Nathaniel is a member of the Club at The Falls. He joined after he graduated from Harvard Law. He'd gotten scholarships to both undergrad and graduate school. Once he passed the Bar, he was kind of unbearable. Didn't hang out at family parties or visit much."

"Jerk." The word slipped from her mouth, and she glanced down to see if Tanner had been following their conversation. His rocking had slowed to the pace of the music Sara still played.

"I think Helene had something to do with that. They met and got married while he was in law school. We were never quite good enough for her." Sara made a face.

"You didn't like her? I mean then? Obviously, now she's persona non grata."

"Helene is beautiful and had impeccable manners and everything Nathaniel wanted in a wife."

"Everything, except fidelity. He must have been pissed when she cheated on him." Darcy wanted to call her a nasty name, but the kid in her lap had her holding her tongue.

The music notes segued into another tune, and Tanner grew heavy in her arms. His eyes fluttered and his head settled against her shoulder.

"It hurt him, but not for the reasons you'd think. I don't know that he ever truly loved her, and she obviously didn't love him. They wanted to be that showcase couple. But Nathaniel's business partner came from a super wealthy family, and I guess that was a bigger draw for her. Too bad she didn't figure that out before they got married."

Darcy shifted, allowing Tanner's head to rest in the crook of her arm, his stuffed dog tucked tightly to his chest.

The music continued, but it was only a simple children's tune now.

"Nathaniel really is a great guy, and Helene is such a huge bitch."

Darcy's head popped up. "Whoa, did you just use the B word? I may have to tattle on you. That's hardly 'family friendly' language there, boss lady."

Sara smirked and pointed her chin at Tanner. "He didn't hear me, and I doubt you care."

"Nah, nothing new to me. But the divorce, did that make Nate drop the pretense? 'Cause he's still pretty uppity."

"Nathaniel was hurt because Helene cheated on him, and with his business partner. He trusted them both. It took a while and lots of barging in on him and letting him know we all still love him and accept him."

"For the starchy, uptight dude he is."

"It's a show for his clients, but I think he got so used to dressing and acting that way, he doesn't know anything else now. He has money and a beautiful house and a fancy car."

"And now he has a kid. Must cramp his style. Unable to wow all the ladies with his shining reputation."

"It's been four years, and honestly, I don't think Nathaniel has dated anyone since. Certainly not anyone steady."

Rocking the boy back and forth, Darcy thought of the child's dad. "Why the heck would anyone cheat on your cousin? He's wealthy and well-dressed. Somewhat droolworthy. He has a great job and belongs to the country club. Isn't that what all women want?"

"Not all women," Sara replied. "I doubt it's what you want."

What did she want? Not GQ, that's for sure. The man was trouble in a million-dollar suit.

"I don't want a man full time. Too much hassle."

Sara shrugged and stopped playing the piano. Tanner didn't stir.

"Maybe someday you'll change your mind. When you find the right guy."

"Like you and the boss?" Darcy snorted with mock derision.

Sara shook her head, ignoring her. "You'll find someone, too. Now, how about we put Tanner on the couch to finish his nap, while I make us some lunch?"

Darcy shuffled to her knees, then managed to stand. She wasn't used to carrying around dead weight, but the kid felt nice in her arms. The last time she'd held a child, the weight had been considerably less. Like seven pounds, two ounces.

Pushing back to the present, she gently lowered Tanner to the cushions, then relaxed on the couch next to him. "I'll stay right here. In case he wakes up."

The sound of the back door opening and voices in the kitchen had her craning her head to see. TJ was back. Freckles padded into the living room and settled on the floor at her feet.

A few minutes later, the door sounded again, then Sara came in with a tray in her hands.

"It's only sandwiches. I hope that's okay." She set the tray on the coffee table and took the chair opposite the couch.

"Where's the boss? What did he say about Freckles?"

Reaching down, Sara scratched the dog's head. "He had to go back to work. And it looks like we'll have some puppies in early July."

"In a month? That's pretty quick." Unlike the nine long months a woman carried her child. Nine months of feeling that baby move inside. Of thinking and rethinking all the good and bad choices you'd made in your life. Of the choices you were gonna make. Forced to make.

"Darcy." Sara's voice drew her out of her memories." I don't want to bring anything up if you don't want to talk about it, but I overheard you talking to Nathaniel. About your brother."

Her brother. Yeah, she could talk about her brother. "Zane."

"If you ever need anything, let us know. TJ appreciates your loyalty to the shop and how much you do for us."

She shrugged. "No sweat. He's been good to me. And he's so much nicer now he's getting it regular, you know. The guy totally needed to get laid."

The red on Sara's face matched her shirt.

They finished eating, chatting about the new album Sara was planning to record and some of the newly hired summer staff. When she glanced down, Tanner's eyes were open, though he hadn't moved at all.

"Hey there, kid. What do you feel like doing now?"

He looked around and hugged his dog tighter. "Fwecko."

Sara petted the spaniel. "Would you like to play in the sand? Freckles loves to go outside."

"Fwecko."

Darcy ruffled his curls. "Okay, outside it is. Do you have any pails and shovels? Me and the kid here could build a sandcastle." She'd spent many hours on the beach building sandcastles the last few years, wishing she had a child to do it with.

Sara put the dishes on the tray and picked it up. "We bought some when we knew Nathaniel and Tanner were coming. They're on the front porch."

Darcy stood and pulled the child next to her. Sara mentioned a diaper change and sunblock, then left with the tray. "I'll be out in a minute, if you don't mind taking him. I need to return a call from my manager."

Easily enough, she found the drawer with Tanner's beach stuff, changed him, then headed out to the porch facing the ocean. Man, this view was incredible.

"Let's go build something cool." She picked up a small pair of gardening gloves next to the planters on the porch and tossed them in the bucket. Zane didn't always like sticky sand, so Tanner might not either.

Freckles walked with them to where the tide had gone out, and the sand was still damp. Perfect for building with. Being early June, the water was cold, but the sun today felt great.

They filled the two buckets with sand, patted them down, then Darcy turned one over, giving it a second to set. As she was lifting the plastic form, Nathaniel came out on the porch and strolled toward them.

Holy Pop-Tarts, the man wore a pair of shorts like he owned them. Those legs, trim and muscled, and too damn long. As he got closer, Darcy focused on the castle.

"Hey, buddy. Are you having fun?"

"Casso." Tanner patted the sand in the other bucket.

"Yes, we're making a castle." Carefully, she removed the bucket.

"I'll be right back to help you. I'm going to jump in quick. Long drive back from Boston with that warm sun beating down on the car."

Darcy glanced up as Nate pulled his shirt over his head, and she almost choked. Her hand slipped and crushed the mound of molded sand.

Nathaniel Storm was no ordinary desk jockey. The chiseled muscles of his abs, dotted with light brown hair, had her salivary glands working overtime. His back was equally amazing as he jogged toward the water and dove head first into the waves.

CHAPTER SIX

*N*athaniel broke through the surface of the waves and sucked in a long breath. God, the water was cold, but it was exactly what he needed.

After a morning full of Stan Jablonski, then driving through bumper-to-bumper traffic to get back to the Cape, he wasn't in a great mood. Knowing he had to deal with Tanner, and whatever new behavior he threw at him, had him tense and also disgusted with himself. This was his son. He should want to be with him all the time. Guilt ate away at him, causing his stomach to clench and his jaw to ache.

Everything would be okay. He just needed to clear his head.

When he'd gotten himself in control and felt a little more relaxed, he wandered back to where Darcy and Tanner dug in the sand. His son, wearing over-sized gloves, scooped and dumped in the bucket, scooped and dumped, rhythmically. Every few shovelfuls, Darcy patted the top quickly, making some sort of 'boop' noise. Each time she did, Tanner lifted his shoulders and squeaked.

It wasn't what you typically saw with children, but it was

a reaction to something she was doing. How did she do that? How did she get inside this kid's bubble and make him see her? He'd been trying for months, and he swore his son didn't even know who he was most of the time.

Darcy looked up from her creation and squinted in the sun. She looked different, almost as if she'd left the vampire look in its coffin for the day. Though still dark, she had less eye makeup on. Her lips were bare, and her hair didn't stick up quite as much. Probably due to the salt air and wind. His eyes dipped lower, taking in her snug tank top and tiny, stretchy shorts. He had moved further south, his gaze sliding over her legs, when she caught him, and her lips puckered in that way when she was about to say something snarky.

"Gym much, Biff?"

"What?" Not exactly what he was expecting. He was no ninety-eight-pound weakling, but he was hardly jacked.

"I hadn't expected a desk bound lawyer to have abs like that." The gleam in her eyes was normal, but he couldn't be sure if she liked what she saw or was making fun of him.

"I play racquetball in the cooler months. In warmer weather, I kayak a lot and then swim once the water's not so cold." After shaking off the ocean water, he slicked his hair back, knowing it would get crazy wavy if he didn't get a comb through it soon. Doubtful Darcy cared what he looked like.

"I'm thinking that ocean water's still pretty chilly. You're a better man than I, diving in."

Looking at her shapely figure in the tank top and shorts, no one would ever mistake her for a man. His eyes kept dropping to her lips. He wondered if he needed another quick dip. He glanced down at Tanner. "Guess I won't be getting as much of the swimming and kayaking done this summer."

Her lips pursed again. The ones that weren't black or Blood Red today.

"Be a shame to ruin that." She pointed to his chest. "You simply need a better nanny than the crap ones you've been choosing."

What he needed was someone like Darcy who could get through to his son. Someone who, for some reason, seemed to get inside his world and understand his needs.

He picked up his shirt, shook it out away from Tanner, then slipped it back on. Discussing his abs felt strange, especially with this vampire of a girl. Plopping into the sand beside his son, he picked up the extra shovel and started digging a moat around the castle Darcy had started.

"Are we about ready to put that castle on?" Darcy asked, tapping the top of the bucket a few times. Tanner filled his shovel one last time and dumped it on top, even though the bucket was already overflowing.

Darcy placed her hand on Tanner's and helped him pat the top, packing the sand tighter.

"Can I help, too? I'm pretty strong." The desire to somehow connect to his son raged through him.

"Are you?" Darcy smirked.

"I'd say you think so, since you were ogling my chest only a minute ago."

"Pfft. That wasn't ogling by any means. If I wanted to ogle you, you'd know it. Now, use those muscles and help us with this castle."

She took his hand and placed it on Tanner's, and all three of them patted the sand.

"Ready to flip it? You help us. Flip." She was talking to Tanner.

They all held onto the bucket and turned it over. Darcy gave it a few more pats, then slowly lifted it off until the sandcastle stood next to the other one she'd made.

"We still need a moat." Nathaniel grabbed the shovel again and started digging around. Thinking of what had happened, he handed Tanner his shovel. Then using Darcy's method, he placed his hand over his son's, and they dug together.

"Dig. Dig. Dig," Darcy chanted, and soon Tanner began saying it.

Might as well join in. Each time he and Tanner scooped the sand from around the castle, they called out, "Dig."

To make it easier to move around as they created the moat, he slipped Tanner on his lap, holding him with one hand and digging with the other. It took a while, but they finally got all the way around the castle. By now, the tide was coming in and getting closer to them.

"Hey, I have an idea," he said. "Maybe we can use the tide coming in to fill the moat."

Depositing Tanner on the sand, he ran around to the ocean side of the creation and began a trench down to the sea. Soon enough, a large wave came in, and the water swirled up, then all around where they'd dug.

"Water, Tanner. Look at the water." Darcy splashed her hand in the liquid filling their moat.

"Water." Tanner tentatively stuck his hand in, then pulled it out again. Yeah, it was still chilly this time of year.

But when the next wave rushed in, Tanner laughed as the moat filled up once again. The sound of his laughter took Nathaniel's breath away. He wanted to hear it all the time.

"Daddy's smart, huh?" Darcy gave him a wink. "He got us that water. Good job, Daddy."

"Daddy. Daddy."

Nathaniel's legs gave out at the name tumbling from his son's mouth, and he dropped to his knees beside the boy.

"I'm Daddy. And you're Tanner."

"Tanner." The boy repeated his name as he stuck his finger in the water. "Dig."

Darcy's hand came down softly on his shoulder. "Don't get discouraged. Keep repeating words to him. Use simple sentences for now. He'll get it."

Clenching his jaw tight, he inhaled through his nose, hoping for strength. "But will he ever get me? Get exactly who I am? His father? Was all this screwed up because his shrew of a mother doesn't know how to tell the truth and only cares about herself?"

The hand on his shoulder flexed and massaged the muscle there. God, that felt good. It had been too long since he'd had any kind of human touch. Aside from the obligatory hugs from his family, he'd pretty much closed himself off to anyone else physically. Yet somehow this vampire sprite, whose crazy insults and sarcastic barbs shot out like arrows, somehow understood what he needed right now.

Lifting his hand, he covered hers.

"Thanks. I needed this right now, Elvira."

As she walked away, she pushed her foot through the water, splashing him. Tanner laughed.

∼

Darcy rolled her eyes as they pulled up to the enormous Victorian house in the quaint little town all the Storms had grown up in. The place was larger than the apartment building in New Bedford they'd lived in when she was a kid, and that had housed five units. Despite that, all the Storms seemed like great people, except the annoying one sitting next to her in the back seat of Sara's SUV.

TJ pulled a u-ey, then parked on the street in front of the house.

"I'm so excited Alex and Gina got engaged," Sara squealed as she jumped out of the passenger side and hustled to the back to get the cookies she'd baked for the party.

Darcy pushed open her door, glancing at Nate. "Do you want me to get the kid from the car seat?"

It was the only reason she'd allowed herself to be dragged along on this family jaunt. Sara had argued that her cousin wouldn't be able to enjoy being with his family, if he had to keep an eye on Tanner all day. She'd played the guilt card about how his evil ex-wife had kept him from seeing them for so long.

Well, the kid was his son, and he should be responsible for watching him. Still, she got that he often didn't feel qualified to interact with Tanner in an appropriate way.

Earlier this week, they'd had fun building sandcastles on the beach, and Darcy had been surprised by the emotion she'd seen on Nate's face when Tanner had called him Daddy. Well, repeated the word. Doubtful he'd made the connection yet. Unfortunately, when Nate had realized, too, the pain had been obvious.

"No, I'll get him. I might let him sleep a bit longer. You guys go ahead in without me."

"You brought me along to watch him, so why don't I sit here, and you go socialize with the fam?" She started to get back in the car, but Sara intercepted her first.

"No, come meet everyone. You'll love Gina. She marches to the beat of her own drum."

"I met them all at your wedding. That was only three weeks ago." Darcy didn't do family, apart from her brother. Everything was for Zane. All her sacrifices.

A small cry came from the car seat that had kept Darcy from having to sit right next to Nate on the way down. Big thanks for small favors. It was bad enough she had to inhale his tantalizing scent the whole way.

"There, now we can all go in together." TJ's voice rumbled with slight annoyance as he balanced the food Sara had handed him.

Darcy wiggled the stuffed dog from Tanner's grip, so his father could undo the straps on the seat. When the child started to whine, Nate thrust a small car into his hand, heading off the impending tantrum.

"Hey, buddy. We're here. You get to see Mimi again. You like being with her."

As Nate maneuvered Tanner from his seat, she stuffed the dog in the diaper bag and slung it over her shoulder. She'd liked Nate's mom, Anna, when she'd met her at the bridal shower. She'd gotten to know her a little better at the wedding when they'd worked together to keep Tanner occupied, so Nate didn't have a breakdown.

The boy slumped on his father's shoulder as they walked up the driveway following Sara. He wasn't quite awake yet. The few times she'd been with him during a nap, he seemed to take a few minutes to fully wake up.

"Let's go in through the house. Knowing Alex, he's got all the food set up in the kitchen. He'll want it to stay warm."

"Isn't he still recovering from surgery? The fire was only a few weeks ago. He and Gina were almost killed." Nathaniel shifted Tanner in his arms.

Darcy glanced at the Victorian next door. The turret and top floor were blackened with soot. Plywood covered many of the windows on the top part of the house. Scary what had happened, and right after Sara and TJ's wedding. She'd volunteered to watch some of the Storm children over at Nathaniel's house, while Alex's immediate family waited at the hospital for news of his condition.

Sara nodded. "Yes, but my mom and yours and Aunt Luci told him they'd do all the cleaning and make all the food, so he didn't have to do anything. It's just us."

Just us. Sara made it sound like there were only one or two people. Her grandparents had three sons, who each had a wife. Then, there were ten grandkids. Two of those grandkids were married—Sara and her brother, Erik. And then the four great grandkids, with another on the way. Darcy had a hard time fathoming that many family members.

She had a hard time keeping up with only her brother, with whom she should be spending time with today. But Mr. Peabody was going to an event with his old army buddies and asked if Zane could go with him. The old man couldn't always push his wheelchair by himself. It had left her without an excuse not to come with them. Additionally, Nate had said he'd pay her for her time. Money wasn't something she could afford to give up.

"Sara, TJ, you're here!" Sara's mom greeted them as they cut through the dining room into the kitchen in the back of the house. "Thank you so much for baking."

"Hey, Aunt Molly. I slaved all day over food, too." Nate winked, his grin wide as he handed her a bag from the grocery store. They'd stopped down the street, and he'd picked up some fried chicken from the deli.

Holy Pop-Tarts, he could be charming when he put his mind to it. She'd have to watch herself. She'd been lured in by charming men before. It had caused more heartache than most people could handle in a lifetime.

"Nathaniel, I'm so glad you came. And Darcy, what a nice surprise. It's great to see you again."

Molly Storm pulled her in for a hug and kissed her cheek. *Geez Louise*. Who did that to someone you barely knew? If she'd been on fire, her mom wouldn't have hugged her to put the flames out.

"Nice to see you again, too." See? She could do manners. She didn't like 'em, but she could do 'em.

Tanner seemed more awake and rolled his car along his father's arm, from elbow to shoulder and back. Nate didn't seem to notice. Or if he did, he wasn't responding. She had to give the guy credit. He was trying.

"Where's the happy couple?" Sara asked, taking the food from TJ's hands and setting it on the counter.

"Out back on the deck. Your aunts and I told them they weren't to do any work today. It's their day to celebrate. But you know Alex. He's got to be involved in every little detail. I gave Luke the job of sitting on him."

"Bet Gina would like that job better," Darcy mumbled, and Molly laughed. Okay, she hadn't insulted Sara's mom. Good to know.

"Everyone's back there. Go on out. I saw Erik and Tessa's van pull up. I'm going to go help get my grandkids out." Molly headed back through the house.

As they stepped onto the deck, she turned to Nate. "Do you want me to take him so you can congratulate your cousin?"

Tanner draped comfortably on his shoulder, still running the car up and down his father's arm. Nate looked torn. Because he wanted to keep hold of his son? Or because he didn't but felt guilty that he didn't?

"It's what you brought me here for. Otherwise, I could have stayed home and watched Creature Double Feature. It was Son of Godzilla and Swamp Thing this afternoon."

"What? No Dracula? Is the moon not full enough for that?"

Lifting Tanner into her arms, she snorted. "Full moons are for werewolves, GQ. You need some serious schooling in the art of horror movies."

"I bet you think you're the teacher for the job."

"Forget it, Biff. You couldn't be teacher's pet in my classroom, even if you brought in candy corn every day for a year."

"Who actually eats candy corn?"

"The cool people do. Now, go congratulate your cousin and his wife-to-be."

Plunking down into a chair, she settled Tanner in her lap. Sara was hugging her brother, who had his arm around his fiancée.

Gina was definitely one of the cool people. In her book, anyway. With long, wavy dark hair and clothes Darcy would die to have. She wore a tie dye halter top with fringe on the bottom and a pair of dark blue harem pants sporting an elephant print. Her feet were bare, and her toenails were painted lime green.

Darcy had gone for more black today. Mostly to piss GQ off. Her tattered crop top, with the cut-out neckline, hung off one shoulder. She'd made sure to wear a tube top underneath. For propriety. 'Cause she knew so much about that. Her ripped skinny jeans stopped short of her ankles. Just as well, since she'd worn her black high tops today in lieu of combat boots.

She'd gone heavy with the black lipstick. Nate had stared at her lips too much this week when she'd neglected to wear it at Sara's house. Having that man's gaze on her lips had done something to her insides. Something she couldn't afford and didn't want to admit she might have liked.

"Congratulations, Alex. Gina." Nate shook his cousin's hand, then pulled the woman in for a hug. "Did Sara and TJ's wedding give you ideas to run out and get married, also?"

"No," Alex replied, "The idea of Gina selling her grandmother's house and leaving finally got through to me. Luckily, she's crazy enough to love me."

"Loving you is easy, Felix." Gina wrapped her arms around Alex's waist. "Living with you, that might be a little harder."

"Tell me about it." Luke, Sara's youngest brother grunted. "It's the nagging. The constant nagging."

Alex narrowed his eyes at his brother.

"He's all yours now, Gina." Luke continued with a smirk.

Greg tipped his chin up at Luke. "You still looking for a new place? My parents are moving to those fifty-five plus condos both Uncle Pete and Uncle Kris have. It'll free up a bedroom or two. If you're real nice, I could rent you a few rooms for cheap money."

Luke nodded. "Yeah, but if Aunt Luci isn't there to make food, then what's the point. At least here, Alex cooks every night."

Everyone laughed. Sara rolled her eyes. "Have they given you any idea when they can get your house fixed up?" she asked Gina.

As Gina talked about the insurance claim and construction times, Darcy rocked back and forth with Tanner. The little boy ran the car over his legs as they went from right to left, then left to right.

Lulled into the hypnotic movement, she took in the people on the deck and started noting their rhythm and mannerisms. Especially Alex. She'd wondered about the odd couple. Gina was free-spirited and unique. Alex was as buttoned down as Nate. But after a while, she saw his little stims. That's what the therapists had called it when Zane had tapped on his fingers or traced shapes in the air. Sometimes, he clicked his teeth together in rhythm. Stimming. Self-stimulatory behavior. Things to keep him calm and help his anxiety. Evidently, Alex needed some self-calming coping mechanisms, too.

He tapped his fingers to his thumbs, back and forth from pinky to forefinger. At a guess, his apparent neatness and need for organization were neurological and not from a desire to be perceived as superior to someone else. There was a huge difference. Nathaniel Storm didn't exhibit signs of any disorder. He was just pretentious.

Though looking at him now, hugging the very pregnant

Tessa and shaking Erik's hand, you wouldn't know he was Mr. High and Mighty.

After congratulations were passed around, everyone wanted to touch Tessa's belly, poor thing. She looked completely uncomfortable, but Erik held her hand and smiled encouragement. Another one with a sad backstory. Dumped at a hospital as a kid, she'd been shuffled through lots of not-great foster care. Her whole life, she'd had a hard time when people touched her, until Erik had shown up needing help with the kids. And look at them now. They were all blissful and shit with a new baby on the way.

Stupid happy endings. She never should have come today. Too many nice people having great stuff happen to them. Not that they didn't deserve it. The Storms were good people. But, too often, bitterness rose up from the depths of Darcy's soul. She wished she'd had even a fraction of the good fortune they seem to have had heaped upon them.

"Hey, Tanner, let's go run in the yard, okay?" The kid had been cooped up in a car seat for two hours. He needed some movement.

She was about to yell out to Biff, then decided to behave. "Nate, I'm gonna take him to run around the grass." She wasn't asking permission, but she waited until he nodded and smiled.

Greg's son, Ryan, came down with them, and soon Erik's adopted kids, Matty and Kiki, showed up, too. Erik limped over to the shed near the driveway, reached in, and pulled out a large kid's ball, before throwing it in their direction.

Matty, who had just turned four according to Sara, picked up the ball and held it out to Tanner.

"You play ball." Apparently, Matty was still learning the language. Erik had rescued him and his sister from a bombing in Kandahar last year, and he and Tessa were in the process of adopting them.

Tanner placed his car on top of the rounded toy and ran it along the top. "Play ball."

"Matty, why don't you show Tanner how to kick the ball?" Darcy instructed the child.

Matty held out his hand, and she put Tanner's into it. "Go play. Matty is your cousin."

"Cousin," Tanner repeated and allowed Matty to lead him away to where Ryan stood waiting.

"Hey, cutie." Gina sauntered over and scooped up the toddler, Kiki, in her arms. "Let's hang out with Auntie Gina." They settled on the grass beside Darcy. "The guys are starting to talk sports. I needed to get away."

"Embracing the auntie roll already, huh?"

"You know it." Gina hugged the little girl, then planted kisses all over her face. Kiki giggled and squirmed. Gina loosened her hold, and the toddler wobbled to where her brother and cousins played.

"Are you and Alex planning on having kids soon?" She was a masochist. She had to be. Why else would she put herself through the hell of talking about kids?

"Not immediately, especially since I can't talk Alex into getting married right away, and he'd never go for a kid—" She placed her hand flat on her chest and made a face. "—out of wedlock."

Darcy's heart froze, her nerves on edge. "Yeah, only terrible people do that."

Gina giggled. "Are you kidding me? It's not a big deal, and Alex doesn't care about anyone else. But he's old fashioned in so many ways, so it matters to him and his kid."

"You don't seem like the old-fashioned type. You're okay with that?"

The grin on Gina's face told the answer. "I've loved Alex since I was a kid. He is who he is, and that's the man I love. I find him absolutely adorable."

"Well, it's obvious he loves you. I hope you're both happy together." So many good manners today. She should get a bullshit award or some sort of recognition.

"Thanks," Gina said with a smile. "I love the earrings."

Darcy ran her fingers down each ear, touching the studs embedded there. "It's a statement."

"A great one. I love the nose ring, too."

Stroking her finger over her right eyebrow, she grinned. "I used to have one here, as well, but I took it out a while back. It was a bit too much. I needed to tone things down."

Gina tipped her head and pressed her lips together. "I love the makeup, but am I seeing maybe an Asian look about you? I ask because my grandmother was Japanese."

"My dad was Korean."

Gina's eyes lit up. "Oh, did he—"

"I don't know. He took off shortly after I was born, and my mom never mentioned him much. Unless it was accompanied by a string of curses."

"Oh." Gina's lips made a great big bow. "Never mind, then. Let's talk about Nathaniel. He's a pretty cool guy, huh?"

Darcy squinted at her. "Are we talking about the same Nathaniel Storm? The GQ wannabe, pretentious corporate attorney who's got his head so far up his ass he can't see straight?"

Gina laughed. "Yep, that's the one. If you feel that way about him, why'd you come with him today?"

"I work for TJ and have been helping with Tanner. Sara guilted me into coming, so Nate could have quality time with his family."

"So you and he aren't a thing? Because he keeps staring over here."

"Probably upset I'm not with Tanner right now. But the kid needs to interact with other kids. See the type of stuff kids do. Sounds like his stuck up priss of a mother had him practically locked in the mansion with staid old nannies."

"Yeah, Alex told me what she did. Poor Nathaniel."

"It sucks that she kept his kid from him for so long, but he's hardly poor. He's paying me a shitload to hang out here today. Otherwise. you wouldn't find me anywhere near his majesty."

Because he looked and smelled too flippin' good, and she didn't need any more pain in her life caused by handsome men.

CHAPTER SEVEN

Nathaniel looked over to the grassy area of the yard to check on Tanner again. Darcy had her eyes on him, so he shouldn't worry. Ever since Helene showed up on his doorstep last Christmas Eve, his anxiety level had gone through the roof. Was he doing the right thing? Would he be a good father? What did Tanner need that he hadn't given him? And the big question…how could he possibly get his son to love him?

Watching Erik as Matty looked up at him with adoration, or Tessa as Kiki clung to her neck after falling and scraping her knee, made him wild with envy. Kiki wanted her mom and trusted Tessa to take care of her and love her. Matty thought of his dad as a superhero. Tanner didn't seem to even realize who was taking care of him.

Maybe he was being too dramatic. His son certainly recognized him. But there was no connection. No *"you're my dad, and I know what that means"* look in his eye.

When Darcy had first let Tanner go off with Matty, Nathaniel had wanted to rush over and stop him. But Ryan was there, too. He was about nine, and Greg had raised him to be sensitive to the needs of other children. Maybe Greg could give him some pointers on this dad thing. His cousin had done it without a mom for Ryan. He'd also had the kid from the moment he was born. Damn Helene.

"Nathaniel, honey, so glad you made it up from the Cape. How's it going down there?" His mom walked up behind him. He gave her a hug, then shook his dad's hand.

"Okay. Sara's been great helping out with Tanner, and they've got a dog who he seems to be enamored with. It's a black and white Springer Spaniel that looks similar to his stuffed pup."

"That's wonderful. Have you been taking it easy and relaxing or working too much as usual?"

"Believe it or not, I've actually taken a little bit of time for myself and Tanner. We built sandcastles earlier this week, moat and everything."

"How fun. And I see you brought Darcy with you today. Are you getting to know her better?"

Not by choice. "She seems to get Tanner, so she's been helping Sara and me with him."

"That's so sweet of her to do that for you."

His mother better not be matchmaking. Especially with Darcy. "I'm paying her. TJ says she could use the money, so it's hardly altruistic. She's got a brother with some special needs."

"It's still quite nice of her. I think I'll head over and get reacquainted with my grandson. I've missed him these past ten days."

His father watched as his mom picked up and kissed Tanner. "How are you doing, bud?"

Nathaniel released a big sigh. "I don't know, Dad. I feel like an utter and complete failure here. You always knew exactly what to say and do with me, Kevin, and Amy. I'm barely hanging on with Tanner."

"You'll be fine. Give it time. Pretty sure I messed up everything I tried to do for the first two years of your life. Your mother wouldn't leave me alone with you, until Kevin came along. By then, you were almost three, so no diapers or bottles. Ask her. She'll confirm every word."

He laughed. "Thanks, Dad. Not sure that makes me feel better. Guess I'll have to keep trying."

"You trying anything with that Darcy girl? She's definitely unique, and there's something about her that sparkles."

"Sparkles? Maybe she's got glitter hidden under all that black makeup. And no. Like I told Mom, I'm paying her to help me with Tanner. She's hardly my type."

His dad gave him a strange look, patted him on the back, then went to join Uncle Pete and Uncle Nick at the grill.

"Hey, cuz, we're starting a game of hoops. You up for that?" Luke trotted past, headed for the driveway.

"Um, maybe." He glanced to where Tanner was surrounded by Darcy, his mom, and Gina. Aunt Molly was also nearby, holding Kiki. "Let me make sure the kid's all right first."

Alex cruised by, cocking his thumb behind him. "You might also want to say hi to Gram and Gramps before you jump into the game. They're up on the porch. You'll catch hell later if you don't."

Nathaniel trotted over to the porch, gave his grandparents and his sister a quick greeting, then made sure Tanner was okay.

"There's plenty of us here to keep an eye on him," his mother said, waving him off. "You go play with the boys. We'll be fine."

He kissed her on the cheek, then hustled to the driveway where Kevin had shown up, along with his cousins, Erik, Alex, Luke, and Greg, and Sara's husband, TJ.

"Okay, teams?" Erik looked around and grabbed TJ's arm. "I want this guy on mine."

"Is he any good?" Nathaniel had been living with the man the past ten days but hadn't spent any time on the court with him.

Luke scowled. "He's too good. Why do you get him on your team?"

Erik shook his cane in the air. "Because I'm a cripple, and I need extra help."

"That's bullshit. You still get all the three pointers." Alex bent to pick up the basketball and grunted. "But I guess it doesn't matter to me. I'll have to sit this one out."

"I'm still playing, even with my cane. Using your injury as an excuse?"

Alex smirked at his older brother. "I had abdominal surgery three weeks ago. You really want me throwing a basketball? When I start bleeding internally again, I'll be sure to let Mom know you said it was okay."

Erik whipped his head to look at Aunt Molly, who stood glaring at them.

"Alexander Peter Storm, don't you even think about playing basketball, young man."

Erik frowned. "Okay, okay, you get a pass. How about you be ref? I'm not sure how honest these jokers will be."

Alex smirked, then pointed at him. "Nathaniel, why don't you go with Erik and TJ? That leaves Greg, Luke, and Kevin on the other team."

"Shirts versus skins. Who's losing 'em?" Kevin pulled a quarter from his pocket. "Call it."

He flipped the coin in the air, and Erik yelled out, "Heads."

Kevin laughed as the coin landed tails. "Loser. Take 'em off, boys."

Nathaniel tugged on his polo shirt as did TJ and Erik,

then they tossed them onto the grass next to the driveway. As he moved into place for the jump ball, he felt eyes on him.

Darcy stared over at them. Specifically at him. Sara's eyes were glued to her husband's chest, and even Tessa peeked at Erik. The shirt thing had never been a problem when it was only the cousins.

"Let's get this game going," Luke shouted, moving in to jump against him.

It had been a while since he'd played hoops with his family. He'd forgotten how much fun they were, and TJ seemed to fit right in. Throwing the odd elbow or hip checking the other team, not much was sacred. Even Erik took his brunt of the tough stuff. He landed on his ass a time or two, but everyone helped him back up and got on with the game. He wasn't against using his cane to trip up an opponent, either.

At a break in the game, Luke and Kevin ran in to get water and beer. The rest of them took the opportunity to check on their family. As he walked toward Tanner to make sure all was okay, Darcy's eyes opened wide, then she quickly glanced away.

"Hey, buddy, how's it going?" He knelt on the ground next to his son.

Tanner stopped, then held out his hand to touch Nathaniel's chest. "Wet."

"Yeah, kid, Daddy's a little sweaty from playing ball."

"Ball. Play ball." The boy ran over to the lightweight ball they'd been kicking around and carried it back.

Tanner knew what that meant. Ball. Nathaniel sat down, unable to hold himself up.

"That's right. Ball. Tanner play ball." Darcy had said keep the words simple. What would he do now?

"Ball," Tanner repeated, then kicked at it. It didn't go far, but the boy seemed pleased and ran to get it again. When he brought it over to him, Nathaniel placed it on the grass and gave it a tiny whack.

Tanner followed it again and retrieved it. Again and again. Like a puppy.

Erik was also checking on his wife and kids. Tessa gazed back with love and happiness. Something he'd never gotten from his ex. Should he get back in the dating game? The thought of it scared him spitless.

"Liquid refreshment," Kevin called out as he and Luke dragged a few coolers toward the driveway. "Half time break is over. Let's play."

Nathaniel hated to leave Tanner, now that he was actually playing with him. Turning to find the child, his lungs deflated. The ball had been abandoned, and the boy drove his car over the seat of his grandmother's chair. Nathaniel's mom smiled down, then gazed at him with a thumbs up. Maybe she didn't realize he'd wanted to continue playing with Tanner.

"You coming?" Erik asked, limping past after kissing his wife and kids.

"Guess so." It wasn't like his own kid wanted anything to do with him.

As the ball began bouncing around, conversation started. They were all a little slower than before.

"What are you doing with Gina's house?" he asked Alex as he dribbled past for a layup.

Greg captured the rebound and took it out.

"We need to get the insurance settled first. They're pushing it through fast, since we outed the bad guys who robbed a few of the town shops."

Luke jumped to get the ball Greg passed to him and hurled it up to swish through the hoop. "Maybe once it's livable, I can move in there and leave you two to hump like bunnies all day long."

"You're one to talk, Romeo." Erik set his feet, took the ball TJ threw his way and let it fly. The net never even moved as the ball swished through. "Someday, all these quick and easy relationships are going to bite you in the ass."

"Does Luke actually call them relationships?" Kevin drove in for a layup. "At least, I date them for more than one night. But I'm happy to be single and available whenever a nice lady has need of me. To protect and serve."

Nathaniel hip checked him, then pulled in the rebound. "Bet you serve them well, little brother."

Kevin laughed, then turned toward Greg. "What about you, cuz? Anyone in your life. It's been a long time. You've been living like a monk."

Greg frowned. "I have a kid at home I have to be with and take care of. You two," he gestured at Luke and Kevin, "go out with enough women for all of us combined."

"Nathaniel's got a kid. Is he cramping your style, bro?" Kevin dribbled past him. "Anything between you and Darcy? Because I gotta say, she's not really your type."

"No, to both." God, what a thought. "She's helping me with Tanner, so I can play ball with you clowns."

Luke paused near the edge of the driveway, smirking. "She's definitely interesting. I bet she'd be a fun night."

For Luke, she probably would be. But why did he feel like punching his cousin for the comment?

~

At the sound of footsteps behind her, Darcy froze, bent over the box of coffee lids. She'd been expecting this.

"Hey, Darcy?"

"Hey, boss. I'm kind of busy."

"Don't give me that. I spent months playing with coffee cups and napkins to avoid Sara. I know the drill."

"Oh, I do it so much better than you. I actually organize them. See?" The coffee cups were stacked in neat rows of ten each. Covers next to them.

TJ sighed. "I was wondering..." He looked through the door into the shop, then back at her.

"No, you weren't. You were gonna order me to go hang out at Story Hour and babysit Tanner again."

His face filled with surprise. "I'd never order you to do anything. If you're uncomfortable watching Tanner, say so. But you've been helping Sara and Nathaniel the past three weeks, so I thought it was okay."

"It's fine, boss. I've gotten to like that little Storm kid. It's all the rest of the brats I could do without." Especially since Hope had latched onto Tanner and decided she needed to be best buddies with him. There was a two-year age difference, but Hope was small and introverted, and maybe that was the attraction with a younger child. Having her snuggled up close to Tanner, who typically sat in Darcy's lap, was what had her on edge.

"Most of them don't bother you. Well, Hope has gotten attached to Tanner, but she's harmless. You could do worse."

He had no idea why having Hope next to her was so bad. It was a constant reminder of what she could've had. What she gave up. All the bad decisions she'd ever made rolled up in one miniscule, dark-haired girl.

"Sara and I both appreciate what you've been doing, and I know Nathaniel is thankful at how much time you've taken to get to know his son and work with him."

"That's me. A wonder of nature. Now, let me finish up these cups, so I can hang with the kiddies."

Ignoring the cups, she took off her apron, hung it on a hook in the back, then hustled into the bathroom. She'd need to darken the makeup around her eyes if she wanted to keep her composure. Maybe even more black lipstick, so Nate wouldn't stare at her mouth. Like the few times he'd done it at the beach house. At least, he'd have his shirt on today. Last week, when they'd gone to New Hampshire for Alex and Gina's engagement party, the basketball game had gotten interesting. When Nate had come over to check on Tanner, his chest glistening with sweat, it was all she could do not to drool.

Once she'd donned her protective armor, she took a deep breath and headed to the carpet in the children's area. Nate sat on the floor with Tanner and Freckles in his lap. Dropping onto the rug next to them, she stretched out her legs, showing off her black combat boots proudly.

"Feeling festive today?" Nate glanced at her outfit. "You've got a little color going on there."

The socks sticking out from her boots were a bright yellow paisley. Her capri leggings were dark blue with burgundy paisley, and her blouse finished up the ensemble with burgundy background and navy paisley.

"It's paisley on parade."

"What's paisley?" Hope's sweet voice caressed Darcy's ear, and she stiffened. She hadn't seen the little girl enter the store. What was wrong with her? She always watched the door on Story Hour days.

"It's this swirly pattern." Darcy pointed to her pants.

Hope checked it out, looked at Tanner in his father's lap, then back at her. And frack, she climbed into Darcy's lap, then reached over and took Tanner's hand. The boy took his Hot Wheels and ran it along Hope's fingers. She giggled.

"Do you want me to take him?" Anything to get Hope off her lap.

"I'm good for a bit. He had a moment earlier. I want to make sure we're okay."

Great, now she was stuck here, hip to hip with GQ

smelling like a frickin' aftershave ad. That, along with Hope in her lap, didn't exactly make for a relaxing day.

Sara sat on the floor at the front of the children's area and greeted the kids. Darcy felt ridiculous, sitting here listening to another adult read children's books. Glancing around, she searched for some emergency that would require her immediate attention. A book emergency. Or a coffee emergency. Like they had so many of those.

Instead, she found Jodie smiling at her. Really? Why didn't this woman want her as far away from her child as possible? Yes, they'd agreed on an open adoption, and Jodie constantly sent her pictures and videos of Hope. She'd seen Hope's first words, first steps, and so many other milestones. But she hadn't been there. Hadn't held her child when she'd cried after scraping a knee. Hadn't rocked her to sleep when she was tired.

Wasn't Jodie afraid Darcy would simply grab hold of Hope one day and take off? So many times she'd dreamed of doing that, of taking her little girl and becoming a real mom to her.

But what about Zane? He could come, too. Yeah, right, and where would that leave them? Darcy supporting Zane and Hope on minimum wage?

Another smile, then Jodie headed up the stairs to the next floor that held all the fiction books. Maybe while she was up there, Darcy could…no, she couldn't.

But she did, anyway. Wrapped her arms around the child in her lap and gave her a little squeeze. Stuck her nose in Hope's hair and inhaled the bubble gum smell of her shampoo. Memorized her feel and scent and the sound of her little voice telling Tanner to listen to the story. God, she wanted this so much. All the time. But she couldn't have it. She'd signed away her parental rights before she'd even given birth to this child.

Maybe it would have been better if the hospital staff had simply taken the baby away as soon as she came out. But Jodie and Sharla had insisted she hold the child. They'd even taken a picture, one Darcy stared at every night before going to bed. They'd been there in the maternity ward, Jodie holding her hand as she went through labor and delivery. Jodie had made sure Darcy got to hold the infant before anyone else.

And when she had, she'd cried. Hadn't wanted to let the baby go. Held her and let the tears fall for all the mistakes she'd made in her life. Except one of those mistakes had created this perfect human being. No matter how much she wanted to raise the baby and give her everything in the world, she also knew it would never happen. Her mother and brother had needed her, and there was no way she could take care of them and a child at the same time, not in any decent way that a beautiful new baby deserved.

As she'd cradled her precious gift, she'd whispered to her, "I hope you'll always have all the things in life I can't give you, and that you'll know how much I love you and why I'm giving you away."

When she'd handed the baby over to Jodie, she said, "Here's my hope. Please, take care of her and love her as much as I do."

The fact they'd named her Hope had nearly killed her. But they'd been true to their word and sent her pictures and encouraged her to visit if she wanted.

But Darcy couldn't do it. Not back then and not now. Holding this little girl in her lap was torture. The most beautiful agony she'd ever felt. But it wouldn't last. She had no claim on Hope and never would.

CHAPTER EIGHT

*N*athaniel was on his own, and it scared the hell out of him. He'd been alone with Tanner plenty of times since his son had come to live with him, but his mother had been right around the corner if he'd needed help. Now, she was a two-hour drive away. Sure, he could call her, but managing a child didn't work well over the phone.

Sara had a concert up in New Hampshire tonight, and she and TJ had left early this morning so she'd have time to get acclimated to the venue and rehearse. They planned to stay at Alex's house tonight, since the concert would run late.

And if taking care of his son wasn't hard enough, Freckles was due to have her puppies possibly this week. He didn't dare leave the house for fear she'd have them the second he walked out.

What the heck did he know about puppies? As much as he knew about raising a child.

"Fwecko." Tanner sat on the kitchen floor, running his stuffed dog over Freckles' head and back. The spaniel didn't seem to mind.

"Be gentle with Freckles. She has puppies in her belly."

"Puppies."

Was the kid asking a question or merely repeating words? How could Nathaniel tell the difference?

He'd chatted with his sister, Amy, at the engagement party. She was currently in school majoring in Communication Disorders. Lots of what she said was exactly what Darcy had mentioned. Repeat words often. Use only a few words at a time, so he understands each one. Build up to larger sentences as his vocabulary grows.

"Here, Tanner. Eat." He held out the rolled-up ham and cheese, and his son took a bite. He couldn't always get him to sit still long enough to eat a full meal, so Nathaniel had taken to giving him protein snacks throughout the day. The kid's range of food he liked was limited, but luckily, he ate a few things in each food group, so Nathaniel could give him a balanced diet.

After taking another bite, Tanner left the room, and Nathaniel followed him. He hated to nag at him to stay in one place. The boy's mind worked in a different way, so he'd been told. Who knew what he was thinking?

TJ's house was fairly spartan, so there weren't too many things Tanner could break. Sara was in the process of redecorating and making it a home, but she hadn't done much yet since she'd been busy with her concerts and the wedding.

Nathaniel trailed his son into the music room and sat on the piano bench, holding out the food. "Hey, buddy, eat."

The boy took another bite, then gazed around the room. The black and white keys caught his attention, and he was riveted. Nathaniel held the food near his mouth again and said, "Eat."

Once Tanner had chewed, Nathaniel pressed down on one of the keys. Tanner straightened at the noise, his gaze intent on the piano. Nathaniel repeated the action.

"You press it." He took the child's hand and touched his

finger to the key. When the tone sounded again, Tanner's eyes lit up, and he started bouncing on his toes.

Nathaniel played the next step up. The note was slightly different. Tanner cocked his head, then look at his father. Was he asking for permission to touch it? It should be fine, right?

"Take a last bite." Tanner finished the roll-up, his eyes never leaving the instrument.

"Each one makes a different sound. It's music." Was that too much for him to understand? Taking his son's hand, he pressed down on the keys starting at one end and moving to the other. As each note rang out, slightly different from the one before, Tanner tipped his head back and forth. When they got to the end, the child's brow wrinkled, and he looked to where they had started.

"You can do it again, if you want. Again." He had to remember small sentences. Simple words.

"Again," Tanner repeated, moving back and pressing each key down the line.

Nathaniel scooted the bench back, so his son could move easily as he touched the black and whites in order. After a dozen times, Nathaniel decided to try something. Who knew if it would work, but it probably couldn't hurt.

Calling up the lessons all the Storm grandchildren had been given, courtesy of Gram and Gramps, he plucked out the beginning of a simple tune. Seven notes, using only a few keys. He played it twice and waited to see what Tanner would do.

His son stopped at the last key on the keyboard and watched Nathaniel's fingers move. He played it again. Then, the boy squeezed in front of him and touched each of the keys in the same exact order. E, D, C, D, E, E, E.

Nathaniel's heart raced as Tanner played the notes again.

In perfect order. Did he understand what he was doing? Or that it created a song?

He let Tanner practice those notes a few more times, then added the next line of the song. After playing the whole thing three times, he sat back and waited. Tanner stepped up to the keys and repeated the entire section he'd just heard.

Seriously, the child was only three years old. He'd have to ask his mom, but he was pretty sure that was fairly young to be playing even the small amount he had.

When Tanner had played the two lines a half dozen times, Nathaniel stepped in and added two more lines, then repeated them twice. Was that too much for him to remember at once? None of the cousins had started piano lessons until they were closer to five or six.

But Tanner reached up and fingered the keys, playing the lines perfectly. All of them. There was only one line left to finish the song. Nathaniel played the entire song this time, but only once. Could Tanner pick it up that fast? He'd been watching intently as the keys were pressed.

He did. Nathaniel sat in amazement as his son played the entire song perfectly from start to finish. The staccato notes didn't flow together like music typically did, but he was still awestruck at what the child had done. Of course, Tanner was excellent at repeating things over and over.

"Great job, Tanner. Music. You played music."

"Music." The boy's soft voice repeated the word as he plucked out the song again.

Something flittered in Nathaniel's chest and started growing. He'd call it pride, but he'd been proud of accomplishments before, and this was far stronger. Warmer and deeper. It grabbed at his heart and made the blood pump faster. It connected him to this child, who still stood playing a children's tune on the piano. Connected them in a way he'd never experienced before.

He wanted to pull Tanner into his arms and hold him tight, to feel the child's energy mingling with his. Would Tanner even notice? Could he take that kind of disappointment again? It felt like rejection, though he knew it wasn't meant that way. The boy's disability somehow kept him from feeling the emotions coursing through Nathaniel. Or did he still have them, but they presented in a different way? He wished he knew.

As Tanner repeated the song over and over, Nathaniel wondered if it had been wise to teach him. This song could drive him crazy in a short period of time. Would the boy be able to learn something else as easy as he'd picked up the first one?

"Tanner, how about trying this?" He pressed the beginning notes of another easy tune.

Before the child could start, a whining noise drifted from the kitchen.

"Fwecko."

"No, not now." Please, not while he was here alone with Tanner.

He took Tanner's hand and they walked into the kitchen to find Freckles in the extra-large box Sara and TJ had placed in the corner. It was filled with blankets and Freckles rested right in the middle, panting like she'd just run along the beach.

"Dog. Fwecko." Tanner sat next to the box and ran his hand gently along the animal's head.

Shit. Was the dog in labor or resting up for the big event? Nathaniel fished his phone from his pocket and started Googling dog birth stuff. When Freckles stuck her nose between her hind legs and started licking her privates, he knew he didn't have time for the internet.

Flipping through his phone, he tapped out a text to TJ's number, not wanting to bother Sara if she was busy rehearsing but needing someone to tell him what to do.

—*Think Freckles is having the puppies. Help! What do I do?*—

The reply came back quickly.

—*Animals don't need help like humans do, but Darcy has experience with pets. I'll call her.*—

Not Darcy. Of all the people to call for help, she was the last on his list. Maybe his brother could talk him through it. Cops helped deliver babies at times, didn't they?

Before he could press the button for Kevin's number, another text came in from TJ.

—*Darcy's on her way. Hold tight.*—

~

DARCY'S TWENTY-YEAR-OLD Ford sputtered as she put it in gear. "Come on, you shit box, you can do it. TJ's house is only a mile down the road."

She'd already clocked out when the boss man had called. So much for the Devil Dogs she was looking forward to when she got home from work. GQ couldn't handle a little dog delivery? Hadn't she seen enough of him lately?

Story Hour was three times a week, and he and Tanner often hung around afterward for a bit. Then, she'd watched Tanner a few times when Biff was busy with lawyerly duties and Sara had errands to run. Most of the time, he'd still been in the house on the phone or a video call, that accursed scent of his swirling around, bewitching her.

Most likely, Nate heard the clattering vehicle as she pulled into the driveway. She half expected him to be outside, clutching his pearls in fear. Instead, he had Tanner wrapped tightly in a quilt sitting on the kitchen floor. She used to do that to Zane when he got overstimulated.

Freckles licked something near her feet.

"She already had the first one. I wasn't sure what to do, but apparently Freckles knows. Unless they aren't supposed to clean the puppy off with their tongue and eat the placenta."

"Nope, perfectly normal. See? You didn't even need me. I can go."

The look on GQ's face was priceless. In one swift movement, he stood, never even jostling Tanner in his arms. Well done. The kid had to be close to thirty pounds. Kudos to those arms, the ones she was definitely not ogling.

"No, please. Stay. Tanner got a little upset when the first puppy started coming out. I'm not sure how much he understands what's going on. Then, at one point, I thought I was going to have to break the placenta to get the puppy out. Poor little guy. He was squirming, but it wouldn't pop. Finally, it did, but Freckles may need help with some of the others."

He gazed down at the dog who was now licking the small pup all over.

"There will be more, right? I mean, don't most dogs have at least a few puppies?"

Kneeling next to the spaniel, Darcy stroked her head and down her back. Her panting had slowed for now.

"According to TJ, the vet said she's having four or five. They weren't positive. Average for this breed is about six, but it's her first litter and that often means fewer puppies."

"Her *first* litter?"

Darcy shrugged. "First and last. I have a feeling the boss man will have her spayed after this. He hadn't really planned on this pregnancy." Like so many other people.

She slipped her hands into a pair of latex gloves from a box on the counter. TJ and Sara had been prepared in case they needed to help the dog during her delivery. Nate eyed her curiously.

"How do you know so much about animals?" He crossed his legs and sat on the floor near her again. Nice and cozy.

"In high school, I worked at a shelter for a while." Even with the money she made at that job, they'd barely had enough to pay for rent and food. Dear old mom would take the welfare check and spend most of it on drugs and booze. She used to bring Zane to help, until he'd tried to steal one of the dogs and take it home.

Nate cocked his head like he was waiting for her to say more. Sure, fill the space with verbal spillage. No need to get into real conversation.

"A few times we had animals that were having babies. Usually, they're able to do it all themselves, but every now and then they can use a little assistance. Especially if they're having multiples. They get tired after the fifth or sixth one and don't always clean them off as well. Or they eat too much placenta, which can make them sick. You need to keep your eye on them, just in case."

"You sound like you know your stuff. You didn't think about becoming a veterinarian?"

As if college had ever been in the cards. Setting aside her complete lack of cash, she hadn't even finished high school with her class because of her pregnancy. The GED had come later.

"I didn't have the right grades for that kind of thing."

His eyes narrowed. "Really? Because, despite your vampire tendencies, I still get the impression that you're highly intelligent."

Blinking away the tears that sprang to her eyes at the compliment—if that's what it was—she shook her head. "Yeah, I'm a regular genius."

Fact was, she'd done well in school when she had the chance to go. Meaning, when her mother wasn't too sick to feed herself or trying to set the house on fire, and Darcy didn't have to keep an eye on her. But she'd made sure Zane went every morning. Thank God for Special Education services and the bus that picked him up right at the apartment.

"Puppy." Tanner squirmed in Nate's arms, his gaze never leaving the small black ball of fur Freckles was still licking.

"Why aren't the others coming out? Do you think they're stuck? Should we do something?"

GQ's concern was cute. Unfortunately, she needed to not desire him in any way.

"The poor dog is recovering from the first baby. The rest will come. Don't worry your pretty little head about it. If there's something more important, go do it." Please, let him go. He could even leave Tanner with her and she'd be happy, as long as she didn't have to put up with his annoyingly endearing presence.

"It's Saturday. I don't need to work."

"I thought all hot shot lawyers worked a bazillion hours to keep up the image."

Nate glanced down at Tanner. "I promised myself I'd cut back this summer and spend time with my son, so that's what I'm going to do. Even if that time includes watching puppies being born."

"Puppies, puppies," Tanner chanted, causing the brooding dad to grin.

And frack if that grin didn't do something to the wall around Darcy's heart.

"So, Darcy, what do you like to do in your spare time?"

Her head whipped up and she eyed him strangely. "My spare time? Like when I'm not working overtime at the store? Or babysitting your kid? Or helping pregnant dogs give birth? Or taking my brother to his counseling services? You mean then?"

That wretched grin again. "Yeah, then."

"Why do you even want to know?"

He lifted one eyebrow, and it made his face even more devilishly gorgeous. "Making small talk, Elvira. No need to throw garlic at me."

She couldn't stop herself from rolling her eyes. "You wear the garlic around your neck, Biff. That's to ward off vampires. Or you can use a cross or a stake to the heart."

"For you, I'd think a lacy, pink dress might work just as well."

Okay, he had her there. Her mouth twisted into a smirk. "True, but what do I use to ward off pretentious corporate attorneys?"

"Why would you want to ward me off? I'm being my absolute, most charming self at the moment."

"That's your most charming? No wonder your ex went shopping elsewhere."

"Ouch."

Okay, maybe that went beyond the snark zone and into bad manners territory, but she had to get him out of her hemisphere. He made her want things she wasn't allowed to have.

"Ouch. Boo boo?" Tanner gazed up at his father, his tiny lips bowed in a pout.

"I'm fine. Don't worry." Nate hugged him closer, his face a mask of emotions.

She needed to apologize. That had been beyond cruel, especially knowing what she did about the man's ex-wife and what an unfeeling bitch she was.

"Look, Nate, I'm—"

Freckles whined and started panting again.

"I guess the next one is coming." He wouldn't look at her. Shit, what a jerk she was.

"I'm sorry—"

"Don't," he interrupted, his gaze swinging to her for a

second. "If you were actually nice to me, I'd wonder what you were up to. Like you were setting me up for sacrifice to some ghoulish monster."

His eyes gleamed as he focused on her. So, not pissed at what she'd said, even though she had to admit it was over the top.

"Believe me, no ghoulish monster would have you. They'd take one lick and realize you were too tough and tasteless, even with your million-dollar suit. The whole village would be doomed forever."

"Poor village." Freckles whined and panted rapidly. "Poor doggy."

Darcy rested a hand across Freckles' belly. More contractions rippled underneath. Stroking the dog gently, she cooed soothing words of encouragement.

"It's okay, sweetie. You're doing fine. You've got another little baby on the way." And someday the babies would be taken away from her and given to other people. Guess life wasn't any easier when you were a dog mom. You didn't even get a choice to give your kids up, but then you didn't have to live with the guilt of it either. Just the horror.

As the second puppy appeared, and Freckles started the process of cleaning it up, Darcy peeked over at GQ and the kid. Tanner leaned against his dad, mesmerized by what was going on.

"Do you know if they're boy or girl puppies?"

"I can check in a minute, once she's finished cleaning this one off. The first one needs to nurse a bit first. It only just found the nipple. Must be a male. They never stop to ask directions."

She leaned in and gently lifted the first puppy to check under the tail. "Yup, this one's male. Called it."

Nate chuckled, shaking his head. "That's a boy puppy," he told his son.

"Boy puppy," Tanner repeated like the little magpie he was, and Nathaniel didn't seem upset at the constant repetition. He actually looked pleased with the new vocabulary. Had he remembered what she'd said about simple words spoken often?

"How long does this type of thing usually last? I mean, until all the puppies are born?"

Shrugging, she kept her eye on the sac that hadn't opened yet with the newest birth. Freckles was licking, but the puppy didn't seem to be wiggling as much.

"It could last up to ten hours. Sometimes more. Each puppy usually takes anywhere from forty-five minutes to an hour. The mom needs that long to clean the afterbirth off and then recover before the next one comes along."

"Ten hours? Man, that's a long time to be in labor."

"Lots of women labor that long to have babies. First babies, in particular. And that's for one child." She'd been in labor for about twelve. Often, she wondered if subconsciously she hadn't wanted to let go of her child, so her body had kept the baby inside for as long as possible.

"Hear that, Freckles?" Nate tilted toward the dog bed. "It could be a lot worse."

Freckles didn't stop licking the new member of the family, but Darcy didn't see it moving. Shit. She didn't need Tanner to see one of the dogs die.

"Do you think you could get me a glass of water, please?" She used her most pleasant tone as she picked up the puppy and started massaging it with a small towel.

"Sure." Nate's voice stretched out the word, and she frowned at him, continuing to rub the puppy. He picked up Tanner and stepped over to the sink. He took his time getting a cup from the cabinet and filling it with ice, then water.

"Thanks." Her tone was tight as she ran her hand over the

soft form. "Put it right there." She didn't even look at it as she felt the bundle in her hand start to wiggle. The breath she'd been holding escaped in a sigh.

"Here you go, mama. This one's ready for a bath now, too."

Freckles got busy licking and cleaning up her newest arrival. Darcy picked up the first pup that had fed and then wandered off to another part of the blanket.

"Everything okay now?" Nate had started rocking back and forth with Tanner, and the child slumped in his arms, his eyes fluttering closed.

"I think so. I hope so. The little guy took a few minutes to get going on his own." When she glanced at the puppy, he was now sucking furiously at his mother's milk.

Nathaniel reached out and touched her arm. The contact sent excitement coursing into her veins. Dangerous man. She had to remember that.

"Thanks so much for coming out to help. I don't think I could have handled…that…and Tanner at the same time. I wouldn't even have known what to do to help."

"You can get out of my way and stop distracting me with chatter." And his perfect scent.

"Sorry, I didn't realize I was talking too much."

Keeping her eyes on Freckles, she shrugged. "Not too much. Just more than I want from you. Why don't you put the kid down somewhere? He must be getting heavy."

"I don't mind. I like holding him. When he's asleep, I can pretend he knows I'm his dad and loves me like a kid should."

Then, the flippin' GQ model went and gazed at his son like he was the most precious thing on Earth. The vulnerability of that confession ripped into her heart, reminding her that no matter how much she'd loved her mom, the woman had never said it back.

CHAPTER NINE

Nathaniel placed Tanner's stuffed dog on his right side and three cars on the table to his left. The red racer, the yellow bulldozer, and the purple roadster. As long as those things were in place, in the correct order, the child went to bed easily and stayed in bed until Nathaniel came to get him in the morning.

As he walked down the stairs, Nathaniel listened for commotion in the kitchen. Darcy had been here since this afternoon, and she had to be exhausted. Heck, Tanner had taken a short nap in his arms, woken up, had dinner, and gone to bed again in that time. Not that it had been easy getting him to eat when Freckles and her puppies were nearby.

"How we doing?"

"I'm not doing anything, but Freckles is getting tired. Four down and one or two to go."

"How do you know when she's done?"

Darcy looked up at him, her eyes twinkling. "She stops having puppies."

"No shit, Sherlock. But is there some indication that she's delivered them all?"

How could he believe anything when she smirked like that? "You mean, like the last puppy coming out with a sign that says, 'I'm the last. Close up shop'? Or Freckles barking three times?"

"Okay, no need to get snarky with me."

"Oh, there's always a need with you, Biff. It's what I live for."

"Are you hungry? You didn't have anything when I fed Tanner, and it's past nine now."

Surveying the dog and her puppies, Darcy stroked her hand down Freckles' back and side. "Well, she seems to be taking a short break. I suppose I could grab something quick."

As she pushed to her feet, Nathaniel grasped her elbow to help. She allowed it but sent him a death glare, warning him not to do it again.

"I can get the food for you. Why don't you relax for a few minutes on the couch in the living room? Is there anything you don't like?"

"Pretentious, snotty lawyers."

"I already knew that. I meant is there anything you won't eat?"

"Pretentious, snotty lawyers." She was too much.

"Noted. Too tough and tasteless, even in a million-dollar suit."

Her eyes lit up. "He learns fast. Anything they have in their fridge is fine. I didn't have the option of not liking any food when I was a kid."

He left that comment alone, but by the time he'd heated up some leftover chili and brought it to her, his curiosity had gotten the better of him.

"Was your mom one of those who made you eat everything on your plate?"

She spooned in a mouthful of the spicy mixture. "My mom wasn't strict about making meals or even providing food. If you couldn't smoke it, drink it, or inhale it, she rarely bought it."

"I'm sorry, Darcy. That must have been tough." Shit, why had he brought this up? Sounded like her early years sucked big time.

"Nah, it made me tough enough to handle anything."

"Including delivering puppies."

Her head popped up, and she started to put the bowl down. "Is Freckles having the next one?"

Once he'd glanced into the kitchen and assured himself she wasn't, he pressed Darcy back into the seat and settled next to her. "She's resting. The puppies are eating. I can probably handle it, if she starts contractions again. Take it easy for now."

"I've already made arrangements for Mr. Peabody to check on Zane, so I may as well earn my keep here."

"Will your brother be okay by himself? Does he need another person with him at all times?" Mostly, he was asking for himself. Trying to see what Tanner's life would be like when he grew up. Would he be able to go to a regular school and participate in a traditional class? Or would he need specialized educational services his whole life?

"Zane can handle himself fine for a while. I've been away overnight before, and he doesn't mind. He has a phone and knows how to answer it if it's me, or to call me if there's an emergency. We practice this often. But most of the time, I like to have another person be around to check on him. Just in case."

"So if he's stayed by himself before, does that mean he can get something to eat and do all the daily routines?"

"He's perfectly capable of getting himself dressed and ready, along with all the hygiene stuff that goes with it. He can make a sandwich and even microwave food. His reading level isn't exactly where it should be, but it's enough that he can read instructions on cans of soup or frozen dinners. He's had jobs before and is fairly self-sufficient, but he doesn't always make the best choices with some things, so I like to keep him close by. Plus, he's my only family."

That was the most serious thing he'd ever heard Darcy say. There wasn't a snarky word in there.

"He's no pretentious, snotty lawyer, but he's doing okay."

There it was. The sass was back.

They lounged on the couch for a while, Darcy with her head back and eyes closed. He didn't dare say anything to disturb her.

A whine from the kitchen an hour later had them both hustling in to see Freckles' tongue hanging out and her sides heaving again.

"Baby number five. Last one, or do you think there's another?"

Darcy's lips twisted to the side. "Did you want to make a bet on it?"

"I'm not really a gambling man, and I know nothing about birthing dogs, but sure, if it'll make you happy. I'll take a bet."

"What would make me happy is if you went to bed and left me with the dogs."

"But what if you need my help?"

"Pretty sure I won't need a corporate attorney to get the last baby or two out. Case dismissed."

"It still wouldn't feel right leaving you here to do all the work, while I shuffle off to watch TV or go to bed."

Darcy crooned a few soft words to the mama dog as she stroked her head and back. "I can manage just fine. I don't need a babysitter."

"That's obvious, since you've been the one babysitting for me these last few weeks."

"Fine, if you want to help, maybe you could get a few treats for Freckles and some water. We need to keep her hydrated."

"Sure thing."

Over the next few hours, the dog delivered two more babies. Watching Darcy with the animal showed a side of her that surprised him. It shouldn't. She was super patient and knowledgeable when dealing with Tanner, and despite her claims that she can't stand the brats at Story Hour, she still teased and joked with them while they were there.

Once a few of the pups were done eating, Darcy settled them near mom on one of the blankets.

Picking up an almost all black pup with small tufts of white on the nose and belly, Darcy held it in front of him. "This is the one you and Tanner should take. She's similar to Tanner's stuffed puppy."

"You want me to take a puppy?" He stared at her. "Are you crazy? I can barely get by right now, never mind adding in something that drools and slobbers and needs to be taken on walks every day."

She scowled. "You shouldn't talk about Tanner that way."

"I wasn't. I was talking about the..." Heat rushed to his cheeks. "I can't believe I fell for that. Must be more tired than I thought."

Her eyes lit up as she laughed, but it was clear she was starting to droop. It was after midnight, and she'd been up helping Freckles for a while. He'd been up, too, but she'd been doing most of the work.

Glancing at her watch, she yawned. "I should go, but I want to make sure she's completely done. I think she is, but there's always a chance of another. Plus, I'm not sure if she's pushed out all the afterbirth yet."

"I don't like the idea of you driving home at this hour."

She quirked her head and made duck lips. "Believe it or not, I've stayed up past midnight before. You know, we nocturnal creatures love being awake during the witching hour."

"You've also been yawning for a while. Why don't you stay here for the night? You said Zane was all taken care of, and Mr. Peabody was planning on checking on him."

"Yeah, they probably watched a movie together before bed."

"There are two extra bedrooms upstairs. Take your pick. Tanner and I are in the front ones."

Crossing her arms, Darcy frowned. "What, I can't have one of those? I'm not good enough?"

The mischief in her eyes did something to his insides. He could play that game, too.

"Tanner's already in bed, and I'd hate for you to wake him. He'll think it's morning and want to get up. But I suppose I could move over and make some room, if you really need an oceanside view."

The face she made bent him over in a laugh.

"I'll take the couch. That way I'll be nearby if Freckles or her babies have any kind of problems."

"Suit yourself. I'll grab you some pillows and a blanket."

When he came downstairs, the kitchen lights had been turned off, except the dim light over the stove. Darcy was sprawled on the couch, eyes closed. He'd wanted to suggest she could use a t-shirt of his, but her leggings were soft and her shirt stretchy. They'd do. He wasn't sure he could handle seeing her toned legs peeking out from one of his shirts. Those were ideas he definitely didn't need.

Without the constant flood of attitude and the impish grin, she actually looked kind of sweet. Innocent. Pretty. He wondered what she looked like under all that black makeup.

Nathaniel checked on Freckles and made sure all the doors were locked. When he re-entered the living room, Darcy hadn't moved. He tucked the pillow under her head without her even batting an eye, then covered her with his grandmother's quilt.

Bending over, he pushed a long lock of black hair behind her ear. It was soft and silky and gave him pause.

He leaned in and kissed her cheek with a whispered, "Thanks."

A tiny smile appeared on her peaceful face, and a feeling stirred deep within him. It was warm and surprising, followed by thoughts he had no business having.

Whatever it was, he pushed it far into the back of his mind and climbed the stairs to his room.

～

DARCY WOKE from a dead sleep when a low whine penetrated her dreams. She bolted up and glanced around. TJ and Sara's living room. Oh, yeah, puppies. The whine sounded again, and she ambled toward the kitchen.

Mama and babies snuggled together in the cushy box, but when she walked in, Freckles rose and padded to the back door. Darcy opened it. Unsure, the dog kept looking outside, then back at her babies.

"It's okay, Freckles. Go pee. I'll take care of them."

Leaving the back door ajar, she moved to the cabinet, took out a can of dog food, emptied it into the dog's dish, then refilled her bowl with fresh water. Once that was done, she inspected the litter. They all squirmed and wiggled and tried to find their mama. Within minutes, Freckles was back in, wolfed down some of her food and water, then rested on her side. The puppies scampered to try and reach her first. Looked like everything was good.

BROKEN DREAMS

When she entered the downstairs bathroom, she almost had a heart attack. Makeup was all over her face. She'd been so tired last night she'd fallen asleep without removing it. Something she never did. Where had she left her purse?

The kitchen table. Grabbing it, she made quick work of washing off the old makeup. Unfortunately, she didn't have everything she typically used. That was stupid, but she hadn't expected to stay over. She couldn't face GQ lawyer man in less than her full armor.

She quickly flicked the mascara wand through her lashes, then used the eyeliner to outline the shape of her eyes. It wasn't the one she used to create the exaggerated designs she usually wore. Could she still make do? And why the heck wasn't her black lipstick here?

Footsteps carried down the hallway, and she penciled a few more lines under her eyes. Hardly enough, but it would have to suffice for now.

"Darcy, are you in there?"

"Right here, GQ. Can't a girl use the toilet without being accosted?"

"I hardly accosted..." His mouth hung open, and his eyes almost popped out of his head.

Narrowing her eyes, she frowned. "What?"

Juggling Tanner in his arms, he shook his head. "Nothing. Thanks for staying last night and helping out."

"Whatever. I should get out of here."

"How about I make you breakfast before you go? It's still early. You told me your brother slept late in the mornings."

Had she told him that? Maybe, at some point. "No need to bribe me with food. I did it for Sara and the boss. Not for you."

"Oh, I'm aware of that. But I'm making pancakes, eggs, and bacon for Tanner, anyway. It's one of the things he loves, so you're welcome to join us. There'll be plenty."

She followed him down the hallway to the kitchen. Bacon, eggs, and pancakes. She loved that shit. Didn't make it often, since cereal and oatmeal were cheaper and easier. Zane typically slept until almost nine every morning, and he knew how to dress himself and go next door to Mr. Peabody's. Often, she started at the coffee shop at six-thirty, so he'd had to learn.

"Are you taking orders, or do I just get what I get?" She sat next to Tanner at the table, while Nate pulled out some frying pans and a griddle. "Do you need me to help?"

"If you want to chat with Tanner while I get started, it would be helpful. He likes his eggs scrambled, but if you want them another way, let me know."

"Scrambled is fine." Honestly, the fact someone else was making her breakfast, even if it was only because he was already doing it for himself and his son, was a milestone. She couldn't remember anyone ever doing more than pouring her a bowl of cereal or handing her a package of Pop-Tarts.

"Hey, Tanner. Smooth." She rested her hand on the table, and they went through their routine. The boy's gaze, however, kept darting toward Freckles and the squirming little nuggets next to her.

"Can I bring him closer to the puppies while you're cooking?"

Nate nodded distractedly as he whisked some flour into a bowl. Was he seriously making pancake mix from scratch? Was that even a thing?

"You sure you don't need any help there, Biff? Doesn't your housekeeper usually do all that for you?"

"I don't have a housekeeper. Just someone who comes once a week for the big stuff like floors and bathrooms. And I like cooking. As the oldest, I had to help my mom get meals ready for the others fairly often."

Well, well, well. The GQ model loved and wanted the best

for his son. He had porn-worthy arms, occasionally excellent comebacks, and now the ability to cook. Any more and she'd need to move him to the not-so-horrible side of her checklist. That wouldn't do. She'd have to look deeper for those faults. Rich corporate attorneys did not give poor-as-dirt, borderline Goth, barely-made-it-out-of-school, sarcastic store clerks a second glance. The only reason he was now, and not in a romantic sense, was because he needed her to watch his kid and help deliver puppies.

As he reached up to a cabinet, the muscles under his snug t-shirt rippled, and she made sure to look. Deeper.

Eye candy. Okay, so yes, she could do that. She didn't even feel guilty.

The bacon was crispy and the eggs cooked to perfection. The pancakes were super fluffy, and there was even real maple syrup from New Hampshire. On the rare occasion she splurged on frozen waffles, she usually bought the stuff made from high fructose corn syrup. No maple need apply.

Nate cut up Tanner's pancakes into bite-sized pieces while she poured milk for everyone. Actual milk. Water was the beverage of choice in the Marx household. Straight from the faucet. Nothing better.

The whole scene was so domestic Darcy almost choked on her food. It was like something out of an old TV show. It certainly wasn't something she or Zane had ever experienced. Or ever would, aside from today. Might as well make the most of it.

"What do you want to do today, Tanner?" Nate tried for eye contact with his son. "Beach? Pool? Play ball?"

He kept the list of choices limited. Good for him. Tanner's gaze swung to the dogs. "Puppies."

Sighing, he followed where his son looked. "Puppies. Yeah, I guess we can't leave them alone, huh?"

Darcy scraped her fork along the plate to get the last of

the maple syrup and licked it. "You don't have to watch them every second. Just make sure the pups can't get out of the box and leave water for Freckles. Did you need to go somewhere? It's Sunday, and you said no working on weekends."

"No, not really. I honestly don't want to sit here and stare at the dogs all day, either. If Tanner had his way, I have a feeling that's what he'd do."

"So compromise. Set a timer for twenty minutes of dog watching, then play on the beach for a while. A few minutes of dog watching and then a fun activity."

"You're brilliant, Darcy. Hopefully, that'll work."

"If it doesn't, I don't want the blame. My suggestions come with no guarantees and no money back."

"Good thing I didn't pay for it."

"Good thing. Now, I do need to go. It's been real. It's been fun. But it hasn't been real fun. Time to skedaddle."

Nate picked up Tanner and walked her to the door.

"Say bye to Darcy."

"Darcy." Tanner held out his hand, palm up, his eyes wide in anticipation.

"Smooth, my little man. Smooth." She slid her hand over his, then tickled his palm. Giggling, he repeated the gesture.

Her car backfired a few times before she got out of the driveway, and she swore she saw GQ grimace. Too bad. Not everyone could own a flippin' BMW.

Zane was getting out of the shower when she entered their apartment. Peeking into the bathroom, she noted he'd hung up his towel and even put the cap back on the toothpaste. Today. From experience, she knew tomorrow could be a different story.

"Darcy. You are home. I took a shower, and I made sure to get all the shampoo out of my hair like you told me."

"That's awesome, Zaney. And you cleaned up after yourself. I'm real proud of you, especially after staying here by yourself."

"I know. I didn't even get scared. Mr. Peabody let me watch a movie with him last night. I helped him get into bed, and then I remembered to lock the front door in his apartment. He told me to leave the door that goes up the stairs to our apartment unlocked in case I needed him in the middle of the night. But I didn't, because I'm not a kid, and I can go to sleep all by myself."

Reaching for the young man who was only a few inches taller than she was, she pulled him into a hug. "I know you can. That's why I didn't worry about you." Only, she had. She worried about him every minute of every day.

"Mr. Peabody said you had to help a dog deliver puppies."

"I did. You remember Freckles, right? I've told you about the dog my boss brings to work."

"Yes. You took me to work one day, and I got to see her."

"She had six puppies last night, and it was late by the time they all came. I needed to stay to make sure they'd be okay their first night."

"Because they're only babies. I'm not a baby. I'm all grown up."

"You sure are, Zaney. Now, I need to be a grown up and take a shower, too. I don't have to work until this afternoon, so if you want some free time, I'd be happy to help Mr. Peabody this morning."

"I want to see the puppies. Can I? Please, Darcy? I love little puppies. They're so cute."

"Maybe later, when they aren't so new. I'll talk to the boss and see what he says."

"Okay. I'm going to get my breakfast now. Is it okay if I make oatmeal? I need to use the stove to heat the water. You said to let you know."

"Go ahead and put the water in the kettle and turn the

burner on. Make sure to use the correct burner. I'll be out in a minute."

Zane had already moved to the kitchen area and held the kettle under the faucet in the sink. Quickly, she ran to the bathroom and turned on the shower. It would take a few minutes to get warm, but she didn't have time for that today. Not if she was gonna be out by the time the water boiled. She wanted to be nearby to keep an eye on Zane as he poured the steaming hot liquid into his bowl.

Before she left for work, she also wanted to practice having Zane use the phone to call her. In case of an emergency. One she hoped would never happen.

CHAPTER TEN

"Hi, Tanner." Hope's soft, sweet voice drifted down to where Nathaniel sat on the floor with his son. Sara was prepping for Story Hour, which started in about ten minutes. A few of the children had already arrived and gathered on the carpet.

The little girl plopped herself next to them and held out her hand. "Smooth."

Tanner smiled and slid his hand along hers. This had been their routine for the past month. Three times a week. Hope was one of the children who showed up for every Story Hour, along with Jasmine and Eddie, who he found out belonged to TJ's cousin, Gabby.

Nathaniel slid out from underneath Tanner. It was time to see if his son would stay on his own, without him or Darcy to supervise.

Darcy was currently helping a few customers at the coffee counter, a group of college-aged guys, who all seemed to want her undivided attention. He could see the attitude exuding out of her from here. Flirty, sarcastic, audacious. They ate it up and punched each other, laughing.

Her makeup was dark as ever, accentuating her eyes. It had surprised him this past weekend, after their night of delivering the puppies, that she hadn't been in full war paint. When she'd fallen asleep on the couch, her makeup was still caked on, but when he'd come down in the morning, the eyes sported significantly less. It had definitely been a different look. But she'd thrown that attitude straight at him, so he hadn't commented on it.

"Tanner's dad?"

Spinning around, Nathaniel saw Hope's mom. One of them. She had two. At a guess, Hope was adopted, because she didn't look like either of them. Jodie had fair skin and light hair, while her wife was dark-skinned with short, curly hair. Hope's hair was jet black and pin straight. If they'd done in-vitro, the little girl must take after the biological father. None of his business, so he simply said, "Hi. Yes, I'm Tanner's father. Nathaniel."

"I'm Jodie Benedict, Hope's mom."

"Yes, I've seen you here before. Tanner seems to like it when Hope sits near him."

"She's very introverted and quiet. I love seeing how she's taken the initiative to sit near him. It isn't something she's done in the past."

Nathaniel merely nodded. Small talk wasn't his thing, unless he was at a party looking to impress prospective clients.

"I was wondering if Tanner would be able to come to Hope's birthday party. It's in a few weeks at our house."

Oh, wow. How could he get out of this? He didn't know this woman, other than seeing her in the store, and the last thing he wanted to do was hang out for a day at a kid's birthday party.

"I know it's a little awkward, but Hope has always been so shy. She doesn't make friends easily. She's been in school this past year, but only one other child has responded yes to the invitations."

Okay, now he felt bad for the poor kid. He'd had some so-called friends in high school not want to hang with him because he wasn't wealthy. It totally sucked.

"She's taken a real shine to your son. You don't have to stay long or bring any kind of present, but I know she'd be thrilled if Tanner stopped by for a short time."

"We could probably do that." He was clearly a masochist.

Jodie handed him a small envelope. "The details are on the invitation. Our address, too."

"Thanks. I'll check my calendar once I get home and let you know."

Jodie looked around, and her gaze paused on Darcy wiping down the counter. "Actually, I was wondering if there's any way you could convince Darcy to come to the party, too. I've noticed over the past month that she seems to help you out during Story Hour. Hope is intrigued by her. Maybe she could even bring Tanner, if you have other things to do."

Hmm. Get Darcy to go with them, so it wasn't as awkward, but have to put up with her flip mouth. Or go by himself with Tanner and stand around totally clueless. He discounted the possibility of having Darcy take Tanner. It didn't sit right with him. The boy was his son. He shouldn't pass him off just to avoid a kid's party.

"I'll mention it to her. I'm not sure what her schedule is here at the store."

"Thanks. I'll let you go, since it looks like Sara's about to start."

Hope sat next to Tanner, her arm around his shoulder. Not that the kid noticed. He was happy driving his car over the little girl's leg.

Nathaniel backed up a few more steps and settled into a

comfy chair. Sara had the children mesmerized. All but Tanner. He was focused on spinning the wheels of his toy car.

"Sharla and I would love to have you at Hope's birthday party." Jodie stood on the other side of a nearby bookshelf talking to Darcy in a soft voice.

"A kid's birthday party really isn't my thing. Thanks for the invite, though." Darcy's voice lacked its usual cutting sarcasm.

"Come on, Darcy. Hope will be starting first grade in the fall, and she won't be able to come here during the week. The only day we'd get here is Saturday. If she starts other activities, they might be on Saturday mornings. You should spend some time with her now."

When he peeked over, Darcy was looking down, her face solemn. What was up between her and Hope's mom?

"Maybe it's best if I get used to not seeing her."

What did she mean by that? Jodie followed Darcy down the counter still talking, but he couldn't hear what was said. What was the connection between Darcy and Hope's family? Were they related somehow? Old family friends? Jodie looked to be in her early forties, and her wife, Sharla, seemed even older. Maybe closer to fifty. Darcy had said she was only twenty-four. Had they known Darcy's mom before she died?

Why did he even care? Darcy had been great in helping him with Tanner, but she still drove him absolutely crazy. John Michaels, the guy doing his renovations, had said it should only be a few more weeks until he could move back in. Once he was home, he wouldn't need to think about Darcy.

Nathaniel pulled out his phone and checked his e-mails, returning some of the most urgent ones. Sara's voice floated across the room, soft, loud, sometimes silly, always enthusiastic.

After the hour was done, he looked up and realized Tanner had stayed the entire time on the carpet with the kids. A little weight lifted from his chest. No, he hadn't been listening to the stories, not that he could see. But he hadn't melted down or gotten up and walked away.

"He did great today." Darcy showed up at his shoulder, her grin wide on her urchin-like face.

"Yeah, he did." His voice stuck for a second, so he cleared it and glanced away.

"He's getting comfortable here. It's becoming a routine. Lots of kids with special needs like routines." She squeezed his shoulder and the touch set something off inside. And it wasn't anything bad.

"Good to know. Hey, are you working…um…" He retrieved the invitation from his pocket and read through it. "Sunday, August first?"

Her eyes narrowed, and her lips formed a straight line. "Is that for Hope's party?"

"Yeah, her mom invited Tanner."

"Then, take Tanner. It might be good for him, seeing other kids somewhere that isn't Story Hour."

"She said only one other kid from her class responded they'd go."

Darcy shifted her gaze to the little girl who still kept Tanner company on the rug. Her expression grew thunderous, and her shoulders heaved up and down.

Reaching out, he took Darcy's hand. "Would you go with us? I don't know these people, and I have no idea how Tanner will react someplace new. Sometimes he's fine, and other times he throws a huge crying fit. I'll pay you. Double because it's the weekend, if that'll make you say yes."

Darcy crossed her arms over her chest. "You didn't pay

me double when we went to Alex and Gina's engagement party. That was a weekend."

He stopped himself from rolling his eyes. "Please, Darcy. I could really use a friend to go with us. Is there a reason you don't want to?"

"It's a kid's birthday party. Why would I *want* to go?"

"To see Hope. And help me with Tanner. Did you know Jodie and her wife before they started bringing Hope to Story Hour?"

Her head snapped up, and she scowled. "Why would you ask that?"

"You seem different with them than with most of the other customers. You aren't as snarky."

"There's only so much snark to go around. I have to make sure I conserve it and use it at the right time with the right people."

He laughed. "Don't I feel special. You never answered my question. Is there a problem with Hope's parents that I should know about?"

Her eyes closed briefly, and she took a deep breath before opening them again. "No, Jodie and Sharla are great people. Great parents to that little girl. She's lucky to have them."

He squeezed her hand, realizing he still held it in his. "So you'll go with me?"

She pursed her lips and glared. "Fine, I'll go with you. Double time."

"So, you did know them before they started coming to Story Hour."

Slipping her hand from his, she turned away but not before she muttered the cryptic answer, "We'd met."

∽

"This is getting to be a habit, boss."

Darcy tugged her bag over her shoulder as she and Zane walked inside. TJ held the door open for them.

"Hi, Zane." TJ stuck his hand out, and Zane paused for a second. Darcy nodded at him, and he placed his hand in TJ's and shook. "Good to see you again."

"Good to see you, too. Darcy said I could see the puppies because they're older now."

Sara greeted them. "Hi, Zane. Yes, the puppies are adorable, and now that they're a few weeks old, it's safe to play with them. That's Tanner sitting next to them. You can look if you want."

Zane's smile was huge as he knelt next to the large box in the corner. Freckles rested with her six puppies, all vying for premium space near mom.

"We appreciate you helping out again, Darcy," TJ said as the door closed behind her. "If it weren't for the fact Erik and Tessa's house is over three hours away, we'd try and do it in one day."

"Luckily, we only have to do it once," Sara said, packing up a batch of what looked like cookies. She'd left some on a plate on the counter. Yum. "Matty's birthday is in June and Kiki's is in July, so they're combining the two."

"And they've got one who'll have an August birthday, right? Isn't Tessa ready to drop the next one?" Darcy tossed her bag on a stool by the island.

"She's got about three weeks left to go, but she's feeling pretty uncomfortable right now, which is why they aren't coming down to New Hampshire to do the party. Erik doesn't want her on a long trip so near the end."

Darcy remembered those last few weeks, with the reality of what she was about to do heavy on her mind and the baby heavy on her bladder.

"Maybe you should consider buying a helicopter, boss. Bet you could do the trip a lot quicker."

TJ tipped his head. "But then I'd need someone to fly the helicopter."

"Pay for me to take flying lessons, and I'd be happy to be in stand-by mode when you need to go somewhere. Think about it. You could take Sara all around the country for concerts and still be home by bedtime."

"Yeah, I'll give it some thought." He faced his wife. "Are you about ready to go? It's almost two."

"I'm ready. Thanks, Darcy."

"No worries. I never had slumber parties as a kid, so I'm making up for it now."

"You've got Nathaniel's cell number, right? He should be back in a few hours, but he said he'd need some quiet time to finish a few other customer accounts."

"Don't sweat it."

Sara and TJ said goodbye to Tanner and the pups, then pulled out of the driveway in TJ's truck. The man had tons of money, and he drove an older model 4 X 4. If she had that kind of cash floating around, for sure, she'd have a nice, new sporty number. Not the beater she'd driven over here, after stalling four times.

"These puppies are so cute, Darcy. Can we have one?"

And so it begins.

"I've explained it a few times, Zaney. We can't have an animal in our apartment. Plus, we don't have the space for one or the money to pay for food. Pets cost a lot of money." She made sure to say pets, because they'd had this conversation before. Zane would start at dog and try and talk her down to a hamster or goldfish. She worked so many hours, she didn't have the time or patience to care for an animal, even if she wanted one.

Tanner looked up from his spot in front of the box and his face scrunched up. He jumped to his feet and bolted toward her, his gaze back on Zane.

"Tanner, this is my brother, Zane. Brother. Zane. He's staying with us tonight."

The boy clung to her leg tightly. "Puppies."

"Yes, Zane wanted to see the puppies, too."

"My puppies." His arms grew tighter.

Bending down, she removed his arms from her leg and replaced them around her neck. "Freckles' puppies."

"Fwecko. Puppies."

"Yep. Let's put a timer on watching them. Ten minutes and then we'll do something else. Do you understand, Zane? We can't sit and watch the puppies the whole time we're here."

"You said we could go in the pool or the ocean."

Naturally, he'd remember that casual comment. She had no idea if Tanner tolerated the water. It would be easier to keep an eye on Zane if he was in a fenced-in pool rather than on the beach. He was a strong swimmer, but riptides could be fierce.

"I'll set the timer, then we can use the pool."

When she tried to set Tanner on the floor, he gave a huge scream and wrapped his arms around her shoulders, burying his face in her neck.

"It's okay, little man. I've got you." Carrying him on her hip, she stepped to the counter and scooped up the timer, setting it for fifteen minutes.

Nate said he kept cars all over the place to distract the boy, so she pulled open a few drawers until she found one. Sara and TJ would be finding Hot Wheels long after Biff and the kid went back home.

With a car in Tanner's hand, rolling up and down her arm, Darcy settled on the floor a good three feet away from her brother. Nate had mentioned Tanner had inconsistent reactions to new people. He either didn't acknowledge them and had no reaction at all, or he got severely agitated and didn't want to be near them. Zane was highly sensitive to people's feelings, and she didn't want him to get upset thinking Tanner didn't like him. Unfortunately, Zane wouldn't understand it was Tanner's disability that caused the outburst and not his dislike.

When the buzzer went off, she climbed to her feet. "Zane, grab our bag and we'll go upstairs. You can pick out which bedroom you want to sleep in tonight, okay?"

At the top of the stairs, she pointed to the two rooms on the left. "Either one of those is fine. I'll take the other one."

"Where does he sleep?" He pointed to the child in her arms.

She peeked into the rooms and saw the toys in the second room on the right. "In here. His dad has that room." Pointing to Nathaniel's room, she walked into Tanner's and started looking for a bathing suit. His clothes were all organized and put away neatly. Shocker. GQ was as structured and stiff as he seemed.

"Take the bag, Zane, and get your bathing suit on. I'll change Tanner."

Once Tanner had his suit on and she'd lotioned him up with sunscreen, she grabbed her own suit and quickly put it on in the adjoining bathroom between Tanner's room and his dad's. The scent of GQ's aftershave lingered in the small room. The bottle sat on the counter, and she reached out to touch it, then stopped herself.

"Stop getting distracted. Men are all trouble."

"Darcy, who are you talking to? The little boy is in his room playing with a car."

"Just myself, Zaney. Are you ready to go swim?"

Her brother nodded and took his towel out of his bag.

"Can you grab mine, too? I need to get one for Tanner."

Digging in the closet, she found a dozen towels. All were brand new and thicker and fluffier than she'd ever seen. She took a few of them, thinking Tanner could lounge on one on the deck if he didn't want to go in the water.

Who the hell was she kidding? She wanted to use one. And why not? Coming over here to babysit the kid and the puppies was becoming a regular occurrence. She should get something out of it. A fluffy, new towel wasn't a huge price to pay.

After carrying Tanner down the stairs, with Zane holding the towels, they crossed through the kitchen to the back door. The puppies were napping. Their mom, too.

"Can the puppies sleep with us tonight, Darcy?"

She closed the door behind them and padded across the patio. "They need to sleep with their mom. They're still babies."

A sad expression crossed Zane's face. He missed their mom, even though she'd sucked at being a mother in every way and never actually did anything for them. Never gave them any love. But she was their mother, and Zane knew that and cared about her anyway.

Would her kid love her, even knowing she'd been given up, or hate her for not being around? What did it matter? She didn't plan on Hope ever knowing the truth, and Jodie and Sharla said they'd never tell her, unless Darcy said it was okay. It would never be okay.

"Go ahead in and start swimming, Zaney. I'm not sure if Tanner likes the water, so it may take me a while to get in."

A silly grin broke out on her brother's face, and he jumped into the water cannonball style. Water splashed toward her, and she quickly moved so Tanner didn't get wet. When she turned around, Zane was already swimming into the deep end. She'd made sure to take him to the beach often and had taught him how to swim. If he could handle the rough waves of the ocean, he could manage the calmer water of the pool.

Darcy sat down, placing Tanner next to her, and tapped on his car. "Pool, Tanner. Swim in the pool."

"Pool," he said without looking up from the toy.

The mid-July sun beat down on them, and she gazed longingly at the cool water nearby. After about fifteen minutes of watching Tanner play with his car, she scooped him up and walked over to the wide, built-in steps.

On the first step, the water only covered the top of her feet. Refreshing, but it didn't do anything for the sweat running down her back. Zane played around in the deep end, keeping the spray of the splashes on that side.

She took a few more steps, until she was on the bottom stair and the cool liquid swirled around her hips. Tanner lifted his feet and wrapped his arms around her neck.

"You don't like the water, sweetie? It's nice and cool."

"Cool."

Dipping down slightly, the water surrounded her chest, but Tanner screamed and tried to climb her like a monkey in a tree.

"It won't hurt you. It's water. Like when you take a bath."

"Bath."

"Yes. Do you like your bath?"

"Bath."

That didn't answer her question. Not that she expected one. But the kid didn't smell, so she assumed Biff bathed him often enough.

"How about we sit here on the steps?" Lowering herself to the third step, she placed Tanner on the top one. He frowned at the water lapping against his legs, then focused on the car as he rolled it across the deck next to him.

Darcy submerged herself in the water up to her neck, then settled back on the step below Tanner. The water barely covered her hips. At least, this way she could keep her eye on both her brother and the kid.

Zane kept jumping into the deep end and making some strange noise when he did. It was good to see him having so much fun. If she didn't have to work all the time, maybe she could find more stuff for him to do that he enjoyed.

"Well, that whole vampire myth of not being out in the sun has gone straight down the tubes."

The droll voice came from the direction of the driveway. How had she not heard the car? Zane yelled and jumped into the pool again. Oh, yeah. That.

As she glanced up, Biff, looking more GQ than ever in off-white pants, a navy polo shirt, and Docksiders strutted through the gate into the pool area. The way he stared at her was dangerous.

CHAPTER ELEVEN

A strangled cry and the sound of a splash caught Nathaniel's attention as he got out of his car. Who was in the pool? Sara and TJ had gone up to Maine to stay overnight. Darcy was supposed to be here babysitting Tanner. Was she jumping in the pool? With his son? The boy could barely handle a five-minute bath without going into hysterics.

As he opened the gate into the backyard and pool area, he noted a young man frolicking in the deep end. Dark hair, dark eyes, and a slight frame. Obviously in his twenties, but who…

As he drew closer, he noticed features similar to Darcy's. This must be her brother. And Darcy…Holy Toledo. She lazed back on one of the steps near Tanner in an emerald green tankini.

Darcy in this suit…wow. What the hell was up with him lately? And if he kept staring at her, something would definitely be up.

"Well, that whole vampire myth of not being out in the sun has gone straight down the tubes."

Those darkly lined eyes turned his way, and she pursed her lips. "I thought you'd be gone all day. Forget your golf clubs?"

"They're in the trunk of my car." He hated golf, but often it was essential when trying to gain a new client. Luckily, it made them happy to have him suck and lose. "My meeting finished up quicker than I'd planned. Hi, Tanner. Do you like the pool?"

His son actually looked up, and a tiny smile crossed his face. He lifted his Hot Wheels and said, "Car."

When Nathaniel came closer to the water, Darcy's brother swam to the shallow end and gazed curiously at her.

"Darcy, who is this?"

"This is Tanner's dad."

"Hi, Tanner's dad. He likes to play with cars. I like to jump in the pool. Darcy said I could come and see the puppies, too."

"Nate, this is my brother, Zane. The boss said he could stay."

"Nate, do you want to swim in the pool?" Zane tilted his head.

Nathaniel started to correct him regarding his name, but the young man spoke slower and more precisely than most people. Would his full name be too hard to pronounce? Would this be the type of thing he'd have to worry about with Tanner?

"Um, maybe." He really should spend some time working on Stan's account.

Darcy leaned back on the stairs, the straps of her top shifting, exposing a small rounded section of skin. "Feel free to do more lawyerly work. I've got everything under control out here."

Too bad he didn't.

"You know, I might take you up on that, Zane. It's warm

today, and a dip in the pool could be exactly what I need to recover from my long drive."

Darcy's expression wasn't in favor of him joining them. Too bad.

"I'll be right back."

"Take your time. Like, a few hours if you need it. You don't want to come back without being perfectly pool ready."

When he gazed over his shoulder, she lifted her hand in a salute. Cheeky. She did make him laugh at times.

To annoy her, he donned his swimsuit quickly and dabbed on a touch more of his aftershave. Grabbing a towel, he skipped down the stairs, checked on the puppies, then headed to the patio around the pool.

"Was I fast enough? I know you were anxious to have me back."

Darcy rolled a car next to the one Tanner was using. "Did you hear something, Tanner? Sounded like a big gust of wind."

His son shook his head and repeated, "Wind."

Pushing off the deck, Nathaniel dove into the deep end, making sure to avoid Zane who was bobbing under the surface holding onto the side. When he came up, he swung his hair out of his face. It was probably a mess, but if he attempted to finger comb it into place, Darcy was sure to give him crap.

He'd probably deserve it. The elite persona he'd worn for so long had gotten ingrained in him. Nasty, teasing comments about his blue-collar family and not being good enough still rattled around his head, making his stomach clench with anxiety.

These days, he had a successful law practice with many corporate clients who approved of his work for them, yet it felt like nothing had changed. Many of the CEOs and upper management still liked to play the rich boy games he'd learned early on in order to be accepted. Sometimes, he felt if he slipped even a tiny bit, it would all be flushed down the toilet.

"Do you know how to swim?" Zane tread water next to him. "Darcy taught me when I was little, and she makes sure we swim all the time, so I can practice and I won't drown. It would make her sad."

The siblings had many similar features, yet the innocence in Zane's eyes was so opposite from his sister. She looked like she knew too much about too many things. Had she grown up too fast trying to take care of her brother when her mother wasn't capable of it? Or was there more?

The ride back from his appointment had been long and hot, so he ducked under the water and swam a few laps to try and release the tension. Darcy in her bathing suit was making another kind of tension seep in.

Swimming over to the steps, he watched as Tanner dropped the little car into the water with a splash. The tiny smile that peeked out every now and again crossed his face.

"What are you doing with the car, buddy?"

The boy dropped the car again and chuckled. Darcy handed him the car she was using and floated away.

"You play with him for a while. I need to cool off."

"Are you going under the water? Your makeup is going to turn the pool black."

"Not quite, but you're right. I will need to wipe it off, or I'll look like the Joker." She dove under the surface and came out on the other side. A towel already lay there. She tugged on it, wiped at her face, then popped under the water again. Lather. Rinse. Repeat.

"That towel's going to be ruined."

Turning, she peeked through a hole in the middle of the terry cloth fabric. Her finger poked out of another one. "Yeah, that's a big concern of mine. And it's my towel, so there's no need to get your panties in a wad. I'm not destroying anything of Sara's."

After tossing the towel back on the deck, she ducked under the water and swam the entire length of the pool, surfacing near Zane in the deepest part.

She chatted with her brother quietly for a bit, while Nathaniel dribbled small amounts of water on his son. They lived on a lake, so it would be nice if Tanner didn't fuss every time he went near it. He'd been sitting on the first step, water lapping against his legs, so Nathaniel figured he'd try for something more.

Picking him up, he waded into the shallows. "Let's cruise around the pool, okay?" Tanner's car started its well-worn path up his arm and over his shoulder. He'd been reduced to pavement.

Darcy dove under the water and surfaced near him. His breath caught, and his mouth hung open. God, she was gorgeous. Makeup all gone. Hair slicked back. Water dripping off her silky skin. He remembered the feel of it from dancing with her at Sara and TJ's wedding.

The Darcy he knew was still there, but a protective layer had been peeled back. The vulnerability in her eyes shown bright as she waited for him to say something. Nothing even remotely snarky came to mind.

"Thanks for keeping an eye on Tanner today."

"Whatevs. Zane wanted to see the puppies. And he doesn't get a chance to swim in a pool often, so he's pretty happy about that. As you can tell."

Her brother had gone back to yowling and jumping in the deep end. Nathaniel couldn't take his eyes from Darcy's beautiful face.

∽

"Come on, Zane, puppy time is over."

"But, Darcy, they're so cute."

"I know they are, but you've been staring at them for like half the day. Give poor Freckles some privacy, huh?"

Zane patted each of the babies and then the mom one last time before rising. "I really want a puppy. Can we get one, please?"

"I really want to be a billionaire and travel the world in a yacht, but that's not gonna happen either."

Darcy finished putting the last of the supper dishes away as Zane tipped his head. "You could marry a billionaire, and then you could travel in a yacht. What's a yacht?"

"It's a huge boat. And my chances of marrying a billionaire are even worse than your chances of getting a puppy."

"Is Nate a billionaire? You could marry him. Maybe he'd buy you a big boat. Then, you'd also have a little boy."

After drying her hands on a towel, she faced Zane. "I'm guessing Nate's probably got some cash, but I doubt he's a billionaire. As for him marrying me, I've got a better chance of marrying Elvis than Nathaniel Storm. Besides, I already have you, so I don't need anyone else."

She could see the gears grinding in her brother's head as he processed that information. "Yeah, I guess if you got another little boy, you wouldn't be able to take care of me. I would miss you."

Her gaze darted to the living room where Nate and Tanner sat watching TV. Was Zane remembering when she was pregnant? It had been six years ago. She'd been able to get by for most of the pregnancy without him asking about her growing belly, but at the end, she'd had to tell him something. He'd believed her when she'd said she was carrying the baby for a couple who couldn't have one. Which was technically true. She wasn't sure how much he understood of their mother's babble about her being a no-good slut. Most of the time, the woman was barely conscious.

"Let's go watch TV and leave the puppies alone."

In the living room, Nate sat with Tanner on his lap, their attention on the screen. Nate had a conference call to California tonight at ten, thus the reason for her overnight stay, and earlier he'd attempted to work on his laptop. But his full attention was now on his son. The way it should be. Every time Tanner plunked himself inches from the cartoon playing, Nate scooted him right back.

As much as she wanted to give GQ a hard time, about anything because it was fun, she couldn't seem to find fault with his parenting. Sure, he was new at it and made some rookie mistakes, but frack it all, he got points for intent.

Had he tried this hard to keep his marriage together? Or had Miss Stick-Up-Her-Butt been too hard to please?

"Hey." Nate twisted his head in her direction. "Thanks for doing the dishes. I'll get them next time."

"Of course, you will. I'm not your maid. But I'll forgive you this time. The kid needed some movement."

"I had him run around on the beach for a bit. Now he's gearing down. The show will be done in about ten minutes, if you want to watch something."

Zane plopped onto the end of the couch, leaving only the space in the middle for her. If she could bring herself to sit next to Biff.

"I don't bite. Not hard, anyway."

His smirk made her decision for her. Settling between him and her brother, she leaned back, put her hands behind her head, and stretched out her legs. "Maybe *I* do. Are you up-to-date on your tetanus shot?"

"Do I need to get the crucifix off the wall in TJ and Sara's bedroom?"

"You might be all right for tonight. The moon isn't full,

but I am. Good thing you made those hamburgers rare and bloody." They hadn't been that rare, but they certainly were good. Any kind of red meat was a treat for her and Zane. Peanut butter was a good source of protein, was fairly inexpensive, and didn't need to be refrigerated for the times when theirs was on the fritz.

"I thought full moons were for werewolves. Who's mashing up their horror movies now?"

"Full moons have a place in most paranormal stories."

"I'll make note of that." Tanner drooped against his arm and Nate kissed the top of the boy's head. "I think it's time for this one to go to bed."

"Will that take a while?" Hopefully, it would, so she didn't have to ignore all the bells and whistles going off in her girly parts.

"A few minutes, as long as I follow the routine. Once he's in bed, he'd doesn't usually get up. The remote's on the coffee table if you want to change the channel. You don't have to continue watching cartoons. Unless you want to."

Zane might want to. He loved cartoons. But maybe she could find something they'd all like. Picking up the remote, she clicked through the eight million cable channels TJ paid for. The perks of being rich. Who could even watch this many shows? You could channel surf for months and not get through them all.

By the time Nate came down, she'd settled on an old George Hamilton spoof. It was safe enough for Zane to watch and hopefully understand, and the silliness would make him laugh.

Nate sat down next to her again and leaned in close. What the heck?

"Hey, so I was wondering about this party," he whispered. "What should I get Hope for a present?"

He must have brushed his teeth while he was upstairs

because his breath was minty fresh. Question. Wait. He'd asked her a question.

"Present? I'm sure Sharla and Jodie don't expect one. Hope will be thrilled to have Tanner there, if her reaction to him at Story Hour is anything to go by."

"I have manners, Elvira, which means we need to get her a gift. What do you buy a six-year-old girl? I've never been one, and it's been years since my sister was that age."

"What? You can't dig back in your memory for what you bought her when she was six?"

He chuckled. "I was fifteen. I doubt I bought her anything. Any money I made at that age was put aside for a car. What did you want when you were six?"

"Food. I think Hope has plenty of that. Sharla is a chef here in town. Maybe a doll or some crayons?" She'd thrown out the other ideas, so he wouldn't comment on her first answer.

Nate's face fell, and his eyes grew softer. No, no, no, he didn't need to feel sorry for her. That wasn't the point of saying that. Her stupid sarcasm jumped in the way again. Why couldn't she keep it contained like she did everything else?

Because it protects you most times. Yeah, it did, but it had kind of bitten her in the ass today.

"Do you plan on getting her a gift?"

Excellent. He'd kept the subject away from her ridiculous mutterings, except now she had to come up with a gift. For her daughter. The one she'd given away at birth. Who ever had to make this kind of decision? It must be God's way of punishing her for her misdeeds. No other explanation.

"I'll grab something at the dollar store. Kids love that crap." But she wouldn't. Her present would have to be something perfect. Not necessarily expensive, but a special gift.

With only one week to figure it out, it was time for panic mode.

Biff grabbed his laptop from the nearby table and settled next to her again. Wouldn't he be more comfortable somewhere else? Like Mars? Or at least the dining room?

Zane's laughter tickled her ears. Yet, she couldn't get her mind off present ideas for a six-year-old girl.

"This is a vampire movie." Guess Nate hadn't been paying attention either. "What happened to evil creatures who invoked fear and horror? This guy looks like he's spent too much time in the tanning booth, and he's disco dancing."

"It was the late seventies. Everybody discoed."

"The original Dracula movies were so much better. Classic. Not like this cheesefest. When they began the sexualization of vampires, it really went downhill."

"Downhill? How can you say *The Lost Boys* was downhill? So cool."

"Vampires are despicable creatures, Elvira. They drink the blood of humans, leaving them undead for eternity."

Darcy snorted. "First, you know this is a spoof, right?"

Nathaniel waved his hand at the TV. "It has George Hamilton in it. Of course, it's a spoof."

"Glad you noticed. Second, you know vampires aren't real?" She glanced at her brother to make sure he understood he didn't need to be afraid of blood sucking creatures.

Nate leaned in to whisper. "Is he a vampire, too? Like his sister?"

"You should sleep with one eye open tonight, just in case."

Laughing, he concentrated on his computer again. Nothing but words covered the screen. Looked totally boring. Good thing she'd never had the urge to be a lawyer.

As they sat watching the movie, she took note of Nate's movements. He had a habit of raking his fingers through his hair to give it a smoother look. She'd noticed his hair had a tendency to curl if it got wet. Did he spend time getting the waves out when he dried it? She didn't even spend that much time with her hair. A few dabs of mousse, ten seconds of a blow dryer while she dangled her head upside down, and she was ready for the day.

The eye makeup was another story. It was almost always black and a good half inch around the rim of each eye. On special occasions, she did something fancy in the corners or add a splash of colored eye shadow. Like the pink at Sara and TJ's wedding.

Biff's long, thin fingers caught her attention as he rapidly typed. His gaze was glued to the screen, never looking down. Bet he aced keyboarding in school. But could he text at lightning speed like she could?

When the final dance scene in the movie came on, Nate checked his watch and frowned. His hand gripped her thigh for a second as he said, "My conference call starts in a few minutes. Do you mind keeping an ear out for Tanner? I'd prefer not to interrupt the call, if possible."

The skin of his hand on her bare thigh caused all sorts of reactions in her. Responding to his question didn't seem to be one of them. When he squeezed her leg again, it broke the spell.

"Sure, kid duty. You go do your lawyer thing. I've got it."

After patting where his hand had just been, he balanced the laptop and stood. Once he'd left the room, she pressed her fingers to the spot. It was only a touch. By a guy she didn't even like. Why did it feel like she'd been burned?

CHAPTER TWELVE

"Thanks for coming with us, Darcy. I owe you one."

Nathaniel shuffled Tanner to his hip and grabbed the birthday present for Hope from the back seat of the car.

"You owe me way more than one, Biff. I've been covering your a…uh, behind for two months now. I think we're getting into triple digits on the owing thing."

Had it seriously been two months since he'd been down the Cape? Man, time flew when you were having fun. He'd been more relaxed down here than he'd been in the last ten years. Maybe longer.

"Keeping track are you, Elvira?" Today, instead of black, she wore a bright orange halter top with tassels around her ribcage and a pair of orange flowered yoga shorts that emphasized her curves nicely. Hardly vampire-like. "I've paid you for lots of the babysitting. Did you want me to add today to the payroll as well?"

He would, if she wanted him to. The thought of coming to the house of virtual strangers and hanging out while little kids ran around playing strangled him around the throat and chest. Kevin was the outgoing one in the family. Nathaniel much preferred to sit back and listen if in a group, or better yet, stay out of places with lots of people. It was one of the reasons he became a corporate attorney, so he rarely needed to appear in court.

"Nah, I'll give you this one as a freebie," she said in an oddly stiff voice.

Darcy was hardly an introvert, but for some reason she seemed more anxious than him as they approached the front door. Was it the house? It was massive and in an impressive neighborhood, and Darcy had insinuated her childhood home had been less than pristine.

"Did you grow up around here?" She'd never said, and he wondered about her. Only because she spent so much time with his son. No other reason.

Her eyes darted between him and the door. "No, I grew up in New Bedford. We moved here when I was about eighteen."

Probably after she graduated from high school. New Bedford was a fairly large city, a bit west of the Cape and certainly more populated than the small town of Hyannis where she now lived.

The front door opened before he could ask any more questions. Jodie wore a wide smile as she stepped back to let them in.

"Hope has been waiting for you to show up. Thank you so much for coming. All of you."

As they entered, Hope rushed into the foyer, eyes alight with excitement. Nathaniel placed Tanner on the floor and handed him the present.

"Give this to Hope."

Tanner stared at the gaily colored gift bag intently, repeating, "Hope."

"Thank you, Tanner." She took the gift, held it by her side

with one hand, and grabbed Tanner's with the other. "Come see the great cake my mom made for me."

Nathaniel watched anxiously to see what Tanner would do. The child knew Hope and would sometimes smile when she sat next to him at Story Hour, but too often his actions were inconsistent.

"He'll be fine." Darcy nudged his side, her own face tense.

The kids wandered down the hall, and Jodie gestured to them. "Come on in. Sharla has tons of food. Hope only cares about the cake."

The kitchen had top of the line everything. Stainless steel appliances, pots and pans hanging over a granite center island, cherry cabinets his mother would kill to have, and one of those fancy double oven things Helene had insisted they get in their monstrous home, even though she didn't actually cook.

Darcy seemed to grow smaller the more they saw. Placing his hand on her back, he rubbed his thumb down her spine. Surprisingly, she sent him a grateful smile instead of the snarl he was expecting.

"Sharla, you remember Darcy, and this is Tanner's dad, Nathaniel. I think you met him one time at Story Hour."

The tall, slim woman stood behind the counter, dicing up vegetables.

"Great to see you again. Please, have some food. I made enough for an army."

"I heard you're a local chef. Can't wait to try some."

Sharla and Jodie introduced them to the dozen or so women mulling around the kitchen. All friends. So far Nathaniel was the only man here. His eyes roamed to the room off the kitchen the children had gone into.

Jodie's face fell a little as she followed his gaze. "Only one other child was able to make it. Granted it's the summer, and people go away a lot, but I was hoping at least a few children from her class would be able to come."

One of the ladies next to Sharla pursed her lips. "You don't need small-minded, bigoted people who can't accept who you are."

Jodie sighed. "Honestly, I think a lot of it is that Hope's so shy she hasn't made many friends. And the afternoon Kindergarten class had less students because most people wanted the mornings. She'll make more friends this year in first grade."

Darcy picked up a small paper plate and filled it with appetizers. He followed suit and ambled to the doorway of the family room. Tanner was on the floor, pushing a pink Barbie car back and forth. Leave it to him to find a vehicle he could play with. Hope sat next to him, a doll in her hand, making it talk and move.

Noise in the kitchen had both he and Darcy twisting to look at the new arrivals.

"Hey, Mom, we're here. Did Hope open up her gifts yet?"

A couple a bit older than him came in with two small children in tow.

Jodie made introductions. "This is Sharla's son, Kobe, his wife, Lora, and their kids, Kansas and Asher."

He nodded as she continued. "This is Nathaniel Storm. His son Tanner is the one Hope can't stop talking about. And this is Darcy. She's—"

"I work at the bookstore where they take Hope for Story Hour," Darcy interrupted. Was she afraid they'd mistake her for his wife or something?

Sharla laughed, then hugged her grandkids. Someone obviously hadn't come out until later in life. Good for Sharla for finally doing what was right for her. He had a college friend who was miserable, because he wouldn't admit marriage to a woman wasn't what he wanted. His father was a bigwig lawyer, and Ford didn't have the guts to let his father know he didn't want the big house, lovely wife path that was expected of a young attorney on the rise.

Marriage was hard enough without trying to pretend you were in love. Nathaniel had learned that the hard way. He was only now realizing he'd never been in love with Helene, just the idea of her.

Kobe shook his hand. "Glad to have another guy here. It gets a little one-sided at times. But we love Hope, and my kids love playing with her."

Hope came running out, gave hugs to the new adults, and pulled Kansas and Asher into the family room. Tanner was preoccupied with the Barbie car rolling back and forth. As long as he wasn't crying, Nathaniel was happy.

After a few minutes, Jodie rounded up the kids and brought them outside to where several games had been set up. Some sort of obstacle course involving balls, hula hoops, and frisbees. God bless Darcy, she helped Tanner navigate the path he needed to follow.

"It's good to see Darcy finally stopping in. Jodie's been inviting her for years." Kobe stood next to him on the edge of the games.

Chuckling, Nathaniel nodded. "Yeah, she acts like she can't stand kids, but she's been great with my son, Tanner. He's got some special needs, and it's not always easy taking care of him. I'm still learning."

"My sister has had some recent medical issues, as well. Mom's been cutting back on her hours at the restaurant to try and help out."

"Family's great that way. My mom's been a godsend with Tanner."

As Hope squealed with delight over finally getting through the course, Kobe grinned. "Hope's a cutie. I still find it hard to believe my mom agreed to Jodie adopting her. She was already over fifty and had raised my sister and me. We'd just had Kansas when she told us she and Jodie were getting married. And that Jodie wanted a baby. They tried in-vitro a few times with Jodie, but she ended up miscarrying each time. That's when they decided to adopt. They met—"

"You two aren't talking sports again, are you?" Lora asked, coming up behind them. "I'll be so happy when baseball season is over. That's all he talks about."

"It's better than talking about soap operas." Kobe ribbed his wife, then followed her, throwing Nathaniel an apologetic look.

The early August sun beat down on them, and Nathaniel searched the yard for shade. There were a few trees close to where Darcy kicked a ball back and forth with Tanner.

"Can I play, too, buddy?"

"Play. Ball." His son sidled up to the large globe, brought his foot back about three inches, and then tapped it with the toe of his sneaker. The ball rolled about five feet.

"Great job, Tanner. Nice kick."

"Nice kick. Tanner."

At his sigh, Darcy edged closer and ran her hand down his arm.

"Sometimes, I wonder if he'll ever understand who we all are."

Tanner picked up the ball and handed it to Nathaniel. "Play. Ball."

Darcy's hand stroked one last time, then lifted away. "He might not say the name, but he sure as shootin' knows who you are."

He wished he could believe it.

~

"IT'S TIME TO OPEN PRESENTS!" Hope yelled. She clasped Tanner's hand and led him into the house. "Come on, you can sit next to me."

Darcy held her breath as the little boy followed her inside the house. Nathaniel looked tense, also. The schoolmate and Sharla's two grandchildren followed behind.

"He looks like he's doing okay, but we should probably catch up to them."

"After you, GQ." She'd rather stay out here by herself than go in and watch her daughter hang around with her new family. But what choice did she have? Most likely, Nate would ask questions she didn't want to answer. Seemed she rarely had choices she liked.

Hope was already ripping through the wrapping paper of her presents. After each one, she'd hop over to the person it was from and give them a great big hug and thanks. When the child picked up the gift with the penguin wrapping paper, Darcy wanted to dash from the room.

"I love these books!" Hope squealed as she hopped across the room in her direction. "These are some of the ones Miss Sara reads at Story Hour. See, Mama?" She waved them in the direction of both her parents.

Jodie flipped through them. *Hop on Pop. Go, Dog, Go.* When she got to *Are You My Mother?*, she eyed Darcy and smirked. "Great books. Did you say thank you, Hope?"

"Thank you, Darcy. I love them." The child flung herself into Darcy's space, and she had no option but to hug her.

Holding tight, she replied, "I work at a bookstore. Great discount. I think you have a few more gifts to open." Get Hope out of her proximity. It hurt too much to hold her for a few seconds when she knew it might never happen again.

"Nice present," Nate whispered in her ear. He and his masculine aroma were far too close again. "We only got her some coloring books and crayons. Sara told me little kids never have enough of those."

"I have it on good authority that Hope loves to color."

"Oh, well, as long as you have it on good authority."

"Are you making fun of me, Biff? I came here today as a favor to you. Do you really think I want to be hanging around a house full of snot-nosed brats?"

Nate gave a harsh laugh. "Brats? Don't think I didn't see you get misty-eyed when Hope liked your present."

Frack. Had he really seen that, or was he only ragging on her?

"A Barbie coloring book," Hope announced as she opened her last gift. "Thanks, Tanner. Barbie is my favorite."

Tanner never even glanced up from Barbie's Corvette. Hope hugged him, anyway. She and Nate both stiffened as Tanner's face grew tense. Fortunately, Hope released him quickly and bounced over to Jodie and Sharla.

"Can we have the cake now?"

Everyone congregated in the dining room, where a huge ice castle sat on the table, surrounded by two princesses and a funny looking snowman. Nate scooped Tanner up and held him so he could see. When the crowd belted out the birthday song, Tanner grunted, clapped his hands over his ears, and stuck his head against Nate's chest, humming.

Darcy shuffled over and nudged him back into the kitchen. "It's okay to step away, if the noise agitates him."

"I didn't want to be rude."

"And I'm sure Jodie and Sharla don't want Hope's party ruined with Tanner having a meltdown. It's called compromise. You should learn about it someday."

Nate's eyes narrowed. "I'm a lawyer. I think I have a minute understanding of what compromise is. Thank you very much."

She twisted her lips to the side. "Anytime I can help."

Nate sat at the table with Tanner when they got a piece of the cake. Darcy settled in a corner of the family room, hoping no one would try chatting with her. Fortunately, Jodie and Sharla were busy taking care of the other guests.

"You have a big H on your shoulder." Hope appeared by her side. She was fixated on Darcy's tattoo. "My name begins with H. Then, you got a O and a P. And then you got a E. That spells Hope. That's my name. Why do you have my name on your shoulder?"

God, help her. What did she say? The truth? Yeah, that would go over big at the little girl's birthday party. Did Sharla's family even know who she was? Hope still stared at her, waiting for an answer.

"I think everyone should have a little hope."

The child laughed. "I'm a little Hope."

"You certainly are. Did you like your presents?"

"Uh huh. Especially the book you gave me. *Are You My Mother?* I like that one, because my mamas adopted me. That means my mama who I was borned from couldn't keep me, so she let my mamas take care of me."

Jodie sauntered over, her eyes questioning. "We read Hope a book on adoption last year. We've read it to her a few times now, so she'll understand." The child had dug into a bag looking for her crayons and wasn't paying much attention to them.

"What exactly did you tell her?" Darcy kept her voice low.

"Why don't you ask her?"

The girl glanced at her mom, who responded, "Hope, Darcy was wondering about your adoption story. Perhaps, you could tell it to her."

Jodie maneuvered back across the room to where Sharla stood. Both women peeked at her, simultaneously trying to appear as if they weren't looking. Wasn't working. Darcy felt as if the entire room was staring at her. Even if they weren't.

"My story," Hope announced like she was ready to start a performance. She crawled onto the couch next to Darcy and folded her hands in her lap. "Once upon a time, there was a nice lady who had a baby in her belly. She really loved that baby, but she was still a teenager and had to go to high school."

Hope tilted her head and made a sad face. "She also had a sick mama and a brother she had to take care of. She knew the baby would need lots of food and diapers and baby stuff. But she didn't have enough money for all that if she had to take care of her mama and brother, too. Then, she met *my* mamas. They wanted a little girl just like me, and they couldn't have a baby in their bellies. So my borned mama gave me to Mama Jo and Mama Shar, so I could come live with them if they promised to give me a good life. She didn't want me to be poor and sick. She wanted me to be happy."

Why was the room suddenly a hundred degrees and blurry? "You are happy, right?"

"Oh, yes." The delight in her little girl's face almost doubled Darcy over. Which was stupid. She wanted Hope to have the best life ever. It's why she'd made the decision to give her away. Still, somewhere in the back of her mind, she wanted the child to long for her real mom. Yeah, stupid.

"I'm glad you're happy. All little girls should be happy."

"Yup." Hope smiled, but then leaned closer, her eyes worried. "But sometimes I wish my borned mama would come live here. I wish I had money, so she could live in our nice house and take care of her mama and her brother here. We could all be a family, and I wouldn't have to think about her and miss her. She'd be here."

What? "You miss your real…birth mother? You don't even know who she is. What if she's mean?"

Hope laughed like that was a silly thing to say. As she hopped off the couch, she chirped, "I know she's not."

Jodie found Darcy a few minutes later hiding on the porch overlooking the blurry backyard.

"You should tell her who you are."

Darcy's head whipped around at the suggestion. "Why would I do that?"

"I told you we want to be open and honest with Hope. We won't do it until you're ready, though. Just say the word."

She planned to keep that word out of her vocabulary. Forever.

"I'm not ready. I don't think I'll ever be ready."

"It's certainly your decision, Darcy. Just know that you have our blessing to tell her."

It didn't matter if she had the whole world's blessing. What if she told Hope the truth? And what if she hated her for it?

CHAPTER THIRTEEN

"Oh, my gosh! He's here. He's here."

Nathaniel wheeled around at Sara's excited exclamation. "Who's here?"

TJ shrugged. "Who was on the phone, Sunshine?'

"Erik. Tessa had the baby."

"I thought she had another few weeks to go." Not that Nathaniel paid close attention to the reproductive dates of his cousins.

"They must have forgotten to tell the kid that." TJ grinned as he sipped his tea.

"By the 'he's here', I'm assuming they had a boy." Nathaniel held a piece of toast out to Tanner for him to take a bite. The boy never looked up from the black and white puppy he held on his lap.

"Joseph Peter Storm. After both his grandfathers. They're going to call him Joey. Six pounds, four ounces. Ten fingers and toes."

Nathaniel chuckled. "Did they actually count them all?"

Sara crossed her arms over her chest. "I would. Mothers like to know these things."

"All's good with Tessa?"

Sara nodded. "Erik says she's tired, but there weren't any complications. He's been a wreck ever since she was in that terrible car accident back in January and almost lost the baby."

TJ slipped his arm over his wife's shoulder. "I understand how he feels. I'd be a mess if anything happened to you."

Standing on her toes, Sara tipped her face and TJ kissed her. Very sweet, but it was also a reminder of how badly Nathaniel had screwed up his own marriage. Mostly, by marrying the wrong woman.

"TJ, I was wondering…"

"You want to go up and see the baby," he finished his wife's sentence. At her nod, he frowned comically. "You know it's a three-hour drive? One way."

"I know."

"We were also up there two weeks ago."

"I know, but it's my brother—"

"Of course, we'll go see them."

Nathaniel swiveled his attention back to Tanner, who wouldn't take his eyes off the puppy in his lap. TJ had lost his sister when he was younger. The man understood the need to see family as much as you could.

Amy might be nine years younger than Nathaniel, and they didn't have much in common at this point in their lives, but if anything happened to her…yeah, he'd have a difficult time, too.

"Why don't you see if you can book us a room at that hotel near the harbor?" TJ suggested. "I'm off today, but we'll need to get someone else to help open up tomorrow, since I was scheduled to."

Swiping across her phone, Sara suddenly looked up. "Oh, Nathaniel, you had that conference call first thing tomorrow morning. Can we get Darcy to watch Tanner for you?"

A serious expression crossed TJ's face. "Monday is Darcy's regular day off. I'm not sure if she's got something planned. I hate to ask her. I think she says yes because I'm her boss. I don't want her to feel pressured."

Nathaniel pulled out his phone. "How about if I text her? She's not afraid to tell me where to get off. If she can't do it, I'll figure something out."

—*Elvira, are you available early tomorrow morning?*—

Maybe that wasn't the best way to get on her good side when he was asking for a favor.

His phone pinged.

—*Depends. What for and how early? My coffin usually doesn't open before a certain time.*—

—*I have a conference call at eight. Sixty to ninety minutes max.*—

As an afterthought, he typed in —*Please, I could use your help.*—

Dots jumped on his phone, stopped, then danced again.

—*Zane has an appointment at ten. I don't think I could make it in time. TJ's house isn't on the trolley route, and my car is in the shop.*—

Damn. Now what? Unless...

—*Can you bring Zane? I'll give you a ride to the appointment after my call.*—

"The hotel has one room left." Sara looked up from her phone. "Should we take it? Can Darcy come over?"

"We're in negotiations."

TJ chuckled. "Good luck. She's a wheeler and dealer, that one."

His phone pinged again.

—*That's awfully early to be up and awake. And the trolleys don't run until after nine. Cab fare is kind of expensive.*—

Wheeling and dealing was right. Either that or she really didn't want to help. Could he sweeten the pot?

BROKEN DREAMS

—I'll come get both of you today. Zane can go in the pool and play with the puppies. You can stay over, then I'll drive you to his appointment and back to your place. Or spend another day in the pool here, and I'll drive you home later.—

Would that do it? When her brother was here a few weeks ago, he'd been so happy and he could tell Darcy was thrilled with that.

—Where's the boss and Sara all this time?—

—In Maine with Erik's new baby. How about I throw in pizza for dinner? You said Zane loves it.—

—You're vicious using that information against me.—

—Maybe I just want to spend time with your charming personality.—

—LOL Laying it on a bit thick. I'm gonna need a machete to cut through all this bull. Fine. I'm in.—

The funny thing was Nathaniel had started to enjoy the give and take of being with Darcy. She was unique and so different than anyone he'd ever known. Her sarcastic humor challenged him to come up with responses that didn't make him look and feel stupid.

—I'll come get you and Zane. What time?—

—Give me an hour. We've got stuff to do.—

He sent a smiley emoji, then slipped his phone back in his pocket. "Tanner, let's finish eating. It's time to let the puppies eat, too."

Grabbing a toy car, he drove it up and down Tanner's leg as he gently lifted the tiny pup from his son's hands. There was a small tussle and a few whines, but Sara moved in, took the puppy, and placed it near Freckles.

As Nathaniel lifted the child into his arms, TJ perused the scene. "I think you might need to adopt one of these puppies when they're ready to leave the nest."

He whipped his head around and scowled. "Yeah, exactly what I need is a puppy to take care of. Like I don't have enough to deal with finding a nanny who's capable of looking after my son."

"The puppies certainly keep Tanner occupied for long periods of time." Sara stroked her hand over Freckles' head. "Maybe it would help."

"Help send me to the funny farm. Who else are they going to?"

Sara's eyes gleamed. "I think I can talk Erik into one. Later, when they're ready to leave their mom."

Nathaniel laughed. "Good luck with that. Did you get the hotel booked?"

"I did." She eyed her husband who had just finished the dishes. "When would you be ready to go, TJ?"

"I'm ready now. Becca's in line to help Mary open the shop tomorrow. I'll switch a day with her later in the week. So, whenever you want to leave."

Popping to her feet, Sara embraced Nathaniel and Tanner in one big hug. "Darcy will know what to do with the dogs, if you don't feel comfortable with them."

"I think Freckles does everything that's needed at this point. All I have to do is give her food and let her go outside a few times a day."

Nathaniel got Tanner cleaned up and changed, then got Darcy's address from TJ. As he got in the car, Sara and TJ were ready to head on their trip, too.

"Give Erik and Tessa my congratulations and best wishes. Hopefully, I'll get the chance to meet the little tyke soon. Once everyone's feeling better and full strength again and things have died down. Before they get the puppy."

"Puppy," Tanner yelled, and they all laughed.

With his son in his car seat, Nathaniel programmed his GPS and drove down the road. Darcy didn't live in one of the fancy neighborhoods Hyannis was so famous for. Not that he'd expected her to, but the house in front of him looked like it could use a little TLC. She and Zane waited outside for him.

After throwing their bags in the back seat, Zane climbed in and began chatting to Tanner. Darcy open the front passenger door and settled in. Her long, nicely tanned legs stretched out, attracting his attention more than they should. She wore some sort of romper dress that allowed her tattoo to play peek-a-boo.

Why did he even care? He'd never been attracted to a woman with ink. Or a jewelry store attached to her ears.

"Erik and Tessa had the baby? I want deets."

Putting the car in drive, he glanced at her. "Deets?"

"Details, Biff. I've met Tessa a few times, and she seems like a decent person. I want to know if everything's okay."

"Um, yeah." He rattled off the sex, name and weight of the baby.

"That's all you've got? Women need more info than that. Someday, when you have a kid, you'll—" Her eyes flew up, anxiety on her face. "I'm sorry. That was stupid. I didn't mean—"

"Don't sweat it, Elvira. I'm still trying to adjust to being a parent myself."

The rest of the ride was quiet, but as soon as they got out of the car, Zane asked, "Can we go in the pool now?"

"Zaney, we just got here." Darcy slung her bag over her shoulder.

"It's okay." Nathaniel extracted Tanner from his car seat. "It's hot today. The pool will help cool us all down."

"Woohoo!" Zane tugged off his shirt, tossing it on a chair as he ran across the deck. With a loud warrior cry, he cannonballed into the water.

Darcy huffed. "Sorry about that. He likes the pool, because it doesn't pull him under like the ocean waves. Do you want me to take Tanner, so you can get work done?"

Nathaniel placed his son on the ground. "I'll get him in his suit first. Why don't you stay here, so Zane isn't by himself in the water? Safety first."

At her nod, he hustled into the house and changed into a bathing suit, then got Tanner suited and sunscreened up.

When he returned, Darcy was on a lounge chair by the pool, her eyes on her brother, a tiny smile on her lips.

"You should ask TJ and Sara if you can bring Zane here more often. They'd love someone to actually get use out of the pool."

"I'll think about it." He had the feeling she didn't ask for favors too often from anyone. She's been doing tons of them for him lately. Didn't seem fair.

"I've got Tanner and Zane for now, so if you have something you wanted to do—walk on the beach or read a book—take advantage of it."

"Thanks. I'll bring our bags upstairs. I assume we'll have the same rooms as last time?"

At his nod, she strolled into the house. He scooped up Tanner and headed for the pool steps.

"Water. No." Tanner clung to his neck like a snake coiled around a branch.

"We won't go all the way in, I promise. You can hang on to Daddy, okay?"

"Daddy."

Every time his son said his name, his stomach clenched. How would he ever know if he was simply repeating what he'd heard or if he actually knew what that word meant?

Slowly, he lowered himself into the water, letting it touch Tanner's toes but not much else. "See, the water is nice. It cools us off when the sun is too hot."

"Sun. Hot." Tanner lifted his face and squinted.

Nathaniel froze. His son knew what that meant. It had to be. It couldn't be a coincidence that he'd looked up. Darcy had said he'd learn new words, if he heard them enough. He certainly had *Freckles* and *puppy* down pat. As they floated around the shallow end, Tanner's death grip loosened.

The back door to the house opened, and Darcy stepped out. Her black hair was slicked back and her face was free of makeup. Wow. It still shocked him how perfect her features were.

"Hi, miss, can we help you with something? Are you lost?"

She made a duck face, then an impish grin appeared.

"That's Darcy," Zane called out, splashing to the side. "She took her makeup off, so she looks different. But it's still her. I see her every night like this."

"Ah, thanks for clearing that up, Zane." Nathaniel couldn't take his eyes off her. This bathing suit was electric blue with a tie dye pattern splashed across the front. Boy shorts were topped with a halter that covered her middle. Interesting that many of the outfits she wore were quite sexy and alluring, but her bathing suits he'd put in the modest category.

Cocking a hip to the side, she planted a fist on it. "Anything else you want to say, GQ? Let me have it."

Shifting his son higher in his arms, he whispered, "Look at Darcy. So pretty."

Tanner clapped his hands and laughed. "Darcy. Pwetty."

The face she made was incredulous as she ran a few steps and dove into the water. But before she'd done that, he thought he'd seen tears in her eyes.

∼

"Is this seat taken, Miss?"

Darcy glanced up as Nate stepped onto the front porch. Her mind battled back and forth on whether she wanted him intruding on her space out here or not. Her stupid heart gave a big rousing cheer. When had Nate's presence become bearable? Almost...desirable?

"Depends on what you want to do with it." She couldn't give in too easily. He'd get suspicious. Especially after the stupid tears that had sprung up this afternoon when Nate had called her pretty. Okay, Tanner had said it, but she'd seen Nate whisper it in his son's ear first.

She wasn't sure how she felt about GQ man staring at her like he did when she wasn't wearing her battle armor. His expression was different. Softer. That wasn't good. Softer was never good. She'd been building up a wall of defense her whole life to stay strong. Chiefly, against the charm of a good-looking guy.

"I was hoping to watch the sunset. You can see it over to the right against the horizon."

"You can. It's kind of cool. We're on the east coast of the country, but because we're on the southern part of the Cape, we get a sunset on the water."

"Do you mind if I join you?"

His manners sure were coming out strong tonight. She waved her hand indicating the seat next to her on the bench swing. "Suit yourself. I've got to warn you, I'm here for a smoke break."

After pulling a candy cigarette from the pack resting near her hip, she inserted the end in her mouth.

Nate's chuckle sent electricity along her nerve endings. His deep voice had a habit of doing that, too.

She held up the pack. "Did you want one?"

His crooked grin made him seem more relaxed than ever. And too darn sexy. "Sure, why not? It's never too late to start bad habits."

When he stuck the thin white stick into his mouth and licked it, images of what he could do to her with that tongue invaded her brain. *No, no, no, stupid girl. Don't fall for those tricks again.*

"I haven't seen you use these in front of Tanner or Zane. Is there a reason?"

"Zane's seen me smoke them at home, but I always make sure to explain they're only candy. Tanner's still too little to understand the difference, and kids like to mimic grown-ups, no matter if the action is appropriate or not. Took me years to break Zane of the habit of swearing. Our mom had a potty mouth." She'd had to break her own habit as well and had come up with some strange substitutes.

Nate gazed at the horizon as the sun lowered behind the waves. "I'm sorry you had such a sucky childhood."

"Why are you sorry? You didn't get my mom addicted to drugs. Or treat me like shit because I wore dirty, ripped clothes to school."

"Was it the other kids, or did the teachers treat you poorly, too?"

She peeked behind her through the window into the house. "Is Tanner all settled for the night?" Avoidance technique number twenty-seven.

"He's in bed, already asleep. The water and fresh air seem to tire him out. Zane's watching TV in the living room. Some cartoon. Looked harmless."

"Yeah, I checked what it was before I headed out here. He doesn't always make good decisions."

"I worry about Tanner, because of that. Will he ever be able to live on his own and function in the real world?"

She patted his hand. "Raise him with lots of love, and he'll be great."

Turning his hand, he clasped hers and squeezed. "Thanks, Darcy. Seriously, for everything you've done for me. And Tanner. It's been super helpful. I don't know how I would have gotten through these past two months without your assistance."

"Eh, it's what I do." She shrugged it off, knowing she didn't handle praise well. Helping someone else with their kid was the least she could do, since she wasn't taking care of her own.

"I got a call from John today, the guy who's doing my renovation. He says it'll probably be ready by next week. Then, I'm sunk. I've got to find a new nanny to take care of Tanner. I've enjoyed spending more time with him, getting to know him. I think I may have connected with him a little more. Who knows?"

"I know." She squeezed his hand back. Why hadn't they let go yet? "He may not show it or say it, but he knows you're here to take care of him. He looks for you when he feels uncomfortable or unsafe."

"Do you think so?" His voice cracked on the words. Yeah, this was one of the reasons her shell had started to weaken around him. She hadn't even put her makeup back on after swimming. She'd told herself it was because she still needed to take a shower, and it would be a waste. That wasn't exactly truthful. The man had shown vulnerability to her, so she could at least let a bit of hers show through, also.

"I know so. You'll be fine."

"Unfortunately, my job isn't one I can always do from home. My partner's been picking up some of the slack while I've been down here, but I can't continue this way. I don't know what I'm going to do about finding the right person for Tanner. I did a lousy job the last four times."

"Move down here, and you can hire me." What the hell? Why had that come out of her mouth? She gave a smug grin to throw him off track. "But you'd have to pay me more than the boss does. Way more."

Nate laughed, and his hand tightened on hers. The innocent contact was killing her.

"Maybe you could clone yourself. Without all the jewelry and sass."

She snuggled close to his side, breaking her own rules of intimacy. "Admit it, you like my sass."

He leaned closer, too, and smiled his killer grin. "Okay, I'll admit it. I do."

CHAPTER FOURTEEN

*D*arcy ducked behind the counter as Nathaniel stepped into Tea and Tales holding Tanner's hand. The memory of him holding her hand a few days ago at Sara and TJ's house blasted through her mind, no matter how much she tried to ignore it and the feeling it had evoked in her. The same feeling she told herself was ridiculous. Because even if she suddenly decided she needed a man in her life, no way in hell would it be GQ.

He'd never be interested in a person like her. Not refined enough or classy enough or educated enough. Doubtful her GED counted for much.

As Sara prepared for Story Hour, Nate settled on the carpet next to Hope with Tanner in his lap. Hope immediately did a smooth five, and Tanner giggled when she tickled his palm.

Turning away from the sight, she convinced herself it didn't bother her. Tanner was enjoying himself with other people, as he should. Hope had a new friend. Something all mothers wanted their children to have. Even mothers who gave up their children.

BROKEN DREAMS

TJ bounded down the steps from his office upstairs. The boss sure loved to see his wife read to the kids. But he crossed the store, headed straight for her, a serious expression on his face.

Pointing to the back wall, he said, "Zane's on the phone. He sounds pretty upset."

Oh, no. Darcy rushed to the phone and pressed the button to connect this extension.

"Zaney, what's happening?"

"Darcy. I need you to come. Mr. Peabody got sick, and I don't know what to do." Zane's voice was panicked and shaky.

"What do you mean sick? Like throwing up sick?"

"No, he said his front hurt, and he's breathing funny."

Frack. What did she do from here? "I'll call for help. You stay there."

"No, Darcy, I called nine-one-one, and they said people would be here soon. I hear the sirens outside. But Mr. Peabody doesn't look good. He's all crooked in his wheelchair."

"Okay, Zane, listen to me. You did what you were supposed to. Good job. Now, you need to make sure the door is unlocked and open so the emergency people can get in."

"I did that. The people on the phone told me to. You said always listen to police and firemen."

"Good, Zane. Stay out of the way while they do their work."

"I will, Darcy, but I'm scared. I don't like to be scared."

Tears burned her eyes. Her brother needed her. "I'll try to get there, sweetie, but for now, sit down and take deep breaths."

"They're here, Darcy. What do I do?"

"You said the door is open, right? Talk to them and tell them what happened."

"I don't know what happened. I don't know." Zane was crying, and it was all she could do not to bawl herself.

A touch on her arm had her glancing up. TJ stood in front of her, his eyes intense. "If you need to go, then go."

Holding the phone away from her mouth, she took a deep breath. "My car is in the shop, and I brought my bike today." A quick peek out the window showed rain pouring down.

"I can..." TJ perused the store.

Darcy shook her head. "You're the only manager here right now. You can't leave."

"I'll drive you," Nate volunteered. Where had he come from? Had everyone stopped what they were doing to listen to her conversation. "Right, buddy, we can take a drive." He juggled Tanner on his hip.

Sara trotted over. "Let me take Tanner. He and Hope can be my helpers today. Nathaniel, take Darcy to do whatever she needs to do."

She could hear the paramedics in the background talking to her brother, trying to calm him down and find out what had happened, but his anxiety was building up. She knew the signs.

"Do you mind? I have to get there soon. He's about to have a full meltdown."

Nate kissed Tanner's head, then swung him over to Sara. "Daddy will be right back."

"Back." Tanner rolled his car up Sara's arm.

"Let's go. My car's on the side street."

Grabbing her purse, she followed Nate to his vehicle and jumped in quickly. The whole time they were driving, she worried what she'd find when they got to the house. Was Mr. Peabody even alive? If he wasn't, how would Zane handle that? He'd feel responsible.

An ambulance and a police car sat out front with the

lights on. Nate had barely put the car in park before she was out and running to the apartment downstairs from hers.

Zane rocked back and forth, his hands scratching over his forearms.

"I'm here, Zaney. You're fine." She pulled her brother in for a hug and patted his back firmly. After a minute, she eased back but kept hold of his hands.

"How's Mr. Peabody? Is he gonna be okay?"

The paramedic, who'd just strapped the elderly man onto a stretcher, stood. "Looks like a possible heart attack. We won't know until he gets to the hospital. Are you family?"

"No, we live upstairs. My brother, Zane, helps Mr. Peabody out during the day."

"Do you know if he has any relatives?"

Mr. Peabody reached out, his voice rough. "My son lives in Connecticut. His number's on the fridge."

Darcy took Mr. Peabody's hand and squeezed. "I'll call him and let him know what happened."

The return pressure on her hand was weak. "Thank you, Darcy. Zane, don't you worry. You did the right thing. You're a good kid, and you did the right thing."

Zane only nodded as he continued to rock back and forth. The police officer took down some information and thanked them for their help. When everyone was gone, she hugged her brother again tighter.

"Darcy, I'm scared. What do I do if I don't help Mr. Peabody?"

"It's okay to be scared, Zaney. Let's go back to our place, and you can rest for a bit. I just need to get that number." She took the slip of paper off the fridge and headed out into the hall. Nate stood there, leaning against the wall. How had she forgotten about him?

"You're still here?"

"Figured I'd stay out of everyone's way. I wanted to make sure you and Zane were okay."

"I was scared, Nate," Zane said. "Do you get scared sometimes?"

Nate clapped him on the shoulder. "I do, and it doesn't feel good. I'm sorry you were scared. I hope Mr. Peabody will be all right."

Darcy held up the slip of paper. "I've got to call his son. Do you mind taking Zane into our apartment for a bit? He's got a stuffed tiger that usually helps him calm down."

"Sure. Come on, Zane."

The two men trooped up the stairs on the right. Pulling her cell phone out, she called Mr. Peabody's son. He was understandably upset but thanked her for being there. He planned to head straight to the hospital. Darcy asked him to keep her apprised of the man's condition.

When she entered her apartment, embarrassment settled in. Nate sat at her card table and folding chair in the kitchen area. He and Zane had jelly jars filled with milk and a paper towel with cookies on it in front of them. She'd splurged for the cookies with the extra money she'd earned from babysitting Tanner this summer. Zane had been thrilled.

God, what GQ must think of her dumpy little place. Now what did she do with her brother? No way she could leave him by himself. He was a mess.

"Zane, grab your raincoat. I've got to get back to work. You'll have to come with me."

Nate narrowed his eyes. "Wait, you're going back to work?"

"I'm still scheduled to work for another six hours."

Nate planted his hands on his hips. "I'm sure TJ will let you have the rest of the day off."

"Whether he will or won't isn't the issue. I can't afford to lose the money from not working. Or didn't you notice the palace I need to pay for?"

The place was clean, because she made sure she and Zane kept it that way, but the furniture was sparse, the curtains threadbare, and the appliances ancient. Doubtful it matched up to his standards.

"You're bringing Zane with you?"

"I can't let him stay here by himself when he's this upset. He's been there with me a few times before. He won't cause any problems, I swear."

"I believe you, Darcy. I just want to make this easier on you."

She eyed him and his perfect hair and clothes. He didn't have to have perfect manners, too.

"Well, you'd be the first.

∽

"Okay, Tanner, keep your fingers crossed this works." Nathaniel unbuckled his son from the car seat and lifted him from the car. "Maybe if you do something super cute, Darcy will agree to my suggestion."

"Darcy." Out came the Hot Wheels, up and down his arm.

"Let's walk. Show Darcy you have some skills, and she won't need to be lugging you all over the place." He hated to admit he liked carrying Tanner, because it made him feel closer to the boy. Like there was some physical connection. There certainly didn't seem to be any emotional one. Not an obvious one on Tanner's part, anyway.

Taking Tanner's hand, he entered the coffee shop and glanced around. Zane was quietly tucked in the children's area looking at a picture book. TJ's friend, Jim, sat next to him, chatting. Darcy waited on a customer at the bookstore counter.

"Hey, Nathaniel, I didn't know you were coming in today." Sara bent over a table, wiping it with a cloth. "Do you need to me to take Tanner while you work? Or just looking for a cup of coffee?"

He peeked over his shoulder. "I was hoping to talk to Darcy for a few minutes, but she's busy right now."

"If it's important, I can take over for her."

He threw his cousin a smile. "It's not vital. I can wait. Maybe I'll read a book to Tanner."

Nodding, she picked up the trash at one of the low tables and brought it behind the coffee counter to throw away. Nate led his son to the children's carpet.

"Hi, Nate. Hi, Tanner. I get to read lots of books today, while Darcy is working. TJ said I could." Zane held up the book he'd been looking at. Tanner plopped down on the floor in his usual Story Hour spot and rolled his car along the lines on the rug. Would he start to fuss if there was no Story Hour? He liked his routines.

"Nate? Sara's cousin, right?" Jim held his hand out, and Nathaniel took it.

"Nathaniel, yes. And my son, Tanner. You were TJ's best man. Jim, right?"

Nathaniel's gaze swung to Zane, then back to the older man. "You don't know how Mr. Peabody is, do you?"

Zane swiveled his head. "Mr. Peabody is in the hospital. He was sick, and it scared me."

"I know, Zane, but you were brave and did the right thing by calling an ambulance."

"Yup, nine-one-one. Darcy taught me to call that number, but only if it was a real emergency. Mr. Peabody being sick was a real emergency. But now I don't have a job. Helping Mr. Peabody was my job."

"Would you like another job, Zane?" Jim offered. "I own a store and could always use a good worker."

Zane's expression grew conflicted. "I have to ask Darcy first."

"Ask me what?" Darcy sauntered over from the counter after her customer left. She nodded at Nathaniel, then tipped her head at Zane.

Jim got to his feet. "Zane was telling me about his job with your neighbor. You know I own Hyannis Home Center. I've always got a need for workers."

Darcy's lips pinched. "Zane needs a good amount of supervision when he works. He can't be left on his own for too long."

"I completely understand. Mary's grandson has some issues as well and needs the same kind of supervision. He works for me a few days a week. Zane could come in on the other days and do the same job. It's mostly cleaning up the boxes after shipments come in and things like that."

"Darcy," Zane said. "Will I help Mr. Peabody again? Is he going to stay in the hospital?"

Nathaniel listened closely. Would this impact his plans?

"I talked to Mr. Peabody's son this morning. They think he'll be going into a nursing home once he's out of the hospital. I'm sorry, Zaney, but he won't need you to help him in there. The nursing staff will do it."

"So I will need another job."

Darcy glanced over at Jim. "What's this job entail? What days and times? Zane can't get there on his own. Plus, he goes to a day program twice a week so he can get Occupational Therapy."

"Tanner's pediatrician said he'd need that," Nathaniel interjected. "OT services. I'm not really sure what it is."

"For Zane, it's helping him with daily living skills."

Jim nodded. "We can work around Zane's schedule and yours."

Darcy's face tightened. "I'll have to think about it. Everything happened so fast I haven't had time to even look at my options."

"Know the offer is there if you need it." Jim patted her shoulder, then crossed the room to where Mary stocked postcards.

Nathaniel needed to talk to Darcy before she made any other arrangements. Would she go for the one he wanted?

"Zane, would you read a story to Tanner? He likes listening to books." Mostly, he looked at the pictures. It was difficult to know exactly how much of the stories he understood.

Zane held up a simple rhyming book. "I can read this one."

Nathaniel positioned Tanner closer so he could see the pictures, then took Darcy's hand. "Can I talk to you for a second?"

Her mouth twisted. "Seems you just did."

His head dropped, and he sighed. When he looked up, she was grinning. That was a good sign. Moving a few feet away, he took a breath and bolstered his courage.

"Listen, I wanted to let you know the renovations on my house are complete. Tanner and I will be moving back in a few days."

She blinked a few times. "Well, have a great trip back."

"Thanks, but I'm still in a bind on finding someone to take care of Tanner. I was wondering..."

"You want me to help you find someone? I can cut through BS better than anyone. You got anyone lined up to interview?"

"Actually, I was hoping I could talk you into coming back with me and being my nanny. You kind of mentioned it the other day."

"I also said you'd have to pay me way better than the boss."

"How much do you make here?"

She named an amount, and he sighed. It was doable. "Okay, I'll pay you a hundred dollars more a week. Plus, you get room and board and the use of a car."

"Whoa, wait. You're serious?" Her head bobbed back and forth, eyes frantic. "I can't up and move to New Hampshire. What the heck am I supposed to do with my brother? He can't live on his own, and he doesn't even have Mr. Peabody around anymore to take care of him."

"I know. I thought about that, too. I've got a four-bedroom house. He's welcome to come live there, also."

Her eyes narrowed. "You want me so badly, you're willing to take on another disabled kid? Wow, Biff, you're desperate. Either that or you've discovered you like the dark side of the moon and want to explore it a little more."

He wouldn't mind exploring Darcy and her intriguing mind some more. Nathaniel reached for her hands. She stared at his like they might bite her, but she didn't pull away. "You're one of the only people who gets Tanner and knows how to engage with him. I need that. I can't take the chance someone will treat him as poorly as the others have. They won't understand what he needs."

Darcy glanced at her brother again. "As much as that's a seriously sweet offer, I don't think I can do it. It took years for Zane to get accustomed to his OT. He loves her and trusts her. It takes him a while to get comfortable with new people. I can't pull up roots and drag him someplace new."

Crap. He was hoping the offer to take Zane would clinch it, and she'd take the job. How did he work this little kink out?

He squeezed her hand tighter, his desperation apparent in his grip. "Please, Darcy. I need you. Tanner needs you. I'll help you find a new therapist for Zane. Someone he likes and trusts. Please, consider my offer."

Her eyes grew misty and her lips pulled together. It didn't bode well for his needs. If he couldn't convince her to come work for him and take care of Tanner, he was sunk.

CHAPTER FIFTEEN

A hundred dollars more a week. Plus room, board, and use of a car. All that would be amazing...if it didn't mean she and Zane had to pack up and move.

Her brother loved the day program he went to and liked being useful. If he lived with them in New Hampshire, he wouldn't be able to get a job. It would take a while to get to know and trust someone enough to help Zane work.

She said she'd get back to Nate later today with her answer. It had to be no.

"You okay, Darcy?" TJ sat next to her at one of the tables in the coffee area.

"Yeah, boss. Thinking about some things I got to do. I'm off the clock now. I'll take Zane home in a minute."

"There's no rush, if you need a few minutes to unwind. You seemed to get distracted after Nathaniel dropped in. Was he saying goodbye?"

"Actually, he offered to steal me away from here. To take care of Tanner. You gonna come back with a better offer?"

"Do you want to be Tanner's nanny? You're amazing with him."

"You couldn't make it here without me. Who'd keep all the summer staff in line?"

TJ laughed. "There is that."

"Yeah." She made a face, playing up the goofball act that made so many people think she had no brains.

"But if this nanny position was something you wanted to do, I could probably step up and handle the riff raff for the next month, until they all left."

"Why would I want to take care of some rich snob's rug rat all day, when I can flirt with the sweet beach bums who hang around here?"

"Because I think you've started to care for that rug rat. Maybe a tiny bit."

Yeah, maybe a smidge. But if she went to live in New Hampshire, she wouldn't be here for Story Hour. And Hope.

For years, she'd been telling herself she needed to cut ties and stop torturing herself with glimpses of her daughter from across the room. Since GQ and his kid had come along, she'd gotten roped into sitting next to Hope or having the girl on her lap. She'd even been coerced into showing up to her birthday party.

Eventually, it all had to stop. Maybe moving to another state was the right answer. It didn't help her with what to do with Zane.

"Darcy, did you and Zane need a ride home?" Mary offered. Jim stood behind her. Her shift had just ended, too. "Jim can drop you off when he drives me."

"Thanks, but Nate's coming to give us a ride. We gotta talk about some things."

At the tilt of Mary's head, TJ said, "Nathaniel's trying to steal Darcy away from us to be Tanner's nanny."

Mary's eyes lit up. Sara hurried over. It was a rainy day, and the store wasn't full. Too bad. Then, she wouldn't have to be the center of attention like she was now.

"I don't think I can. Zane has his day program and his therapists are here."

"Hmm." Jim crossed his arms over his chest, then whispered something in Mary's ear.

The woman grinned. "We could do that."

"Do what?" Darcy asked, not sure she wanted to hear the answer. She hated when others made decisions for her.

Mary pulled out the chair on Darcy's other side, sat, then patted her hand. "First, I guess we should tell everyone our good news."

"Okay. Slight segue, but whatever keeps the conversation away from me."

"Don't worry, we'll get back to you." Mary tapped her hand again. "Jim and I are getting married."

TJ smirked. "Took you long enough."

"Shush, you." Mary slid a side eye at the boss. The woman was like a mom for many of the staff who worked here. "Jim plans on selling his condo and moving into my place as it's much bigger. But I have that small apartment over the garage. It would be the perfect place for Zane to live. He could work on being independent, while still having us nearby."

"I don't know…" Zane had never lived on his own.

"It doesn't have a full kitchen, so you wouldn't have to worry that he'd burn the place down. There's a microwave and small fridge, but I'd expect him for dinner every night. I love to cook, and I haven't had anyone to do it for in so long."

"I don't know. He's used to our apartment." Their craphole apartment.

"Can we ask him?" Mary said.

"Knock yourself out." Zane wouldn't want anything to change, would he?

"Zane," Jim called out. Her brother got up from his spot on the floor and loped over. Jim explained the situation to him. "Do you think you'd like to come live with us? You could work in the home center store a couple days a week and help Mary around the house on the other days when you don't have your day program."

Zane looked interested. What?

Darcy stood and paced. "But how's he gonna get to his day program and this new job you've got for him? He doesn't drive or have a car."

Mary waved her hand at her soon-to-be husband. "Jim will drive him to work when he goes in, and I can drop him at his day program and therapists and pick him up. I'm sure TJ wouldn't mind shifting my schedule here and there to accommodate that."

TJ laughed. "You've always made your own schedule, then told me what it was. Why would we do anything differently now?"

"Don't you be fresh, young man." Mary's eyes sparkled. "Now, Darcy, we've worked out your problems with your brother. What other objections do you have?"

"How about everyone wanting to get rid of me? Do I smell that bad? Or is it the makeup? It can't be my shimmering personality, because that wouldn't make any sense."

"No one wants to get rid of you, Darcy." Sara touched her shoulder. "I think we all want Nathaniel to have the best care for Tanner, and we want you to do something besides serve coffee all day. This could be a good step for you."

"Maybe I like serving coffee. Besides, today is Friday the thirteenth. I shouldn't be making decisions on a day like this."

TJ frowned. "What does the day have to do with making decisions?"

"Come on, Elvira," Nate said, from behind her. When had he shown up? "Friday the Thirteenth should be a great day to make decisions for the mistress of the dark."

"Not the way to talk me into taking the job, Biff. You should be throwing compliments and bonuses at me."

"I should be throwing thanks at Mary and Jim for figuring a way to work it all out. What do you say, Darcy? It's more pay than you make now, plus you won't have rent or food costs."

"But I won't see Darcy ever again." Tears came into Zane's eyes.

"Of course, you will, Zane. My house is only two hours from here. She can visit you every weekend if you want. Or you can come up to visit us."

"He doesn't drive, and my car won't make that kind of trip for very long, genius."

"I've been planning on getting a new car sometime soon, so I'll let you use mine. I wouldn't want Tanner in your death trap, anyway. You can come back here every Saturday or Sunday if you want. I'm not in the office and usually have dinner with my folks, so I won't need you for Tanner. Does that work?"

"Why is everyone so fired up to get rid of me?"

"I'm not." Nate grinned. "I'm trying to get you to come with me."

If only that were true. Well, it was but not for any reason other than he needed a nanny who wouldn't be nasty to his kid. The money was tempting. If she didn't need to pay rent, not to mention heat, electricity, water, and food, she could actually save some money. Get training in something that would pay better than serving coffee. But how long could she do this? And if she came back on Saturdays, then maybe she could drop in at Story Hour and see Hope.

You just said it was time to cut ties.

Maybe they needed to be broken slowly.

"Well?" Nate's crooked smile dug into her heart. She'd be doing this for his son, not him. She had to remember that.

"What happens if you find someone better? I'll be out of a job and an apartment."

"Is there anyone better than you?" His eyes glowed with a challenge.

"No, but the kid will be going to school soon enough, and then I'll be out of a job. Boss, if I go, and the kid doesn't need me anymore, do I get my old job back?"

TJ nodded. "Darcy, you've got a job here any time you want it."

"So…?" Nate crept closer. Maybe she should only take the job if he agreed to stop smelling so good.

The decision wasn't solely hers. "Zane, would you be okay living with Mary and Jim? I'd see you every weekend. And it might only be for a short time, until Nate gets someone else to watch Tanner."

"I would have my very own apartment?"

Darcy nodded.

"And I would have a new job with Jim?"

"Yes, and he and Mary would make sure you still got to your program and therapists. But I won't go if you don't want me to."

"If you don't go, who will watch Tanner? He's only little. Not like me. I'm all grown up and can live in my own apartment."

"You are all grown up, Zaney." Tears rushed to her eyes.

"I think I want to be all grown up in my own apartment. With my new job."

Darcy slowly spun to face Nathaniel. "Fine. I'll do it for the short term, but you start looking for a real nanny. I'll help interview and even train her, and I won't leave until I know Tanner's in good hands. Does that work?"

"Perfect. Thank you, Darcy." He held out his hand and when she put hers in it, he tugged and leaned in. "FYI, the nanny uniform is pink with lace."

BROKEN DREAMS

～

Nathaniel plumped the throw pillows on the couch, then paced in front of the windows again, peeking toward the driveway. He'd left Darcy his BMW and driven back home in a rental he'd used until he'd bought something new. She'd texted that she was leaving two hours ago, which meant she was due any time.

It had been five days since she'd agreed to be Tanner's nanny. Temporary nanny. Until he found someone who could do the job as well as Darcy. He wasn't sure that person existed. And wasn't that a change from their first meeting at Sara and TJ's wedding? Where he'd been, he hated to admit, a tiny bit afraid of her. Maybe he'd gotten used to having her around.

She had a softer side to her startling appearance. He'd gotten used to the clothes, piercings, the spiky hair, and even the dark makeup. And the few times he'd seen her without it? Slinking out of the pool dripping wet, her hair slicked back, water running over her tanned skin and curves. Droplets clinging to her eyelashes. Whoa.

He shook himself loose from his memories. She was arriving soon. He was about to be her boss. Of course, according to her, she was only here to help him choose and train a real nanny. That made her more his HR person than his employee, and TJ had promised her she could have her job back whenever she needed it. She wouldn't be working for him forever.

Except, some strange part of him wanted her to stay here with him. And Tanner. Tanner needed her. The thought of not having her nearby...

The sound of a car engine caught his attention, and he trotted to the front door, hoping his son would stay napping until he got Darcy settled.

His silver BMW pulled in alongside the newer Toyota Highlander. The SUV was larger and safer, the sort of thing he needed to consider now that he was a father. It was a family car.

"Sweet ride, Biff." Darcy pursed her lips as she tossed him the keys. He tossed them right back.

"It's your ride while you're here. I told you I'd get something newer."

Her eyes narrowed as she cocked one hip to the side. "Wait. You're letting me drive the Beamer, while you drive a dad car? Groovy. And you live on a lake. This is seriously one cool job. I may never go back to serving coffee."

That's kind of what he was hoping for.

"Are all your bags in the trunk?"

She hauled a large duffel from the back seat and smirked. "Only the one. I travel light."

He slung it over his shoulder. "I figured you'd have a few for your makeup and another couple for the earrings."

"Not very observant, are you, Biff? I wear the same earrings every day. I rarely take them out, and I never change them."

"Why not?"

"Have you counted them? Half a dozen in each ear. My delicate skin doesn't do cheap jewelry, and the good stuff is too expensive for multiples."

"But your delicate skin does an inch of black makeup."

She tilted her head. "I make sure I get the brand that's hypoallergenic."

"Well, come on in. I'll give you the two-cent tour."

He took her in the front door and tipped his head to the right. "That's my home office. I've used it a bit more since Tanner came to live with me, but I still need to go into Portsmouth most days."

Darcy peeked in. "Leather and oak. Nice details."

"The room on the left was a formal living room, but I had John fix it up so Tanner can use it as his playroom." John was in the process of building a loft with a slide and a small play area underneath. As soon as the materials came in, he'd attach it to the wall. Hopefully, his son would use it.

"Where's the kid now?"

"Napping." He glanced at his watch. "He's pretty structured with his sleep schedule. Most likely, he'll wake up in about a half hour."

She nodded approvingly as they moved down the hall.

"Master bedroom suite on the right. Full bath and laundry room on the left."

She took a quick peek in each, then continued after him.

"And that brings us to the big room."

Her eyes opened wide as they stepped into the enormous, open space with floor-to-ceiling windows that overlooked the lake. "As you can see, the kitchen and dining area are up here on the landing. John added a half wall around them, so Tanner doesn't accidentally fall off. Then, you take the few steps down into my favorite room."

"Wow. You could fit my entire apartment in this room. What do you do with all this space?"

He gestured to the left where a flat screen was mounted on a wall above a fireplace. A couch, love seat, and a few comfy chairs formed a grouping around it. "Space to relax. I haven't decided what to do with the right side yet." That half of the room sat empty.

"Um, boat, bucking bronco, jungle gym, spaceship. Just a few things that come to mind."

Nathaniel laughed. "Hmm, I'll have to think about those. I had thought about a piano. Nothing quite as big as the one TJ has."

"Do you play?"

"All the Storm kids had lessons. Gram and Gramps made

sure of it. I haven't played much lately, but I taught Tanner a song on TJ's piano."

Darcy cocked her head. "Seriously? Like he played it, or you took his fingers and pressed the correct keys?"

"I played a few notes a couple times, and he copied me. I repeated them and added a few more notes. We got to the point where he played Mary Had a Little Lamb all by himself."

"Frack, really? You know I've heard of some autistic kids doing stuff like that. Music is very mathematical and repetitive."

"I was kind of surprised when he did it. We were playing with the piano, and he got really excited about the sound."

"Excited?" Her lips twisted to the side.

"Well, as excited as Tanner ever gets. But his eyes lit up, and he started bouncing. Once I taught him the song, he played it over and over. He only stopped because Freckles started having her puppies."

"Cool. Maybe Tanner can give me lessons."

He could give her lessons. The two of them seated side by side on a piano bench, fingers almost touching, his pulse racing. He'd been out in the sun too long if he was thinking of tickling the old ivories with the moon goddess.

The thought came and went in a moment. Luckily, Darcy hadn't noticed anything amiss. She stared out the windows at the yard and lake.

"This is great. Do you own all this land?" Her voice held disbelief.

"Yeah, it's only an acre, but it gives me some privacy when I want to go outside and relax."

"You've got a dock. Do you have a boat?"

He sidled up beside her. "There's a small rowboat in the shed that was left here by the previous owner. I haven't taken it out yet. I've also got a few kayaks. Last summer, I took one out almost every day. Haven't even touched them this year. My brother, Kevin, and his work partner, Mitch, come over to use them a lot, though, so if you see them, don't worry."

"Oh, no worry from me, Biff. They're not my kayaks."

"If you take one out, make sure you and Tanner wear life vests. There are a bunch of them in different sizes in the shed."

"You have lots of kayak parties, do you?"

He grinned. "No, but I do have a big family who enjoy hanging out at the lake."

"Do you like them hanging out here?" One eyebrow rose in question.

He crossed his arms over his chest and sighed. "I didn't for a while. Helene and I lived in a bigger house over in Rye. She wasn't very welcoming to the rest of my family."

"Holy mansion, Batman. You and the bitch had a bigger house than this one? Did you rent it out for parties?"

"Helene liked to entertain. As for me, I haven't felt like partying much in the last four years."

"She did a number on you, huh?"

He shook his head and snapped out of his pity session. "I'm fine. Hopefully, I can make it up to my family now that the house is renovated. We've still got a few more weeks until Labor Day we can enjoy."

Darcy glanced outside and indicated the shed. "So, is that where I'm staying?"

He laughed. "No, I've got three bedrooms upstairs. There's only one bathroom, though. You'll have to share with Tanner."

Darcy rolled her eyes. "Oh, man, with Tanner. That kid likes to stay in the tub so long, I'll never get in."

"Sorry," he teased. "Them's the breaks."

"Any other rules I need to know about."

Rules. He hadn't thought about that. The other nannies

had seemed to come with their own set. For Darcy, he wanted her to keep interacting with his son the way she had been.

"There are times I have to work late, so I'll need you available to watch Tanner until I get home. But I'll always let you know if I'm planning to be late. You're welcome to use the car even when you aren't on duty. Just be sensible and no drinking or drugs while driving. Or really at all while you're around Tanner."

"Yeah, after my mom, alcohol and drugs aren't high on my list of must-do things. Candy cigarettes are my only addiction. Can I go out at night, hang with friends?"

Did she have friends in the area? He'd never heard her mention any or even a boyfriend.

"Of course. You aren't in prison, Darcy. Nevertheless, I'd prefer you don't hang out with guys while you're in charge of Tanner. And don't bring them to the house."

Her eyes darkened, and he knew he'd worded that wrong. She planted her hands on her waist.

"What? I can watch your kid *and* screw a guy at the same time. I'm multi-talented that way, I assure you. Want a demonstration?"

Aw, crap. The hurt in her eyes couldn't be hidden, even by all the black makeup. Why did he have to go and sound like such a douchebag?

Stepping closer, he touched her arm. "I'm sorry, that was uncalled for. I just figured all the guys would be lusting after you once you put on the lacy, pink uniform I picked out for you."

CHAPTER SIXTEEN

*L*acy, pink uniform.

He better the hell be kidding. Especially after the crack about bringing guys to the house. He wasn't the first person to assume she was easy. The way she dressed didn't help any, but it was the part she was meant to play. One she'd gotten herself into a long time ago. When she was young, innocent, and stupid.

Maybe not so innocent. She'd seen too much growing up with a drug addled mother, who did anything she could to get her daily fix. But stupid? Uh huh, that word fit like a glove.

"Pink lace to me is like garlic to a vampire, so you'd better be joking, GQ, or you won't have a nanny to take care of your kid."

Nate's eyes showed his regret for what he'd said. Cocking his head toward the stairs that ran along the back wall behind the dining room, he pressed his hand to her lower back. "Come on. I'll show you the rest of the house."

She followed him up the stairs and down a hallway. Were the rooms up here as nice as the ones downstairs? The master bedroom in this place was huge, and she'd gotten a peek at the walk-in closet. Bigger than her bedroom. Well, her old bedroom. She couldn't afford to keep paying rent when she wasn't living there. Zane had loved his new little place over Mary's garage, and she had to admit she was a bit jealous. Zane was in his glory.

Here, she'd most likely get a ten by ten foot room with a single bed. Not that different from what she'd had.

"This is Tanner's room. I usually keep the door open a crack, even though I have a video monitor set up in there."

Darcy peered inside. "Where's the video feed go?"

"I have it in my bedroom, but there's an app you can put on your phone that enables you to see him if he's napping."

The blinds were down but tipped open enough that light filtered in. Tanner slept on what looked like an adapted crib. It had three sides, with the fourth side open. He could easily get out of bed if he wanted to. Nate had hinted that the boy had a scheduled sleep time and he stuck to it.

"Why is he in a crib?"

Nathaniel backed up, stepping away from the door. "When Helene dropped him off, I needed something fast. Greg had this from when Ryan was small, and it converted to a child bed. He seems to like it, and I don't worry about him falling out as much since three sides are covered."

"Makes sense."

"Your room is next door. The bathroom's across the hall. Feel free to put anything of yours in the cabinets. Tanner's only got a toothbrush, paste, and a few tub toys. You've seen how much he likes water, so you can imagine they don't get used all that much."

Nate pushed open the door on the left, and she followed him. Holy Chihuahua.

"This whole room is mine?"

"It's the biggest one up here. Sorry you have to share the

bathroom. I had my cousin, Sofie, decorate it for you. I think they ran out of pink, so you'll have to make do with this."

A queen-sized bed sat between two windows and sported a black and white comforter with a geometric pattern. A dozen fancy pillows with shams in the same pattern were tossed across the top. Shear black curtains draped the windows, allowing light to filter in. The white walls had pictures and decorations in mostly shade of black and gray, with the occasional splash of red.

Over in a corner was a large upholstered chair, also black and white, with a footrest in front of it. A small writing desk sat in the other corner. She meandered through the room and opened the double doors across from the bed. The closet ran almost the length of the room.

"I don't have enough clothes to fill this up."

Nate appeared at her shoulder. "Don't worry. I ordered about fifty pink uniforms. That should take up plenty of space."

God, with this room, she'd almost be willing to wear a stupid pink, lacy dress.

"Oh, one more thing." Nate pressed his hand to her back and guided her toward the bed. When he closed the door, she snapped her head up to stare at him. Was he expecting something more from her than nannying? Shades of the past flashed through her mind.

"I had this in my office, but I moved it up here. I thought it fit with your stuff better."

He...what? On the back of the door was an old movie poster in a frame. All red and black. Bella Lugosi in Dracula. Seriously? Why had he done this?

Suddenly, tears started to leak out. *Cut it out*. It was a flipping room, not a diamond ring.

"Darcy, are you okay? I thought you'd like it. I can have Sofie redo it, if you really hate it."

"No." She grabbed his arm and flashed him a genuine smile. "It's amazing. It's absolutely perfect. Especially this poster. It's...this is nicer than anything I've ever had before. Thank you."

"It's the least I can do after all you're giving up to help me with Tanner."

She explored the room for a few more minutes, taking in every little knick knack and trinket. The movie poster was so great. The fact he'd taken it from his office astounded her and pleased her all at once.

"There's one more room up here. It's the room I would have put Zane in, if he'd come."

The next room was empty, but almost as big as the one he'd put her in.

"If you want more space, you can use this room. I don't need it for anything. If you'd like your own sitting room, we could get you a couch and TV."

"This is where you would have put Zane." He'd actually considered allowing her brother to live here, as well. That said a lot about his character. The gesture pulled at her heart.

"Yeah, I would have gotten a bed and a dresser obviously. I can still do that if you want. For when he visits here. All you have to do is let me know."

"I'd like him to visit."

More tears, and this time they found their way down her cheeks. She missed her brother already.

Strong arms wrapped around her from behind. They were perfectly muscled with the right amount of hair sprinkled on them. She should pull away. Why would she ever think Nate holding her was a good idea? For some reason, she liked it. Aside from Zane, it had been an extremely long time since someone had held her simply to console her.

Had anyone ever held her like this? She couldn't remember. It felt nice. Warm. Comforting. She wanted more of it, and maybe that wasn't a good thing. Wanting something you knew you couldn't have and certainly didn't deserve.

A soft whine drifted down the hall, and Nate loosened his grip. Tanner was awake. It was time for her to get to work.

∼

NATHANIEL SWORE as coffee splattered on the cuff of his white shirt. Why was he so nervous? It was simply a meeting to get Tanner ready for school. Granted, he had no idea what the specialists would tell him about his son. He'd taken Tanner in a few days last week for testing. They were meeting today to discuss the results and options for school.

"I've got to change my shirt. Do you mind getting him ready?" Darcy sat at the table, sipping a cup of tea and chatting quietly to the boy. "His khaki shorts and that navy polo shirt, I think."

"Yes, we discussed this yesterday. I made sure it was clean and pressed."

She had actually ironed some of the laundry for him and Tanner. What *she* currently wore needed some work. She was in her typical sleepwear, tiny shorts and a loose T-shirt with the neck and arms cut out. Not that he didn't appreciate how she looked in the skimpy outfit, but it got his mind circling in directions he didn't have time for.

Glancing at his watch, he sighed. "We've got to leave in about twenty minutes. I don't want to be late. Will you have enough time to get him dressed and you, too?"

Getting dressed wasn't what he worried about. It was her donning her makeup. Every night for the past five nights, she'd taken a shower before bed and come down with a clean, scrubbed face, yet every morning, she'd have it layered back on again.

"We'll be fine, if I hustle right now and leave the breakfast dishes. Don't sweat it. We'll make it. Although, I don't know why you need me at this meeting."

"You're the one who'll be dropping him off and picking him up on the days he goes. Plus, I want you to hear what they say about Tanner and what he'll need. It's always good to have an extra set of ears to catch everything."

"Come on, Tanner, let's head upstairs." She slid the child onto her hip and trekked over to the stairs.

"Um, his boat shoes with the blue socks."

"Yes, Biff."

"And Darcy…?"

She swiveled on the top of the stairs with an indulgent smile.

"I'm not making you wear the pink uniform, but do you think you can please not look like a vampire?"

Her eyes narrowed. "A leopard can't change his spots, but I'll make a valid attempt."

Shit, he'd done it again. He knew he was being testy, but he couldn't remember ever being this anxious. He hated the unknown, and this meeting was like nothing he'd ever done before. What if they told him there was nothing they could do for Tanner? Or what if they thought he should be in a residential program? He couldn't do that to his son. Locked away without his family. Tanner had finally gotten used to being with his father. His real father. Because the one he'd originally had obviously hadn't been there for him, even when he thought the kid was blood related.

As he slipped a new shirt off the hanger, he clenched his teeth thinking about Helene and all she hadn't provided for their son. Which was laughable considering how much money she and Bryce had at their disposal.

With his new shirt on and tucked in, he gave his hair a last comb and headed back to the kitchen. Darcy appeared at the top of the stairs with Tanner's hand in hers. The boy had on the suggested outfit and looked perfect. Darcy—he stared at what she'd put on—it could be worse.

A black denim skirt was topped with a magenta T-shirt, which displayed a large peach flower on the front. The skirt went almost to her knees. Her feet were covered in black high tops. She'd applied makeup, but it was subtler today. A much thinner line around the eyes and her lips were dark red instead of black.

"Do I pass muster, Biff, or do I need to go and put on the pink lace?"

If only he had a pink, lace uniform for her.

"You'll do. Let's go."

Once he'd pulled onto the road, Darcy asked, "Are you sure you want me there?"

Reaching over, he took her hand and squeezed. "Yes, you should know Tanner's routines. Plus, I need your support. I mean…uh, if Tanner starts acting up, you'll be there to take care of him while I talk to his teacher."

The pressure from her hand took some of the anxiety away as he maneuvered through the streets. They arrived at the school with six minutes to spare.

"Okay, buddy, this is your new school." Nathaniel held his son's hand as they walked up the front steps, Darcy on Tanner's other side. "You'll meet new friends here, like you did at Story Hour with Hope."

"Hope." Tanner sang out. Did he miss the little girl? They'd seen each other three times a week for two months.

When they reached the front office, he approached the desk. "I'm Nathaniel Storm. I'm here to meet with the Director of Special Education, Peggy Ramirez."

The secretary smiled. "Yes, I remember when you first came in back in May. You and Mrs. Storm can take a seat over there. Mrs. Ramirez will be right out."

Nathaniel led Tanner and Darcy—not his wife, that

would have to be cleared up—to the seats against the wall. He pulled his son into his lap. Just to keep him from wandering. He wouldn't admit holding the child was all that was keeping him together.

"They obviously don't know you well enough yet," Darcy whispered as she sat next to him.

"Why do you say that?"

"She thought you'd be interested in someone like me for a wife. That's a hoot."

"Yeah, a hoot."

"Hoot," Tanner yelled out. "Hoot, hoot."

Before he could respond further, the door behind the secretary opened and Mrs. Ramirez walked out. They'd met at Tanner's eligibility meeting before the summer started.

"Mr. Storm, nice to see you again," the mature dark-haired woman commented. She smiled at Darcy and Tanner, who stood up next to him. "And this must be—"

"Darcy Marx. She's Tanner's nanny. And this is Tanner."

"Nice to meet you." The women shook hands, and Mrs. Ramirez squatted in front of the child. "It's nice to meet you, too, Tanner."

She didn't hold out her hand, rather watched to see what Tanner would do. He reached up and touched a large dog pin on her lapel.

"Dog. Fwecko."

"We spent the last two months with my cousin. She has a dog named Freckles."

"Yes, that's right. You mentioned you were having renovations done on your house. Are they finished?"

"They finished last week. I have the forms you wanted me to fill out, as well as the paperwork from the pediatrician who diagnosed Tanner's disability."

"Excellent. I'll give it to Maggie, and we can take a walk down to see Tanner's new class and his teacher."

After giving the envelope to the secretary, Mrs. Ramirez led them down the hall, pointing out the classrooms as they marched past.

"While we still haven't officially placed him in a classroom until after the IEP meeting, Mrs. Adams runs the morning four-year-old preschool, and that's the most likely spot for him."

They entered a large room with colorful pictures and decorations on the walls. Tiny tables and chairs littered the room in between low shelves stuffed with blocks, books, and tons of other child stuff.

"Joanne, I have a new customer for you. Tanner Storm. Once all his paperwork is finished, he'll be added to your roster. I'm not sure which days yet." She introduced Nathaniel and Darcy, also.

Nathaniel released his breath. Which days? So, not being recommended to an outplacement at a residential school. Good to know.

A petite blonde jumped down from the stepladder she was on and approached them. "Storm? Any relation to our Kindergarten teacher, Leah Storm? She's right across the hall."

"She's my cousin." Maybe he could ask Leah to check in on Tanner every now and again. It would certainly ease his mind.

Mrs. Adams shook his hand, then bent at the waist, waving.

"Hi, Tanner. Want to take a look around the room?"

The child's eyes were already swiveling in every direction, taking in as much detail as he could. When his gaze landed on a bucket of Hot Wheels cars, he began to shake and flap his hands.

"Car. Car."

"Um, yeah, he really likes cars. He could play with one for

hours and not get tired. I often use them to get him calm, if something traumatic happens."

Darcy stood to the side, quiet and attentive, observing everything.

"Darcy will be bringing Tanner to school and picking him up at the end of the day."

"He won't be taking the bus? The school does provide transportation." Mrs. Ramirez said.

"He might in the future, but for now I'd prefer to bring him and pick him up. When I talked to the bus company earlier to discuss the routes, they said because we're over on Exeter Pond, near the edge of town, his ride could be thirty minutes at times. I don't want him so stressed out from the bus that he has a terrible day in school."

"Understandable."

Mrs. Ramirez glanced at the clock on the wall. "The rest of the team should be arriving in the conference room, so if you're ready, we'll head there. It's only two doors down. Tanner can stay in here and play while we meet."

These people didn't know Tanner, and he wanted Darcy in the meeting with him. How did that work out?

"I'll stay here with him, Nate." It was the first time she'd said anything since the brief interaction in the office. "You go take care of business. We'll be fine."

Mrs. Ramirez said, "We'll rotate out in the meeting, so the specialists can come in here and visit with Tanner again. Once he's comfortable, Ms. Marx can join us if you'd like that."

"Sure." He knelt next to his son and kissed his forehead. "I'll be back in a few minutes, buddy." Tanner had already picked through the toy cars and chosen half a dozen to play with. Sometimes, Nathaniel wished he had four wheels and an engine, so his son would concentrate on him.

When they entered the conference room, the number of

people sitting around the table floored him. Mrs. Ramirez introduced them, but his mind was trying to keep track of what they did. As a result, their names flew right past. Special Education Director. Special Education Teacher, who was also the case manager. Occupational Therapist. Physical Therapist. Speech Language Pathologist. School Psychologist. It made his head swim. Which basically set the tone for the rest of the meeting.

Mrs. Adams, the preschool teacher, joined them a few minutes later, and they finally got started. He was given a booklet outlining his rights as a parent. Attendance was taken. He was asked about Tanner's history, which spawned another painful recitation of the whole sordid story. Tanner's mother, her new marriage and subsequent abandonment of her child, instant fatherhood, the current custody arrangement, and Helene's rights, or lack thereof. All of Nathaniel's dirty laundry laid out for a room full of strangers.

The faces around the room were sympathetic, their voices understanding. Then, the School Psychologist reviewed the testing she'd done last week. Nathaniel tried to focus on the results, but as another specialist went through her report and talked about the goals they had for Tanner, he became more and more overwhelmed. If he was this confused, what would his son be when he had all these people coming in and out of his life on a frequent basis?

Some of the specialists left the room, then returned for another one to leave. Were they rotating out to visit with Tanner as Mrs. Ramirez had suggested earlier?

"How much time will he spend in school? He's still only three. He won't be four for another month."

"Many of our special needs children come five full days, in order to receive the maximum benefits."

"A full week? He's never even been to school before. Doesn't he need consistency? He's finally feeling comfortable with me and Darcy. I'm not sure how he'll react with so many new faces all at once."

"Has Ms. Marx been with you since you retained custody?"

Did he tell them he'd been an utter failure at hiring appropriate nannies? Just what he needed, more of his dirty laundry to throw around the room.

CHAPTER SEVENTEEN

"He seems to be comfortable in the classroom right now." The woman, who'd introduced herself as Libby the OT, sat on the floor pushing a car next to Tanner's. These people all had a nice manner with him. Except he hadn't paid all that much attention to any of them, not with a whole bin of race cars nearby. "Why don't you join Mr. Storm in the meeting? It's a good idea for you to hear what's going on if you'll be taking care of Tanner when he's not in school."

Darcy got to her feet but hesitated. She didn't belong in a school meeting as a responsible adult. What was this world coming to?

She stroked Tanner's head and told him she'd be right back. He looked up and actually made eye contact for a fraction of a second.

Libby grinned, her eyes widening. "Second door on the right. Just go in. I think the inner door to the conference room is open."

Darcy exited the room, glancing back at the boy playing on the colorful carpet. It was similar to the one TJ had in the children's section at Tea and Tales. Was that why Tanner had adjusted quickly?

When she arrived at the conference room, the inner door was ajar. Nate was speaking. The deep, rough voice he used when he talked about his son drifted out to her and made her shiver. Too much about the man caused that reaction. It needed to stop. She was only staying until he found a suitable substitute.

"I know he should have started therapy before now and didn't because of his mother, but he finally seems comfortable with me and Darcy. She's amazing with him. He responds better to her than anyone else he's been around. Darcy gets inside the little bubble world he lives in. I haven't even been able to do that. I don't want Tanner pulled away from something that seems to be working to spend all week with a slew of new people."

Heat rushed to her face at his clear confidence in her. When Mrs. Ramirez glanced up and waved her in, her cheeks got even warmer.

A smile crossed Nate's face when he saw her. He pushed out the empty chair next to him and stood while she sat. Did men really do that anymore? Apparently, this man did.

The Speech Path spent some time going over the goals they had for Tanner, and Darcy paid close attention. She wanted to do as much as she could at home to help Tanner communicate better. Nate nodded at everything she said, but Darcy could tell his anxiety was growing. Sliding her hand over, she placed it on the chair beside his thigh and gave a gentle stroke, letting him know she was here if he needed her.

Once the Physical Therapist talked about his goals, a forty-somethingish woman introduced herself to Darcy. "I'm Trish Longwood, Tanner's case manager. If there are ever any problems, or you need something, I'm the one to contact."

"Thank you." Darcy felt completely out of place here.

"We were about to discuss Tanner's schedule."

Nate tensed. "What are my options here? Or do I have any?"

The options were staggering, it turned out. Half-day, full-day. Most of the children in the inclusion program attended full-day, but with Nate's concerns, they recommended the morning preschool. It was an integrated classroom, with typically developing children, as well as children with special needs like Tanner. There were also Developmental Support Classes in the afternoon, to focus on skills Tanner would need as he continued in school.

Nate gripped her thigh as the conversation went on. He was obviously overwhelmed and invested in making the best decision for Tanner, with no clue what that might be.

Observation and push-in services were discussed. Darcy patted his hand on her leg. His hold loosened but didn't leave. Thinking back to her brother and the services he'd gotten, and the anxiety Nate confessed to, she asked another question.

"Can we start Tanner off with a few mornings and maybe only two afternoons for his supports, then work his way to more as he settles into the routine?"

Nate let out a breath and gave her a quick nod. "I'd like that better than having him attend five full days right away. Especially since he's never been to school before. I don't want my son to feel like I've abandoned him like his mother did."

The nods of the others in the room lessened her concern.

"We can do that, certainly. Why don't we start with Monday, Wednesday, and Friday? And we'll set his afternoon Developmental Support Class on Wednesday and Friday."

Nate grimaced. "He still takes a nap every day after lunch. I'm not sure how well he'll do without one."

"We provide the students with a mandatory rest time every day. He'll have a mat in the classroom, and you can send in a blanket and a stuffed animal or other comfort item if he needs it."

"He's got a stuffed dog that helps him sleep."

"Good. Feel free to send that in his bag, along with an extra set of clothes in case of an accident."

Nate stiffened. "Oh, uh, he's not potty trained yet. He doesn't seem to get the concept of going on the toilet."

Trish chuckled and it lit up her eyes. Darcy liked her. She was genuine.

"Many of our special needs students are still potty training. We'll work on it in class. If he sees the other children doing it, then it might give him incentive to learn."

"That would be great. If you have any tips you can pass along to me on how to get him to actually pee on the pot, I'd appreciate it. I'm flying by the seat my pants, here."

Darcy enjoyed the seat of his pants, very much, thank you. Today's were navy blue and fit him well without being too snug.

"We're here to help. Feel free to ask any of the therapists for advice, also. Oh, and Libby, the OT, only works here part time. She's available for home visits, if you ever think Tanner needs a little more in the way of services."

Mrs. Ramirez gave Nate a school handbook, then went over a few of the rules and explained the drop off and pick up procedure. For Darcy to enjoy in her new fancy Beamer. Well, not hers exactly, but hers for now. She'd take it. Beat the broken-down piece of shit she'd left behind in Mary's garage.

"School starts a week from Wednesday, and we have an

Open House the night before. It's all in the information packet I gave you. Do you have any other questions?"

Nate's eyebrows drew together intensely. "What do you do if he has a meltdown? If he won't stop crying? I hate seeing him so upset, but I won't be here for him."

"We're trained to take care of children who have special needs. Tanner isn't the first child on the spectrum that we've had here."

Shaking his head, Nate said, "I'm sorry. Of course, you're trained for this. I'm being ridiculous."

Darcy thought he was being incredibly caring. Her own mother had never cared what kind of help Zane needed. If she'd ever been to an IEP meeting, doubtful she understood a word of what was said.

"No, you're being a good parent. And we're here for any questions. Mrs. Adams usually sends a daily notebook home letting you know how your child's day was. Any therapies or activities he's engaged in during the day should be in there."

The meeting was wrapped up, with the school secretary, Maggie, getting their emergency contact info card.

They picked Tanner up from his classroom. Once in the car and on the way home, Nathaniel touched her elbow. He needed to stop. It did things to her that she couldn't deal with. Things she liked too much.

"Thanks for coming with me today, Darcy. I appreciate the support. And the help when you spoke up about Tanner's schedule."

"No sweat. The kid needs a bit of time to adjust to school. They knew that. It wouldn't have been a problem."

They drove the rest of the way in silence, with Tanner humming in the back seat. It sounded like happy humming. He wasn't stimming.

After they got back, and Tanner had been sprung from his seat, Nate stepped closer to her. "I want to apologize about earlier. The comment about your clothes. It was inappropriate, and I never should have said anything. Not that it's an excuse, but I've been a mess all day, thinking they might suggest putting Tanner in a residential facility."

Who in the world had given him that idea? It was absurd.

"You're a mess, huh? Kind of hard to believe when your pants still have a crease in them."

He closed one eye and pursed his lips.

"One of these days, I'd love to try and really mess you up." Reaching up, she tousled his hair with her fingers. "It could be fun."

∽

NATHANIEL SIGHED as he wiped peanut butter off Tanner's hands, then glared at Darcy who bent over to pick up the crumbs she'd swept from the floor. The sight of her backside almost made him forget what he wanted to say.

"Why in the world did you agree to this ridiculous party? My birthday was five days ago, not today."

Darcy dumped the contents of the dustpan in the trash. "It wasn't my idea, GQ. It was your mom's. And it's today because it's Saturday, and most people have the day off, unlike your birthday which was Tuesday. Not key birthday party time."

He watched as Tanner skittered down the three steps into the family room. Right to his car so he could roll it across the coffee table. "We didn't need to have a party at all. I'm okay with ignoring it."

Darcy crossed her arms across her chest. He wasn't sure if that was good or not. She wore a loose pair of overall shorts in a camouflage pattern that showcased her amazing legs and kind of hid her chest. Kind of. If you didn't look at her from the side to see she only had a black tube top on under it.

"First off, it's your thirtieth birthday. That only happens once in a lifetime. Got to live it up."

"So when you turn thirty, I can give you a huge shindig?"

She looked at him funny. Yeah. What was he thinking planning something for Darcy that wouldn't happen for another six years?

"Second, your mother wanted the party. She says you've been stressed lately and needed something to keep your mind off everything."

"I wasn't stressed when I was down the Cape. I took time off work to play on the beach and build sandcastles and swim in the pool."

"Number one rule: don't argue with the mom. If she says you need a birthday bash, then I throw you a birthday bash. What's the big deal?"

"First," he threw the list back at her. "It's at my house, which means I need to make sure the place is all picked up and perfect."

"Hey, I'm the one who spent all day yesterday cleaning it. And face it, you never allow the house to even get dirty. Tanner's not the type of kid who's bouncing all over the place, shedding dirt on the carpet."

She had him there. He wouldn't mention that the cleaning lady came every Thursday to do the floors and bathrooms. Didn't mean he wanted a party. He hated being the center of attention.

"Second, this week was a busy one with the meeting at Tanner's school and trying to catch up with everything I've missed at the office. I'm exhausted and was hoping to relax for the day."

Darcy walked closer, and he took a step back. Those dark red lips were asking for trouble. Trouble in the form of a kiss. And wouldn't that be a big mistake.

She squeezed his arm. "I'm sorry. I thought I was doing

the right thing. But all you need to do is sit back, relax, and chat with your relatives. I'll take care of everything else. No sweat."

"Everything?" He grinned, knowing his mother had made arrangements for the food.

"Well, all the hostessing sh…stuff." Her gaze flew to where Tanner rolled his car around. "Your mom and aunts are bringing all the food, and Amy dropped off the paper goods yesterday. I think Kevin is in charge of drinks."

"Guess we'll have beer, then. Kevin might be a cop, but he likes a good brew when he can."

"Is he gonna give everyone a Breathalyzer before they leave?"

"He might."

"I'll be on my best behavior." Her eyes flashed attitude.

"Listen, Darcy, it's Saturday, and you've been amazing all week with Tanner. I know I said no drinking and stuff with Tanner around, but I'll be here and so will my mom, so if you want a few drinks, go for it. It's not like you need to drive home after."

"Thanks, Biff. I'll keep it to a few. Can't have the hired help dancing on the tabletops. Though I gotta tell you, I do a mean sprinkler."

"What does a sprinkler have to do with dancing?" The visual of Darcy swinging her hips on his picnic table was one he needed to obliterate quickly.

She pursed her lips. "It's a dance move, Biff. You need to get with the program. You're too young to be this stiff."

After skipping down the steps into the family room, Darcy turned the stereo to an upbeat tune, then put one hand behind her head and started jerking the other one in the air from her side to the front. Her hips popped in rhythm with her arm. It took him a second before he realized…sprinkler.

What would they think of next? He had to admit she made the silly dance step look kind of sexy.

Tanner watched her, and she gently took his hand and moved it in the same motion she'd been doing. Nathaniel chuckled as the child attempted to copy her. They danced around for a while, before Darcy gathered his son and trotted up the stairs for a nap.

His mom and dad showed up about an hour later, carting in bowls and plates of food.

"Happy Birthday, Nathaniel." His mom kissed his cheek.

"You already said that when you called me Tuesday night."

She gave him the mom eye. "I can say it as many times as I want."

"Of course, you can, dear." His father patted his wife's shoulder. "Nathaniel appreciates it, I'm sure."

Way to put him in his place.

"I do appreciate it. I'm sorry, Mom. It's been a busy week, and I'm a bit grumpy." They should know that. It was nothing new. He'd been grumpy for the past four years, maybe longer.

"Which is why you needed a party. Good food and family always make everyone feel better."

His mother was such a people person. His dad, too. Nathaniel sure didn't get his personality from them.

"Luci and Molly are bringing more food. I arranged everything so Darcy didn't have to take time away from Tanner to cook." She looked around. "Where are Darcy and my grandson?"

He pointed to the stairs. "Darcy put Tanner down for an early nap. We figured it would be easier than keeping him up and having him cranky while everyone is here."

"So thoughtful. How's she working out? Better than your other nannies, I'd wager."

"Much better. She seems to really get Tanner."

His dad twisted his head to gaze out the window. "Glad it's working out for you. Pete and Molly are here. I'll go give them a hand. Knowing Molly, she brought enough food for an army or two."

"Or three." Aunt Molly was the sweetest and always made sure everything was organized to the last detail. When they were teenagers, Erik had complained to him a time or two that his mother's love of lists could get tiresome at times, especially when he'd wanted some non-family time with a local girl.

He turned to his mother, who was putting bowls in the fridge. "What do you need me to do?"

"Absolutely nothing, sweetie. I want you to relax and enjoy being with your family. I think most of your cousins will be coming, and you used to always have such a great time when you were with them."

Sure, before he'd gone to Brookside Academy and started worrying about what people thought of him. Then, Helene had come along, and he'd slipped even further from the family who loved him. He just wanted to enjoy life again. He'd gotten a taste of that this summer.

"There's my grandson. Hello, sweetie, did you have a good nap?"

Darcy trotted down the stairs, Tanner in her arms. At the bottom, she handed the child over to his grandmother, who pulled him in for a tight hug. He'd discovered that Tanner preferred deep pressure rather than a loose embrace.

"What can I help you with, Anna?"

Nathaniel frowned as he noticed Darcy's face. She'd applied more makeup in the short time she'd been gone, really accentuating her eyes with a thick black outline. Her lips...Damn, they were painted completely black again. The war paint was on full force.

"Oh, you've helped so much already just being here for Nathaniel and Tanner."

"But you've got the kid now, and I'll bet you want to spend some time with him. That frees me up to get this party rockin'. Does some of this food need to be kept cold?"

His mom pointed at a tray on the counter as Aunt Molly and Uncle Pete strolled in, hands laden with more food.

"I don't think I have enough room in the fridge for all of that," Nathaniel said.

"Don't worry." Uncle Pete cocked his thumb toward the patio, visible through the back windows. "We brought a few large coolers. Molly wanted to put the desserts in here on the dining room table first."

"Let me give you a hand with that." Darcy bounced over and took a large platter from Uncle Pete, then stalked over to the door. Was she as anxious with so many people as he was?

"I'll help, too." When his mother started to object, Nathaniel shook her off. "I can't stand around doing nothing. My parents raised me better than that."

Grabbing a large salad bowl, he trotted off behind Darcy. He'd said the perfect thing to keep his mother from arguing with him. Outside, he slid up behind Darcy and placed the bowl inside the enormous cooler that had been deposited on the patio.

"Did Tanner wake up on his own?"

Darcy ran her hand through her spiky hair, then shook her head, the strands rustling like dark wheat on a windy day. "Nah. I rubbed his back, so he came out of it slowly."

"How'd you get him to nap earlier than usual?"

"Classical music. Didn't you notice he likes it? It seems to calm him down. I've been playing it for him at night, too. I know you've heard it. You usually help to put him down and at least kiss him goodnight."

"Yeah." He shook his head. "I hadn't connected the two

until now. Could be why he used to play with my stereo all the time. I had John build the cabinet with the higher shelf, so he couldn't keep fiddling with it. I was afraid he'd break it."

"Don't beat yourself up over it, Biff. It's a parent's job to keep their kid from breaking all the good stuff. You're doing brilliant." She patted his arm, and some of the stress of the day eased out of him.

Taking her hand, he pulled her closer. Why did he like having her near? It transcended common sense. Could he convince himself it was simply the unique scent that was Darcy? Her dark-rimmed eyes scrutinized him, and he admired her boldness. They stood for a while, her soft skin warm against his. Had he ever felt this comfortable with Helene? And frazzled all at the same time?

No. Helene had been an expensive decoration he'd appreciated for her beauty. Unfortunately, there hadn't been much more to her. Tanner had paid the price.

Rubbing his thumb over her hand, he squeezed Darcy's shoulder with the other. "I'm only surviving because of you. You've taught me so much about my son. Not sure how I'll ever repay you."

The gleam in her eye glistened bright. "You can make sure I get two pieces of cake. I hear Luci's quite the cook."

He laughed. If that's all she wanted, he could make it happen. "You've got it. If for some reason there isn't enough, I'll let you have mine."

"The birthday boy giving up his own piece of cake? Radical. It's a deal."

Her grip loosened and melted away. Disappointment filled him. Too many people were arriving to examine this thing, whatever it was between them.

Kevin arrived, hauling a large cooler. Darcy's eyes appraised the muscles bulging under the weight. Yeah, Kevin worked out. Nathaniel played racquetball and kayaked, but the weightlifting his brother did had resulted in a different physique. Did she prefer that kind of shape?

"Hey, bro, happy birthday. Got a six pack of your favorite imported beer."

"Sounds great." He slapped Kevin on the back, then shook his hand.

Most likely, he wouldn't be indulging in the alcohol if he had to stay aware of Tanner. He'd given Darcy the green light to drink, but he wasn't sure how much she'd actually consume, and he didn't like to take chances.

Two more cars drove along the road. One pulled up the driveway. Striding over, he greeted Erik, Tessa, and the kids.

"I can't believe you drove all the way down here with a new baby to wish me a happy birthday."

Erik released Matty and Kiki from their car seats and unclipped an infant seat from the middle. Tessa slid out of the front gingerly, hefting a large diaper bag over her shoulder.

"Happy Birthday, Nathaniel." Tessa leaned up to kiss his cheek. A far cry from the shy teenager who'd come to live next door to Gram and Gramps over a decade ago.

"Thanks. Let me take that." Tessa handed over the diaper bag, then gave Erik some sort of look that Nathaniel didn't understand, but Erik obviously did.

"I'll be in the house. Come on, Matty. Erik, you have Kiki and Joey."

The pretty brunette shuffled up the walkway with the little boy. Kevin bounded up behind them and grabbed Kiki, swinging the toddler up into the air. The little girl shrieked, then giggled.

Erik shifted the infant seat to the hand opposite his cane. "It was a long drive. She and Matty both need the bathroom. Joey's going to need to nurse soon."

"How's Tessa feeling?"

Erik monitored his wife and son's progress into the house. "She's recovering. I wish I could do more to help."

"Well, let's find someplace private for you guys to get set up."

Kevin plunked Kiki on his hip. "We're all family here. No one's going to care if she's feeding the baby."

Erik frowned. "No one else will care, but have you met my wife? It took forever for her to even hug the family."

Kevin smirked and stroked the baby's closed fist. "She did a bit more than hugging to get this little guy."

Erik shook his head. "That's because she likes me better than the rest of you schmucks."

Cocking his head, Nathaniel headed toward the house. "She can use my room."

He wanted to offer to carry the infant seat as he saw his cousin struggle. But he also knew Erik. He'd hate anyone thinking he couldn't cope with a small child.

"You came a long way."

As they entered the house, Erik handed the baby seat over to Uncle Pete. Aunt Molly immediately dove in to release her grandson from the constraints.

"We're actually staying at Alex's tonight. Joey's being baptized tomorrow at the family church."

"Not only Joey," Molly said, holding the baby to her shoulder and rubbing his back. "Matty and Kiki are being baptized as well."

Erik grinned. "Yup, the adoption was finalized last week. The kids are officially ours."

Nathaniel clapped Erik on the back. "Congratulations. You went from being a father of none to the official father of three in a few weeks' time."

"It's pretty great. Tiring but great."

Tessa strode in holding Matty's hand. Nathaniel pointed

the way she'd just come. "My bedroom is that door on the left. There's an upholstered chair in the corner or you can use the bed. Whatever works best."

"Can you make sure Kevin still has Kiki?" Erik asked. "I'll be out as soon as I get Tessa settled."

"Sure. Why don't I take Matty and Tanner out there, as well? Looks like Greg and Ryan are here. That kid is great in getting them all playing together."

His mom set Tanner on the floor as Matty skipped over and took his hand. Nathaniel held his breath waiting to see what his son would do. He wasn't sure if he remembered the boy.

"I'm your cousin, Matty."

"Matty. Cousin."

Tanner took the boy's hand and together they trooped outside. Nathaniel followed behind.

CHAPTER EIGHTEEN

*D*arcy pulled a soda out of the blue cooler. The red one held beer. As much as Nate had given her the okay to have a cool one, she wouldn't. She never wanted to take the chance of getting addicted to anything. Alcohol, drugs, Biff.

Ha, that was a ridiculous thought. Not that she couldn't get addicted to him.

The fact was it might already be too late.

Gulping back a huge swig of soda, Darcy shook her head. Maybe the beverage would explode inside her and take out the rest of her brain cells. 'Cause she couldn't have many left, if she was having lustful thoughts about Nate.

Another car pulled in front of the house, and long blonde hair flashed in the sunlight. Sara. A friendly face. If she'd brought the boss along, then two friendly faces. No one could claim the Storm family weren't friendly. They were. To a fault. But the Happy Days vibe always got her twitching, wondering if she was trapped in a time warp. Maybe Fonzie would zoom by on his bike and take her away from all this.

Sara pulled a platter from the back seat as TJ rounded the

car to help her. Behind him was...Zane. OMG. They'd brought her brother with them.

"Zaney!" Running across the yard, she plowed into him, wrapping her arms around his neck. He clung to her as tightly. "I didn't know you were coming. I was planning to drive down tomorrow to see you."

TJ shrugged. "Figured since we were heading up today, we'd bring him along. We're staying overnight at Alex's for the baptism tomorrow. Hopefully, Nathaniel has room for Zane here. Not sure how many beds are left after Erik and his crew get at them."

"There's a pull-out couch in the spare room next to mine. Nate had it delivered yesterday in case Zane came to visit. So groovy you brought him."

Sara smiled what the boss man called her 'ray of sunshine smile'. "We want you to be happy, Darcy. We figured you missed him." Sara dropped the food on the picnic table.

"I missed you, too, Darcy." Zane still held tight. Had she made a mistake moving here without her brother? She'd promised Nate she'd stay until he got a decent nanny for Tanner. Had he even looked since she'd been here?

"You know you can come here to live, right, Zane? Nathaniel has another room if you aren't happy where you are."

Zane's eyes widened and almost sparkled. "No, Darcy, I love my new apartment. I get to stay in it by myself." His hands started to vibrate, and she hugged him tighter to get him settled.

"Mary and Jim are so nice to me, and Jim brings me to my new job every day. I get to help him pick up all the cardboard boxes and even put some of the boxes of nails on the shelves. I have to make sure to check the numbers carefully, so they are the same. But I'm good at that. Remember how good I was at matching in school? Jim says it made me perfect for helping him put the boxes of nails away."

"So, you like your new job?"

"Yup, and Mary is a really good cook. She makes my favorite, macaroni and cheese, but she doesn't use the box and the orange powder like you do. She uses real cheese, and it tastes super good, Darcy. You should try to make it like Mary does. She can give you the recipe if you ask her real nice."

"I'll do that, Zaney. I'm sure it's great." Was it great that her brother didn't need her anymore? He was being useful and a contributing member of society. It had been her goal for so many years. Her whole life it seemed. Why did it make her feel like crap right now?

"We'll stop by and pick him up tomorrow late afternoon," TJ said. "That way you'll get a good long visit with him. Unless you'll be coming to the party after the baptism. You could bring Zane then."

Nate hadn't said anything to her about a party. Was she not invited? Why would she be?

"Mary and the others at the store all say hi. It's not quite the same without you there."

"Better, less stressful?"

"No." TJ stared at her, his eyes warm. "Quiet. Kind of boring, believe it or not. Has Nathaniel started his search for a new nanny?"

She lifted one shoulder. "Why would he when he has me?"

"Why indeed?"

"Well, come on, Zane, boss, there's tons of food to be eaten. Anna and Molly already brought a ton, and there's Luci pulling up. I hear she's the one you really want to get friendly with."

Darcy held Zane's hand and introduced him to the people who had shown up. Nate's sister, Amy, immediately began talking to him, asking him all sorts of questions about where he went to school and what he'd learned. She was in college studying Communication Disorders. Was she studying Zane? Since she was being super nice and seemed truly interested, Darcy didn't care.

TJ brought Zane's overnight bag inside, and Darcy lugged it up to the guest room.

"Good thing we got that pull-out couch." Nate appeared behind her in the bedroom doorway.

She pivoted and stuck her hands on her hips. "Did you know they were bringing Zane today?"

Nate shook his head. "I thought you were planning to visit him on the Cape tomorrow. Now, you don't have to."

"Right. Cool. But I'll need to get him back to TJ and Sara, so they can drive him back to the Cape. Is the party after the baptism at Alex's?"

Nate ran his hand over his neck. "Yeah, I didn't tell you about it because it's your day off. I thought you'd be visiting Zane, and I didn't want you to feel obligated to go."

She pushed one shoulder up in the air. "Totally get it. It's not my family, and I'm the hired help. No reason for me to go, unless you want a body to watch Tanner."

A strange look crossed his face as he trudged forward. "I don't want you to think of yourself as the hired help. I mean…yes, you're helping me. And yes, I'm paying you, but… okay, bad example. What I'm trying to say is I hope you're here as a friend who's doing me a favor."

His hand lifted and stopped short of her face, then landed gently on her shoulder. "I'd love for you to come with me tomorrow, and not just to help with Tanner. I know my family all think highly of you, too. You and Zane are welcome. But if you'd rather have the time with your brother by yourself, I understand, too."

Darcy wasn't sure how to respond. And for her, that

never happened. But frack, his hand on her shoulder almost seared right through her bare skin. Why did this spiffy lawyer have such an effect on her?

Taking a deep breath, she managed to twist her mouth sideways. "No sweat. I'll chat with Zane and see what he wants to do."

Dropping his hand, Nate spun and took her hand to pull her along. "Whatever you want. Now, let's get this party started."

He kept hold of her hand until they got to the bottom of the stairs. So many people. Aunts, uncles, cousins, and their kids. Darcy's head spun with the magnitude of it.

For the next few hours, she got pulled into conversations with Alex's future wife, Gina, whom she really loved. The woman was unique in so many ways.

Darcy helped Tessa with her kids, even holding the new baby for a few minutes. As she stroked the infant's face, memories of cuddling her daughter seconds after she was born floated through her mind. The pain of loss ripped through her, and she soon found another willing adult to take the child.

She made sure Zane had enough to eat without overdoing it. He didn't always remember to limit his food. Luckily, he had a fast metabolism, which kept him thin. That and the running around he did with the kids. He loved kicking the ball to Matty and Tanner, who surprised everyone by chasing it a few times. Of course, then Tanner would stop and run the Hot Wheels that was never far from his hand over a chair or table.

Nate, Kevin, and all the cousins shot hoops in the driveway for a while after they'd eaten. She moseyed over every now and then, subtly ogling the shirtless ones.

"Those Storm men do take your breath away, huh?" Gina

sighed from beside her. "If I weren't so in love with Felix, I'd make a move on one of the others for sure."

Laughing, Darcy eyed the men. "Which one?"

Gina crossed her arms over her chest. "Hmm, let me see. Not Erik, since he's already married. Plus, he was always a bit too cocky before he was injured."

"You've known them all a while, then?"

"I lived next door until my father died, then I'd visit my grandmother anytime I was in my mother's way."

No father and a mother who couldn't be bothered to parent. Gina's life wasn't that far from her own. Except Darcy didn't have a grandmother to take her in.

"What about the others?"

"I didn't know Nathaniel and Kevin as well, since they didn't live on the same street. But Nathaniel always seemed a bit shy. He didn't put himself out there much. Very serious. Unlike Kevin who is undoubtedly a good-time party boy. It's funny he became a cop."

"Yeah, Nate and Kevin have the same coloring. That's all they seem to have in common."

"Then, there's Luke. He's the playboy. He was always chasing some girl. Still is. Who knows if he'll ever grow up and settle down?"

"That leaves Greg. Would he be your choice?"

Gina's eyes never left her fiancé. "Greg is great. Kind of sucky losing his wife when Ryan was only a few months old. But he's steady. If you ever wanted to make a move, I'd go for Greg."

"We weren't talking about me."

A smirk appeared on Gina's lips. "Weren't we? You can't go wrong with a Storm. The family is the best I've ever run across."

"Thanks for the tip, but I'm not in the market."

The guys finished up and started pulling their shirts back

on. Gina winked at her before strutting over to Alex. "Neither was I."

Darcy zeroed in on Nate and the snug T-shirt now clinging to his sweaty torso. She shouldn't, but it was getting harder and harder to deny the pull he had on her.

"Everything okay?" he asked as he sidled up next to her and placed his hand on her shoulder. He'd been doing a lot of that lately. Did he know how much it freaked her out? Did he sense the electric charge that surged through her skin?

"Yeah, I think your mom wants to do cake and ice cream now." Good excuse. Sounded valid.

"Sure, let me cool down first."

He joined his brother and cousins in running the hose over his head, then shaking like a dog. Anna, Molly, and Luci rolled their eyes and shook their heads at the antics of their children. And the boss, who fit right in with the guys. Darcy was glad to see him feeling so comfortable with this family after all that had happened to him in the past. He was a good man and deserved good things.

Darcy found Tanner with his grandmother and led him into the house to grab the present they'd made for Nate. She waited until he'd opened his other gifts, a few ties and sensible things but a few gag gifts, as well.

"Give this to Daddy." She directed Tanner to hand his father the wrapped present.

"Thanks, buddy." Nate kept Tanner against him as he tore apart the paper. When he opened the box, his face tightened, and she swore his eyes turned misty.

"Did you make this?" He held out the picture of Tanner's handprints turned into several animals.

Tanner pressed his hand up against the print that looked like a dog. "Woof. Fwecko."

"This one does kind of look like Freckles. Thank you,

buddy. I absolutely love it." He pulled Tanner in for a tight hug and kissed his head.

She'd never tell Nate how much Tanner had hated having the paint on his hands. The look in his eyes as he beamed at his son was beautiful. Every father should look at his kid that way.

As wrapping paper was cleaned away, Nate held the framed painting and marched her way.

"I assume you did this with him?"

"I helped a bit. The handprints are all Tanner."

"These are perfect. Something I'll cherish always. Thank you."

Leaning down, he placed his lips on her cheek. It was only a tiny peck, but his mouth lingered for a few seconds longer than she would have expected. The contact set her heart racing, and she knew she was in trouble. She needed to get this strange reaction to him under control.

CHAPTER NINETEEN

"Let's go. Let's go."

Nathaniel picked up Tanner's new backpack and whirled around the see where he was. In the family room with his toy car. Big surprise.

"Biff, where's the fire? They told us at the Open House last night, if we were driving our kid to school today, to wait until after all the buses had left. It gets too congested with people trying to bring their kids into the school while the buses are offloading."

"I know, I heard them. I don't like being late. I love my mom, but she had a habit of being late every time we needed to be somewhere. I used to try and get rides from other moms who ran on time, so I wouldn't get noticed for slipping in after start times."

"You know, for a hot shot, big wig lawyer, you sure don't like to be the center of attention."

Picking up Tanner, he headed for the door. "You finally noticed."

He knew his mom had only started her tardiness after she had her third kid, but at nine, he'd hated showing up last to baseball practice or needing a tardy slip if he'd missed the bus.

"Do you actually need me to help you walk him into the building?" Darcy paused by the car door as Nathaniel buckled Tanner into his seat.

He motioned for her to get in, then settled in, also. "Don't you want to see him on his first day at school?" She'd referred to the boy as 'our kid' a few minutes ago. It was possible she'd simply been quoting what the teacher had said last night. Either way, he wanted her there.

"Of course, I do." Her voice was soft and filled with emotion. "Are you gonna be all right?"

"Why wouldn't I be? Kids start school every day. It's nothing new. It's not a bad thing to want to be on time."

As he steered down the street, Darcy rested her hand on his forearm. "It's okay to be nervous, but I liked the teachers and specialists we met last week. I think they'll do a great job with Tanner."

"I know. I know. Thanks. I'm being a wuss."

Her hand continued to warm the spot on his arm. God, it felt good there. Comforting. Strange coming from the vampire sprite, yet lately he'd had this desire to touch her. And he had. He kissed her on the cheek after he'd gotten his present from Tanner. He knew he'd lingered a bit too long, but aside from a flush to her face, she hadn't said anything. Maybe that alone said plenty. Rarely was Darcy speechless.

When they pulled up to the school, a half dozen yellow buses were entering and exiting and blocking the parking lot. Cruising past, he pulled into the church parking lot on the other side of the street. He didn't dare look at Darcy. She'd have something to say.

When he did skim past her to check on how Tanner was doing, her lips twitched in a smug grin.

"Fine. You were right. Happy?"

"No, because now we have to sit here and wait until all the buses leave. Not that I have anything better to do. Nannying doesn't work too well when the kid you nanny for is at school."

"How about I take you for a late breakfast once we drop him off? Will that make up for making you wait?"

Her eyebrows knit together. "Aren't you heading into work today?"

"Not this morning, no. I wanted to make sure Tanner is okay at school."

"He'll be okay, Nate. In about ten minutes, you can stop worrying."

He lifted one shoulder. "I thought I'd pick him up today, too. 'Cause it's his first day."

She folded her arms over her chest. "Then, what did you hire me for if you planned to do everything for him, anyway? I could have stayed in bed and gotten my beauty sleep."

Heaving a deep sigh, he closed his eyes for a brief moment. "I'm only doing this for his first day. I do need to get back in the routine of going to my office in Portsmouth. But don't parents want to see their kid's first day of school?"

Her face tightened. "I wouldn't know. I'm not a parent." She shifted and stared out the window.

God. Her mom had probably never spent any time taking her to school. How could he have forgotten that?

"I think I'll stretch my legs for a minute. The buses look like they're almost done unloading."

He got out of the car, and a minute later Darcy did, too. She opened the back door and unbuckled Tanner. Nathaniel reached in to get his bag.

When he bent down to pick up his son, Darcy shook her head. "He needs to learn independence. I know you love carrying him around, but at school he should be walking by himself and carrying his own backpack."

She was right. He needed to stop treating Tanner like a baby. But damn it, he'd never had him as a baby. Helene had robbed him of three years of his child's life.

They each took one of Tanner's hands and crossed the street to enter the school. After checking in at the office, they headed down the hall to the classroom. His cousin, Leah, stood in a doorway, greeting children as they came in.

"Nathaniel, is today Tanner's first day?"

"It is. I think I'm more nervous than he is."

Darcy laughed. "No doubt, Biff."

"Darcy, it's great to see you again. If you're in the building, stop by or at least wave if I'm in the middle of something."

"I'll do that."

Another child shyly shuffled toward Leah. She leaned over and welcomed her to class. Nathaniel gave a wave of his hand and crossed the hall to Tanner's room.

Mrs. Adams stood inside the doorway with a huge smile on her face.

"Good morning, Tanner. I'm so happy to see you here today."

His son stared straight into the room, his gaze zooming in on the shelf where the Hot Wheels were held. Figures.

"We showed you where your cubby is last night. You can put your backpack in there and go sit in the circle area."

Nathaniel took the boy's hand. "When he's dropped off in the car loop, who's going to help him do this? Should Darcy come in and help?"

"Nope, we'll have several adults bringing the children in, and we'll help them. Hopefully, after a while, the routine will become something they do on their own. It's all part of the goals for these children."

Darcy touched his back as he helped Tanner slip his backpack off and hang it up. The contact was nice. Supportive. Something he needed at the moment.

One of the classroom aids came over and encouraged Tanner to go sit on the carpet. When the child did as told, Nathaniel reached to say goodbye.

Darcy stopped him. "Don't make a big scene. He's distracted by the toys, and that's a good thing. We'll be back soon enough to get him. He's only here a half day today."

He allowed himself to be led from the room but couldn't help glancing back in to see how Tanner was doing. His son sat near a few other children who all had some sort of puppet in their hands. Tanner did, too. He was inspecting it closely.

"He's gonna be fine. You promised me breakfast."

"I did." As they went back down the hall, the sound of excited children echoed around them. Leah was now in a rocking chair, a dozen or more little faces gazing intently up at her.

"I hope that comes with bacon, because I could really use some salted pork right now."

He chuckled and set his hand on her back until they got to the car. Before he could open the door for her, she slid into his arms and clung to his waist. Immediately, his own arms surrounded her.

Maybe Tanner wasn't the only one who liked pressure when they were held. His anxiety seemed to release its hold on him and slip away.

He pressed his lips against her hair. When he'd kissed her cheek the other day, he hadn't wanted to stop. He'd desired to skim his mouth over her face and take hold of her lips. They'd been covered in black lipstick, and he should have been revolted. But all he could think of was kissing her until her lipstick was gone. He pondered how long it would take until her lips were all soft and pink again. Like he'd seen them each night after her shower.

Today, she wore the deep, blood red again. It seemed to be her concession for being seen with him in public. The eye makeup was also softer than typical. Like Darcy. She wanted everyone to think she was this tough as nails, street smart punk. And maybe she was. But he'd seen a much softer side to her.

He couldn't deny how she interacted with Tanner and connected on a level he only dreamed of and longed for. With her brother, she was fierce and protective, yet loving and compassionate all at the same time. Such a mixture.

And with him...? The teasing and sarcasm were still strong, but something had cracked in the wall she'd erected between them. Erected between many of the people in her life. Why? Why had she built this wall? And why was it now starting to crumble?

He wouldn't push the last question. Didn't want her aware her wall had weakened. He liked what he saw peeking out from behind it and was afraid if she knew, she'd fortify the battlements and build it even stronger than before.

~

Soft jazz filled the room as Darcy and Nathaniel tag teamed Tanner into his pajamas.

"Where's the dog?" Darcy crouched on the floor and stuck her head under Tanner's bed. Her delicious ass stuck in the air. God, the effort it took to look away.

"Dog." Tanner yelled and reached into his hamper to pull out the black and white stuffed animal.

"Oh, there it is, buddy. Does it need to be washed?"

Darcy stood up. "I'll see if I can do it tomorrow while he's occupied with something else."

"Tomorrow's Saturday. I'll be home, so you're free to take some time for yourself if you want."

"Time for myself? What in the world would I do with that?"

The music softened into a slow, sensual number, and his feet simply took over. Grabbing Darcy's hand, he swept her into his arms and swirled to the erotic beat. Her eyes widened and her dark red mouth formed an O when he pivoted, bringing her closer to his body.

"You could go dancing."

"I'm dancing right now. Why would I need to go again?"

"You could go with someone you actually like and whose company you enjoy."

Her hand rested on his shoulder, then her fingers sifted through the short hair on the nape of his neck. God, that felt like heaven.

"What if I enjoy *your* company, Biff?"

He laughed. "Have you finally cloned yourself and this is the non-sassy version?"

Her body swayed to the jazzy number floating through the room. "Maybe I'm just feeling the music deep in my soul."

As much as he'd love to keep her exactly where she was, they had a little boy to get to sleep. He spun to find him, and nearly fell over.

"Look," he whispered in her ear.

Her eyes searched for what he'd pointed out. Tanner held his black and white puppy and swayed to the sound like they'd been doing.

"Aww, that's beautiful, Biff. Can we let him continue for a little bit?"

"Only if we can, too."

Those dark eyes bore into him, but her hands never left his shoulders. Guess that was a yes.

What in the world was he doing slow dancing with the mistress of the dark without some formal occasion where he was required to? And he'd started it. For some reason, he'd needed to hold her in his arms.

"Not too bad, Biff. Was this part of GQ training when you started hanging with the rich boys?"

"No, this was my mother insisting we learn, because she loves to dance and wanted her kids to love it, too."

"Do you love it? You're good. Quite the smooth mover. Maybe where Tanner gets his smooth moves from."

Did he love dancing? Right now, the answer was yes. Because of Darcy. And wasn't that a kick in the pants. With Helene, he'd always been too conscientious of making a wrong step or missing a beat, but dancing with this little sprite was relaxing.

"With the right person I like it." That would have to do for now.

"Tanner is so adorable." Darcy's head lowered to his chest with her eyes peering in the direction of his son.

The boy hugged the stuffed animal close to his chest and kissed its head. Drawing Darcy nearer, he repeated the action with her. Even with her hair standing up almost straight, it still felt like silk, and the product she used to get it that way smelled like something floral. The scent of it made him grow hard. Or could that be Darcy's compact little body sliding against his?

Whatever it was, he was having a hard time remembering that he didn't like her, that they were polar opposites in every way. Except right now they both seemed to enjoy dancing with the other. They both cared deeply for Tanner and wanted the best for him. And they both liked watching vampire movies. The classic Dracula was on tomorrow night. Could he get her to watch it with him? Did she have plans for her Saturday night?

She'd been here a little over two weeks. Her first Saturday, she was still getting used to the routine and getting her room settled. This past Saturday had been his birthday party and his family had hung around until almost ten. His cousins, all of them, had made it a point to catch up and check on how he was doing, with Tanner, his law practice, and his personal life. The fact he'd been divorced over four years and it was only now they were touching base again, just showed what an asshole cousin he'd been in ignoring his family.

Keeping in closer contact with his cousins was a priority. Growing up as close as they'd all been, there was no reason for them to drift apart now. Why hadn't he used them for support when Helene betrayed him? Because he'd wanted to show he was strong enough to handle it on his own. And he was embarrassed. That he'd chosen someone as shallow and unfaithful as Helene.

The beat of the music picked up, but the tones were still a haunting jazz melody. Darcy's body wiggled in his arms, and he twirled her left and right. Tanner spun his dog, then slid into his bed, holding the stuffed animal next to his face. The boy reached out, touching the red racer, yellow bulldozer, and purple roadster, then closed his eyes. His routine. It was like magic once he touched that last car.

Now that Tanner was asleep, or close to it, he found he didn't want to let Darcy go. Had she even noticed Tanner was asleep? Her eyes were closed as well, yet her fingers still sifted through his hair.

Bending his head, Nathaniel lined his cheek up near her ear and inhaled her intoxicating scent. When he thought back to their first dance at Sara and TJ's wedding, he realized he hadn't seen her at all. The real Darcy. She was her own person and didn't give a shit what anyone thought of her. That alone was what made Darcy so different from him.

He'd cared too much what others thought. Being one of the popular crew in high school had been such a rush. Of course, it had taken a few years and lots of hard work to scrape up the money for the right kind of clothes and tickets to the notable events. Luckily, he had good genes, so he'd had an advantage there. The difficult thing for him had been pushing past the introversion and desire to be alone, in order to make it with what he'd considered the 'right' friends.

And where had it gotten him? His career was due to good grades at an excellent school. His acceptance was most likely from the Storm name in town. Being one of the popular kids had only led him to Helene or led her to him. He liked to think she'd cared for him at some point. But with her actions, both to him and their son, he seriously doubted it.

His hands skimmed down Darcy's back pausing right above her bottom. They wanted to continue farther, but Nathaniel called on all his control and kept them where they were.

A soft groan drifted from Darcy's lips, and she stirred. When she saw Tanner asleep in his bed, she eased away. He kept his arms around her.

"He went to bed on his own," she whispered, staring up at him. Her eyes held a dreamy expression. What had she been thinking about while he'd been kicking himself in the pants over his past mistakes?

"He did." Still he swayed to the rhythm of the sensual music filling the room. Confusion crossed her face, but she didn't remove her arms from around his neck.

"Should we let him sleep?" She peeked over his shoulder at the child.

"I don't think we'll wake him. Dancing hardly makes a sound, except for the music, and we know Tanner likes the music."

"Do you need the practice for some reason? Got a hot date at the newest dance club?" Her eyes sparkled with mischief.

"No hot date. It's been a long dry spell since Helene walked out." Now, why'd he go and confess that ridiculous and embarrassing fact?

Instead of the laughter or derision he expected, her face softened, and she stroked his cheek. "I'm sorry she did such a number on you. It sucks. I understand, though. I'm glad you aren't one of those guys who works out his frustration by using women for sex because of the shitty one who crapped on you."

The vehemence in her tone made him wonder if she'd been used that way in the past. He hoped not. It was hard to imagine anyone getting away with something like that with Darcy, but there was a reason she was tough as nails.

This time she did pull out of his arms, her gaze darting around the room. "I guess I should jump in the shower. It's been a long week, and I could use a good night's rest. Unless you needed me to do something else tonight."

What would she say if he said he needed *her*? Probably laugh in his face and call him Biff or GQ. Then, add a scathingly flippant comment that put him in his place.

As she spun to leave, his tongue got the better of him. "Darcy?"

Pausing, she cocked her head. "Yes?"

"The original Dracula is on tomorrow night. If you don't have any plans, would you like to watch it with me once Tanner goes to bed?"

A tiny smile played about her mouth. Did she need more convincing?

"We can debate the nuances of the classic Dracula movies versus the newer sexier vampires."

"Sounds good. I'll be ready to get my debate on." She disappeared into the hallway.

As he picked up the odd toy from Tanner's floor and tidied things up a bit, he heard her get her stuff from her room. The bathroom door closed and the shower started. He pressed a kiss to his son's head and turned down the light and the music.

Tomorrow. Tomorrow night would be different. They'd sit on the couch together and enjoy the movie and some hot debate.

He wondered if he could interest her in anything else.

CHAPTER TWENTY

*D*arcy rubbed the towel through her hair and gave her head a shake. The dark strands floated into place. Spike it up or leave it down? She said she'd watch a movie with Nate as soon as Tanner was down for the night. She'd jumped in the shower, as usual, but couldn't decide if she should don her armor or not.

In the few weeks she'd been living here, her routine had been taking a shower at night and being scrubbed clean. No hair gel and no makeup, other than some moisturizer for her face. Nate had gotten used to her that way. If she suddenly went fully done up again, he'd know something was up.

It's not like it was a date or anything. Was it? He'd asked her last night about the movie. But they'd watched TV together a couple times since she'd been here. Usually with her picking up or cleaning something. Him with a laptop typing away during commercials. It had never been the two of them making plans to sit and watch a movie and discuss it.

Okay, no makeup. Keep the hair flat. The least she could do was comb it back behind her ears. It hadn't been cut in a few months and was starting to get long. When she brushed it back, she realized it didn't look so bad. Maybe a darker version of Molly Storm's adorable pixie cut.

Digging through her drawers, she picked out a loose tank top and some comfy shorts that didn't show her ass in all its glory. After peeking into Tanner's room and ensuring he was asleep, she padded downstairs. Maybe she should have put some socks on. Her toenails were painted a bright pink, and she had a feeling Nate might have something to say about that.

He stood at the fridge in the same cargo shorts and navy polo shirt he'd had on earlier. Tanner had worn a matching set. Even though she'd had today off, she'd still hung around the yard, reading a book. It wasn't too much of a hardship, sitting on the dock dangling her feet in the water while the sun beat down on her. Nate had gone out for a kayak ride with Tanner cradled between his legs. It had been utterly adorable. And some strange feeling inside her wished she'd been the one sandwiched so close to him. He'd invited her along, but she'd spent tons of time with Tanner all week and felt the kid needed some dad time. Without her interference.

He retrieved the pitcher of iced tea she'd made this afternoon. "Want a glass?"

"Sure. What time does the movie start?"

Glancing at his watch, he answered, "In about five minutes. Do you need snacks?"

She sauntered toward the couch, picked up the remote, and settled close to one side. "How about some garlic?"

His chuckle echoed through the large room. "I think I'm all out. Can we make do with an onion or scallions?"

"I don't know, Biff. Don't think the effect is quite the same."

After flicking on the TV, she picked up the glass he'd placed on the coffee table and took a sip. Was she honestly nervous? Why would she be? It was GQ and a movie, for

Pete's sake, not a date at the Ritz. Still, her stomach did a little flip thing that she hadn't felt before.

When Nate sat next to her, her breath hitched. He pressed some buttons on the remote, and the channel flicked to a black and white screen. His head cocked to the side, and he jumped up. Too close to her. He must have finally realized.

But he merely moved to the wall and dimmed the lights.

"Here we go." Nate settled back mere inches from her location and rested his arm along the back of the couch. "Now, this is how Dracula is supposed to be. None of this modern crap with touchy feely vampires."

"For your information, vampires have emotions, too. They're quite misunderstood."

His crooked grin flashed her way, and she almost swooned. Like she was a Victorian heroine in a novel. God, she was going soft. She should've put her makeup on. The pink toenail polish must have leeched into her veins.

They watched for a while silently, but every so often she had to laugh. "Dramatic much?"

"What are you talking about? This is some of the best acting of its time."

"Good thing time passed."

"Oh, shush." He grabbed her hand and squeezed it. "Here comes a great part."

The great part was he didn't let go of her hand. She shouldn't like his touch so much. There was no way in heaven or hell that Nathaniel 'GQ' Storm would ever think about Darcy Didn't-Finish-High-School Marx in any way other than as his kid's nanny or someone who worked at a bookstore. She could dream, though. Just for a minute.

When Dracula threw a hypnotic stare at one of the lady victims, Nate gazed at her. "You know, your lips are such a pretty color. I don't know why you hide them under the dark lipstick."

How did she respond to that? If it had only been a dig at the lipstick, she could have thrown something sarcastic back, but he'd called her lips pretty.

"I'm not wearing lipstick."

He smiled. "I know."

Her heart beat erratically as his gaze lingered on her lips. Movement from the screen had her jerking her head that way. "Oh, look, poor girl. She's done for now."

Dracula had the heroine in a hypnotic trance.

Nate followed her gaze, his hand still holding hers. "In these classic movies, the vampires aren't really sexy or appealing in any way. There are experts who feel—"

"There are experts on vampires?" she interrupted.

"Well, experts on vampire movies. They often felt the early vampires were feared by people because their evil intentions were clear."

"That's why I'd take Brad Pitt any day. He's my kind of vampire."

"You probably liked Spike and Angel, too. I figured you for a Buffy kind of girl."

"I certainly wouldn't mind giving them an interview."

Nate laughed. So he wasn't only a classic vampire fan. He'd obviously seen the more modern ones, as well.

"Many argue that the modern interpretations of vampires are way too heavy on sex appeal of creatures who are inherently evil and not something to find attractive."

Scooting back on the couch, she faced Nate as he waxed on about vampire theory, mesmerized by this corporate attorney and his being serious about the issue.

The movie played on, and they watched. They also debated the merits of the classics versus the more modern views of the creatures.

Could she inch a tiny bit closer? He'd also taken a shower, and his natural scent rose to the surface and got her hormones itching. "You really know a lot about this subject. It's kind of surprising."

"Well, there are those who say lawyers are blood suckers by nature. Guess it's a natural attraction. I draw the line at biting a client on the neck."

"I vant to suck your blood." Her vampire accent was atrocious, but Nate laughed anyway. "You should try it sometime. You might like it."

"Try it, huh? Sure." He held out his hand in a claw shape and growled, "Come here." Just like Bela Lugosi on the screen. His eyes grew fierce as his fingers beckoned, and he repeated the command. "Come."

God, she wanted to do exactly as he asked. Follow him anywhere he wanted her to go. Where would he take her? And would she regret it later?

"Your will is strong." Nate's voice was low and rough. "Do you have wolfsbane to ward me off?"

He continued to stare, his hand signaling for her to move near. "I vant to suck your blood."

She grinned at him as he mimicked her previous attempt.

As he dove her way, his hands curled into claws, she careened sideways. Grabbing her shoulders, he laughed, then set his teeth against her neck. Her laughter died with the touch of his lips on her skin.

Darcy couldn't control the moan that escaped her lips or the tremor that rocked her body as his teeth scraped along her throat. Oh, Lord in Heaven. She arched her neck hoping he'd continue. He did. But soon the playful bites turned into sensuous nips and his tongue poked out to lick the spots he'd tormented. Was that groan from him?

Her eyes fluttered closed as Nate sniffed her hair and pressed kisses along her jaw. "God, you smell so good."

That was her thought of him as well. Poised above her, his nose nuzzled her cheek, the sensation causing ripples of pleasure to dance through her veins and zero in on the part between her legs. Holy shizzle. It had been a long time since she'd allowed any feelings to go there. But here they were, shouting to the world that they were still alive and in need of stimulation.

"You're right. I do like it." His eyes never left her face.

His deep voice had her clenching her thighs. Sliding her hand into his hair, she urged him even closer. "See? I told you."

As she guided his head, she aligned her lips directly with his.

∽

NATHANIEL SIGHED as Darcy's lips touched his. All he could concentrate on was the perfect body beneath him and the soft, enticing lips moving against his. The tart taste of the lemon from the iced tea mixed with whatever special ambrosia Darcy exuded. He couldn't get enough.

"So sweet," he mumbled against her lips.

Her eyes opened and some emotion he couldn't read crossed them. Was she regretting this?

Stroking the side of her face, he slipped his fingers through her silky hair. This time his tongue roamed along her bottom lip, then explored the top one. A gasp escaped from her mouth and he slid inside. Her tongue welcomed his and a battle ensued.

His cock hardened at the sensual sounds coming from her mouth. Her body shimmied next to his.

"You're driving me wild, Elvira. Must be a full moon."

"That should be my excuse." Her lips continued to torment him, push him deeper into needing her.

He stroked her neck where he'd lightly bitten a few moments ago, then caressed her shoulder, pushing the strap off. Following his fingers, he licked down her neck and along the arm that was now wrapped around his shoulder.

His other hand traveled across her throat, down to the valley between her breasts. The tiny breaths coming from Darcy's lips urged him on. He pressed his mouth to hers again. His hands stroked her sides, slid under her top, then paused as they found the curved underside of her breasts.

"This wasn't what I'd planned when I suggested the movie."

"No." Regret filled her voice. That he'd started it or that he'd stopped?

"Kind of a nice distraction, seeing as you've been tempting me for the past few weeks. Truthfully, it's been months."

"I haven't done anything to tempt you." Her eyes gleamed and her mouth twisted. "Unlike you, who struts around looking perfect and smelling like the god of passion."

He chuckled at her statement. "The god of passion? I'm a bit rusty on my mythology. Who is that again?"

She glanced up for a second, then grinned. "I think it's Eros, but I could be wrong."

"Eros?"

"Son of Aphrodite."

"That makes sense." What didn't make sense was how he couldn't get enough of her. He nibbled on her neck again, and she tipped her head to the side. Was that a hint? He didn't need it etched in stone.

Darcy's hands ran over his back as he sucked on a spot he'd discovered. Tiny whimpers drifted his way as her body shivered. God, he loved how responsive she was.

"You're not afraid I'll turn you into a vampire, are you?" he whispered into her ear.

"I'm not afraid of anything." She cupped his face and

kissed him. "It's far more likely you'd turn me into a corporate attorney. That would be kind of scary."

The movie played in the background as they pressed their lips together and stroked overheated skin. But he hadn't prepared for this and wasn't sure Darcy was ready either.

Shifting on the couch, he settled so they both lay on their sides, her in front of him facing the TV. "I need better instruction on this neck biting thing. Dracula's just the vampire for the job."

As he nibbled on her neck, she sighed. "You're a fast learner."

Darcy must have gotten the slow down message, because she focused on the screen after sending a questioning glance over her shoulder.

Don't make this weird. Let her know you wanted this.

"I guess I lost control tonight."

She stiffened. "Heaven forbid you lose control, Biff."

Crap. He didn't want her to feel slighted. Running his hand down her arm, then over her hip, he said, "Maybe I can lose a little control, if it's all right with you. But I don't want to overstep. I'm sorry if I did."

Her eyes darted in his direction, her mouth pursed. "I was hardly fighting you off."

"I know, but I wanted to be sure you weren't participating solely because you work for me."

She resettled on her back, a frown on her face. "Yes, you're paying me for a job, but I'm not doing this for you. It's for Tanner. I can leave at any time and go back to my job on the Cape, so I seriously don't feel the need to please you in any way, especially physically. Believe it or not, I find you attractive."

"You aren't too bad yourself."

"You've got some mad kissing skills, GQ. A girl could get used to that."

Shit, she'd said exactly what he wanted to hear. Still, he wouldn't rush her. As much as he'd love to take her into his bedroom and discover all that passion he'd felt bottled up in her kiss, he'd take his time with her.

Leaning in close, his nose to hers, he cupped the side of her face. "I wonder, if we do it more, we could get even better."

A smirk appeared on her kiss-swollen lips. "I thought you wanted to watch the movie."

After glancing at the screen, then back at the sensuous expression on her face, he shrugged. "I've seen it a few dozen times. Kissing, though. It's been a while since I've practiced any of that."

Her arms wrapped around his neck and tugged. "I'm all for helping you practice, until it's absolutely perfect."

CHAPTER TWENTY-ONE

*N*athaniel set his car in park, turned off the ignition, and tucked his keys in his pocket. After quickly checking his briefcase, he hopped out of the car and strolled into the house.

He'd had a little more pep in his step since Saturday night. Even his client, Stan, had noticed and commented on it. He'd waved it away, blaming it on the gorgeous weather.

When he opened the front door, he stopped and cocked his head to listen. Perfect. No sounds of a sad little boy crying or humming in distress. It had been this way since Darcy had arrived to oversee the care of his son. Three weeks tomorrow since she'd moved in and helped him get Tanner into a routine. Over three months since he'd seen how well Darcy interacted with him.

The boy had attended school three times now, and the notebook sent home from Mrs. Adams showed only a few tense situations. How each event occurred and how it was handled was all included in the daily notes. But today was Tuesday. Tanner had spent today home with Darcy.

After peeking into the playroom and seeing it empty, he

continued to his room. He tossed his briefcase on the bed, loosened his tie, and shrugged off his suit coat. Once he'd hung it up in the closet, he dug in his case and took out the presents he'd bought.

Soft music drifted his way, and he followed it to find Tanner swaying to a slow beat with his stuffed dog in his arms. Darcy was at the sink, rinsing something off. As much as he wanted to go over and nibble on her neck, something he'd done frequently the past two days, he needed to make his son a priority. Especially since Helene had never done that.

"Hey, buddy. Did you have a good day with Darcy?"

He stepped down into the family room. It took a moment, but the boy tipped his head up and parroted, "Darcy."

"How was your day?"

"Puppy." The animal flew into the air only to be caught in the child's hands.

Nathaniel held out one of the bags he'd brought in and shook it. "Tanner. For you."

His son paused and cocked his head. "Tanner."

"I got you a present. See?"

The boy inched forward and peered inside the bag. A big smile lit his face when he saw what it was.

"Go ahead. They're for you." He held out the bag for Tanner to take.

Tiny hands reached inside and pulled out two new Hot Wheels. A shiny red corvette and a green jeep. In an instant, Tanner had them rolling over the coffee table, his eyes glued to the moving wheels.

As much as he'd love a nice thank you and a hug, he knew the excited smile was the best he could hope for. It was far more than he'd expected.

Standing, he climbed the few steps back into the kitchen,

where Darcy snatched a look at Tanner. She ignored him as he approached, but he could tell she was aware of him.

When he reached her, like the past few days, he leaned in and kissed her neck, then nibbled on the soft skin.

"I'll make you a corporate attorney yet."

"You'll have to try harder than that."

He nipped a bit deeper and was rewarded with a shiver that shook her entire body. God, that turned him on. Helene had been more prone to fake gasps. He didn't even want to think about Helene anymore, now that he had Darcy. It was still early, and he had no idea how they'd even gotten here, but he hoped something good would come of it.

"I got you a present, too."

Spinning quickly, her mouth opened in a cute bow. "What? Why?"

"I can't buy you a present?"

Her eyes narrowed. "You don't need to buy me something because we've been kissing."

He handed her the bag and pecked her cheek. "I bought them as a thank you for taking such great care of my son. I appreciate it, Darcy. You have no idea how much. I used to come home from work, and he'd be standing with his sad face pressed against the window anxiously humming and rocking. It killed me."

She reached up and patted his cheek. "I'm happy to do it. I have fun with him."

Standing back, he crossed his arms over his chest. "Well, open it."

Darcy reached inside the bag and removed the flat, square box. Handing him back the bag, she lifted the lid. Another O crossed her lips.

"Now, you have earrings for all occasions. And they're hypoallergenic. Do you like them?"

"There's got to be a few dozen pair here. Do you hate the earrings I have so much?"

He touched her ear and caressed the side of her face. "No, they're beautiful. But I saw these and they reminded me of you. See this frog one? Remember last weekend down by the lake?"

Her laughter warmed his heart. He wasn't sure how she'd react. She wasn't as prickly now as she'd been when they'd first met, but she still had her moments.

"I do. And the butterflies and dragonflies and, oh, look at the flowers. Like the ones growing next to the shed."

He pointed in the box. "And here are some of the strawberries you like to eat so much. And the fish. And look, there are even a few moons. They aren't full moons, though, because then we'd be in real trouble."

Her eyes shown as she smiled at him. "I think you're real trouble, with your nibbling on my neck all the time. Now, you're giving me presents that have special meaning. Are you trying to make me cry, Biff?"

He stepped back. "What? No. I thought they'd be a good reminder of what you've done while you were here with us. A memory."

"A memory? Have you hired a new nanny? Do I even have time to pack before you boot me out the door?"

She thought…Whoa, he needed to back up a bit. Taking the box from her hand, he placed it on the counter, then ran his fingers down her arms.

"I was buying Tanner a few new cars, and when I went past the jewelry counter, I saw some of those earrings. I remembered what you said about the expense, because you have so many in your ears that replacing them wasn't something you did often. I made it a point to choose styles that would mean something to you, so you didn't think I was simply trying to get you to wear different earrings."

"So, not being booted out the door?"

"The truth? I haven't even had a chance to put an ad in anywhere for a new nanny. I refuse to use the same agency I did before. They were all unqualified disasters."

"I'm sure if they came from some fancy agency, they were highly qualified nannies."

"Yet still disasters when it came to giving my son what he needs. You're the best thing that's come our way lately, Darcy. The gift was merely a small appreciation for what you've done."

Her lips twisted to the side. "Then, I'll just say thanks and accept them graciously."

"Graciously?"

The attitude returned to her expression. "I can do gracious when I want to. Don't I look gracious?" She struck a pose with her hip cocked out and her fists on her waist.

He laughed. "Very gracious. The absolute picture of graciousness."

"Good, now be gracious enough to set the table. Dinner's almost ready."

He finally realized what the aroma was circling the room. Tomato sauce. It smelled like his Aunt Luci's recipe.

Moving to the stove, he lifted the lid off the pan and sniffed. "Did you make this?"

"Pfft. Me make homemade spaghetti sauce? No. Your mom dropped this off today."

After taking a tiny taste with the wooden spoon, he sighed. "Let me guess, Aunt Luci made a huge batch, and mom got more than she and my dad needed. She brought the rest over here for us."

"Bingo. You win a prize."

"What do I win?" He placed the cover back on the sauce, then swaggered to where she stood by the sink, lifting a bowl of spaghetti she'd poured from a colander.

Elbowing him out of the way, she placed the spaghetti on the table in the dining area, then went back to turn the stove off. She rotated and stared straight at him, her grin sly. "What do you think would be a suitable prize?"

He slid his arms around her waist and drew her close. "I think I'd like another shot at turning you into a corporate attorney."

Tilting her head to the side, she smirked. "You can certainly give it a try."

⁓

"What in the world, GQ?"

Darcy watched as delivery men rolled a large wooden box up the driveway and down the walk, toward the double back doors into the family room.

"It's Tanner's birthday present. I'm glad it got here while he was napping. I was hoping it would. I wanted to surprise him."

"How in the world did you get them to deliver it on a Sunday?"

"Money talks. When you buy something this expensive, they give you delivery when it's convenient for you."

Her mind whirled trying to figure out what it was. More climbing stuff for the playroom? Doubtful anything else could fit in there. Nate's friend, John, had installed some cool climbing equipment that went up to the cutest loft area. She'd spent the last few days sitting in it with Tanner, reading stories and playing with cars.

The men pushed the item into the large open area where she'd suggested a spaceship or a jungle gym. Okay, the box was too small for a jungle gym and wasn't the right shape for a bucking bronco. They set it close to the wall and started to remove the packaging.

"What is it?" She tugged on Nate's arm, needing to feel his skin against hers. It was becoming an addiction. One she didn't want to be cured from.

"You'll see. Have a little patience."

"All out of patience today, Biff. I had to clean the house for yet another birthday party. That's two parties in a two-week period of time. I also changed my day and visited Zane yesterday, so I could be here for Tanner's party today. You really owe me."

"I do." He bent and kissed her swiftly. She wanted to pull him back and continue. Unfortunately, they had company who looked at Nate for directions.

"Right there is perfect."

As they lifted the front cardboard panel off, Darcy finally saw what it was. A piano. Not the huge honking kind like TJ had in his house, but a square upright.

"You got Tanner a piano? This thing must have cost some bucks. The kid's only four."

Nate handed one of the guys a wad of cash as they picked up the scraps from the packaging and left.

"I know it's a bit outlandish for a four-year-old, but when we were at Sara's, he seemed to be interested in TJ's piano. And he was able to copy that song easier than I would have thought. He kept going back and playing it over and over. I didn't need to show him how to do it again. I thought, if I had a piano here, it might be something else he could do. Besides watching the wheels on cars."

"Do I get to use it, too?"

The cutest grin crossed Nate's face. "I'd be happy to teach you. It's been a while since my lessons, but I took advantage of TJ's Steinway and brushed up a little. I do a mean Chopsticks. We could start now, if you want."

She glanced at the clock on the wall in the kitchen. "Tanner will probably sleep another twenty to thirty minutes, and your family shouldn't be here for at least an hour."

Laughing, Nate pulled her to sit on the bench in front of the piano. He pressed his fingers to the keys and played something pretty. Darcy watched as his long thin fingers lifted and lowered, and notes floated through the room. He obviously wasn't as rusty as he'd made out.

Darcy settled beside him on the narrow bench and set her fingers on the keys. "So, what's my first lesson, maestro?"

"Do you know how to read music?"

She made a face at him.

"I'll take that as a no. Doesn't matter. I don't have any sheet music, anyway. I'll have to get some. I'd bet my mom has some of our old music that we used when we were learning to play."

He pulled out his phone and sent a text, then pressed a key in the middle. "The keys are A, B, C, D, E, F, and G. The black keys are the flats and sharps."

"Wait, how can they be both flat and sharp?"

He looked about to explain, then stopped. "That's kind of a long explanation for a first lesson. How about if I play you a tune like I did with Tanner and see if you can repeat it?"

His fingers pressed a few keys in the tune of Mary Had a Little Lamb. "Great. If I can't do it, I lose in my own version of Are You Smarter Than a Four-Year-Old?"

Nate pressed a series of keys babbling letters as he did. Was she supposed to remember these letters?

"Now, you do it."

"Do I have to spell whatever the heck you were spelling, because it isn't any word I've heard before?"

He glared at her, then took her hand and pressed the keys again, with the same alphabet soup. Then, he did it again. It was only seven notes.

"I can do this." Was she trying to talk herself into it?

Following Nate's lead, she pressed the keys in the same order. Not too bad.

"Good. Do it a few times."

Taking a breath, she repeated the notes again, then again. "Okay, I'm ready for the next part."

"You need a reward for doing so well with the first part."

"Was I better than Tanner?"

His lips twisted. "About the same."

"Did you reward him?"

Nate shrugged. "I played more notes. He seemed to like that. I was thinking of something a little different for you. To motivate you better."

Licking her lips, she smirked. "I like motivation. What have you got in mind? Something I'll like I hope."

"I hope you like it. I know I'll like it."

"But it's my reward and my motivation. Why should you like it?"

"Well, I need a reward and motivation to keep teaching you, don't I?"

She crossed her arms over her chest. "I guess. You still haven't told me what this reward/motivation even is."

He leaned closer and his lips closed in on hers. "Are you getting a hint yet?"

She licked her lips, hoping he'd take the hint. "Maybe."

When Nate's mouth touched hers, she released a sigh. His kisses had been so sweet, and she had a feeling she was getting addicted to them. He nipped at her lips, then eased away.

"Is that motivation enough?"

"I could certainly be coaxed into playing more piano, if I got a few of those after every practice."

"Tough negotiator. I think I need to see more practice before I hand out any more kisses."

She stuck her hands on the keys and pressed them in the

same pattern as before. He showed her the next few lines, which were fairly repetitive. It wasn't so bad. They stopped to go over the layout of the keyboard, and Darcy almost forgot the pattern entirely.

"You might need to teach me from a distance, Biff."

He sat up and cocked his head. "What? Why?"

"Because you distract me, and I can't think when you and your aftershave start working on me. I get hypnotized."

"My aftershave is hypnotizing?" His eyes gleamed. "Hmm, wonder what I could get you to do. Act like a monkey? Bark like a dog?"

"I bet you could get me to kiss you. Way better than barking like a dog in my opinion."

His hand slid behind her ear and cupped her head, drawing her near. This would never grow old. Not that she expected to still be here with him when she was old. But wouldn't that be a kick in the pants? Darcy and the corporate attorney. What a thought. Maybe a dream. A broken dream, more likely.

As Nate's tongue teased her lips, a cry came from the baby monitor sitting on the kitchen counter.

"Right on schedule." Her voice was breathy and soft. Sheesh, it's not like she hadn't been kissed before.

"I'll go get him. I want to see if he'll use the toilet again."

Darcy nodded, hoping her heart wasn't thumping as loud outside her body as it was inside. "He's used it a few times at school, too. He'll get there."

Nate squeezed her shoulder as he got up. After he trotted up the stairs, she played the tune one more time, then got up and went into the kitchen. Anna was bringing the cake and a few side dishes. Amy was scheduled for paper goods again. As a college student, she claimed it was all she had time or money for. Kevin, as usual, insisted he bring the drinks.

Hot dogs and hamburgers sat in the fridge ready to go on

the grill, so all Darcy needed to do was pull out the condiments and some serving dishes and utensils.

Nate's voice drifted down as he talked to Tanner in that tone she recognized as caring and patient. Who'd have thunk it? The man who'd almost fallen on his ass when he'd seen her at Sara and TJ's wedding rehearsal was a kindhearted soul who loved his son. One he didn't even know about until nine months ago. With what his ex had done to him, it was surprising he didn't have a huge chip on his shoulder when it came to the boy.

"Here's the birthday boy, and he used the bathroom. Great job, Tanner."

"What a big boy," Darcy crooned as she tickled him on the belly.

"Pee pee." Tanner bounced in his father's arms.

Nate smiled, and it lit up his entire face. Every time Tanner associated a new word with an actual item or event, his pride shown bright. What would it be like to have a parent do that with all your accomplishments? Her mother hadn't even realized she was there most of the time.

"I have something special to show you, Tanner." He carried the boy down into the family room and sat at the piano bench with the child on his lap. "Music. Remember?"

Tanner pressed the key in front of him, then paused. Darcy stepped closer and pulled out her phone to record. The expression on Tanner's face couldn't be anything but excitement.

Touching the black and white keys, the child tilted his head, then froze. Suddenly, he started playing the children's tune Nate had just taught her. Hot dog. The kid remembered it from a few weeks ago. She wasn't sure she could remember it from a few minutes ago.

When Tanner repeated the song, she turned the video off,

but continued to watch as Nate's eyes filled with tears. Frack, this guy needed to stop all the emotional crap.

He glanced up at her and grinned, apparently not caring if she saw his vulnerability.

"Proud daddy, huh?"

"Daddy," Tanner parroted as his fingers kept up the pattern on the keys.

Nate kissed Tanner's head and nodded. "Yes, very proud daddy. I love you, Tanner."

"Love Tanner." The child played his song. No interruption.

Now, Darcy had tears in her eyes. Not something she wanted GQ to notice, so she patted him on the back and went back to fiddling in the kitchen. Maybe it wasn't such a good idea to hang around here. This family reminded her too much of what she'd never had and most likely never would.

CHAPTER TWENTY-TWO

Nathaniel held Tanner snugly in his lap as the child played his new piano. Okay, maybe the piano was also for him. He might have fought against the lessons when he was a kid, but he had to admit the thought of starting up again excited him. Especially if it was something he and his son could do together. He'd start teaching him for now and decide later if he wanted to get a real piano instructor. One who truly understood an autistic child.

"Hey, Biff, your parents just pulled up," Darcy announced from the kitchen.

"Let's go see Mimi and Pop."

"Mimi. Pop."

His little magpie repeated those words until they arrived outside to greet them.

"Happy Birthday, Tanner," his mom sang out, holding her hands up. Universal sign for *Give me my grandchild.*

Depositing his son in his mother's arms, he kissed her on the cheek. "Hey, Mom. Dad. Thanks for coming over."

His dad lifted one eyebrow. "Like you could keep your

mother away when it's her only grandchild's birthday. She already missed the first three."

Knife to the gut. "I'm so sorry."

Kris Storm's eyes opened wide, and he frowned. "*You* have nothing to apologize for, Nathaniel."

His mom snuggled Tanner to her chest, kissing his cheek a few dozen times. "We have him now, and that's what's important."

"Come on inside and see Tanner's big gift," Nathaniel said.

His mom followed after him. "Is it the pu—"

"No," he cut in quickly, not wanting his son to hear the other present he was getting today. "Sara plans to bring that gift up later this afternoon. I haven't told this guy yet, because sometimes he doesn't understand today, tomorrow, yesterday, and other time units."

"Have you spoken with your sister lately?" His mom asked as they entered the kitchen. Darcy was nowhere to be seen.

"Yeah, she should be here shortly. She has today off." Over the summer, Amy worked at a residential camp for people with severe disabilities. He'd been picking her brain lately for ideas and information about adults with autism. Tanner was only four, and Nathaniel already worried about his future.

His dad set the cooler he'd been carrying down on the floor, then took the bowls from inside. "Where do you want these?"

"I guess the fridge until Kevin and Amy get here." He hadn't invited all the aunts, uncles, and cousins today. Tanner seemed to get overwhelmed when there were too many people around, and his family's numbers were not small. Since they'd all gotten together two weeks ago for his birthday, everyone seemed okay with not having to show up again. Not that any of them would have minded. He'd missed a lot by secluding himself after Helene left. While he'd been with her, too.

His mom lowered Tanner to the floor, and the child ran off, down the few stairs and over to the piano. Nathaniel's heart skipped a beat. Seemed he liked the gift.

"Oh, my. Would you look at that? You bought a piano. What made you decide to do that?" They followed Tanner down into the family room.

Before he could answer, his son started plunking out the tune he'd been taught.

His mom gasped. "How in the world did he learn that?"

Nathaniel explained about TJ's Steinway Concert Grand.

His dad shrugged. "When you're a famous songwriter, I guess you need something like that. How long did it take Tanner to learn the song?"

"About five minutes."

His mom appeared skeptical. "He's only four. None of you even started piano lessons until you were five."

"He hasn't done it since we left the Cape almost a month ago. But when I showed him the piano earlier, he just started playing."

Crossing her arms over her chest, his mom grinned. "We've got a prodigy maybe?"

"I haven't tried teaching him anything else yet. It may be the only thing he can play."

"He's already better than me." Darcy strutted down the stairs. She'd put on her war paint. Did she feel so uncomfortable around his family she felt she needed it?

His mom drew Darcy in for a hug. Her body tightened, her expression forlorn. What was that about? It was like she didn't want the contact, but she also desperately needed it.

A knock on the double family room doors had them all rubbernecking that way. Amy stuck her head in and asked, "Should Kevin put the cooler out here?"

"Sure," Nathaniel replied. "Since we're all here, might as well start cooking."

Amy joined Darcy and their mom and started pulling things out of the fridge. His dad marched outside to get the grill going

"I'll need the burgers and dogs. Do we want the rolls toasted?"

Amy tossed him a few plates and the bags of rolls. "Not me, but you know Kevin likes his charbroiled practically into ashes. Better do a few of each."

When he brushed by Darcy to get the meat, he whispered in her ear. "Toasted roll or not?"

She sent him a scathing look. Was he not supposed to flirt with her in front of the family? It wasn't something they'd discussed. Would it look bad that he was kissing the nanny?

"It's no biggie. I'll take whatever is left."

"Gotcha." After grabbing the meat, he skimmed past her again, allowing his hand to caress her back. The thin tank she wore over the black skirt didn't hide her taut muscles.

As the afternoon progressed, Darcy had a few cheeky things to say, but she seemed more subdued than in the past. She spent most of her time chatting with Amy about ways she could work with Tanner on his language skills. The speech pathologist at his preschool had sent home suggestions, and Darcy had been vigilant in following them.

"Are we ready for the cake?" His mom asked after they'd had time to digest some of the meal.

Darcy and Amy brought out the cake and a few containers of ice cream. His dad lit the four candles. They flickered in the air, but luckily the breeze was mild today.

When they began to sing the birthday song, Kevin at the top of his lungs as he'd done since he was a child, Tanner started rocking back and forth and covered his ears. Nathaniel immediately scooped him up and glared at his brother. Darcy insinuated herself closer to Kevin and whispered in his ear. His voice lowered as he threw Darcy his trademark smirk. Probably the one all the girls went nuts over, right before they agreed to date him.

His mom cut the cake, and Nathaniel let Tanner eat it on his own, in his own way. Which was not the way he'd seen Erik's kids eating cake. Tanner scooped a small amount onto the end of his fork, held it gingerly in front of his mouth, then stuck his tongue out to lick it. His son didn't like to have any food residue hanging around his lips. He and Darcy had been teaching him how to use a napkin to wipe his face.

"Nakkin," Tanner squealed when frosting dotted his upper lip. His panicked eyes darted back and forth until Amy tossed one in their direction. Maybe they'd better teach him how to lick food off his mouth, as well.

"So, uh, these birthday gifts we got the kid," Kevin said, leaning on the back of the chair Darcy sat in. "You said he was getting a pu—"

"He is," Nathaniel stopped him from giving away the secret. No sense getting Tanner all worked up until Sara and TJ arrived. Glancing at his watch, he said, "They should be here within the hour. I think they were bringing one to Greg and Ryan first."

Darcy pushed out of her chair and held out her hand. "Why don't I kick the ball around with Tanner while you get everything cleaned up?"

He smirked. "What if I want to kick the ball around with him while you clean up?"

The expression she leveled at him was comical. "You pay me to be the nanny, not the housekeeper, even though I do that, anyway. Today, I do the fun stuff. Problem with that?"

"Not at all. Just checking."

She pulled Tanner's favorite ball from the shed and gave it a little kick, and Nathaniel watched for a few minutes. The short, flirty skirt she wore flapped in the breeze, showcasing her amazing legs. The nights had started to get cooler, and he feared she'd be wrapped up in more concealing clothes soon.

A touch on his arm had him tearing his eyes away to focus on his mom.

"You seem so much less stressed than you've been since Tanner got here. I'm glad to see it."

"Yeah, well, Darcy keeps Tanner happy. Happy boy, happy father."

"It's wonderful that Darcy has worked out so great. I like seeing that smile on your face again. I've missed it."

He drew his mother in for a hug and kissed her head. "I'm so sorry I've been such a terrible son the last six, seven, eight years." How long had it been since he'd started dating his ex?

She reared back. "What are you talking about? You've never been a terrible son. Maybe a bit distracted, but you've never done anything to hurt me."

God, she was such a beautiful person. "I allowed Helene to distance me from the family. And then after she betrayed me, it still kept happening. I couldn't face anyone for the longest time."

"But you've fixed all that. You're starting to realize your family is here to help you. No matter what."

He hugged her again. "Thanks, Mom. I'll try to make sure not to push anyone away again. Except maybe Kevin." His brother had been kicking the ball around with Darcy and Tanner. The flirting between the two adults irritated him. Darcy was supposed to be watching Tanner, though deep inside he knew that wasn't the reason he was annoyed.

"What is Kevin doing now?"

"He's putting the moves on my nanny."

His mom smiled. "She is an interesting girl. I'm sure she has many guys wanting to get to know her better. Does she have a boyfriend?"

Had he ever asked her that? She'd been here a month, and there'd been no mention of one. And they'd been making out like freakin' teenagers this past week. If she had a guy in her life, they couldn't be very committed to each other. He should clarify that with her before they moved any further. And shit, it suddenly hit him that he did want to move things further.

His mom stared at him, and he shook his head. He hadn't answered her question. "I don't think she does."

"Then, is it a problem if Kevin gets friendly with her?"

Friendly? Not the way his brother thought of friends.

"Darcy is essential to keeping Tanner happy, and I don't need Kevin swooping in with his brand of friendship, then tossing her aside when he gets bored."

"I don't imagine Darcy would ever get boring, but I understand your concern. Kevin hasn't had the best staying power when it comes to women. I've learned not to get my hopes up too much when he brings one home."

They swiveled to look at the sound of a car in the driveway. Sara's SUV pulled to a stop.

"Darcy," he called. "Can you bring Tanner over here? His other present has arrived."

Her eyes sparkled, and she skipped over to the child. You'd think she was getting the puppy. She'd been more than excited when he'd told her he'd decided to go ahead and take one of Freckles' offspring.

While Darcy carried Tanner over, TJ and Sara strode up the walkway into the backyard. Sara's arms were filled with a wiggling black and white bundle of fur.

"Tanner, you have another birthday present, buddy." He ruffled the boy's hair, then pointed to Sara. "Remember Freckles."

"Fwecko. Puppies."

"That's right, Freckles had some puppies, and they're big enough to leave their momma."

"Momma."

Did the boy remember his mother? Miss her? Had Helene been in his life enough that he knew who she was? He'd never asked for her in the nine months he'd been living here.

When Sara lifted the puppy and put it near Tanner, his expression brightened. "Fwecko. Puppy."

"Yes, this is one of Freckles' puppies." Sara held the squirming animal, while Darcy took Tanner's hand and allowed him to stroke it. "Your daddy said you could keep him."

"Daddy. Puppy."

Nathaniel slid his hands under the tiny dog and cocked his head for Darcy to put the child on the ground. He knelt down and placed the pup on the grass next to Tanner.

"Tanner's puppy. This is for you."

A shrill laugh pierced the air, causing the other adults to wander over. His son had been mesmerized by the animals when Freckles had delivered them, and they were tiny. At this moment, he was exhibiting behavior Nathaniel hadn't seen before. Did he understand they were keeping the puppy?

Glancing over to Darcy, he raised an eyebrow. She shrugged one shoulder and made a duck face.

As Tanner sat on the grass and let the small pet scamper over his lap and around him, Nathaniel stood and thanked his cousin.

"I appreciate your bringing the dog up here. I'm not sure I could have gotten Tanner to leave the dog alone on the drive back here. As it is, I wonder if he'll go to bed tonight."

"It wasn't a problem. We dropped this little gal's brother off at Greg's. You should have seen Ryan running around the yard with him. I think they'll both sleep well tonight."

"How's Freckles doing with all her puppies missing?" Darcy asked. Did she have tears in her eyes? Or was it from the bright sun?

TJ slid his arm around Darcy's shoulder and gave a squeeze. "Freckles still has all but these two. We decided to rehome the puppies a few at a time so it wasn't so hard on her. We've been taking Freckles and the pups to the shop the last few weeks to get them accustomed to lots of different people. You saw them the last time you came up to visit Zane."

Sara reached into the carry case at her feet and drew out a small blanket. "This has been sitting with Freckles for a while. I figured the smell and feel of it will help this new lady to feel at home. Have you decided on a name yet?"

He grinned. "I'm not sure I want to leave it completely up to Tanner, but we may give him a few suggestions and let him decide which one he likes best. Did Ryan pick a name yet?"

TJ laughed. "Apparently Greg's deal with his son was that if Ryan got the puppy, Greg got to pick out the name. They took the black and tan male."

"And…" he prompted.

Sara rolled her eyes. "They named him Guinness."

Kevin's loud laugh startled Tanner, who started to rock back and forth. Darcy slipped onto the ground next to him and brought the puppy up to his face.

"Are you interested in a piece of cake? There's plenty." Nathaniel asked the newcomers.

"I could be convinced.," TJ said.

At the table, Nathaniel slid a piece onto a small plate and handed it to the man.

"Zane said Mary and Jim are getting a puppy, too." Darcy appeared behind him, sliding her finger through the frosting.

When she popped it in her mouth to lick it clean, Nathaniel nearly groaned out loud.

TJ nodded. "Yeah, Mary and Jim. Erik and Tessa. Alex and Gina, we're pretty sure. We're also keeping one of them for ourselves. Mary used to have a dog years ago. I think she's excited about having one again."

"Zane said they let him pick the one they'll keep. He liked the light brown one and has already named her Cinnamon. He's having a blast living on his own."

Her lips tightened into a fake smile.

"That's good, isn't it?"

"Of course, it is. And he's been wanting a puppy forever. Granted, if he learns to take care of it, he'll want one of his own. When I move back, I won't have any place to keep it. Most of the places I can afford don't allow animals."

TJ bent his head toward her. "I'm sure Mary would let him visit as much as he wanted. She's also mentioned bringing Cinnamon to work to spend time with her mom."

"Like doggy daycare," Nathaniel said.

"Darcy's talking about moving back, Nathaniel. Does this mean you've found a new nanny for Tanner?" TJ asked.

Darcy snorted. "Pfft. Nate likes to interview new employees about as much as you do."

Sara and TJ threw each other a sly look. Obviously, there was a story involved, but it wasn't any of Nathaniel's business. Glancing around, he took note of Tanner still playing with his new pup on the grass. His parents, Kevin, and Amy sat next to him, laughing.

For one of the first times since he'd had Tanner dropped in his lap, he wasn't stressed or nervous. Darcy had a lot to do with that.

"Sorry, boss," Darcy said to TJ, then took Nathaniel's arm in her grasp. "You'll have to do without my charming presence a little longer. Until GQ here gets his act together and actually searches for another nanny."

As he patted her hand, happiness grew and exploded inside. If it was up to him, he'd put off looking for another caregiver for as long as possible. Maybe forever.

CHAPTER TWENTY-THREE

"How's the nose feeling?"

Darcy gazed up at Nathaniel as he trotted down the stairs into the family room and lowered the lights.

"I'll live. It happened a few days ago, so it isn't agonizing every time I accidentally touch it anymore. Zane thought I just changed my makeup a bit."

Leaning against the couch, he winced. "I'm so sorry."

"Stop apologizing. It wasn't your fault."

"But it was my son's fault."

She held up her hand. "No, it wasn't. I've already told you that a dozen times."

After dinner on Thursday, she and Tanner had been frolicking on the floor with Oreo. The black and white puppy had jumped up and licked Tanner's face, and the boy had popped up in surprise. Unfortunately, she'd been poised above him at the time. His head had connected with her nose, sending her careening backward.

By the time Nate had bolted down the stairs, blood had been gushing everywhere. Tanner had freaked, while she'd tried to push past the pain in her face. He'd started rocking back and forth and biting on his arm. It had taken an hour to clean her and the carpet up and refocus Tanner enough to reassure him she'd be okay.

That night, as she'd been icing her poor nose, Nate had put the boy to bed by himself, the puppy on his little dog bed next to Tanner's. The scene on the video monitor had warmed her heart.

The once arrogant attorney had been holding his son tenderly, talking to him.

"We've got to make sure we're real nice to Darcy."

"Darcy," the child had parroted. "Nice."

"Yes, she is very nice. To both of us. And we want her to stay."

"Darcy, stay."

Nate had kissed his precious son on the head, then tucked him in. When she'd attempted to wipe the tears that had fallen, the broken nose she'd sustained quickly reminded her that was a mistake. Unlike the decision to come work for this family. Things had changed immensely since she'd started hanging out with this family. Good things.

"So, the kid and pup are asleep?" Picking up the remote, she flicked the channel to some wildlife special.

"Yeah. How was the traffic back from the Cape?"

"Small talk, GQ? Since when do we do small talk?"

Nate reached out and snagged her hand. "Just trying to segue into making out with you. You're kind of sexy with the black eyes."

She shook her head and smiled. Her eyes and nose had been so sensitive she hadn't even been able to use moisturizer. The bruising had gotten worse, but at least the swelling from the first day had gone down.

"It was quiet with you gone visiting your brother. Luckily, I was able to get Tanner's mind off the fact you weren't here. Oreo helped."

"You're more capable of handling him than you think. Don't shortchange yourself."

His eyes turned a smoky grayish blue, and he stroked her cheek. "I think my fangs have grown too long. I should sharpen them on something. Any suggestions?"

The hot kisses they'd been sharing came to mind. "I may have a few."

Resettling on the couch, she presented him with her back and tipped her head to the side. Immediately, his arms wrapped around her middle and his lips attached right to the spot she'd been dying for him to nibble on. Funny how her feelings had evolved when her first impression had been so negative.

"Bullseye, Biff."

"Happy to oblige, mistress. But I don't want to hurt you."

"I didn't break my neck."

God, his mouth and tongue sent her shivering wildly while the warmth of his arms lulled her into a false sense of comfort. But why false? Hadn't Nate shown her kindness and respect while she'd been living here? He trusted her with his most precious gift. His son. She trusted him, too. Enough to let him see her vulnerability.

Like now, with his nose nuzzling her neck. She'd never allowed anyone to get this close. Not willingly. She trusted Nate, and for some reason knew he'd never intentionally hurt her.

Relaxing against him, she soaked up the affection as he paid homage to the skin from her ear to her shoulder. The gentleness of his lips as they skimmed back and forth touched her heart. Could she let herself get more involved with him? She'd never felt this kind of emotion. It was so much more than sexual. His embrace made her feel safe and cared for.

"Is that a Hot Wheels in your pocket or are you glad to see me?"

"Always glad to see you." He chuckled, then his tongue stroked the back of her neck. "And taste you."

The contact caused her to tremble in his embrace. There were no words to describe it.

"Is this okay, Darcy? You're shaking."

"Yeah, it's okay. And so much more."

"There's a lot more I'd like to do with you." His voice was deep and rumbled in his chest, vibrating against her back.

She wanted more. Was she brave enough to let him know?

"Show me your moves, GQ. Let's see what you've got."

～

Nathaniel chuckled at Darcy's words. "Wait, I need moves? No one said anything about moves."

This woman was so much fun and every second with her was unique and magical. Nothing like Helene and their boring sex life. Forget his ex while Darcy was in his arms and at the tip of his tongue.

"Get back in the groove. You were doing fine." Her sigh drifted to him as he nipped up to her ear.

Fine wasn't enough, but he'd need to take it slow. Give her time. Darcy did something to him, not just physically but emotionally as well. Working together toward Tanner's well-being had made him feel close to her. And when she ditched the heavy makeup, it was like she'd allowed him to scale the walls she'd built around her and get a peek of the real Darcy.

Inhaling her clean scent, he skimmed his lips along her cheek, then tipped her chin so he could reach her naked lips. The moan that slipped from her mouth got him hot and hard, but he wouldn't rush this. Every moment touching

Darcy was one to savor. He shifted and lifted her legs over his, allowing her to rest against the throw pillow on the arm of the couch.

As he gazed into her deep brown eyes, he stroked the smooth skin of her face. So much feeling and emotion stared back at him. Like he could see into her soul. It was the most beautiful sight.

"I need to kiss you."

For once, no sarcastic response. She simply nodded.

He gently framed her face and pressed his lips to hers. Another sigh as she clutched him. The contact burned, setting his desire aflame. *Keep in control. Make this special for her.* As far as she'd allow him to go.

His lips descended again and again, lightly, drawing her in, coaxing her mouth to engage with his. He skimmed his fingers down her throat, caressing until they reached the edge of her tank top. As he brushed the back of his hands over her breasts, she inhaled swiftly. Her nipples puckered and poked against the fabric.

"So beautiful." The soft sighs were gutting him.

Kissing her deeply, he licked along the seam of her lips, tempting her tongue to play. It hesitated, then tangled with his, ratcheting up the passion building along his nerves. Was this what good sex felt like? Or was it the woman coming unglued in his arms who made him feel this way?

As their lips consumed each other, he caressed her breasts. He had to see them. Lifting the fabric, his hands glided over the silky skin. They were round and full and exactly the right size to fit in his hands. When he flicked his thumbs over her rosy peaks, Darcy's head jerked back and her eyes closed tightly. Her gorgeous mouth opened in a gasp, and her hands dug into his back. He loved how she looked, all filled with passion, knowing he was the cause.

"God, Darcy, I need a taste."

Her eyes widened as he lowered his head and his tongue swept around her nipple, circling it like a lion to its prey. Her chest heaved, and her dark gaze never flickered. When he enveloped her bud in his mouth and suckled, a sexy moan erupted from her throat.

His tongue swirled and tormented the tight bud, his hand cupping and teasing the other. Darcy arched her back, her breathing heavy, as she slipped her fingers under his shirt. He loved seeing her lose control and submit to the desire. His own excitement threatened to swallow him up as he fanned the flames.

"You are so perfect, Darcy. I can't get enough."

"Take what you want."

He pressed his lips to hers once more, then slowly explored from her cheek to her throat, her shoulders, down her long trim arms and back up. Every time he glanced at her, Darcy's face glowed with pleasure. He continued his journey. When he ended up back feasting on her nipples, her voice shook.

"Mad skills, GQ. God gave you mad skills."

The part of him that had taken the blame for his marriage's lackluster sex stood up taller and smirked.

Skimming his palm over her bare stomach sent sensations rocketing up his arm. He had to touch all of her. His libido was on fire, and Darcy was the only one who could help him. But she had to be pleased first. Fully and completely.

The tips of his fingers tingled as they maneuvered past her navel, under the waistband of her panties, then infiltrated the valley between her legs. The whimpers coming from Darcy's throat drove him on. He slipped his fingers into her crease and almost lost his mind at how wet she was. Her hips rocked back and forth as she grabbed his hand and held it in place.

"Don't even think about stopping."

He nipped at her lips. "Yes, mistress."

As his fingers got busy, he couldn't pull his gaze from her rapturous face. So gorgeous. Tiny panting sounds spiraled higher and higher kicking him in the balls. All he could think about was her falling apart in his arms.

"God, Darcy. I'm going to explode and you haven't even touched me."

He flicked his thumb over her sensitive skin as two fingers surged in and out. Tilting closer, he surrounded her nipple with his lips and tugged it gently with his teeth.

Darcy cried out, and her whole body trembled. She wrapped her arms around his neck and nipped it.

"Fireworks, GQ. Frickin' fireworks."

~

Darcy sagged against the throw pillow, drawing Nate with her.

The grin on his face turned her insides to oatmeal. Which went along with what he'd done to her other parts. "And here you were being humble saying you didn't have any moves."

"Didn't think I did. You must be an inspiration."

Darcy finally found the energy to sit up. "Yeah, I hear that a lot."

What Nate had just done inspired her in other ways. She pushed him back against the cushions and straddled his lap.

Wiggling his shirt up his chest, she asked, "What can I do for you?"

He stopped her hands. "You don't have to do anything for me, Darcy. I didn't do this to get repayment."

How was she supposed to read that? Didn't most guys want something back?

"Then, thank you." She framed his face and pressed her

BROKEN DREAMS

lips to his. As gently as he'd done earlier. This man did something to her when they kissed. Her insides got all messed up and confused, and she had a hard time keeping up the ridiculous banter she was famous for.

He ran his hands up her back, and desire stirred. She tugged at his shirt and tossed it away. Glorious. His hard chest called out to be touched, and she happily obliged. His chest, muscular arms, those droolworthy shoulders. All screaming for her to explore.

Nate drew her closer as their lips touched. His erection pushed against her thin shorts, and she wiggled her butt to get better contact.

"Seriously, GQ?"

His gaze flew up to hers. "What?"

"You just gave me the most explosive orgasm ever and—" She shifted her hips.

"That was your most explosive?"

"Don't let it go to your head." Another wiggle and a groan from him. "Wait, feels like it already has."

How was she still so in need of him? After ripping her top over her head, she flung it away. Nate's eyes widened as the corner of his lip turned up.

"Trying to tell me something, Elvira?" He slipped his fingers into the back of her shorts and slid them lower. "Am I getting warmer?"

"A freakin' volcano, GQ." She slithered down his body, licking her way to her final goal. As she reached for his zipper, a thought came to her. A terrible thought. Nate had said it'd been a while for him. Did he…?

"Please, tell me you have condoms somewhere in this house."

His face froze, then perked up again. "Kevin comes to the rescue. He said I needed to get laid and left a box of them in my bedside table."

"When was this?"

Nate made a face. "Uh, maybe a few years ago. Before Tanner showed up. I'm sure they're still good."

Was *she* good? Could she take this last step? Just a minute ago Nate had insisted she didn't need to pay him back. She nodded, more for herself than for anything else. After all this time, she wanted the real deal, and she couldn't find a man better than Nate.

As he stood in front of her, he took her hand. "You're sure about this?"

Stepping toward him, she pressed a kiss to his lips.

The grin on his face grew as he scooped her into his arms and trotted up the stairs, then down the hall. His room was dark with only the light from the hallway spilling inside.

He placed her gently on the huge bed, then stood gazing down at her.

No quips came to mind. She patted the spot next to her, and he crawled across the mattress to her side. They both reached out and fell into each other's arms. More kissing. Touching. Feeling Nate's heartbeat against her cheek as he held her and stroked fire into her skin.

The room spun while Nate kissed every inch of her. He teased her senseless as he dragged her shorts and panties down her legs. Then, his tongue got in the act and all she could do was feel.

Pleasure. Ecstasy. Her world spinning out of orbit and colliding in another galaxy. How did he do this to her? So much. Too much. Not enough. He took her higher than ever before and cast her over a cliff. But as she fell, she heard his voice reminding her he was right there for her.

As she opened her eyes, his firm chest pressed to her and he held her tight, giving her tiny kisses on her shoulder. Melting into him, she soaked up every sensation.

"Um, you got sidetracked. That was for me, too."

His eyes gleamed. "I've discovered I like making you scream."

"What? Did I—"

"Not too loud." Nate glanced at the monitor on the dresser. "He's still asleep. Maybe you need to get some rest."

Pushing his chest playfully, she threw her arms above her head. "I'm not done with you yet." She shot a look toward his bedside table.

Nate reached over, pulled out a box, then ripped it open. He retrieved a few packets and tossed them next to her.

"Expecting a few encores? I need to see the actual performance first before I decide if I want the sequel."

He swept his hand over her naked body. "The preview wasn't enough?"

Heat rushed to the surface of her skin. It had been plenty. But she still wanted the big finale. With Nate.

"Lose those and have a seat."

Nate dropped his pants and boxers. Holy hornball, the man was not lacking. When he sat on the edge of the bed, she crawled to him and draped herself over his back, caressing his pectorals. The sensation of skin on skin, her front to his back, was sinful. Sliding back and forth, she enjoyed the thrill and awareness.

Nate clasped her hands and groaned. "You're killing me, Darcy."

Tilting her head, she indicated he should get fully on the bed. Quickly, he responded, reclining against the pillows, his hands behind his head. His crooked smirk dug into her.

Starting at his feet, she dragged her hands up his legs, over his hips, across his delicious chest, then ended with her fingers entwined with his. Their bodies touched from head to toe. As much as she wanted the finale, she couldn't stop the need of feeling him everywhere.

Not a word was spoken as she twisted slightly, rubbing

herself along his hardness, letting the sensations overwhelm her. Nate touched his lips to her cheek, her mouth, her forehead. She'd never felt so cherished.

As she wiggled, his erection tantalized her most intimate space. She couldn't stop. Wanted this so badly.

Nate released one hand and skimmed it down the length of her before picking up the condom. "We'll need this."

Plucking it from his fingers, she said, "I'll take care of it."

Nate helped her roll it on, then lay back again. She kissed him, squirming against him until he was right where he'd been before, teasing her opening. Pressing her hands on the mattress beside his head, she lifted and twisted until he entered her. Oh. Oh, God, yes.

Lowering her head until her forehead touched his, she breathed out his name. "Nathaniel."

She'd never seen anyone look at her like this before—like she was special.

Clasping her face, he devoured her mouth and bucked his hips under her.

Seconds, minutes, hours, they feasted on each other. Touching, twirling, dancing together to the song of love. Desire rose up again and seized her tightly. He'd already gifted her with two amazing orgasms, but she was grabbing this third one by the balls and holding on for dear life.

Together they plunged off the cliff, landing safely in each other's arms.

"Holy shit, Elvira. I think you put me under a spell."

"I tried." If only she really could.

He held her for a few minutes, then flopped to his side. "Be right back."

The water sounded in the bathroom, then he appeared in the doorway, the light from behind him illuminating the room and falling across the bed where she lay.

In seconds, he was back beside her, holding her close, stroking her skin.

"You can't be ready again. I need a rest."

"Rest. I like touching you, if that's okay."

"Very okay."

As his hand caressed her stomach, he paused a few inches below her navel, then squinted, leaning closer.

"What are you looking at? You've done your duty down there. Three times, I might add."

"You've got some little grooves that run along right here. They don't feel or look like scars."

Darcy froze, her lungs filling with ice.

They weren't scars. Not physical ones. But their cause had scarred her heart. Stretch marks. Something she couldn't tell him about without pulling some awfully big skeletons out of her closet.

~

"Get your hands away from there." Darcy pushed at Nathaniel's fingers as they traced the silvery lines on her lower abdomen. With the only light coming from the hall and the bathroom, he couldn't see clearly what they were.

He sat back. "Did I do something wrong?"

Shit, they'd just had the most amazing sex of all time. He didn't want to mess anything up with her. Caressing the side of her face, he kissed the tip of her nose.

"I'm sorry, whatever I did."

Darcy turned her face away and her mouth tightened. He'd never seen her react so emotionally to anything. Typically, she was throwing shade in every direction.

"What did I do?"

"You didn't do anything." When she glanced back, her eyes shimmered with tears.

"I made you cry. I don't like that I made you cry. Can you please tell me what happened? I can't fix it if I don't know what it is."

Her bottom lip trembled. "There's nothing you can fix." A sob tore from her throat, and she collapsed against him, tears rolling down her face.

Oh, God, now what? He tugged her close and stroked her back.

"Hey, it's okay. I'm here. Tell me what to do. I'm a corporate attorney. You know I'm not good at this comfort stuff."

A tiny chuckle intermingled with the sobs it seemed she couldn't control. So he merely held her, pressing tiny kisses to her hair, rubbing her back, whispering those silly words that somehow seemed to ease the pain.

Darcy's nude body pressed against his. He'd never been in a situation like this before. Was he even helping?

After a while, her sobs lessened yet she clung as tightly as before. When her breathing grew less shallow and her body loosened, he lifted her chin and tenderly pressed his lips to hers.

"Can you tell me what that was all about?"

"I'm sorry. I didn't mean to lose it like that. You caught me off guard."

He grazed her hip with his fingers. "It has something to do with those lines on your stomach."

She pressed her lips together and shook her head.

"You don't trust me? I get it. I shouldn't have asked." For some reason, he didn't release her. He should get up and go into the other room, until she composed herself and went up to her room. Obviously, they weren't as close as he thought they were.

"No, you have every right to ask. It's just…it's hard to talk about. Especially naked."

After grabbing a t-shirt from a nearby chair, he helped

slip it over her head. Then, he settled against the headboard and pulled her between his legs.

"Is that better? You don't have to tell me anything you don't want to. I have no right to your personal life."

Taking a deep breath, Darcy squeezed his hands that rested on her stomach. "I've never shared this with anyone. And only a few people know. I need to keep it that way."

"You have my word. Unless you killed somebody. I'd have to throw you to the cops for that. You didn't kill someone, did you? Please, say you didn't kill someone."

"I didn't kill anyone. It's nothing illegal."

"Good. But those lines…you aren't an alien, are you?"

"Are we playing Twenty Questions, or did you want me to spill my guts?"

He pressed a kiss to her cheek but remained silent. Her breathing was steady, in, out, in, out. Like she was trying to psych herself up for the big reveal.

"The lines on my stomach are stretch marks."

"Stretch marks. From being heavier and losing lots of weight? That's hardly something to keep a secret."

"It is, if the weight was from a pregnancy."

A pregnancy? Darcy had a baby?

CHAPTER TWENTY-FOUR

"Pregnancy?" Nate's voice rose with the word. "You have a kid?"

Darcy shook her head, wondering how much to tell him. She didn't owe him anything. She didn't owe anything to anyone. Except Hope. She owed that little girl a perfect life that her biological mother couldn't give her.

"No. I don't have a child. I was pregnant and delivered a baby, but I don't have a child."

"Oh, God, Darcy. Did...did the baby die?" Were those tears in Nate's voice? No, they'd start her up again.

"No, she didn't die. She was absolutely perfect. Ten fingers. Ten toes. A mop of dark hair that stuck up in every direction. And I got to hold her in my arms. For ten amazing minutes, I held her." The tears started again in earnest. Oh, Lord, she hadn't cried this much in years. Working with this family was making her soft.

"You gave her up, didn't you?"

All she could do was nod as she cried her heart out. Nate's arms felt warm and comforting around her. She could almost forget what she'd done. Almost.

"How old were you?"

"Seventeen. So stupid and naive." And thinking she could handle anything.

"Did the teenage deadbeat run off when he found out you were pregnant?"

If only that had been the case.

"He wasn't a teenager. He was forty."

"Forty? Wait, what were you doing with a forty-year-old guy? Better question, what the hell was he thinking having sex with a seventeen-year-old girl?"

"It's a long story."

"Tanner's asleep, and it's barely nine. Plenty of time for a bedtime story."

But if she told him, then he'd know what a fool she was.

"In the fall of my senior year in high school, Zane had this job working at a small insurance agency in downtown New Bedford, not too far from the dump we lived in. Mostly cleaning up. The manager was this guy who was always nice to me when I'd come to get him after work. He'd chat with me and ask about school and shit."

"He put the moves on you?"

"Not really. He'd tried one time, but I got embarrassed and made up some excuse about needing to get Zane home."

"So, how'd you end up pregnant?" Nate's voice grew dark. Was he guessing what had happened?

"One day, when I came to pick up Zane, he asked me into his office to talk about something. Said he'd caught Zane stealing supplies from the office. He said he didn't want to call the police, but he couldn't have anyone stealing from him."

"Did you ask Zane if he'd taken this stuff?"

"No, but I'd found little things around the house that weren't his. He'd done this before. He knew he wasn't supposed to buy anything with his work money unless I was with him. Zane doesn't always make the best decisions. But I wasn't sure what the police would do to him if this guy called them and pressed charges. Zane was over eighteen. Yes, he's got a disability, but that didn't mean they'd let him get away with stealing. I couldn't let this guy hurt my brother."

Nate's breathing had picked up and his arms tightened around her. "So, he basically blackmailed you into sleeping with him."

She nodded. "He said if I was real nice to him, he'd forget about the thefts. He started kissing me."

"Obviously, it was more than kissing."

"I didn't realize it at first, and so I agreed. I kissed him back. He'd been flirting with me for months, and I used to love walking Zane home, because even though this guy was forty, he was hot and super nice to me. Now, I realize why."

"God, Darcy, I wish I could go back and make that not happen."

"We kissed for a bit, and he touched me. I thought maybe that's all he was gonna do. That all he wanted was to play with my boobs. But soon enough I was spread on his desk and he was screwing me."

"That's called rape, Darcy."

"Not if I agreed to it. I let him do it. I never even tried to stop him. I even…"

"You even what?"

"I even liked some of it. Liked when he first started touching me. It felt good."

Nate was quiet, and she wondered if she'd completely lost him. He should kick her out of his bed and toss her to the curb.

"And you ended up pregnant."

"I don't know if it was that time or the next time."

"You did it more than once?"

She nodded. Is this where he pushed her away, wondering if he'd catch some horrible disease from her?

"He wanted me to come back and do it every week. But after the second time, he said something about sleeping with underage girls, and I managed to get it on my phone. I made a copy of it and then let him hear it. I told him I wouldn't share it with anyone if he left us alone. Like his boss, who didn't know he was having sex with girls in the office."

"Did you ever tell him you were pregnant?"

"No, I didn't want him anywhere near me. When I'd played the conversation for him, he told me to get lost, that he didn't want me to come around again. I happily complied, although Zane didn't understand why he couldn't work there anymore."

"You know what he did was illegal. Right? You were underage, and I'm guessing he set up the whole theft thing."

"Yeah, but who the hell cares what happens to an inner-city slut who flirts with an older guy. She gets what she deserves. They wouldn't have done anything to him."

"You aren't a…what he did was wrong. You say you agreed, but it wasn't like he gave you much choice. That's non-consensual. Especially since you were a minor. I don't care how much you liked it or if you agreed to any of it. You were coerced by a person in power over you."

She merely shrugged. It was so long ago. She wished she could forget it ever happened.

"You decided to give the baby up for adoption?"

"I didn't know what to do at first. I took a home pregnancy test, and it was positive, so I went to this nearby clinic after school one day. They gave me a real test and confirmed. There was no way I could have the baby. My mother needed freakin' rehab again. How could I take care of a baby, take care of my brother, and deal with my mother's drug habit all while working a part-time after school job?"

"You didn't get an abortion?"

Heat seared inside her as she whipped her head to stare at him. "I couldn't. It was my *child*. Doesn't matter how she was conceived. She was still a part of me. I couldn't kill her. But I couldn't take care of her either. When I left the clinic, there were some people standing outside who handed me a pamphlet. I didn't even read it until I got home. It was about adoption. People who were willing to help you with medical and living expenses until after you had the baby. I called them."

"I'm proud of you for making that decision. It couldn't have been easy."

"When I called the agency, they had a special set of parents who were very interested in me. Well, in my baby. Still, they were amazing to all of us. They agreed to move us to the Cape and pay for an apartment, until I could get back on my feet and get a job after the baby was born. These people were loaded and could afford it, and a regular adoption agency had put them way at the bottom of the list."

"Were they not good parents? Did you check them out?"

"They offered me everything in the world. A place to stay, good food to eat, even help getting my mother into rehab nearby. And they paid for all this throughout my pregnancy, even helped me get my GED, and then paid for months after until I'd saved enough to pay for our own place."

"So, that's how you ended up on the Cape. You decided to stay."

Picturing her beautiful baby girl, she nodded. "Yeah, these women wanted an open adoption. Meaning they'd send me pictures of the child every month. They even said I could meet with her if I wanted."

"That's awfully generous. But…Wait, women?"

"That's why it was harder to adopt, because it was a gay couple. They'd tried invitro a few times, but it hadn't worked.

One of the moms is in her forties and the other is over fifty, so their age also precluded them from adopting through regular channels."

"And you have a tattoo with the word Hope on your shoulder."

She nodded, another tear leaking from the corner of her eye.

"Does Hope know you're her mom? She hasn't said anything about it?"

"I'm not her mom. I'm the person who carried her for nine months. She has two moms who love her very much and do everything they can for her to have a perfect, normal life. All things I never could have given her."

"She seems awfully taken with you."

Darcy twisted to glare at him. "I never had any close contact with her, until you and Tanner showed up, and TJ wanted me to sit with the kid at Story Hour."

"Wait? What? So that was the first time you'd ever talked with Hope? Jodie invited you to Hope's party. She'd never done that before?"

She shrugged. "She's invited me every year. I always say no."

"But you went this year. Was it because of Tanner?"

"Tanner. And you. You seemed so pathetic and lost at the thought of going. Then, Jodie said only one kid from school was going. Damned if I was gonna have my kid upset, because no one showed up for her birthday. She loves Tanner, and I knew that would make her happy."

"Well, thank you. I'm sorry if it was hard on you. I never imagined…never would have thought. I wondered if you were related when I first met her. She looks like you."

She rested her head on his shoulder. "You think so?"

"Not the ears, but definitely the coloring and around the nose and eyes. She's a cutie."

"Does that mean you think I'm cute, too?"

"When you aren't throwing attitude at me. Maybe even when you are."

His legs rose up on either side of her, reminding her he was still naked.

"Have you ever thought of trying to see Hope more? You said Jodie would consider it."

"No, it hurts too much. Seeing her at Tea and Tales has been so painful. It was masochistic of me to get a job there."

"Did you do it because Hope went to Story Hour there?"

"Yeah." She released the breath she was holding. "And once Jodie saw me there, she made sure to bring Hope all the time. She's bugged me a few times this summer to let Hope know who I am."

"But you don't want to." His arms loosened, and she felt his warmth drain away. Was he thinking of his own circumstances?

Scooting away from his comfortable chest, she faced him. "Do you hate me because I gave up my kid? Like your bitch ex did?"

Nate took her hands and rubbed his thumbs over them. "Helene is a cold-hearted ice queen, who doesn't want a child who isn't perfect. And Bryce is her meal ticket, and she can't go without that. She knew I'd never take her lying ass back."

Darcy had never thought of that. "Did she ask?"

Nate's lips thinned into a straight line. "Yeah, and I let her know where she could go. However, that's the difference between you and her. You loved your child so much, you couldn't think about harming her in any way and wanted her to have the absolute best life ever. You knew you couldn't give it to her and made arrangements so she'd have one."

"So, it's not the same thing, huh?" God, she needed someone to convince her she wasn't a horrible person.

"You're nothing like Helene. That's a good thing. What you did for Hope was admirable. But you know what?"

"What?" Is this where he told her she was scum and needed to leave?

"Even though Hope wouldn't have had the nice cushy life she's had, I think you would have done a fine job of raising her, even in the worst conditions. Because you're a good, decent person, Darcy Marx."

Sniffing, she wiped moisture off her cheeks. "You're just saying this because we had sex and you want it again. I mean, it was crazy good sex."

He drew her closer and kissed her. "It *was* crazy good. Not sure if it's because of you or the fact I haven't had sex in almost five years."

"It's been over six for me, so I'm not the one to ask." She ran her hand over his shoulder and down the strong arm that held her.

"Hold on. You haven't had sex…Hope just turned six."

"I know."

"You haven't had sex with anyone since she was born? Since that douche bag…" Nate's jaw grew rigid and his hands gripped hers harder. "But you dress and act—"

"Like a slut, I know."

"I didn't say that. That's not what I meant."

"Doesn't matter. It's true. That's what I am."

"You've had sex with one guy, and non-consensual sex at that, and you think that makes you easy?"

"I gave it to him easy enough. I never fought or even tried to get out of doing it. Hell, I was flattered by his flirting and charm for months and even envisioned myself being his girlfriend. He was freakin' forty years old. They weren't exactly pure thoughts."

"Yes, he was forty. And you were seventeen. You were

manipulated and taken advantage of, Darcy. You aren't a bad person."

"You won't tell anyone, right?" Her stomach twisted at the thought of others knowing.

Pulling her into his arms again, he kissed the top of her head. "It's not my secret to tell. For what it's worth, I don't think anyone will judge you. Certainly, not as much as you judge yourself."

"Thank you."

"I think it's all an act you put on to hide."

"What are you talking about? An act?"

"The spiked hair, makeup, piercings, weird clothes, the smartass comments. They're to hide behind. It's like a fence to ward people off. If they don't get too close, they can't see your pain. Or the fact that you're actually a nice person behind it all."

God, he needed to stop. "You're being too nice, Biff. I'm gonna melt in all this sugary sweetness."

"Get used to it, Elvira. Now that I know *you* plus *me* equals fireworks, I'm not going to let you get too far."

As he drew her down into the warmth of the bed and kissed her in that spot on the back of her neck, she almost forgot the most important thing.

He'd never want someone like her permanently.

∼

Nathaniel slid the green mask off his face. "Have I done my fatherly duties yet?"

Her eyes shone. Or he thought they did under her red mask. It was hard to tell.

"You wore that for over an hour. I'd say you earned yourself some dad points today. You would have gotten more if you'd done the Halloween costumes a little better. Gekko doesn't wear black jeans."

He sighed. "I don't have any green pants. Isn't the green sweater enough? I did the mask."

"PJ Masks," Tanner chirped and twirled around, his hand clutching his bucket of candy and prizes close to his chest.

"And I'm pretty sure Catboy doesn't wear wind pants, so I should get a pass."

"They're still blue, and you don't have tactile sensitivities. I offered to buy you green Gekko pajamas, but you refused."

"I'm not wearing pajamas out in public, and definitely not to the country club." He observed the other parents milling about with their kids at the club sponsored Halloween event. They thought this would be better than Trick-or-Treating with Tanner tonight after dark. "I do business with some of these people."

"Good thing I don't." Darcy held out the red wings she'd donned today and posed like she was about to take off.

Her cute little body got him revved up in her snug, red yoga outfit. It got him revved up in anything she wore. And didn't wear. But that was all in private. The last four weeks had been amazing with Darcy. The chemistry between them was through the roof. Ever since that day a month ago, they'd been intimate most nights. Of course, Darcy insisted she go back to her room sometime in the middle of the night, instead of staying with him in his bed. She felt she needed to be upstairs when Tanner woke up each morning and to keep an ear out for the puppy, but there were times he wanted her near him when he woke up.

"Okay, Owlette, are we ready to head home? Looks like Catboy needs his nap. We're a few hours overdue."

"I suppose." She slid the mask off her face. Silly woman. Her black makeup was accented with red today. "Are you ready to go home, Catboy? Did you get some great prizes?"

"Car," Tanner called out, pulling a Hot Wheels from his bucket. Nathaniel had made the suggestion to the organizing committee. Tanner definitely didn't need tons of candy.

Darcy stretched out her wings again and twirled in a circle. Tanner laughed and spun around, too. His mask tumbled off his face.

As Nathaniel stooped to pick it up, a pair of three-inch spiked heels came into view.

"Nathaniel?"

The voice was unmistakable. Helene. When he stood, he got the rest of the picture. Perfectly coiffed hair, expensive jewelry, and stylish maternity outfit covering her large stomach. What was she doing in those heels this far along?

"Helene." He kept all emotion from his tone.

Darcy's head whipped up, and her eyes almost glowed as she zeroed in on his ex-wife.

"What are you doing here? I thought you and Bryce belonged to the Wentworth Club in Newcastle."

"We do, but my friend, Yvette, is having my baby shower here, so I needed to make some arrangements first."

"I thought baby showers were surprise things." What did he know? He'd never been to one.

Helene gently shook her head. Never wreck the hairdo. "Maybe in some circles, but not in ours. These things need to be planned."

At that moment, Tanner jumped and squealed in delight. At what, Nathaniel didn't know. Helene gazed over and her eyes clouded.

"Is that…?"

"Yes, it's Tanner. *My* son. The one you deserted and have no say in how he's raised anymore. That one."

"Nathaniel, don't be so…" She trailed off, her tone soft. Did she genuinely regret what she'd done? Then, she straightened her shoulders and took a deep breath. Her eyes held that gleam she'd always gotten when she was about to put someone in their place. He must be the next victim. Too bad. She had no effect on him any longer.

Helene tilted her head. She was staring straight at Darcy, who was making goofy faces with Tanner. "I see you've found your flea-infested alley cat."

Darcy's head popped up, and her face hardened. She'd heard. Shit.

He wanted to wipe the sneer right off his ex's face. "Yet, she still has more class than you."

There was almost emotion on Helene's face as she stepped closer to Tanner. Darcy did a perfect pirouette, placing herself between his ex and the child. She held out her wings as if to hide Tanner from his mother.

The surprise on Helene's face was priceless. Doubtful she'd ever had anyone get in her way before. She took a step to the side and said, "Tanner."

Their son glanced up briefly, then went back to twirling with his bucket extended. It was exactly how he reacted with people he didn't know. Total oblivion.

Darcy still stood in Helene's way, and his ex looked about ready to let go. He reached out his hand for the child. Tanner stopped spinning, took it, then held his other hand out for Darcy, even though it still had the bucket in it.

"Do you know who I am?" Helene's voice was imperious.

The face Darcy pulled was comical, and he almost laughed but caught himself in time. Helene could be brutal when she wanted to be. Darcy didn't deserve her wrath. He started to pull on Tanner's hand when Helene shuffled forward.

"I'm his mother."

Oh, God, Darcy's eyes gleamed and her lips twitched as she dropped Tanner's hand and moved so his son was behind her.

Leaning into Helene like she was about to tell her a secret, Darcy said, "Not a very good one."

"You don't know—"

"Oh, I know plenty." Darcy cut Helene off. "I know a lot more about your son than you do."

"You have no right to speak to me this way." Helene dug out her regal tone.

Darcy wouldn't respond well to that.

"Listen, bitch, I'll speak to you any way I feel like. I don't give a crap that you pushed this kid out. That doesn't make you a mother. Do you know his favorite toy? His favorite food? What outfit he has to wear to school on Mondays? Who his therapists are? His favorite song to play on the piano?"

"Oh, stop." Helene's eyes rolled to the ceiling. "The child is four. He has…issues. I'd be surprised if he could sing a song, never mind play one on the piano."

Darcy crossed her arms over her chest and smirked. "And that's where you'd be wrong, sister. Tanner got a piano for his birthday and can now play over a dozen songs. His favorite seems to be the Tarantella. An easy version, of course, but still. To learn them, all he has to do is watch Nate play."

Helene's eyes narrowed. "I seriously doubt, wait…Nate?"

Now it was Darcy's turn to roll her eyes. "Yeah, now that you aren't around, he managed to get the stick out of his ass and become a regular guy. He plays with his kid and dresses up for Halloween parties and everything. Like a real dad is supposed to. Good ones, anyway."

Helene stayed quiet for once. Nathaniel wasn't sure if he should interject about the stick part, but he was getting turned on watching Darcy let Helene have it.

Tipping her head to the side, Darcy pursed her lips. "You know if you made an appointment with a specialist, I'll bet you could get yours surgically removed. It looks like it's up there much farther than Nate's was. Oh, and while he's in there, you might want to see if he can liposuction some of that fat off. Unless the new hubby is into big butts. Some guys are."

"Well, I never—"

"I didn't think you did. I doubt you ever will. And that's sad. Let me give you a little advice, for the sake of *this* kid." Darcy pointed to Helene's belly. "Learn to be an actual mother to him and not someone who pets him on the head like a puppy. He might turn out to be a better person than you."

Darcy shook out her wings, and Helene took a step back to avoid them.

"Oh, and FYI, I'm an owl not a cat. Tanner is the cat."

"Catboy," Tanner yelled and grabbed his mask to put on. Nathaniel grinned at his ex, who looked baffled. He put his own mask back on as Darcy did the same.

"Yeah, Helene, if you're going to be a real mother, you need to get with the program." Nathaniel peered down at this son. "Are you ready, Catboy?"

"Super Cat Speed," Tanner yelled, then looked at him.

He took the boy's hand. "Super Lizard Grip."

Darcy fluttered her wings. "Super Owl Wings."

They all joined hands, and as they ran, he peeked back at a very stunned Helene.

"Into the night to save the day."

CHAPTER TWENTY-FIVE

*D*arcy winced as the doorbell rang a second time. Hopefully, it wouldn't wake Tanner from his nap. Or the puppy, who was sleeping in his crate in Tanner's room. He was still too small to go up and down the stairs by himself.

She peeked through the narrow windows next to the door. A pale, stout, balding man stood there, arms crossed.

Opening the door, she asked, "Can I help you?"

"Oh, hey, you must be the nanny." The way he said *nanny* didn't sit well with her.

"I'm Darcy."

"Sure, Darcy. Great to meet you." He tromped in before she could stop him.

At her glare, he gave a strange chuckle and held out his hand. "Stan Jablonski. I do some work with Nathaniel. We needed to go over a few glitches in a contract."

"Mr. Storm's not here at the moment."

The guy shrugged and started down the hall. What the hell? He wasn't very tall, but he had some heft to him. Could she muscle him around like she'd done with Nate's ex last week?

"I'll wait. He said he'd be home early this afternoon."

Darcy followed him down the hall into the kitchen. "Can I get you something to drink? Soda? Iced Tea?" She had manners she could use when she wanted to. Not that she wanted to with him.

"You got a beer?"

Just what this pompous ignoramus needed was alcohol. "No, we don't." They did, but she sure wouldn't give it to him.

He made a face. "Storm doesn't have beer? What's he drink? The hard stuff?"

"Milk or apple juice?" She bit her lip to keep from screaming. GQ would owe her time and half for this treatment.

He looked around, his head nodding as he did. "Where's the kid?"

"Napping. Are you sure Mr. Storm said he'd be home soon? He didn't mention it to me." She edged nearer to the sink to see out the window. Would Nate show up soon?

"Oh, sure, I talked to him this morning. Something about a dock."

Yeah, Nate wanted to winterize the shed and boats before it got too cold. It was only the second week in November, but in New Hampshire you could get snow this early.

"If you'd like, you could wait for Mr. Storm in his office." Yeah, that'd be a good place for him. Out of sight and out of her hair.

"Actually, sweetheart, you know what I'd really like?" He shuffled behind her and flipped the hem of her skirt. "How about a little of what you give Mr. Storm?"

She whirled around, but he pressed her against the sink, trapping her. Frack, this guy was stronger than his fat little body appeared.

"Let me go. Now." She kept her voice calm but firm.

"Come on. I'm a little early, and Storm won't be here for a bit. The kid's having a nap. Just flip up that cute little skirt of yours. I can do it fast, if you're worried he'll catch us."

When she pushed at his chest, he grabbed her wrists.

"I'm the nanny here, not the concubine."

"Ooh, big words. An intelligent whore. I like that. Does Storm like your smartass mouth? Does it get his motor running? It's got mine."

"I'm here to take care of his kid."

"Course you are. Doesn't mean you can't take care of him, too. Don't tell me he doesn't get a little somethin' somethin' on the side. He's been a lot happier, since you've been here."

She pulled on her hands, but he held tight. At least with his hands holding hers, he couldn't touch any other part of her.

"You need to leave now. I'll inform Mr. Storm that you were here." Her control was being tested more than it had ever been.

"Oh, don't be like that, sweetheart. What? Does Storm give you extra pay for screwing him? I can throw you a twenty, but you better give me some head for that."

"I'll be giving you something all right." She threw a sexy smile his way and inched her hands up his chest. "I'll need some room."

"Yeah, that's what I'm talking about." Stan backed off and released her hands. She quickly lifted her leg and kneed him in the groin. He went down like a rock.

"You little bitch."

"I won't ask you again. Get the hell out of here."

Pulling himself up by the counter, Stan growled. "I'll make sure Storm takes this out of your hide. Right after I do."

He lunged for her. Darcy opened a drawer, getting in his

way, then she ran to the other side of the dining area table. After shoving the drawer closed, he rushed her again.

Her instinct was to scream, but the last thing she needed was Tanner coming down to see this. She grabbed the vase that sat on the hutch behind her and held it aloft.

"You're gonna get this on your head, if you don't get the fuck out here."

"Oh, that tongue is going to feel nice when it's swirling around my cock, you little bitch."

He pounced in her direction, then jerked backwards.

"Stan! What the hell is going on?" Nate shoved the short man away from her. Thank God.

Stan shook Nate's hands off and straightened his suit. "I was just being friendly with your nanny slut. The bitch kneed me in the nuts. She owes me for that."

Darcy had never seen Nate's face go so red and tight. He took a step forward and *bam*, punched Stan right in the face. She wanted to do a little dance.

Stan staggered back and groaned. When he straightened up, it was his turn for the red face. "That was a mistake, Storm. I'll pull all my business from your law firm."

Shit. This guy was a big account. GQ was sure to be pissed at what had gone down.

"Get the hell out of my house. I don't want to see you again. Find yourself another lawyer."

Stan sputtered and threw a few choice curses her way, mixed in with some incredibly insulting accusations. Nate escorted him down the hall, leaving Darcy standing there holding a vase out in front of her like a weapon. The front door slammed, and she slowly turned to replace the vase.

"Are you okay?"

Why the hell did these stupid tears need to show up right now? All she could do was nod.

He eased up behind her and touched her shoulder, the

pressure gentle. "I'm sorry, Darcy, I had no idea he'd go after you."

"You knew he was coming here?"

"When I spoke with him this morning, he mentioned he might drop by later with details on a problem account. I didn't think he'd be here already. Did he hurt you at all?"

Rubbing her wrists, she shook her head. "Not as much as I hurt him."

Nate took her hands and pressed his lips to where she'd been rubbing. "I'm so sorry."

As much as she wanted to lean in and absorb his strength, she was also pissed that somehow Stan had thought she was an easy mark. What had Nate told him about her?

"Darcy. Time?" The little voice drifted from the monitor on the counter. Tanner had woken and was asking if it was time for him to get up. The boy did like his schedules.

"I've got to get your son."

"I can get him, if you need a minute."

"No, I'll get him. It is, after all, what you pay me for. Right?"

As she trudged up the steps and thought of all she and Nate had been doing the last month, she had to wonder exactly how much her job description had changed.

~

HEADING TO HIS ROOM, Nathaniel tugged his tie down and slid his coat off. What the hell had Stan been thinking coming here and trying what he had with Darcy? After tossing his shirt in the hamper, he sat in the chair next to his bed to remove his shoes. He slumped, holding his head in his hands, a slight ache starting up in the back of his skull.

Stan's account was a huge one and losing him would sting a bit, but what other choice had there been? Darcy did not deserve to be treated like a whore. No woman did. He'd give up all his clients if it meant he could keep her safe.

Of course, it seemed like she'd been holding her own when he'd gotten there, but Stan had still been advancing, his intent apparent. What would have happened if he hadn't gotten home when he had? Not something he even wanted to think about.

He finished changing into jeans and a t-shirt so he could do some repairs to the dock and the shed before winter set in. The weather today was in the fifties, so it would be perfect. He needed to check on Darcy first and really assess how she was.

When he got to the kitchen, she and Tanner were on the floor in the family room, next to the coffee table. Oreo frolicked under the table, chewing on an old sock. Tanner was doing an easy wooden puzzle. He'd taken the pieces out and replaced them dozens of times, but he still loved to work at it. That repetitive thing.

Darcy had changed, too. Removed her skirt and put on a pair of black jeans with an enormous black sweater. She'd layered on more makeup, as well. Shit.

"Hey, buddy. Good nap?" He knelt down and stroked Tanner's curls. Emotion filled up all the deep holes inside him that Helene had created. This child was everything to him. More than anything, he wanted Tanner to feel the same deep emotion for his father.

"Puzzle." Tanner placed the last piece in, tapped the board, and said, "Done.

Darcy gave a strained smile, patting the dog. "Good job, Tanner."

"Puzzle, again." The boy picked up the puzzle and dumped the pieces on the table.

Nathaniel stroked Darcy's shoulder, and she stiffened.

When he tapped her, she finally glanced up, and he tipped his head toward the kitchen.

She followed him up the stairs but didn't go any farther.

"Do you want me to press charges against Jablonski?"

Her eyes shot up in surprise. "What? You'd do that? I thought he was a big client of yours."

"Not anymore."

Lowering her eyes, she tugged on the bottom of her sweater. "Sorry about that."

Nathaniel took her hands and drew her closer. "Don't be sorry. You didn't do anything. Do you want me to press charges?"

She shook her head. "No, there's no need to make it worse."

"You don't seem okay."

Her head whipped up, fire in her glare. "Maybe because you've been telling your clients you're knocking boots with the nanny. So my job description has been altered to mistress now?"

"What are you talking about?" He took a step back, shocked. "I've never told anyone about us."

"Well, you've obviously given Stan some indication that I'm putting out, or he wouldn't have stopped by expecting a free sample."

"I mentioned I had a great nanny for Tanner, and you were amazing. I certainly never told him, or anyone, we were sleeping together."

"So I'm your dirty little secret." Her shrill voice rang through the air.

The pounding in his head intensified. He wrenched his fingers through his hair.

"You can't have it both ways, Darcy." His own voice rose as confusion roiled through him. "Either we tell people we're in a relationship or we don't. What the hell do you want?"

"A relationship? That's a good name for it." Her bottom lip tightened, and her expression grew thunderous.

The sound of the door slamming in the family room broke their standoff. Tanner?

The child no longer played with the puzzle. Through the floor-to-ceiling windows, Nathaniel saw him, hands over his ears, running across the backyard, toward the lake.

"Shit!" He tore off down the stairs, Darcy on his heels. By the time they got outside, Tanner was already galloping down the dock, squealing out unintelligible sounds.

"Tanner! Stop! Don't go any farther."

The child stopped and swiveled, then shook his head back and forth, hands still covering his ears. The fighting. It obviously upset him. Why hadn't he been paying better attention?

"Tanner. Let's go play puzzles." Darcy's softer tone drifted past, but his son stomped his feet and shook his head again.

Nathaniel picked up the pace as the boy backed too close to the side of the dock.

"No!" he and Darcy both screamed at the same time as Tanner tumbled into the water.

Nothing beyond saving his child entered his mind. He flew down the dock, his feet pounding as hard as his heart. He couldn't lose his son now. Targeting where Tanner had gone under, he dove right in. The boy splashed and cried but was soon in his arms, coughing and spitting.

"You're okay, buddy. You'll be okay. Daddy's got you." Thank God.

His son's cries blasted his eardrum, but it was the most beautiful sound he'd ever heard. He was alive. He was breathing. Nothing else mattered.

Holding Tanner in one arm, he used the other to swim to shore. Darcy stood on the grass, holding out her hands.

"Come here, sweetie. Let's get you in the house and warmed up."

Another shrill screech blasted from Tanner's mouth as his little arms clung around Nathaniel's neck, almost choking him.

"I think I'd better take him. I'm already wet." The boy clung to him like a Boa Constrictor wrapped around its prey.

"I'll go get some towels and blankets." Darcy ran off, and Nathaniel realized the water had been damn cold. The chill air didn't help as it blew through their soaked clothing. He needed to get Tanner inside and warmed up.

By the time he got in the house, Darcy was trotting down the hall, a pile of towels and blankets in her arms. The puppy was in her crate in the corner. Darcy must have put her there when she'd come in earlier.

"Let's get his clothes off right here and wrap him in a blanket."

When he tried to lower Tanner to the floor, the boy gave another yell and gripped even tighter, his legs trying to climb up Nathaniel's body.

"I've got you, buddy. Daddy's got you. You're fine." The sobs coming from his son's mouth tore at his insides, slicing him to shreds.

"We've got to get him dry." Darcy reached up, but Tanner burrowed into his chest, still crying.

"He won't let go. Let's see if we can get him undressed from here."

As he attempted to ease Tanner away, the child clutched tighter, screaming, "Daddy! Daddy!"

Nathaniel's heart lurched as his son clung on, chanting his name.

"We need to get your wet clothes off. Wet clothes off." Nathaniel tried reasoning. "Let's get you warm and dry."

Darcy removed Tanner's shoes and socks, then slid his pants and underwear off. Nathaniel grabbed one of the towels and wrapped it around his son's lower half.

Next was the attempt to slide Tanner's shirt up over his head. It took some doing, but they finally managed to get the wet clothes off the child and wrap him in a warm blanket.

"That's better. Right, buddy? Warm now."

"You need to dry off, too, Nate. I can sit with him on the couch while you do."

Nate shuffled over and leaned down, but Tanner's arms slithered out of the blanket, and he clung to Nathaniel's neck again.

"Daddy. Hold Tanner. Daddy hold." His cries were pitiful and tore at Nathaniel's heart.

"I'll hold you. I won't let you go. I promise."

"Promise, Daddy."

"I'll hold you forever, Tanner. I will." Tears formed, and Nathaniel didn't even care about holding them back.

"Daddy hold Tanner. Forever." The little voice finally stopped sobbing and the boy gazed up at him.

Pressing nearer, Nathaniel kissed Tanner on the forehead. "I love you, buddy. So much."

"So much, Daddy." Tanner reached up with one hand and pulled on Nathaniel's head, then kissed his cheek.

How long he stood there, holding his son, soaking in the love that he felt emanating off him, he wasn't sure. Tanner had settled comfortably in his arms yet still gazed at him as if Nathaniel might disappear any second. It would never happen. He and this kid were in it together, forever.

A nearby sniff had him twisting to see Darcy wiping tears from her cheeks.

"You're still soaking wet and dripping on the carpet."

"I don't care about the carpet, but the wet doesn't feel great. Tanner, can you sit with Darcy while Daddy gets dry?"

"Daddy hold Tanner." The panicked response didn't even bother Nathaniel one bit. His kid only wanted him at the moment. Glancing at Darcy to see her reaction, he noticed her nodding, her eyes damp. She understood how much this meant to him.

"Would you be able to get my socks and pants off?"

"I can try." She dumped the extra blanket and towels on the chair and unbuckled his belt. Within moments, she'd managed to get the damp fabric down his legs and wrapped a towel around his waist.

"Sit and I'll get the rest of this mess off."

Following her orders, he settled on the couch, Tanner still snuggly in his arms. Darcy tucked the other blanket around him, then worked on the sodden socks. Once she got everything off and tossed in the same pile as Tanner's clothes, she pulled the blanket away and slipped her hands under his t-shirt.

"Let see if we can get this off, too."

With a bit of fancy maneuvering, the shirt joined the rest of the pile. Darcy scuttled about picking up the wet mess as he shifted the blanket more securely around him.

Holding his son with one hand, he felt the child's skin on his face, arms, and legs to make sure he hadn't been exposed to the cold water too long.

"Hey buddy, are you warm now?"

"Daddy hold Tanner."

Not exactly what he'd asked, but the answer still pleased him.

"I'm here. I'm here."

Ordinarily, Tanner didn't like to be held for any length of time without having something to focus on. The terror of falling in the lake must have had an adverse effect on him.

Darcy ran up the stairs, and minutes later, descended with pajamas for the boy. "I thought something warm and comfortable would be better for him to wear."

"Good idea."

Once they'd gotten Tanner dressed, Nathaniel pulled

Darcy next to him. She tussled for a minute. "I need to put those wet clothes in the laundry first."

"The laundry can wait. I need to make sure my two best people are taken care of. Tanner's not the only one who had a scare today."

Her expression was one of doubt, but she rolled her eyes and gave up fighting him.

When Tanner began to fidget, Nathaniel eased away to get a toy car from the drawer in the end table next to him. The child lunged for him again, whimpering.

"I'm just getting this, buddy."

His son perked up as he took the car, a tiny smile lighting his face. Then, he snuggled back in for the long haul.

Nathaniel found Darcy's hand and squeezed it. "You okay?"

Her lips twisted to the side. "I'm not the one who took a dive in the lake."

He stared at her intently. "Darcy."

"I'm more freaked out that I didn't notice how upset Tanner was. He should never have even gotten to the door."

Her face was a mask of pain and guilt.

"Don't. I'm as much at fault here. Tanner's okay. Though he may have been inhabited by an alien Klingon." He tried pulled the boy away, and his arms tightened again.

Darcy chuckled but looked away.

As they sat on the couch, Tanner's body softened and relaxed. He drove the little car down Nathaniel's arm then onto Darcy's.

"Darcy. Here." He waved his hand to indicate she needed to move closer.

A tiny smile peeked out on Darcy's face as she shifted against him. Reaching his arm around her shoulder, Nathaniel snuggled her in and pressed a kiss to her cheek.

"I'm glad you're here, Elvira. Tanner and I both couldn't do this without you."

As she rested her head against him, Nathaniel knew that was true. Or more precisely, he was realizing, there were many things he needed Darcy for. Not all of them had anything to do with his son.

CHAPTER TWENTY-SIX

Darcy roamed around the family room one more time and fluffed the pillows on the couch. She'd been reduced to this. Pillow fluffing. The house was tidy, the dishes done, laundry washed and put away, and she'd thrown some chicken and vegetables in a crock pot this morning for dinner. She'd even let the dog run around in the yard for a half hour, even though the temps had gone down last night. Look at her, being all domestic and shit.

Tanner had been at school today, and Nate had offered to pick him up. She suspected it was more Nate needed to reassure himself Tanner was okay there. Since the lake accident last week, Nate had been coming with her to drop him off in the morning and coming home early from work to pick him up from school. Darcy had felt like a third wheel and utterly useless.

Not that she hadn't been busy on the days Tanner didn't have school, but when Nate was home, the child only wanted his father.

The night of the accident, Nate had allowed Tanner to sleep in his bed. It had surprised Darcy, because the boy rarely veered from his routines. But falling into a cold lake when you didn't like water and couldn't swim would freak any person out enough to need more comfort. Nate had, too. She took a deep breath, remembering how he'd asked if she'd join them in his huge King-sized bed.

She had, and that was another domestic scene she knew she could get used to. The simple act of being near Nate, with Tanner between them, holding onto both of them, had stirred emotions in her she'd never felt before.

The next morning, Nate had been concerned with how Tanner would behave at school, so he had insisted they both bring him. The teacher and specialists had listened as Nate told them about the accident and Tanner's reaction. They promised to let him know if the child had any issues during the day. He'd been fine.

The sound of the door opening had Darcy glancing up. Nate and Tanner. Father holding son.

"You don't have to carry him everywhere, you know. He has these cool things called legs. I understand they do all sorts of groovy stuff like holding you up and walking. Sometimes even running."

The sheepish expression on Nate's face tugged at her heart. "I know. I missed so much of his life, and we finally seem to be connecting, so I like holding him while he's still small enough to."

She eyed his shoulders and arms. "With those muscles, you'll be able to pick him up for a while."

Depositing Tanner on the floor next to his backpack, Nate winked at her. "Are you jealous? Wish I was carrying you around?"

She pursed her lips. "Maybe." Definitely. His arms felt heavenly when they held her.

His tie was already off, hanging out of his pocket, and his top button was undone. This semi-relaxed Nathaniel

Storm did something to her insides. And between her legs. Not something to think about with the kid right there.

"Let's empty your backpack, Tanner," Darcy suggested.

"Daddy help me."

Nate glanced up at her with an apologetic expression, then knelt next to Tanner and prompted the boy to unzip the bag himself. Nate was getting good at encouraging self-help skills in his son. He'd been avidly reading the comments written in Tanner's school notebook and discussing the therapists' recommendations.

Tanner pulled out his binder and handed it to his father. "Missa Adams."

"That's right. Mrs. Adams gives this to you. All your teachers write in it telling me what you've done in school."

"Fwecko. School." Tanner extricated his stuffed dog and snuggled into his father's lap.

The look on Nate's face as he held his son said it all. For months, he'd been trying to get some sort of emotional reaction from the boy, and he'd finally gotten it. It didn't look like he minded the recent clinginess one bit. She was glad. The man had been struggling to be a good father since Tanner had been dumped in his lap eleven months ago. His efforts had paid off.

But where did that leave her? Yes, he'd still need someone for Tanner while he was at work on the days the kid didn't have school. But his case manager had mentioned full time school was an option.

Nate looked up and caught her staring. Hopefully, the goofy feelings she'd been having didn't show on her face.

"I called the country club today to find out if they have swimming lessons for kids. They do. On Saturday mornings. I thought I'd sign Tanner up."

"You think he'll go in? He didn't even like the pool at

Sara's much. After last week, is it a good idea to jump right into that?"

He gazed down at Tanner, who'd called over the puppy who'd been napping on the dog bed.

"Maybe you're right. They have new classes that start after the new year, although I don't want to wait too long. Having him fall in the water last week took a few years off my life."

"There are ways of making you immortal." She snapped her teeth at him, then trotted up the stairs to the kitchen.

His laugh echoed through the room, sending chills down her spine. Good chills. Ones she'd like to continue having for a long time.

As she checked on the crock pot and set the table, she glanced down at father and son playing on the floor with Oreo.

"Oreo. Tanner puppy." The child giggled as the dog tussled with his old sock.

A hand on her shoulder startled her. Nate stood behind her, his lips descending on her neck.

"Maybe once Tanner goes to sleep tonight, we can work on this immortality thing you mentioned. I'd love to hear more details."

She glared at him, but that didn't stop him from nibbling on that spot that sent her flying. She should. It was getting far too addicting. Realistically, she knew it wouldn't last. Couldn't last. Nathaniel Storm, corporate attorney, would never consider someone like her for any kind of permanent arrangement.

For now, she would enjoy every second she could get. Soon enough, they'd leave her. Everyone always left. Only, in this case, it was his house, so she'd be asked to leave.

Nate should start looking for a new nanny to replace her. She'd mention it to him soon. As his lips skimmed her neck, she decided next week would be fine. It was Thanksgiving in eight days. It could wait until then. It would most likely be a while before he found a person capable of taking care of Tanner the right way. So perhaps she had until the New Year with them. Yes, she'd enjoy her time.

When she was back on the Cape, she'd have to find a new place to live. Ideally, somewhere nicer than the crap hole they'd lived in before. If Zane wanted to stay with Mary and Jim, she could find a one-bedroom apartment, which would be cheaper. Working here with no rent and the food included, she'd saved a shit ton of cash. Yeah, her new place would definitely be an improvement. Darcy Marx would be moving up in the world.

Nate's arms wrapped around her, and he settled his chin on top of her head as he watched Tanner play with Oreo. Times like this, she allowed herself to dream of a domestic life with a loving husband and children.

Settling back against Nate's chest, she gave herself a mental shake. *Don't get too attached. You'll only get hurt again. People don't stay in your life.* Yeah, she needed to leave before she grew to love this family.

But it was a delusion. She knew it was already too late.

∽

NATHANIEL RUBBED his palms on his coat before turning the doorknob into the house. Why was he so nervous? He'd thought this through and noted all the pros and cons. Marrying Darcy was the perfect solution.

While she was hardly the type of woman he'd normally choose to date or marry, she had so many qualities that outshone what he'd thought he wanted.

And wasn't that a hysterical concept considering his first reaction to her. Her spiked hair and plethora of jewelry. The dark makeup and candy cigarettes. He hadn't seen those in months. The makeup still lingered at times when they went out somewhere, but she'd definitely toned it down from what she'd originally worn. Her hair was a few inches longer and she typically wore it tucked behind her ears like a pixie. He didn't mind the short hair. It allowed him access to that spot on the back of her neck. She made the most beautiful little sounds. Tiny little gasps that let him know exactly what he did to her.

Another reason marriage to Darcy would be great. They were amazing together. It would work, and it would be good for both of them.

He closed the door, and Darcy poked her head out of the laundry room, her brows knit together.

"It's only noon. What are you doing here? Tanner doesn't get out of school for another three hours."

"It's the Friday before Thanksgiving. I decided to close the office early today and take all next week off."

She threw her hands out in front of her. "Whoa, GQ. Where'd the workaholic corporate attorney disappear to?"

"He's still in here," he said, pulling his tie off and stuffing it in his pocket. "But I got the A.D.O. account back and felt like celebrating."

She squinted at him in confusion. "A.D.O.? Am I supposed to know what that is?"

"Stan Jablonski."

Her face tightened, and her mouth formed a straight line. That reaction showed she hadn't been as unaffected as she kept claiming.

"You're working with him again?"

"No, but I am working for the company he represented. The CEO was a bit put out at having to find a new lawyer, so he called to ask why I'd quit. I told him the truth."

"That you're screwing the nanny and good ol' Stan thought he could, too?"

Taking her hand, he rubbed his thumb across her soft skin. "No, I never mentioned what we do, only what Stan tried to do. Needless to say, he doesn't work for that company any longer."

"They canned him?" Her face gleamed.

"He's probably in the unemployment line as we speak. But that does bring up something I wanted to talk about."

"What?" Her eyes narrowed again. Suspicious little thing, wasn't she?

After beckoning her over to the couch, he settled next to her and took her hands again.

"I've been giving this a lot of thought lately."

"You're ready to finally look for another nanny?" Was that hope in her eyes or regret?

"No new nanny. But I don't ever want what happened with Stan to happen again."

"I can carry a knife. I saw this one with a pearl handle, and it had the sweetest sheath you could attach to your thigh. I'd look totally badass with that baby on me."

He laughed at the suggestion. He could legitimately picture it.

"No knife. I wasn't thinking of a weapon."

Oreo scampered over and jumped all over their feet. Darcy scooped her up into her lap. "I know, you're gonna get the pup trained as a killer. We can sic her on any deviants that come along."

"She'd probably lick them to death." Nathaniel took the puppy, set her back on the floor, then tossed her an old sock. "No, I have an idea that will keep us on equal ground and discourage anyone from harassing you. In any way."

"I'm intrigued. Go on."

Taking a deep breath, he forged ahead. "Darcy, I was thinking we should get married."

Her eyes opened wide, and her mouth dropped. Obviously, not what she was expecting. It wasn't anything he'd have expected either.

She was silent for a second, then started giggling. "Ha, that's a good one, Biff. You almost had me there for a second."

"I'm not joking. I think we should get married."

She angled in and sniffed near his mouth. "Have you been drinking?"

"No, I'm perfectly sober."

"And you want to marry *me?*" Her eyes softened, filling with emotion.

"It's the perfect solution."

"Solution?" Why was she frowning? "Solution to what?"

"If we get married, we won't have people like Jablonski thinking they can take advantage of you. You and I would be on equal footing. You wouldn't be my employee. You'd be my wife."

"So you never saw me as an equal while I've been living and working here?"

"No, that isn't what I meant. You're certainly more than my equal—"

"Darn tootin', I am."

"Listen, Darcy, if you become my wife, I won't have to worry about anyone disrespecting you for any reason. Mistaking you for anything else. I won't have to worry about Tanner, either. He'll have a mom again, and this time one who actually wants to be with him."

"You want me to be Tanner's mom?" Her eyes grew glossy. Did she like the idea or hate it? He couldn't tell.

"Yes, and that way he'll have someone here for him all the

time. You could even sign things for him at school and make decisions for him, instead of waiting to ask me."

Her head cocked to the side. "So, it's a convenience thing, this marriage?"

He was unsure of her reaction. "Well, it's for a lot of reasons. To keep you safe. Give Tanner a mom and someone who understands what he needs." He drifted in close. "And there are some other perks of being married."

"Sex. I'm so amazing you bought a ring and got down on one knee. Oh, wait, you're sitting, and I don't see any jewelry."

Damn, he hadn't figured her to be the hearts and flowers type. He slid off the couch to kneel in front of her.

"I'm sorry I don't have a ring, but we can go get one soon if you really want it. What do you say?" Usually he could read Darcy, but today she was a closed book.

As she crossed her arms in front of her, she pursed her lips. "Let me get this straight. You basically want a legal nanny for Tanner. One who's hot and will have sex with you. You're already getting that. What's with the marriage thing? Unless you're trying to save money, since you wouldn't have to pay your wife a salary."

Her eyes searched his face. What was she looking for?

"It's not about money, not the way you think. I want to help you, too, Darcy. You'd be covered by my insurance and able to be more involved in Tanner's learning. And once he goes to school full time, if you wanted, you could go to college and take classes. I'd pay for it, if it was something you wanted to do."

"Go back to school? For what?"

He shrugged. "Anything you want. Or not. You don't have to. I make enough you can stay at home and take care of the house. I just didn't picture you as the Suzy Homemaker-type, though I know you love the lacy, pink uniforms."

He winked, and her cheeks turned red.

"This is, uh…I don't know. Probably not a good idea. I mean, look at us. GQ and the vampire. It might make a good movie, but I'm not sure how it would play in real life."

Dipping closer, he drew her face right up to his and leaned his forehead against hers. "I know we're very different people, but we've also got some impressive chemistry. You can't deny that."

He kissed her, and a small protest escaped. A second later, it dissipated, and her hands clutched his hair, hauling him closer. Their lips collided and made beautiful music together. So beautiful he felt like singing. She still hadn't answered him yet.

"What do you say? Will you marry me? Be my Bride of Frankenstein?"

That got her laughing. Good, she'd been a little too serious. Of course, it was a serious subject.

"I need some time. Honestly, I thought you should start looking at interviewing nannies to replace me. This was never supposed to be a permanent position. Definitely not marriage permanent. You'll be home until after Thanksgiving, right?"

He nodded.

"I need to go back to the Cape. Talk to Zane. Figure things out. I mean, you could just have Tanner go full-time at school and hire someone for the afternoon. You've been getting home early lately, anyway. You don't need me."

Glancing at his watch, he said, "We still have a few hours before Tanner gets out. How about I spend some of that time trying to talk you into this arrangement and showing you exactly how much I need you?"

Once his lips met her neck, she didn't object at all.

CHAPTER TWENTY-SEVEN

*D*arcy sat in her car, tapping her fingers on the steering wheel. Truthfully, it was Nate's car, but she'd gotten used to it. Tanner's car seat was still in the back. Because Nate assumed she'd be coming back. She wasn't so sure.

At some point, she'd have to give the vehicle back. Her own car had been totaled once she'd agreed to work for Nathaniel, over three months ago, and even though she'd saved tons of cash from taking care of Tanner, it sure wasn't enough to fork out for a new car.

Unless she married GQ. Biff. Nate. Nathaniel Storm, corporate attorney. What the heck had he been smoking asking her to marry him? Certainly not her candy cigarettes. The ones she'd quit cold turkey to go work for him. Well, maybe she still had one when Tanner went down for a nap, but nothing like the two pack a day habit from before.

Marriage. Since she'd never had any major relationships, it wasn't something she'd ever thought about. Zane had been her whole world, and none of the guys she knew would ever have agreed to take on responsibility of her brother, along with her.

But Nate had. He had made real plans for Zane to live with them before Mary and Jim's offer. That had been one of the first times she'd truly seen him for the altruistic, caring man he was. He was great with Tanner, his own son, but Zane wasn't anything to him. At the time, neither was Darcy, yet he'd still thought enough about her to make arrangements for her brother.

Was she anything to him now? Sure, she was nanny extraordinaire to Tanner and a surprisingly decent housekeeper. The dinner menu could still use some work, but she was getting there. And often Nate helped her throw things in the crock pot the night before, so all she had to do was plug it in and turn it on the next morning. They'd made an excellent team. In many areas.

And Holy Pop-Tarts, in the bedroom they were the best team ever. Darcy hadn't ever imagined it could be so amazing. Nate was such a giving lover. She'd never felt so special and cared for. But what *did* he feel for her? Not love. He'd never mentioned the word in his whole bad marriage proposal. Not that she knew what a good one was like, but she'd seen enough movies to know that wasn't it.

Could she do a marriage without love? One based on a need to take care of Tanner? Erik and Tessa had started their marriage for the sake of the kids. You couldn't tell that now. Those two were so madly in love it was like a freakin' neon sign. They stared at each other like no one else existed. That didn't mean it would happen with her and Nate. Well, it had happened, but only on her side.

Yeah, ridiculous that Darcy Marx, independent woman, was in love. With a corporate attorney. But after months of seeing him with his son, longing for the connection he'd finally gotten, she couldn't keep her feelings from erupting

BROKEN DREAMS

all over and consuming her. Nate was a good guy. A good dad. And she'd fallen head over heels in love with him. Million-dollar suit and all.

Five days later, she still hadn't made a decision. But there was one decision she had made. It was why she was sitting outside Sharla and Jodi's house the day before Thanksgiving. Being with Tanner for so long had made her realize something. That poor child would always know his own mother hadn't wanted him. She couldn't allow Hope to think the same.

She'd gotten a text from Sharla asking if she'd be around this week and, if so, could she stop in to visit. They'd been asking her to visit for six years now.

Getting out of the car, she took a deep breath and adjusted her denim jacket. She could do this. Maybe.

The walk to the door was like heading to the gallows. What if Hope hated her for giving her up? Hated that she'd lied to her all these years when she'd seen her at Story Hour? Could Darcy handle that? She'd have to. Hope needed to know she'd been wanted. Always.

Her hand shook as she pressed the bell. When the door opened, she snapped to attention.

"Darcy, I'm so glad you were able to stop by." Sharla stood back and waved for her to enter. "We've been wanting to talk to you."

"I know. You want me to tell Hope, and I'm thankful you've let me have that decision. I've finally made the choice to tell her. Not sure how she'll take it, but she has to know she was never an unwanted baby."

Sharla's eyes grew damp as she smiled. "That's great. Hope's playing in her room right now. Jodie and I need to discuss something with you first."

Darcy's stomach tightened. "What's wrong? Do you not want me to tell her now?" After she'd wrestled so long to come to this decision?

Shutting the door behind her, Sharla led her down the hall to the living room. Jodie sat on the couch. Her face was pale, and her hair hung limply on her shoulders.

"Darcy. Thank you for coming over. Hope will be thrilled to see you. Sit down."

She sat in the chair opposite Jodie. Sharla ensconced herself next to her wife and clasped her hand.

"Are you all right?" It had been almost four months since she'd seen Jodie at Hope's birthday party. The woman had definitely lost weight.

"It's what we needed to talk to you about," Sharla said.

Jodie smiled up at her partner, then turned back to Darcy. "I've got ovarian cancer."

"What? You'll be okay, though?"

Sharla patted Jodie's hand. "We have every reason to believe she'll be fine. Jodie's scheduled for a complete hysterectomy the day after Thanksgiving. They'll be starting her on chemotherapy as soon as it's medically safe to do so."

Darcy leaned forward. "Is there anything I can do for you? Clean your house, make supper for you? I'm not a great cook, but I can put stuff in a crock pot like a pro."

"Actually, there is something you can do for us." Jodie's voice softened. "Even though we have every reason to think I'll recover, we need to make arrangements for Hope in case something happens."

"Nothing's gonna happen to you, Jodie. You'll be healthy in no time. Plus, Sharla is still here."

Sharla nodded. "Jodie's redone her will and wants to name you as legal guardian for Hope if anything happens to her. Now or in the future."

"What about you? Why wouldn't you raise her?"

Sharla shifted in her seat. "I love Hope dearly, but I'm also fifty-nine years old. I have a daughter with medical issues, who I've been taking care of. There may come a time I'll need to be with her on a more permanent basis. Not that I'd ever kick Hope out of the house, but I want to make sure she has a stable environment to grow up in."

Jodie squeezed Sharla's hand. "What you may not realize is that I'm the one who adopted Hope. As much as she calls Sharla 'mom', legally she's *my* daughter. Sharla already had children and grandchildren and only supported me in adopting Hope, because I was so desperate for a child. Now, it makes sense that if anything happens to me, we'd want Hope with her biological mother."

Darcy wiped a stray tear that had managed to escape. "But it won't come to that, because you'll beat this thing."

"Yes, I certainly hope so." Jodie's voice sounded stronger. "Except I'm not talking about only now, I'm talking about the future. You're twenty-four, Darcy, while I'm forty-seven. We want Hope to have family beside her for her whole life. That's why we wanted you to tell her who you are, and why we want you to be in her life and get to know her better."

"She knows who I am. Well, not that I gave birth to her, but she knows I'm Darcy."

"But she's getting older and won't be going to Story Hour much longer. Besides, you've been nannying for that Storm boy and haven't been here much."

She'd visited Zane almost every weekend but had only dropped into the store during Story Hour a few times. It had killed her not to see Hope, and she hadn't realized how much she looked forward to seeing the girl every week.

"Are you sure about this? What about Koby and Lora? They're great parents."

"They already have two children and another on the way. If you absolutely don't want this, Darcy, we understand. But I thought you'd decided to tell Hope. Do you honestly have no interest in taking care of her if something happens?"

"Of course, I'd want her with me. I've wanted her with me since the second I held her. But we made a deal for you to be her parents. I won't go back on that. I still have nothing to offer her."

"You have love. That's the only thing she needs." Jodie reached over and touched Darcy's arm. "So, you agree."

Darcy couldn't do more than nod. She swallowed the emotion clogging her throat.

"The other thing we'll need help with is being here for Hope while Jodie has her surgery and chemo. Kobe and Lora have offered to watch her over the holiday, but I think it would be better if she wasn't pulled out of the house at night. Is there any way you can stay here until at least Sunday? Maybe longer?"

Darcy had told Nate she'd be down the Cape for a while. Could she stay here? God, too many confusing things going on and all pulling at her heart.

"I promised Zane I'd spend some time with him. Can he stay here, too?"

"Absolutely." Jodie perked up, and a little color came into her cheeks. "Hope enjoyed the few times she met him."

"And maybe," Sharla responded. "You could see if Mr. Storm would be amenable to Hope celebrating Christmas with you at his place, if you have room. Jodie will be deep in chemo at that time and probably won't be feeling too well."

Jodie added, "We don't want Hope being dragged down at Christmas by my condition."

Shrugging, Darcy said, "I'm not sure, but I can ask." Much of that would depend on her answer to Nate's marriage proposal. Even if they didn't get married, she'd find a way for Hope to have a wonderful Christmas.

"Good." Jodie took a deep breath and straightened on the couch. "Now, go tell Hope who you are. Her room is at the top of the stairs on the right. We'll be here if you need us, but I have a feeling it'll all be good."

Darcy wished she felt as confident. Her feet dragged as she climbed the stairs, her heart beating rapidly in her chest. The door was ajar, and she peeked in. Hope was on the floor with two dolls, a tea set in front of them.

"Knock, knock," she said in lieu of actually doing it. Hope's face brightened. *Okay, that's a good start.*

"Darcy!" The little girl pushed to her feet and charged in her direction, straight into Darcy's open arms. Oh, God, this felt so right.

"Hey there, Hope. Looks like you're having a party. I don't want to interrupt."

"You're just in time for the cake." Hope jumped from foot to foot and tugged on her hand to sit next to the dolls. She scurried around and found another cup and plate, then set them in front of Darcy.

"Why, thank you. What's the cake for?"

Hope tapped one of the dolls on the head. "It's Jenny's birthday. We're celebrating."

"Happy Birthday, Jenny." Darcy tipped her head at the doll.

Hope poured pretend tea, then added cream and sugar. Darcy had never attended a tea party before, though she'd seen children having them on tv shows. This was her first.

"I missed you at Story Hour. How is Tanner? Does he miss me, too? Does he still do smooth-five?"

"So many questions."

Hope giggled, and Darcy felt her courage grow.

"Tanner's good. He started school and goes three days a week."

"What kind of backpack does he have? I have a Wonder Woman backpack."

"Uh, he has PJ Masks."

"Oh, cool, I like Owlette the best."

Darcy felt like Hope had meant her. "I was Owlette for Halloween. Tanner was Catboy."

Hope tipped her head. "Who was Gekko?"

"That would be Mr. Storm. Only he didn't wear the green pajama pants."

Hope snickered. "He's a fun dad. Tanner's lucky. And he's got you. That's lucky, too."

"Thank you, Hope. I feel lucky to be with them, also." She did. But now for the moment of truth. "I came to visit today because I wanted to talk to you. Is that all right?"

Hope sipped at her pretend tea, then placed the cup back in the saucer. "I like it when you visit, like at my birthday party. That was fun. I read your books all the time."

"I'm glad you enjoy them. Remember at the party you told me the story of your birth?"

Nodding, Hope said, "Yup, how my borned mama loved me so much she wanted me to not be poor."

"Yes, she did love you so much. She still loves you. And thinks about you every day, wishing she could be with you."

The little girl's eyes popped open extra wide. "Do you know my borned mama? Can you tell her I want her to come visit me?"

"She has visited you. She's visiting you right now."

"Is she downstairs?" Hope jumped to her feet, but Darcy held out her hand.

"She's right here. I'm your mama. The one who gave birth to you, anyway."

The expression on Hope's face went from confusion to excitement all in a few moments. "You are! Really?" Her voice grew softer. "I got my wish. I did it on a star one night. I wished for you to be my borned mama, and you really are."

Darcy nodded, the lump in her throat nearly strangling her. She'd wished on millions of stars over the past six years.

Hope's face darkened, and she frowned. "Your mama was sick. Is she better?"

Darcy shook her head. "No, she died, but I still have my brother to take care of. You remember Zane. You met him a few times."

"I remember." Hope's bottom lip began to tremble, and tears came to her eyes.

"Oh, sweetie. I'm so sorry. I didn't want to make you cry. I know you must be angry with me."

Hope's head shook back and forth as she trembled. "You're my borned mama. I wanted you to come and you did. I missed you so much. I love Mama Jodie and Mama Shar, but I wanted you to come love me, too. And you did."

Darcy held her arms out, and Hope collapsed into them. "I've always loved you, baby. Ever since you kicked inside me and moved all around. When I held you right after you were born, I didn't want to let you go. I wanted to be your mama always and hold you every second. Except I knew I couldn't take care of you and give you everything you needed. Everything you deserved. It broke my heart, but I gave you to your mamas, because I knew they could take care of you better than I could and that they'd love you so much."

"They do love me really good."

"I'm glad. I just want you to know that, even though I wasn't with you, I never stopped loving you. Not once. I even got a job at the bookstore so I could see you. You are my precious little girl, and I love you so much."

Tears poured down her face as Darcy rocked back and forth with her little girl in her arms, holding her like she'd wanted to do every day since she'd given her up. "I'm so sorry I couldn't keep you. I wanted to, and I hope you forgive me."

Hope shifted in her arms and reached to touch Darcy's face, wiping away her tears. "I love you, too, Mama. Don't be sad. Now, we can see each other all the time, right? You can come play with me and visit me or maybe even stay here. We have an extra bedroom."

So much for Hope not wanting her. Was she dreaming? Nah, none of her dreams had ever been this good.

"Actually, your moms asked if I'd stay here this week with you. You know Jodie has to go to the hospital the day after Thanksgiving, right?"

Hope's face fell. "Yeah. She's sick, but the doctor's going to make her all better. Will you stay with me when they're at the hospital?"

"If you want me to."

Hope bounced up and down. "I do, I do. Will you bring Tanner with you?"

"He's with his dad now, but I'll bring Zane if that's all right."

"He's funny. He likes to make weird noises with stuffed animals. He can come stay here, too."

The girl's arms clung to Darcy's neck and squeezed tight. It was perfect. It wouldn't stay this way. At some point, she'd go back to her life, the one that didn't include Hope. But now, at least, she could come visit, hopefully whenever she wanted. It still wouldn't be enough.

When Hope eased back, she pointed to Darcy's ears. "You got new earrings. This is a frog."

"Yep, I got these from Tanner and his daddy. Frogs, to remind me of the time Tanner and I caught a couple frogs by the lake. We went out fishing in their boat, too."

"Here is the fish." Hope found those earrings.

Darcy explained about the flowers and dragonfly, then touched the moon at the top. "These are because Mr. Storm thinks I'm a vampire who comes out in the full moon."

Hope giggled. "You aren't a vampire. They wear black capes and have pointy teeth."

As Darcy talked about the things she'd been doing in New Hampshire, it suddenly occurred to her exactly how much she loved Nate and Tanner. As much as she loved Hope. Would it be so bad to marry him, even if it wasn't for love? When had she ever known love, except for Zane and Hope? Certainly not romantic love.

Could Nate come to love her? Even though they'd had a rough start, things had smoothed out between them, once they'd gotten to know each other. Could it work? But then she wouldn't be as close to Hope, and now that the child had been told the truth, Darcy wanted to spend more time with her. Would that make Jodie and Sharla worry that she was muscling in?

"You know what, Mama Darcy?'

Had her heart stopped? No. There it was, beating so fast she couldn't even tell, like a hummingbird's.

"What my sweet Hope?"

"If you marry Tanner's daddy, then Tanner would be my brother. I'd like to have a brother."

"You have Kobe."

The child's mouth twisted. "Yeah, but it's nice to have lots of them. And Kobe is too old to play with me. I really like Tanner. Can you please be his mom, too?"

She wanted to argue that the decision wasn't hers, but it was. Nate had put that ball squarely in her court.

"Please. Can you be his mom? He needs a mom. I have three moms, and he doesn't have any. Every kid has to have a mom."

Wow, out of the mouth of babes. Her answer to Nate's question was definitely shifting directions from what she'd originally planned.

"And if you marry Tanner's daddy," Hope sat closer and pressed her face against Darcy's. "Maybe he could kind of be like my daddy, too. I don't have a daddy, and he's really cool

323

if he dresses up like Gekko. Because Catboy and Owlette are way better than Gekko, and he's still okay having that costume."

You couldn't fight that reasoning. She'd made the decision to tell Hope because of Tanner and Nate's ex. But Darcy had the power to make Tanner feel the love of a mother...her love. Would he get that anywhere else? Maybe Nate didn't love her now, and maybe he never would, but he loved his son. And Darcy loved his son. And she loved Nate. Hopefully, all that love would be enough to make the marriage work.

"So, will you marry Tanner's daddy, please?" Hope begged.

"I'll see what I can do."

CHAPTER TWENTY-EIGHT

"I'm sorry Darcy isn't here with us today. She didn't want to stay?"

Nathaniel squinted at his mom as she stirred the gravy. His mom's gravy was the best in the universe. Her questions, not so much. Darcy's reason for not being here was one he preferred not to discuss.

"She left Friday for the Cape and is spending the week with her brother."

"Who's been watching this little guy all week, then?" Amy asked from the family room, where she sat with Tanner playing the piano.

"I've been off. I don't go back until next Monday."

"Whoa, wait." Kevin held up his hands in protest. "You've been off since Friday and aren't going back? That's over a week away from work. Who are you, and what have you done with my brother?"

Nathaniel pressed his lips together. Yeah, the old Nathaniel would never have taken that much time off. The new Nathaniel made time to stop and smell the roses.

"I think I left him on the Cape this summer while I was making sandcastles."

"Nuh uh, Nathaniel Storm, Esquire, doesn't make sandcastles."

"Well, the new improved Nate Storm does."

Amy shot him a look. "Only Darcy gets away with calling you Nate. How come you've never given her any noogies?"

Kevin crossed his arms. "You're lucky you only got a noogie. He put me in a stranglehold until I took it back and called him Nathaniel five times in a row."

His mom rolled her eyes, muttering, "Children."

His dad laughed. "Thanks for letting us do Thanksgiving dinner here, Nathaniel."

"Well, the puppy is still too active to take with us anyplace, and it's easier for me so Tanner can take his nap. Plus, it's more familiar to him. He needs that with Darcy not here."

Tanner's head whipped up at her name. "Darcy. Home."

"No, sweetie," Amy answered. "She'll be home soon."

But would she? Did she even consider this her home? She'd given up her tiny apartment easily enough and didn't seem to miss it. Had she ever considered any place home? Knowing what her early life had been like, he had doubts.

"Are you enjoying your break from college, Ames?" Nathaniel walked down the stairs and crouched beside Tanner. He loved listening as his son played tunes on the piano. It still astounded him what this child could do.

"I haven't done much. Got together with a few friends, who are also home. You know me. Such a party girl."

His sister was intelligent and certainly social, way more than him. But she was a straight arrow. He didn't even remember her ever having a boyfriend. Too busy with her studies.

"Glad you're taking some time for yourself."

"If you need any help with Tanner over the next few days, I'd be happy to come over and watch him."

"If you want to, there are a few things I could do. I'd planned to get them done when this little guy napped tomorrow."

"I'll stop in for a bit. I don't get to see my only nephew often enough. And it's doubtful I'll get another one soon." She glared at Kevin, who smirked back.

His mom hit her spoon on the side of the pot. "It's all ready, if you'll give me a hand getting it on the table."

Nathaniel had set the table earlier and put a construction paper turkey in the center that Tanner had made at school.

"My turkey," he said when Nathaniel plopped him in his booster seat.

"It's awesome, buddy. Great job."

Everyone else commented on the craft as they placed dishes of steaming food around it. His dad set the large platter with cut turkey and drumsticks next to him. They passed plates around and loaded up, then held hands as his mother said a prayer.

For a while, no one said anything as they tasted the wonderful meal. Nathaniel had stuck the turkey in early this morning, but everyone else had contributed to the rest of the meal.

He wondered what Darcy was doing now and where she was eating. She hadn't said when she'd left. Or if she'd be back. They'd made love almost frantically that afternoon, like Darcy was trying to get every last memory of him in her mind. He'd done the same, but he fervently hoped he'd managed to show her how good they could be together.

The few texts he'd sent recently had been ignored, until one response came yesterday morning.

—*I need time.*—

He had no idea how to even process this. As he gazed at

his family, he remembered how they'd helped each other when he was younger with any problems. Could they give him some insight now?

"Um...so I proposed to Darcy on Friday." Yup, rip that Band-Aid off.

All eyes flipped to him.

"Darcy," Tanner yelled and banged his fork on the table

Amy was the first to speak. "You guys are getting married?"

"She didn't say yes." His voice was rough.

Kevin made a face. "She turned you down? That's cold."

"She said she needed to think about it."

His dad looked perplexed. "It's kind of sudden, isn't it?"

His mom, Amy, and Kevin all gave Dad the side eye.

Kevin smirked. "You never noticed the looks Nathaniel gives Darcy."

Amy chuckled. "It's pretty obvious you're hung up on her."

Had he been that transparent?

"How did you propose?" His mom asked. "Roses? Champagne? Down on one knee in a romantic setting?"

Amy's eyes opened wide. "What's the ring look like? Is it huge?"

"Uh, I didn't get a ring. I just told her I thought we should get married."

His mother's mouth hung open, and Amy made a face. "God, you suck at proposals."

His sister had a point. Even Darcy had mentioned it.

"Why do you think you should get married? Is she pregnant?" His dad scowled.

"No, of course not." He didn't think so. They'd used condoms every time. "She's good for Tanner."

His mom frowned. "That's why you want to marry her? Not the best reason."

Well, he wanted to protect her, too. From assholes like Stan or anyone else who thought they could take advantage of her. But he wouldn't share that tidbit with his family. It would likely embarrass Darcy, and that was the last thing he wanted to do.

Darcy had made him a better person. One who was able to laugh at himself and have fun again. She'd pulled that stick right out of his ass, and he was man enough to admit it had been a big one. The movie nights, dressing up for Halloween. Having a good time being with his son and with her.

"She's good for me, too. Made me like myself a lot more."

Kevin cleared his throat. "Made us like you more, too, bro."

"Not that we didn't like you before," Amy clarified, her eyes sending daggers to Kevin. "But you could be an old stick in the mud at times."

Great, this from his straight arrow sister.

Kevin grinned. "Yeah, now you're actually tolerable."

Sure, his siblings were kidding, but they weren't exactly wrong. He had been a self-centered jerk for too long. What could he do to get Darcy back?

"Honey." Mom threw him a sympathetic glance. "What are your feelings for Darcy?"

She'd only been gone six days, and he already missed her. Hell, he'd been missing her since Friday night.

"Is it like what you felt for Helene?" His father's question had him remembering his failed marriage.

"No, but let's face it, Helene and I didn't really get married for love."

Kevin's smile grew into a smirk. "And how'd that work out for you?"

"Nathaniel." Dad cleared his throat. Hopefully, words of wisdom to help him out of this dilemma would pop out. "Think about your life with Darcy in it, how you feel when she's here with you, how you feel when you see her with Tanner. Now, compare it to a life without her there."

God, no. He couldn't imagine that. She'd filled up so many parts of him with her offbeat humor and wardrobe, not to mention the makeup shield she hid behind. And the gentle loving nature she had with Tanner spoke volumes about her character.

"She's an unbelievably beautiful person on the inside." He liked what was inside. Liked it a lot. He knew how fortunate he was to have been allowed to see her true self at all.

Kevin laughed. "Dude, have you taken a look at her outside?"

"Yes, and you need to stop looking."

"Have you shagged her yet?" Kevin's eyebrows rose.

"Kevin Michael Storm." Ooh, his mom had broken out the middle name. His brother was in deep trouble.

"Just being honest. I remember you told me after you and Helene split that there wasn't much chemistry between you."

Another failing of his and probably one of the reasons she'd set her sights on Bryce.

"Yeah, because I was a jerk, who only cared about appearances and thought the chemistry didn't matter." Not that his ex had been any better.

Amy tipped her head. "Well, you certainly like sparring with Darcy. Plenty of sparks flying when you're together."

Wasn't that the truth. And one of the things he truly loved about her. She made him work hard to keep up.

"They do. She makes me feel so much when she's with me."

His dad's face was still neutral. "Make sure what you feel for her isn't only gratitude for taking care of Tanner."

"My turkey." His son had continued eating amongst the strange conversation.

Running his hand over Tanner's head, he replied, "Not

gratitude." The image of her riding him in bed flashed through his mind. She made him lose control. In a good way.

"It should also be more than S-E-X." His mom, good preschool teacher that she was, spelled the word, though it was unlikely Tanner understood what it meant.

"It is. Way more than I ever felt for Helene. You can't even compare the two. I want to do stuff for Darcy and not simply give her things. She isn't into material stuff, anyway. She's the most unselfish person I've ever met, and I want her to be safe and happy. I want her doing it here with us. The thought of her miserable is like a stab to the gut."

"Sounds like love." Amy's dreamy eyes showed her romantic streak.

Kevin snorted. "Like you'd know." Their sister shot eye daggers his way.

"I know what it is." Mom threw one of her 'looks' at her younger son. "And I'd say love isn't far off, if it isn't already there."

Love? Did he love Darcy? It wasn't something he'd ever truly thought about. The sensible side of him wanted her here for Tanner. As well as for him. But why? It wasn't the same kind of love he felt for his family. Or for Tanner. But the emotion was just as deep and strong. Maybe that was why it hurt so much when she hadn't jumped at the chance to marry him.

Did she have the same feelings for him? If she didn't, what was he going to do about it? Could she learn to love him the way he was certain she loved Tanner? The way he now realized he loved her?

Guess the first step was to actually tell her.

∾

"Thanks for the information, Alicia."

Nathaniel scribbled a few notes on a legal pad as he juggled the phone between his shoulder and ear. "I owe you one for helping out on this case. I'll talk to you soon and see how it shakes out. I hope they nail him to the wall."

As he swiped his phone off, he peeked into the playroom again, where Tanner rolled his car along the railing of the loft. Oreo scampered up the steps, then slid down the small slide, barking happily.

"Hey, buddy. You okay?"

Tanner glanced up and smiled. Oh, the things that smile did to him. Warmed him so deeply inside he knew he'd never be cold again.

"Daddy, bwoo car." He held up the Hot Wheels in his hand. It was indeed blue. And the response could be considered almost an appropriate answer to his question. The school, and his therapists, were doing a fabulous job with his son.

"I'll be in to read you a story in a minute."

As he walked back to his office to place the notes on his desk, he thought about the phone calls he'd made the last few days.

What had happened to Darcy years ago had plagued him. She'd refused to tell him who the scumbag was, but Zane had been more than happy to tell Mary and Jim where he'd worked when they'd lived in New Bedford. A little digging, and the name of the guy who'd blackmailed Darcy into having sex, which in his book was rape, had come to light. Lo and behold, the guy had been at it again. God knows how many times and how many young girls he'd done this to.

But one of them was attempting to press charges. He'd called his friend, Alicia, who lived in that area. She'd been in Harvard Law School with him, and when he'd told her the circumstances, she'd dug even deeper. Then, she'd agreed to work with the family in bringing this guy to justice. He'd offered to pay for her services, but Alicia hated any man that preyed on innocent young girls and had told him it would be her pleasure to help put this slime bucket away.

What he'd done and what Alicia was doing wasn't something he'd tell Darcy about. Bringing that back up would only cause more pain. He'd keep it to himself. If he ever saw her again.

Swiping his phone, he checked the text message left by Darcy on Saturday. She was staying down the Cape to help watch Hope while Jodie had surgery. He'd tried asking some questions, and even calling, but there'd been no response except her saying she needed some time.

"Did you want a story, Tanner?"

The boy released the car on the slide, so it zoomed down to the floor. Then, he followed.

"Book. Daddy, this one."

The book was one they'd read often, usually with Darcy nearby providing hilarious voices and commentary, much of which went over Tanner's head.

God, he missed her. Her ridiculous humor, her caring nature, the fun and happiness she brought to this house and his life. The sex, too, but he'd gone years without that. He could do it again. He wasn't sure if he could live without her vibrant personality here.

As he read the book to his son, Tanner pointed at the pictures, labeling them.

"Daddy." He pointed to the father in the picture, then patted Nathaniel's arm, giving him chills that his son finally seemed to get it.

When he touched the image of the mother, he cocked his head. "Mama. Darcy?"

Was Tanner equating Darcy with a mother figure? The child was starting to understand the family unit as it was something his SLP was working on in his sessions. Darcy certainly had been his mother figure since she'd moved in. Even longer if you considered the few months she'd helped out when they'd lived on the Cape.

Tanner got up and crossed the room, picking up a colorful bangle bracelet from the end table.

"Mama. Darcy. Find Darcy." He looked around the room, then headed for the door.

"Darcy's not here, bud."

"Want Darcy. Home." Tanner's face crumpled as he looked at the bracelet he held.

"I know. I want her home, too."

The boy placed the bracelet back down, then ran to take his hand and pull. "We go. Darcy mama home."

Nathaniel allowed himself to be dragged down the hall. He glanced at his watch. A little before noon. Tanner could have his nap in the car on the way down to the Cape.

"You're right, buddy. We need to go find Darcy." He had to let her know how he felt. How much he needed her with him. Hopefully, she felt even a tiny bit the same.

"Let's have a quick lunch, then we'll find Darcy. Your mama. I hope. Go get your stuffed dog while I make something for us to eat."

Tanner galloped up the stairs. "Darcy. Mama. Darcy. Mama."

Sandwiches would have to do, because he didn't want to waste any time in getting down there. But where would he find her? At Hope's?

Taking his phone from his pocket, he tapped on Sara's number. Hopefully, his cousin could figure out where Darcy was before he arrived.

CHAPTER TWENTY-NINE

Darcy set her cup on the coffee table and stretched back in the settee to enjoy her croissant sandwich after the lunch rush. Tea and Tales had a few customers, but nothing like this past weekend. She'd brought Hope to Story Hour on Saturday after a quick visit to see Jodie in the hospital. The store had been jam-packed with Black Friday weekend shoppers, so Darcy had grabbed an apron and helped out. The boss had been appreciative and ordered pizza for everyone who'd still been working at supper time.

Hope had been thrilled to play with Freckles and Domino, the other black and white puppy that Sara and TJ had kept, while Darcy had poured coffee. They'd gone in and helped for a few hours on Sunday, as well. It was better than sitting in Jodie and Sharla's huge house by themselves.

But now Hope had been at school the last two days, and Sharla had been at the hospital almost non-stop since the surgery. So Darcy had come back to the store. She should have gone to Nate's to watch Tanner. The guilt of leaving him hanging had been eating away at her. She was a coward and needed to face Nate sooner or later with an answer. As much as she thought she'd made her decision, she was afraid. Still that neglected little girl who'd never had a mother to love her.

Which was why she'd stayed with Hope, who was her child and needed her, too. The girl had started calling her Mama Darcy, and it gave her such chills. Good ones. Hope had even done it in front of Jodie and Sharla on their hospital visit. Darcy had examined their responses carefully, but both had smiled happily. No sign of jealousy or annoyance. These two women were amazing, and she was blessed they'd been the ones to adopt her child.

"Who's been watching Tanner the last few days?" Sara asked, lowering herself to the opposite chair, a muffin in her hands. Cinnamon and Domino scampered over, sniffing at the food. Mary had brought the other puppy here today to be with her mom. Something she did often, apparently. Freckles gave a soft 'woof' and her pups trotted back to her in the children's area.

"Oh, uh, he's in school all day, and Nate's been coming home early recently." It was only a little lie. Nate *had* been coming home early, his home, not hers, but Tanner didn't go to school on Tuesdays. Certainly, someone in his family had stepped up to the plate if he'd gone to work. But she also knew he could do much of his work from home.

"It's sweet of you to help Jodie watch Hope while she's in the hospital." Sara's expression showed her confusion, but Darcy wasn't ready yet to share that the little girl was her child. "What time does she get home?"

Glancing at the clock on the wall, she calculated the time. "Not for a few hours. She's got a Brownie meeting after school today. She's excited about being able to sell Girl Scout cookies this year. You and TJ will buy some, right?"

Sara laughed. "Tons. If she orders extra, we'll let her sell them in the store some weekend. What is the troop planning to do with the cookie money?"

They chatted for a while about Hope and the Girl Scouts, and the concerts Sara would be performing in the coming months. It was great she could perform and record new songs while still being married to the man she loved. Sara had it all. The best of both worlds.

Could Darcy have even one world? Which one? Being Hope's every-now-and-then mom? Or Nate's wife and Tanner's stepmom?

Sara glanced at her phone, then looked up. "If you're hanging around for a while, TJ just got in some Cape Cod Christmas decorations he wants out ASAP."

"You know how I like to keep busy."

After her last bite of lunch, Darcy organized and put out the new display. Mary chatted with her some, then spent a few minutes with the dogs. Freckles seemed to have her offspring under control.

A round of yipping later had her glancing over. Another black and white puppy was frolicking with Domino and Cinnamon. It looked like Oreo, but...

"Darcy!" Tanner yelled from the doorway. The boy made a beeline for her and jumped into her arms.

"Hey, Tanner, what are you doing here?" Nate materialized behind his son, his face anxious. Was he planning to rescind his proposal? Something better? Worse?

Tanner planted his hands on the side of her face, his expression serious. "We find you. Come home."

Nate nodded slightly, the smile on his face forced.

"You came all this way to get me? Thank you. I missed you." She did. But she also missed Hope when she wasn't with her.

"I miss you, Darcy. Mama. Come home."

Had he called her *mama*? Two kids in the span of a week.

She swallowed, trying to keep the emotions from pouring out.

Freckles padded over and nuzzled Tanner's hand. The boy squealed and hopped to where the puppies were all prancing about, happy to see each other. So easily distracted.

"Hey, Elvira."

"GQ."

Nate stepped closer as she rose to her feet. God, he looked frickin' amazing. Snug, worn jeans and a navy Henley. She chuckled when she noted Tanner wore a similar outfit.

"You've been gone for eleven days."

He'd counted. What the hell was she supposed to say? Mary and TJ stood behind the book counter, attempting to look like they weren't listening in. Sara didn't even pretend from her spot near the coffee counter.

"I'll keep an eye on Tanner if you two need to talk. TJ's office is a great place for that." Sara grinned. When she and TJ had reunited after being away for months, they'd hashed things out in his office. Darcy had checked on them later and been scolded by TJ. She had a feeling they'd done more than talk.

Darcy tipped her head at Nate and moved toward the stairs. Once in the office, she closed the door and leaned against it. "I'm sorry I didn't come back to help with Tanner."

"You said something about watching Hope."

"Jodie's got cancer. She had surgery Friday." She gave him the Reader's Digest version of what had transpired last week. He nodded, a frown on his face.

"So, did you tell Hope?"

All she could do was nod. The subject was still a touchy one.

Stepping closer, he stroked her arm. "Are you all right? How did that go?"

"She calls me Mama Darcy now." Those stupid tears started up again.

Nate enveloped her in his arms, and she snuggled close. How was she supposed to do this without him? She wasn't. Taking a leap of faith and accepting his offer was what she'd decided to do. She needed to tell him, but his hand rubbing up and down her back felt too good, and she hated to make it stop.

"I'm glad you told her. Did she take it well? I know you were worried about that."

"She hopped all over the place, saying she'd made wishes about having her birth mother show up. Guess I was worried for nothing." About Hope, anyway. Nate was another story.

"Any child would be lucky to have you for a mother, Darcy." He pressed his lips to the top of her head. "I've been making wishes for you to be Tanner's."

Peering up at his handsome face, she touched his cheek. "I wasn't very gracious with your proposal. I'm sor—"

"You have nothing to be sorry about. I completely botched it. There were so many things I should have said before I asked you to marry me. Unfortunately, some of it I hadn't figured out yet."

"Like what?" Her mind swirled, attempting an outrageous retort, but it was empty. Like her life without Nate standing next to her, teasing her.

"How I feel about you."

She cocked her hip and smirked. "Impressed by my maternal skills, dazzled by my shining personality, maybe even a little annoyed that I'm more stylishly dressed than you, but also totally turned on by my sexual prowess." Yeah, it had come back. She waited for him to roll his eyes.

"Exactly. And more."

Narrowing her eyes, she studied his face. He wasn't kidding. "More?"

Framing her face with his hands, he kissed her sweetly. "Darcy, you are such an amazing, unique woman. It's not surprising that I fell in love with you."

She froze. Not what she expected. "You did?"

"I know you may not love me now, but maybe someday you can look past all my faults and grow to love me like you love Tanner."

"I do love Tanner." And the boy's obtuse father who apparently couldn't see the emotion shining from her eyes. "And I—"

"Listen, I know I'm a bit of a stickler for things and an old stick in the mud—quoting my sister here—but I'll do what I need to do to make you love me. I've changed so much already. You changed me. Made me a better person. Someone who can have fun again and appreciate the things in life that don't cost money. You've made me less selfish and more aware that family is essential. I want you to come back home with us."

"Home? Your home?" It had felt like hers, too.

"*Our* home. You've been so much a part of our lives, and it hasn't been the same. I love you, Darcy. Please, come back. You don't have to marry me, but you need to be with us."

"You don't want me to marry you now? Are we back to the nanny thing?"

"Oh, God, Elvira, I do want to marry you."

"For Tanner's sake?" She had to be clear.

"For me. I'm being absolutely selfish on this. I need you. I love you. I want you. As my wife. We can hire another nanny, if that's what you want."

Hand on her hip, she tilted her head. "No other nannies. I've heard you make wild passionate love to them after vampire movies."

Nate laughed, his face gloriously handsome. "Only the mistress of the dark. Will you marry me? I promise I'll make you as happy as I can. I'll do whatever I need to, so you'll fall in love with me."

"You're too late."

His eyes darkened. "You—"

"I'm already in love with you, GQ. There's no need to do anything else to make me fall. I fell long ago."

"You did?"

Nodding, she said, "I think it was on the beach when Tanner called you Daddy. Then, you realized he was merely repeating words. I saw how much that broke your heart. But it filled mine with love knowing how much you cared for your son."

Nate closed his eyes and rested his head against hers.

She ran her hands up his sides. "It doesn't hurt you've got the abs of a god."

Chuckling, he held her closer, his arms feeling like a warm blanket on a cold night.

"It'll never get boring with you, Elvira. I've got that to look forward to. Um, you are going to marry me, right?"

She pursed her lips and gazed at the ceiling. "You might need to do the proposal thing again. Just so I'm clear on what you're asking."

Nate got down on one knee and took her hand. Definitely better than the first time.

"Darcy Marx. You are the most beautiful person I've ever met. Inside and out. You taught me so many things that I'd forgotten. What's important in life. How to laugh. How to have a good time. That family is more precious than anything else, especially money or status. Will you do me the honor of being my partner in life? In helping me raise Tanner and being the mom he so desperately needs? Will you keep me humble and always let me know when I'm getting too big for my britches?"

"I like that one. It should go in the marriage vows."

"I love you, Darcy. Will you be my wife?"

"What? No flowers or ring?"

He laughed and shook his head. "Sorry. I brought Tanner and a puppy. I didn't get you a ring, because I thought you might want to pick out your own. You don't strike me as the diamond solitaire type."

"You're learning. And yes, I'll marry you, Nathaniel Storm. I don't even need a ring. Only our love for each other. You may rise and kiss me."

"Yes, mistress." He obeyed perfectly and drew her closer, his lips devouring hers.

As they basked in each other's arms, she stroked his face. "I know I like to joke at times, but I promise you I'll do whatever needs to be done for us to be happy."

"All you have to do is be yourself, Darcy. You're who I fell in love with. I'm still not sure how I went from shock the first time I met you to now, not being able to live without you, but whatever happened along that journey, I wouldn't have it any other way."

EPILOGUE

"You are rocking that bride look, Darcy."

Darcy glanced over at Sara as her Matron of Honor winked. Yeah, the exact same words she'd said to Sara at her wedding last year. Who'd have thunk Darcy Marx, independent woman extraordinaire, would take the plunge? With a corporate attorney of all people.

"Of course, I am, boss lady. What else would you expect?"

Sara shook her head. "I'm not your boss anymore. I never was. But now you've got a much better job. Wife and mother."

"I'm not a wife yet. Nate could still change his mind. If he was smart."

Setting the floral headband on Darcy's head, Sara rearranged a few strands of hair that she'd curled loosely. It was still short, but she'd agreed not to spike it today. The softer arrangement didn't look too bad. It went with the softer makeup she'd used. Still fancy and outrageous compared to most, but it wouldn't be her without it.

"Nathaniel is head over heels in love with you. I still can't believe the difference in him between last year and now. You're so good for him."

Darcy shrugged. "Duh. I'm good for everyone."

"Yes, you are." Sara dove in for a quick hug, then stood back and assessed her work.

"Do I pass muster?"

"You look absolutely amazing, Darcy. That dress is something else. I would never expect it for a wedding, but you totally pull it off."

Darcy twirled in the mirror, admiring the yards of silk and lace. The ecru top had a sweetheart neckline and cap sleeves, then narrowed at her waist. The bottom was dip dyed, starting at a lighter blue then getting darker until the last few feet were a deep midnight color. Traditional dress, yet still non-traditional in many ways. Authentic Darcy Marx.

Looking in the mirror, she adjusted her earrings. Wouldn't Nate be surprised when he saw them? The phases of the moon started with the full moon on the top, then waning until only a crescent dangled at the bottom. The flowers in her hair were also dusted with the deep midnight blue.

Sara and Amy, her only other attendant, also wore dresses of deep midnight. The wedding was on the small side, especially compared to the event of the century Sara and TJ had. Besides the Storm family, there were only Zane, Mary, Jim, and Becca from the bookstore.

How they'd managed to get this beautiful place, The Inn at the Falls, she didn't know. Especially the day before Valentine's Day. Apparently, the Storm family had connections. Could be because they'd kept it to twenty-five guests, if you didn't include the kids.

A soft tap on the door had Sara glancing at the clock. "We still have fifteen minutes."

She opened it and cocked her head. "You aren't supposed to be here."

Nate's deep voice rumbled in. "Just one minute. Please."

Darcy called out, "You come to your senses and calling it off?"

"Mama," Tanner yelled from the hall.

"Let the little guy in, not the big one."

Sara stepped into the hallway and both Tanner and Hope came in. They took one look at Darcy and smiled.

"You are beautiful, Mama." Hope sighed, running in for a hug. Her flower girl dress was a lighter shade of blue with midnight accents. Tanner melted her heart in his tiny tux.

Darcy leaned over and pulled Tanner close. "You know what you need to do, right? Walk with Hope."

Tanner nodded. "Hope, sister."

God, not now. Tears filled her eyes and she pushed them back. There wasn't time to fix her makeup. "Yes, hold your sister's hand and walk with her until you get to Daddy. I love you both."

Darcy and Nathaniel had been taking Hope every weekend while Jodie had chemo and was recovering, Fortunately, it seemed they'd gotten all the cancer and her prognosis was good. But not having to run around after a six-year-old for a few days a week would help her get better faster.

Zane also had been coming every weekend, since they were picking up Hope, anyway. Darcy had moved into Nate's master bedroom, while Hope had taken her room and Zane had the extra one. It was a full house from Friday night to Sunday, and she'd never been happier. This was what family was supposed to be.

Nate had even talked about buying a small vacation house on the Cape, so they could be closer to Hope if needed.

Now that I'm not paying a ridiculous amount for a live-in

nanny, I think I can afford it. She'd paid him back for that crack, and he'd loved every minute of it.

"Okay, you two, go get in place. Daddy and I need to get married and make this all official."

Last week, they'd made something else official. Helene had signed away her parental rights, and Darcy had adopted Tanner. Plus, she had Hope now and—

"Come on," Sara interrupted as she shooed the children out. The door closed on Nate as he coerced the children down the hall.

"Are you ready for this?"

Darcy nodded, despite the knots twisting her insides. They shouldn't be there, but too many years of being cast aside by her own parents had instilled this doubt in her. Shaking her head, she pushed them away. Nathaniel Storm loved her. For who she was. He'd never asked her to change at all. For that, she loved him even more.

Amy came to the door and motioned for them. Music started, and Darcy took a deep breath as Amy marched down the makeshift aisle, Sara right behind her. Moving into place, she focused on her end point. Kevin stood next to Nate, both watching the women.

TJ stood waiting to give her away, so she stepped forward and took his arm. Nate's love carried all the way across the room. His eyes gleamed once he got a look at her. Yeah, she'd warned him she wasn't going traditional. He hadn't expected anything else, but also hadn't known what she was wearing.

"You look absolutely stunning. I have to admit I was a little nervous what you'd come up with." He took her hand and lifted it to his mouth. The moonstone engagement ring sparkled in the candlelight.

The minister cleared her throat and began.

"It is my honor to be here today…"

The rest of the words drifted off as Darcy held the hand

of the man she loved. The one who pledged to honor, love, and cherish her forever. It was finally sinking in. This great love they shared. The love they would share with their children.

Once they'd been declared husband and wife, Nate kissed her with one intent. To show everyone assembled how much he needed, wanted, and loved her.

As they danced their first dance, she pressed her lips to his ear and whispered, "I wasn't sure when to tell you this."

His hands tightened, and he pressed his lips to her cheek. "Is something wrong?"

"I don't think so. But you need to tell Kevin one of those condoms he gave you didn't work."

Nate froze and eased away, staring into her eyes. "Are you saying…?"

Nodding, she gave him a tiny kiss. "I am, but I'm not sure I can do this."

"The marriage thing or the baby thing?"

"The baby thing. The memories are so…hard."

"But this time you've got me, and I'll always be there for you, Darcy. We'll do this together."

He reached down and ran his hand over her still flat stomach. "You've got your little Hope. Now, you just have to have a little faith."

∼

Take a sneak peek at the next book in the Storms of New England series, LOST DREAMS book 5.

LOST DREAMS

STORMS OF NEW ENGLAND, BOOK 5

CHAPTER ONE

"The Crisis Team Meeting will begin in three minutes in the office conference room."

Alandra Cabrera glanced up at the speaker in her classroom and frowned. Why couldn't she ever be on time for these things? It would take her that long to hit the bathroom in the staff room, then walk all the way to the end of the hall and down two flights of stairs. If she didn't use the bathroom, she could make it with a minute to spare. But the meeting would run long, as it always did, and she'd never have time to go again before the kids started arriving in her classroom. And it was two hours before they went to Art, which was the first break she had. Her bladder wouldn't last that long.

Grabbing a pad of paper and a pencil, she tore off down the hall. Good thing the kids weren't here. She usually reminded *them* not to run inside. Luckily, she didn't see any of the typically gabby teachers in the staff room and managed to get in and out fast.

She slid into the conference room just as Reggie Thorpe, the principal, started passing out agendas. A quick scan showed her the only seat vacant was…oh, God, right next to Greg Storm, Captain of the Squamscott Falls Fire Department.

It wasn't that she didn't like Captain Storm, quite the opposite. The man was gorgeous and incredibly nice. He made her heart race, but he also turned her into a giddy school girl. No one had caused that reaction in a very long time. Way before Jeff had screwed her over and deserted her and Jillian.

Ali threw Captain Storm a pleasant smile and took the handout he passed her. *Keep your eyes on the paper. Play it cool. Pay attention to the meeting, and don't stare at the handsome fireman.*

While Reggie droned on, as principals tended to do, Ali kept her hands busy taking notes. Fire drills. Lock downs. Fire Safety Week. The new video monitors being installed near all the entrances to the building. Still, she couldn't stop taking peeks at Greg Storm, all in the guise of listening to the other members of the committee as they spoke. Which was ridiculous because they'd both been on the Crisis Team for three years now. She also had his son, Ryan, in her class this year. She should be comfortable in his presence.

Yeah, it had been a fun parent conference last fall. Her stomach had twisted into knots, and she'd been practically punch drunk after it was over. Good thing she'd had all her information in front of her and had gone through the same spiel almost twenty times before. Ryan's conference had been the last of the day, and they'd taken a bit longer than she'd allowed other parents. Not that Ryan had needed extra discussion. He was a great kid and excellent student. His father had been concerned, however, because he didn't have a mom at home and wanted to make sure his emotional skills were on par as well as his academics.

Of course, she hadn't minded. The man was dreamy in so

many ways. His soft, light brown waves were cut short, yet still long enough to have a touch of curl to them. His bright blue eyes, like his son's, shone with intelligence and humor. And those shoulders, God, those shoulders. Broad and strong, they bracketed his defined pectorals that were showcased in his navy SFFD t-shirt. She wouldn't even think about how his blue chinos fit over his firm ass and thighs. No, best not think about those.

God, is it hot in here? Pushing her hair off her neck, she took a deep breath and focused on Reggie. He was going over the fire drill routine for a third time. Like they'd never done a fire drill before. The tall, stick-like principal looked over his glasses at his paper, then smoothed his hand over his bald head.

"Alandra, have you talked to the rest of your team about scheduling a time for your classes to go in the smoke house?" Every year the fourth-grade students got to go in the trailer simulator, learn what to do in case of a fire, and then practice going out through a window with a rope ladder hanging down.

Ali flipped her notebook to the correct page. "I have their schedules here. We can plug them into whatever time frame the firefighters have set up."

Reggie pointed to Captain Storm. "Greg, why don't you and Alandra go over that schedule and make sure Maggie gets a copy in the office?"

Ali turned to the man next to her, but before she could say anything, the bell rang. Reggie, of course, was still talking. Why couldn't he ever let them out of a meeting a few minutes before the bell rang, so they'd have time to get to their classrooms before the kids did?

The specialists who didn't have students waiting for them sat listening to the principal, but Ali and the other classroom teacher on the committee stood and pointed to the door. The sound of kids in the hallway stomping their way to their classes finally made Reggie dismiss the meeting.

"I'm sorry, Captain Storm, I need to get to class," she said as she picked up her notepad and pencil.

"I'll walk with you, and we can figure out a time to go over that schedule."

They left the room and awareness zinged through Ali's bloodstream. Was everyone staring at her? Her face must be crimson by now and sweat trickled down her back. Why did this man send her nerves into a tizzy?

He stepped closer to avoid a group of eager first graders and leaned down. "Please call me Greg. We've known each other a while now. No need to be so formal. I'm still getting used to the Captain title. I've only had it for a few months."

"Greg. And congrats on the promotion. Ryan was so excited when he came in after Christmas break and announced it to the class."

They started up the two flights of stairs, weaving between scurrying little people.

"Hey, Mrs. C."

"Good morning, Aiden. If you get to the classroom before me, make sure everyone's following the routine, okay?"

The boy's eyes shot up, and he grinned. "Will do." He took off walking even faster.

Greg chuckled. "Apparently, he wants to follow your directions."

Shaking her head, Ali said, "He just really likes to tell people what to do."

Greg laughed again and ducked around the kids barreling past. "Boy, they sure are in a hurry to get to class."

"Yeah, get to class, dump their bags, then go meet their friends in the bathroom. Or visit last year's teacher and get something out of the candy jar."

The smile on Greg's face showcased his dimples. Man, those were dangerous.

"You don't have a candy jar?"

"Oh, I do. But they have to work to get a piece from mine. If they had Mr. Lavallee last year, they know he'll let them have one every day just because they show up to say hi."

"It means more if you have to work for it." That grin grew bigger.

As they approached her classroom, the din inside spilled into the hallway. She took a step inside, flicked the light off and on, and called out, "Morning routine. Even if I'm not here, it's the same every day."

The noise level lowered as sheepish kids put backpacks and coats away, took out homework, and got started on their morning work set out on their desks. Stephanie Long, another teacher on her team, peeked through the connecting door to her room and waved.

"I figured you had a meeting this morning. Let me guess. Reggie was running it and it went over?"

"Yep, thanks for keeping an eye out." Stephanie closed her door and Ali swiveled back to Greg, who still stood in the hallway.

"Sorry. It's always crazy first thing." Several students gave her hugs as they slipped past to get inside the room.

"Don't apologize. Makes me have more respect for what you do. What's a good time to get the schedule figured out?"

"I have a prep period from ten to ten-forty and lunch at twelve-thirty for a half hour. If those don't work, school is out and the kids are usually gone by three fifteen-ish."

Greg pursed his lips and glanced at his watch. "I've got paperwork that has to be done this morning as long as we don't get a call. And I hate to take up any of your very short lunch break. But I don't want to keep you from heading home. I know you've got your daughter to take care of."

"I typically don't pick her up until four or four-thirty, since I need to get work done here. Once I'm home, it's almost impossible to do anything. Plus, I want to give Jillian all my attention."

Greg nodded. "I can be here at three-fifteen sharp, and we can whiz right through it."

"Sounds like a plan. I'll see you then." Two more students walked through the hallway and wrapped her in a hug before heading into the room.

"Dad! What are you doing here?" Ryan Storm sauntered down the hallway, his sandy blond hair curling out from under his baseball cap.

Greg scooped the hat from his son's head and held it out. "I had a meeting here this morning, then needed to arrange some stuff with Mrs. Cabrera about the smoke house."

Mrs. Should she remind him it was only Ms. now, since her ex walked out leaving her with a small child?

"The kids are all stoked about that, but I've seen it a bunch of times." Ryan shrugged.

Ali chuckled at the boy's bragging. It must be cool having your dad be the fire captain.

Greg ruffled his son's hair, then swatted him playfully on the back. "Go do your morning routine. I'll see you later."

"And I'll see you right after school, Greg." God, it felt weird calling him that, even though they'd seen each other outside of school during town events often enough.

"I look forward to it, Mrs—"

"Ali is fine."

"Ali. See you after school."

As she pivoted to work with the students who'd all taken their seats, she knew she was looking forward to seeing Captain Greg Storm again, too."

ABOUT THE AUTHOR

Stay in touch with Kari Lemor and find out when her next release or sale is.

Website: https://www.karilemor.com/

Join her reader's Group THE LIT LOUNGE for fun and getting to know her better:

https://www.facebook.com/groups/373521153021256/

Other places to get information on Kari:

- facebook.com/Karilemorauthor
- twitter.com/karilemor
- instagram.com/karilemorauthor
- pinterest.com/karilemor
- bookbub.com/authors/kari-lemor

Made in the USA
Middletown, DE
13 August 2023